Amen and Amen

OTHER BOOKS BY GENE VICKERS

Imagine This: A Tale of Two Bears

Amen and Amen

GENE VICKERS

Mountain Arbor
Press
Alpharetta, GA

ISBN: 978-1-63183-760-9

Printed in the United States of America   0 5 0 5 2 0

∞ This paper meets the requirements of ANSI/NISO Z39.48-1992 (Permanence of Paper)

To Jason

A big thank you to my wife, Elaine, for her support during the writing of this book.

And a thank you to Harold Hogan for suggesting I turn the original short story, *Amen and Amen,* into a novel.

PART I

T he center snapped the ball to Bubba, and Little Jimmy was flat-out gone down the imaginary sideline. Bubba flicked his wrist a couple of times to hold the pass rushers in check and then let loose a bomb, sailing at least forty yards and falling into Little Jimmy's hands over his right shoulder—a perfect strike in full stride.

"Color him gone," Bubba crowed and he was. "Game's over, time to eat."

Bubba jogged over to the cookshed where Clarice, his girl-friend, was sitting with their friends. "How bout that?" he said leaning over to give her a peck on the cheek and a pat on the butt.

"Stop it, Bubba," Clarice said and frowned, embarrassed by the pat.

Bubba grinned his devilish grin and said, "Someone get the dogs and burgers on the grill. Jimmy and I have to be at work at four."

"Grill's ready," Janice said as she began taking the burgers and dogs out of the cooler.

Little Jimmy, seeing Clarice come down on Bubba for the butt-pat, winked at his friend and patted Janice on the butt as she started cooking. She didn't say anything about it, just smiled at her boyfriend.

"See there," Bubba pointed out, "nothing to get upset about." Clarice gave him the what for look and it ended the conversation cold.

The cookshed and the field the locals played ball on most Saturdays was behind Coosa Baptist Church. Bubba's grandmother was a member there, and the church built the cookshed and maintained the field as an outreach for the young people in the community. And it worked. At least half of the Saturday regulars playing ball there would be in church on Sunday morning. Even though Bubba had to work every Saturday until midnight, Granny still insisted he get up and get himself to worship service. She told him a thousand times, "God gave you the body and the ability to work a job, and the least you can do to show your thankfulness is to be in church on Sunday mornings." And he was, every Sunday, probably not so much as a worship thing as not wanting to disappoint his Granny.

The burgers and the dogs were almost done when Eula Johnson pulled up in her dad's old Chevy truck. "Sorry I'm late," she said, setting a large bag of potato chips on the picnic table. "I had to work over for a few minutes."

"Let's eat," Little Jimmy said, "I'm starving and we have to be at work in a couple of hours."

"Hear, hear," Bob said. "I don't have to work this evening, but I'm so hungry my stomach thinks my throat's been cut."

Bubba smiled at the old saying, one he had heard his daddy say before.

"So what's going on down at the Dairy Queen?" Bubba asked Eula as he sat down next to Clarice.

"Same old, same old," she responded, opening the bag of potato chips and passing them around. Everyone was eating and enjoying what Bubba had come to call their po man's country club, the cookshed and grill. It was a great place to hang out, and it kept the kids out of a lot of trouble they might otherwise have gotten into. Using the church-sponsored facility made some feel obligated to go to church on Sunday, and it made them feel like they belonged to something bigger and better than they were. They wouldn't get that hanging around Pete's Pool Room in town or the local drive-in where some kid always managed to slip some booze from his parents' home. This was a far better place for them to hang out and spend time with their friends.

Bubba was the son of Frank and Mary Preston, locals who had lived in the North Georgia mountains for generations. Most of the kids who came here to hang out, play ball and grill were locals as well. The majority of families represented here worked at McClain's Furniture Manufacturing. There was always talk about McClain's closing and going out of business. Overseas competition had just about done the job, and cutbacks due to lost business had already hurt the community as a whole.

Bubba, Little Jimmy and most of the ones sitting around the picnic table went to Union High School, and most of the boys worked part time for minimum wages at McClain's.

Coosa Baptist Church, originally started in the late 1800s, was nestled in a picturesque valley. On the right side of the white frame church was a family cemetery, and the majority of the kids playing ball here had family members interred there. The graves were all facing the East, with great expectation of a better day to come. Because the cemetery was on a hillside, overlooking the ball field, Bubba said the headstones reminded him of bleachers at a stadium and swore the people buried there enjoyed watching them play ball and grill out. Eula thought that was the funniest thing imaginable; dead people watching some kids play ball and grill hamburgers and hot dogs.

Bubba and Eula had always been best friends. She was beautiful, but he had never been attracted to her, other than as a special friend. It was the same for her. She had seen Bubba and Clarice's relationship begin and blossom, and she was concerned about what she thought was happening. One day, she said, "Bubba, I want y'all to be careful. Seems like the two of you are a little too friendly, kinda like married friendly, if you know what I'm trying to say without having to spell it out."

Bubba did what he always did when he found himself in a tight spot—blinked those big ole blues, as Clarice called them, and flashed his million-dollar smile.

"Shucks, Eula, I don't know what you're talking about."

"Sure you don't, Bubba, but mind y'all be careful, or you'll find yourself working at that damned old furniture company for the rest of your life."

Sharing good times with friends is essential to life on all economic levels. Bubba called the people who had the fine cars, big houses, and money the *hootie tooties*, his spin on *hoity-toity*. Eula, while acknowledging the economic differences, didn't seem as absorbed with the issue as he was. She figured it was some kind of male ego thing but had never suggested that to him.

"Yeah," Bubba had responded to her remark about having to work at McClain's for the rest of his life, "that would really suck and would probably land me a single-wide to boot."

Bubba, Eula, Clarice and most of their friends had lived in mobile homes their entire lives. That was about all someone working at McClain's could afford. Bubba, while not voicing it often, said his dream was to one day have a home that didn't have wheels on it.

By the world's standards, they didn't have a lot of stuff that seemed so important to most people. They went to school together, to church together, and enjoyed simple, good times together. Being on the lower end of the economic scale did present its own set of issues, especially at school where peer pressure was great. But Eula chose to be a glass half full person. Once she asked Bubba, "Why's your glass always half empty?" He responded quickly, without even thinking about it, and said, "So your glass can be half full. Someone has to worry about stuff; might as well be me."

Being a good friend, she was forever trying to get him to see life and high school as she did.

"Come on, Eula, take off those rose-colored glasses. High school is a stage and it's kinda like a production or play. We're the extras. The *hootie tooties* need us to fill the hallways, witness their adventures, applaud when they get shiny new cars and fancy clothes or make their plans to go away to their folks' preppy, Ivy League alma maters. Hell, Eula, I'm already at my folks' alma mater—McClain's Furniture Manufacturing."

"Bubba, that's just in your mind. It ain't really like that at all."

"Well, you tell that to Maude when I park her next to a shiny BMW or the new Mercedes convertible Jill what's her name just got from her daddy. Maude feels it just like I do." Maude was Bubba's old Chevy pickup, badly in need of a paint job and new upholstery.

"And how do you know that? I suppose Maude told you, huh?"

"Sure as hell did. Said not to park her nowhere near no BMWs, Mercedes or Corvettes."

"Bubba, you just won't do. If you'd give these kids half a chance, you would see they're more like us than you'd ever suspect."

"Have you ever compared the way we dress to the way they dress? They wear name brand everything and we wear faded-out jeans, T-shirts and work boots."

"Well, that's because most days you and Little Jimmy go straight from school to McClain's, don't you?"

"What's that got to do with anything?"

7

"You kill two birds with one stone. You get to dress for school and work at the same time."

Eula knew she had him going and smiled a devilish grin.

"Eula, you're a piece of work, that's for sure."

The burgers were to die for, and Bubba and Little Jimmy both ate three of them. Clarice, aggravating Bubba said, "If you're not careful, you'll get fat." He started to tell her he had an idea as to how he could burn all those calories up quickly, but thought better of it, figuring Eula would pick up on it and only fuss some more about his relationship with his girlfriend.

"That was a great catch," Bubba told Little Jimmy, changing the subject from his overeating and getting fat.

"Wasn't a hard catch. You couldn't have placed it any better. Your feel and touch for passing the football makes running a pattern and hauling it in look easy."

There were twelve to fifteen guys who met most Saturdays behind the church and played touch football. Most days, their girlfriends would show up with dogs and burgers and grill them while the boys played ball. The majority of the guys working at McClain's were on the 4 to 12 PM shift on Fridays and Saturdays. During the week, they could only work four hours and would get off at 8 PM. Most Saturdays, they'd play right up until time to go to their jobs.

Bubba had boasted many times he thought their team could beat their high school team any day of the week and twice on Sunday. Bob, the center on Bubba's team, asked a question that would ignite a firestorm. "Why don't you and Little Jimmy try out for the high school team? I don't know about the rest of us, but I'm sure the two of you could make it."

Eula rolled her eyes, knowing this would get Bubba started on the *hootie tooties* again. And it did.

"Bob, surely you're joking."

"No, I'm serious as a heart attack. No one wants to play for the school because we haven't had a winning season since my dad played there and that was eons ago. They can barely field a team. Maybe some of the rest of us could help, but they definitely need someone like you who can pass and someone like Little Jimmy who can catch the ball in traffic. Why not?"

"Yeah, Bubba, that's not a bad idea as long as you don't mess with any of those frilly cheerleaders," Clarice quipped.

"Clarice, what's wrong with y'all? Has everyone lost their mind?"

Eula thought, "Here it comes."

"You're probably right, we could make the team. But they'd never let us play. All we'd do is warm the bench. I can't speak for Little Jimmy, but I have better things to do than sit on the sidelines. If I have to be there, I'd much rather be in the stands and pretend I don't know who they are."

"There's a new coach this year. How do you know he won't play y'all in the games?" someone asked.

"Because they already have their starting quarterback, Johnny Kitchens. His dad owns the big hardware store in town and I hear he gives a ton of money to the Athletic Association. Now, honestly, do you think they would pull him and start me? Surely, you jest. Johnny can't hit a bull in the ass with a handful of rice, but he's the QB and he will keep the job no matter what kind of record the team has this year. And Jason Williams, their main receiver, isn't going anywhere. His dad's a doctor. And then there's Rodney Flannigan. He averages only twenty to thirty yards a game rushing, but his dad owns the biggest construction company in the county. How is Little Jimmy going to compete with either one of them? Hell, Rodney hardly ever gets past the

9

line of scrimmage. It's about who you know, who you are, and how much money your folks have in old man Morgan's bank. Always has been, still is, and always will be. End of story."

Eula was smart. While she understood the difference money made in their town, she also knew the *hootie tooties*, as Bubba had so named them, had no more to do with the fact their folks had money than Bubba, Little Jimmy and the rest of her friends were responsible for their families not having money. She wanted Bubba, as her friend, to judge the others on a playing field that wasn't centered around economics.

Someone listening to Bubba rant and rave would have thought he hated the *hootie tooties* and the world in general. He could sound so angry at times, but Eula and the rest of his friends knew he had a heart as big as Texas and would help any-one, anytime, with anything. He was all bark. The entire circle of friends, at times, felt what Bubba felt, like they were on the out-side, looking in. It was tough at school, and Bubba was right to a large extent. The activities and the social functions did revolve around the kids whose parents had money, or at least enough money for them to participate in those activities. It was nobody's fault, it was just the way it was, but it frustrated Bubba and his friends. For some reason, Bubba decided he would be the spokesman for everyone, whether they assigned him that posi-tion or not.

Eula didn't fit in with the other kids either because she didn't have the means to go and do the things they did. But she got along with them and considered them her friends, at least in the classroom. One of the cheerleaders, knowing she and Bubba were good friends, told her she thought he was the most stuck-up person she had ever seen. Passing him in the hall one day, she had said "hello" and Bubba continued to walk as if she didn't exist. After hearing her story, Eula wondered, "So just who is the *hootie tootie?*"

The school's mascot for the football team was a cougar. Bubba said he felt sorry for the poor student who had the task of donning the cat suit, as Bubba had dubbed it, and parading up and down the sidelines, trying to spark enthusiasm in a lost cause. The Mighty Cougars they weren't and hadn't been in years. Eula knew Bubba, Little Jimmy and some of the others had athletic ability. What she didn't know and what she figured her friends wondered as well, "was it enough talent to make the team?" But there was one thing for sure, the team needed help. Bubba was right. The quarterback couldn't hit a bull in the ass with a handful of rice, and she felt like she could probably rack up more yardage than their running back. She decided to challenge the bark and address Bubba in front of his friends.

"Bubba, behind the church, y'all really look good. And you've pointed out often enough, and we know it as well, our high school team has a lot in common with a Hoover vac; they both suck. That's a given. But the question begging to be answered here, is this—how do y'all know you could do any better in a real game situation than poor old Johnny and Rodney do? Huh? How do you know, unless you're willing to go out for the team? We all believe you can, but..." and she left the but hanging, waiting for a response.

"Where's this going?" Little Jimmy asked. Eula had gotten everyone's attention.

"Yeah," Bubba added, "what's the point? School started three weeks ago and they've been practicing for about five weeks all together. We're a little late for this year, don't you think? But let's say, for the sake of argument, we go out for the team, and in your world, we make the team, and in my world, we get to sit on the bench for the entire season, watching what's his name make a fool out of himself and continue the losing streak. They'll never let us play, so what would be the point?"

"I hear you, Bubba, but you'll never know that for sure unless you go out for the team. Someone told me the new coach, even though it's three weeks into the season, is trying to recruit guys right now, and he may not be in anyone's pocket. I dare you, or as we said when we were younger, I double-dog dare you to go out for the team. Y'all put yourselves in the game or quit criticizing those who are willing to try. They may be *hootie tooties*, but they'll get killed and embarrassed all season if someone doesn't step up and help. What do you say to that, Bubba Preston, and the rest of you? Do you have balls enough to try out for the team?"

Eula was on a roll and she knew it.

Bubba stood up quickly and said, "Time to go to work, LJ." Lots of Little Jimmy's friends called him LJ. Squeezing Clarice's shoulder, Bubba headed for the truck. Maude roared to life and he and Little Jimmy were gone.

"Oh crap," Clarice said. "Eula, what have you done?"

The drive to work was only a five-mile trip. Neither one said anything for a few minutes. Finally, Little Jimmy asked, "What was all that about? Who put a burr under her saddle?"

"It's all right," Bubba said, brushing Eula's tirade away as if it hadn't spoken to him. "You know how they get. Every so often, they feel like they have to mother us. I guess it's a female thing, trying to figure out what's best for the ones they care about and, believe me, Eula cares about all of us. That's for damn sure."

"No doubt about that," Little Jimmy said. "But that double-dog dare, that was something else, wasn't it?"

"Classic Eula," Bubba said. "Best friend a person could ever have. Aggravating as the day is long, but she means well, LJ."

⋅⋇⋅⋅⋇⋅⋅⋇⋅

The eight-hour shift seemed exceptionally long. Eula's speech caused Bubba to look deep within himself. After taking Little Jimmy home, Bubba drove a little slower than usual, still trying to make sense of the earlier evening's conversation with Eula. And Little Jimmy was right, that double-dog dare was stuck in his craw.

Parking Maude beside their trailer, he cut the lights off and shut the engine down. It was late and he was tired. Granny would be up and ready in the morning, waiting for him to take her to church, and no matter what else was going on in Bubba's world, his Granny took precedence. In the dark cab of his truck, with no one to see the tears streaming down his face, he dealt himself an honest hand. He wasn't really jealous of the *hootie tooties* and their prominence in the community. Their fancy homes, cars, clothes and money was just that—theirs. In reality, he was ashamed of his family and their lack of status in a world where he had to interact and mingle with those who had so much more of life's goods. The real issue wasn't the *hootie tooties.* They were simply the scapegoats for all the frustration he felt about his station in life and the struggle he saw his parents having, just trying to make ends meet.

Getting out and shutting Maude's door as quietly as he could, he stood looking at the single-wide trailer he had always called home. He often joked about getting a house that didn't have wheels, but God, how he loved this place and the ones sleeping

13

so peacefully inside. They were special and he knew it. Money didn't make special people, heart did, and they had the biggest hearts in the world. Entering the unlocked trailer, he quietly went to his bedroom and collapsed into the hole that had been his mattress for way too many years.

⌀⌀⌀⌀⌀⌀⌀

Granny was hard of hearing, but she could hear Maude's tailpipes barking as Bubba came up the drive to pick her up for church. He saw the front door open on her single-wide, and she stepped out ever so gingerly, onto her deck. Her single biggest fear, at her age, was a fall. "A fall will put you in a nursing home and you usually die there," she said often. "Don't want that to happen to me. Gotta go slow and be careful. Some of my friends have already fallen and are in the home. Not me, if I can help it."

She was feisty, walking over to the edge of her deck. Bubba parked, jumped out, and hurried to the steps to help her down. "Good morning," she said and greeted him with a big hug. "I appreciate you picking me up and taking me to church. Means a lot to me, and I look forward to spending time with you." Bubba didn't realize it, but looking back, this would be one of his favorite memories, taking his Granny to church.

"You tired, Bubba? I know you are. That old furniture plant is a hard place to work. Put twenty years in there myself. But I ain't complaining. Helped me get my home paid off. Should be thankful, I guess. If it hadn't been for the old furniture plant, I might not have a place to live."

"Yes, ma'am," Bubba said, as if hearing this story for the first time. When they got to the truck and he opened Maude's door

14

for her to get in, she said the same thing she always said whenever he picked her up to take her anywhere. "Need a ladder to get in this thing."

She didn't realize the entire scenario was the same each and every Sunday, her words and Bubba's as well. "Better watch it, Granny, Maude's kinda sensitive. You hurt her feelings and she might not crank."

Bubba drove slowly when his Granny was in the truck. On the ride to church, she would point out old, fallen-down houses and barns and tell him who used to live in them. He felt like he knew those folk, people who had passed long before he was even born. There was a hollow sound in her voice, almost haunting, as she took Bubba back to people in another time and a place he could never go. But she had been there. As he drove, the old places would once more come alive as she mentioned the names of those who had lived in them.

Maude didn't have a handicap sticker, but the whole church knew he parked there so Granny wouldn't have so far to walk. Bubba, good-looking, blonde hair and blue eyes, six foot, four inches tall, great physique— teenager with all the answers. With his right arm around her shoulders, holding her left hand in his, he walked his Granny through the doors and down the aisle to the second pew on the right. Her small frame, bent over from ninety-two years of living, moved slowly. The pastor would always smile and think to himself, "Now that's what a grandson is supposed to look like." Along the way, she had to stop and speak to everyone she knew, which was most of the members. Often, Pastor Baker, smiling, would stand behind the podium and wait, out of respect for Granny, until she made it to her pew.

The pastor's observation was correct. Bubba, bringing his Granny to church every Sunday morning, and helping her to her seat, was an example of love at its best, on display for a world seemingly bent on its own destruction. Bubba, the *hootie tootie warrior,* looked more Christ-like walking his Granny down the aisle than he would at any future time in his life. He didn't realize it then, but others did and it made members of the congregation smile at the obvious love and devotion shown by a teenage grandson to his beloved Granny. But more importantly, it made Jesus smile as well.

⚜⚜⚜

Pastor Baker always preached good sermons, and this morning was no exception. Granny Preston loved Pastor Baker, partly because he would stop by several times a month to look in on her. She was still a very good cook and the pastor always went away with a full belly and a package of sweets for his missus. The visit was mutually good for both of them. Bubba figured the pastor got the better part of the deal, considering how good his Granny cooked. She got a visit, which she enjoyed, but the pastor got cake, cookies, and Granny's fried chicken, which made the Colonel's take a back seat.

Going back down the aisle after the service was as slow as coming in. Granny had to speak to all her friends on the way out. Bubba was her favorite grandchild and he knew it. He was never impatient, nor did he make her feel hurried in any way. When they finally reached Maude, Granny said the same thing she'd said an hour or so earlier, "Need a ladder to get in this thing."

Bubba got her into the truck and went around and climbed in on his side. "Well, you finally did it, Granny."

"Did what, Bubba, what did I do?"

"You hurt Maude's feelings, Granny, and she's crying."

16

"Aw, bull, Bubba, you're full of it." She liked to cut up and have a good time. She still had a quick wit and a good comeback. "They say you can go to hell for telling whoppers. You know this truck can't cry. Wait till I tell Pastor Baker. He needs to pray for you. Maybe even a laying on of hands is in order. Maude's crying— who ever heard such nonsense."

They talked about Maude all the way home. As always, she already had some Sunday fixings and tried to get Bubba to stay and eat with her. Before he got so involved with Clarice, he ate with her almost every Sunday. Arriving at Granny's trailer and helping her inside, Bubba replied, "I can't today, Granny, I . . ."

"I know, it's that Clarice girl. She's done took my grandson away from me. I may have to have a little talk with Maude and see what the ole girl has to say about this."

"Well, after I get back from seeing Clarice, I'll send Maude over and y'all can have that little talk."

He had one foot in her trailer and the other on the porch, ready to go. Testosterone had got the best of Granny's favorite grandson. He kissed her on the cheek, gave her a hug and promised her he'd come by in a few days to make sure the preacher didn't eat up all her fixings. This left her with a smile on her face as she waved to Bubba and Maude, tooling down the driveway, headed for Clarice's house.

Clarice lived about eight miles on the other side of town. She went to Mt. Gilead United Methodist Church. Bubba had taken Clarice by several times to see Granny so they could spend some time getting to know each other. When Granny found out she was Methodist, she told Clarice that everyone was Baptist until someone went and messed with them. Bubba knew she was pulling Clarice's leg, but Clarice didn't know what to think about what Granny had said, and asked Bubba to explain it after they left. "You're gonna have to watch Granny closely or she'll pull the wool over your eyes for sure," he told her.

After leaving Granny's, all the things Eula had said the previous day came flooding back into Bubba's mind. He was in a hurry to get over to Clarice's house so they could spend the rest of the day together. Maude was purring along, her tailpipes echoing over the open fields they were passing. Eula had made it sound like all the bad vibes he got from the *hootie tooties* was more his fault than theirs. No way was he going to take the blame for their bad manners and snobbery. Not on his watch, anyway.

Bubba often kidded Clarice about being uppity because she had a double-wide. He said Maude was so intimidated, she usually skipped and sputtered when they turned up her driveway. Clarice's answer was always the same, "You're so full of it, Bubba Preston, you and Maude both."

When a child is scolded or punished by one parent, they often turn to the other for comfort, sort of good cop, bad cop. That's the way he felt as he pulled into Clarice's drive. The previous day, Eula had hammered him quite a bit in front of their friends. He needed Clarice to tell him he wasn't as bad as Eula had made him out to be, or he wasn't crazy with prejudice against the other kids because they simply had things he didn't. For whatever reason, he needed the love of his life to pick him up, dust him off, and tell him it was okay. And Bubba, being Bubba, hoped for a whole lot more.

Parking Maude next to Clarice's father's truck, he bounded up the three steps onto the deck of their trailer. Mr. Smith came to the door and invited him in. "Clarice, Bubba's here," he said loud enough for her to hear him. "She'll be here in a minute. You know how long it takes for the ladies to get all their ducks in a row."

"Yes, sir, I do indeed. Drives my dad absolutely crazy having to wait on my mom. Usually, she's the one who decides where they're going and when, and he has to work around her schedule. When the time comes, he's ready and in the car twenty minutes before Mom walks out the door."

"Know that scene all too well myself," Mr. Smith said. "Well, here comes Clarice. She's a little faster than her mother."

"Give her time," Bubba said, as she walked into the living room. "Just give her time."

"Give me time for what, Bubba? Y'all ain't badmouthing us girls again, are you? Cause if you are, I'll call Mama in here right now and she'll straighten both of you out."

"Oh, nothing like that," Bubba said, grinning. "See you later, Mr. Smith."

Mr. Smith nodded goodbye and they were out the front door.

Clarice knew Bubba as well as anyone and could tell he was not himself. She knew why Eula had challenged him and Little Jimmy Saturday and actually agreed with her analysis. But she also knew that while his bark was ferocious, Bubba had a gentle spirit and got his feelings hurt easily.

Clarice slid over next to Bubba and placed her hand on his leg. A little smile started to creep from the corners of his mouth. Clarice loved his blue eyes and dashing smile. "Gotcha," she said. "Now talk to me, Bubba. I'm sorry about Saturday. But you get so wound up about your *hootie tooties,* it can't possibly be good for you. Eula loves you like a brother and worries about you. Eula's like a sister to me, and we talk about everything. We both just want you to be happy, that's all."

"I hope you don't tell her everything," Bubba said, flashing his million-dollar grin. "Like what you do when—"

"Stop right there, Bubba Preston, and don't make fun of me. You're the one that makes me do that, and no, I wouldn't dare tell her about the only thing her pretend brother seems to have on his mind. She already suspects it, but I'm not telling her and you'd better not tell Little Jimmy or no one else either. Do you hear me, Bubba?"

"I thought about telling Granny," he said jokingly.

"Oh, that would be just dandy. She'd tell the whole church and they'd drag us kicking and screaming to the front and lay hands on both of us. And it's not me that's got the problem, it's you."

"Speaking of laying on of hands," he said, placing his hand on her leg.

"Stop it, Bubba, this is serious stuff. You don't take nothing serious. We're gonna keep on, and there's gonna be a Bubba Junior running around before we're ready for it."

"I bet he'd be beautiful," Bubba said thoughtfully, squeezing her leg and then putting both hands on the steering wheel. "And I resent your remark about me taking nothing serious. I was serious about telling Granny what you've been doing."

"What I've been doing? Have you lost your mind? It's all you. I'm just the innocent victim here."

"Innocent, my butt. Look in the rearview mirror and tell yourself that lie without smiling." Clarice pulled the rearview down and started to repeat her statement of innocence. "I'm just the innocent," then she broke out in a smile that turned into laughter.

"Now, who's not serious here? I'm the only one who's serious in this relationship. That's why I was going to talk to Granny about you and your promiscuous behavior."

"My what?" Clarice said, getting agitated with him. "And how could you discuss something as devilish as your inappropriate behavior with your sweet, little ole Granny? She'd be so disappointed in you, and heartbroken to boot."

"Because she's got experience, that's why."

"You ought to be ashamed, talking any such way about your saintly Granny."

"Well, she's done it at least six times."

Clarice gasped, "Bubba, Lord forgive your evil ways."

"Well, she has done it six times, at least. My daddy is the result of one of them."

"You could aggravate the devil himself," she said.

"Okay, but I refuse to let you drag my granny into serious stuff like your bad behavior. So, let's talk about something silly and meaningless instead."

After a few seconds of silence, he said, "Me and Little Jimmy talked last night on the way to work and at break times. No one, I mean no one, double-dog dares the dynamic-duo. It's probably too late, but we'll talk to Coach Henderson and see if he needs two more people to warm the bench for him. He'll turn us down because, never mind, you don't want to hear why again, but at least we'll honestly tag-team the double-dog dare, pin it on the mat, and then maybe Eula can give it a rest."

"Don't be ugly to Eula and don't forget she loves you like a brother. She's only concerned because you seem to get so upset and agitated whenever anything is mentioned about the school or any kids other than your friends. Hey, I've got a great idea. I guarantee it'll make you feel better."

"All right," he said, placing a hand on her knee. "I bet I know what it is."

"You ain't right, Bubba, and you don't know what my idea is. Put both hands on the steering wheel before you get us killed."

"Okay, what's your feel-good idea?"

"Why don't we go fishing? We ain't been in a while and who knows, we might catch something this time. It's a beautiful day and my blanket and the fishing rods are in the tool box. What do you say, Bubba Preston, would you like to take a pretty girl on a Sunday afternoon fishing trip? Never can tell what you might catch."

"Hey, I like the sound of that!"

"Don't read too much into that. You're already considering confessing your sins to Granny. No need to add any more to the growing list of misdeeds you're rapidly accumulating."

"Misdeeds, my foot, I'll show you misdeeds. You're as guilty as I am, maybe more."

Feeling better, he broke into an improvised song. "A fishin' we will go, a fishin' we will go, high ho cheerio, a fishin' we will go."

"You ain't got a dab of sense. Don't forget the bait. Can't go fishing without bait."

"I'm headed to Harold's, even as we speak. Grab some fresh chicken liver for Big Blue's Sunday dinner and some snacks for our picnic."

"Big Blue's a figment of your imagination. You probably think he's a *hootie tootie*, too."

"Oh, no, Little Jimmy's seen him twice, and I've seen him once. He's four-foot long, if he's an inch."

"Uh huh, in y'all's minds. Little boys dreaming about a monster catfish, terrifying the river folks."

"I'll show you little boys dreaming," he said.

"We're going fishing, Bubba, *F I S H I N G*. And that's all, or I'll tell Granny myself."

Clarice sat in the truck while he went into Harold's to get the bait. He got two cans of Vienna sausage, a box of saltines, two large Hershey bars, and two belly-washers, his nickname for two-liter Cokes. He bought a pound of fresh chicken livers for Big Blue. He'd fed the catfish in the river so much chicken liver, one of them ought to be four-foot long, for sure. Putting the supplies in the tool box, he climbed in and fired Maude up.

"Sing with me, honey," he said and broke into his rendition of

A fishin' we will go. "Got Big Blue a whole box of chicken livers for his Sunday lunch. Who knows, today could be my lucky day."

"Who knows," Clarice said in a Marilyn Monroe, seductive tone. "It just might be."

"That's the last straw. I'm calling Granny for sure now. She has to know about this."

"About what? I'm the one calling Granny." They both laughed. "Where we going fishing today?"

"To our favorite, and I might add, secluded spot, down by old man Jones' farm. Big Blue hangs out there a lot. He likes the bend in the river, and the little tributary feeding into the river supplies him with a lot of snacks. Big Blue says there's a good-looking chick who sometimes frequents the river bend, not at all bad to look at."

"Is that so?" Clarice said with a doubtful look on her face. "I'm starting to get concerned here. Now you're talking to catfish?"

"Not any old catfish, just Big Blue. We communicate because we're both connoisseurs of fine women, of course mine has legs and his has fins, but it's really all about good taste."

 It was secluded. The old county road was mostly dirt with a little gravel here and there. The going was slow because of all the washboard ruts. But it was a beautiful place to picnic or spend leisure time watching the river flow around the bend and head south. The river was about thirty yards across and was partially lined with oaks and scrub brush, making it very private. There was a clearing about twenty yards from where the road ended, an easy walk from the truck. Clarice got the blanket and the two folding canvas chairs he kept in the back of the truck. Bubba got the fishing gear, their lunch and Big Blue's chicken livers. It was a gorgeous day for a fishing trip and a picnic.

Bubba was more interested in helping her spread out the blanket than in fishing. "Bubba, go fish. Big Blue's waiting for his Sunday dinner."

"Are you sure you don't need any help with the blanket?"

"Go fish, Bubba. Fish."

Smiling, he said, "Okay, if I gotta."

"You gotta. I saw Granny sneaking down the path a few minutes ago. She'll get your goat if you don't go fish."

He put the rod-holders in the ground, baited the two spinners with the chicken liver, and cast them out into the deepest part of the river. He used pieces of old pantyhose to wrap the chicken liver in and ran the hook through the liver and the small piece of pantyhose. It helped to keep the catfish from stripping the hook too easily. Sometimes, because the piece of hose would have blood on it from the liver, the catfish would mess around with it, trying to get it off the hook, and would eventually get caught, which was the idea to begin with.

Sitting back in his chair, he waited, but not without comment.

"Come on, Big Blue, dinner's ready. Nice, soft, fresh chicken livers. You know you're hungry, and I know how much you love chicken liver."

Clarice shook her head and thought to herself, "I have fallen in love with a guy who talks to catfish. How smart was that?"

Wearing shorts, and a halter top, she took off her open-front shirt and lay back on the blanket to soak up a little sun and work on her tan. It was one of the last warm, pretty days before fall arrived with cooler temperatures. She kept a book in the tool box for outings like this one and usually fell asleep reading.

It was a lazy kind of Sunday, and Bubba was almost asleep when he realized he was getting a bite on one of his fishing rods. He got up so fast, he turned over his chair. With rod in hand, he was ready. The catfish was playing with the bait. He'd pick it up, swim just a little ways, and spit it out of his mouth, not giving Bubba a chance to set the hook. The commotion woke up Clarice.

"Go ahead, you know you want it. Take the bait, delicious chicken liver, fresh from Harold's. Bought it just for you. Come on, it'll taste so good." The catfish straightened the line for a third time, but dropped the bait again.

Clarice called out, "What's going on over there? This is supposed to be a relaxing Sunday afternoon picnic, and it sounds like someone watching a wrestling match on television. Could we please hold it down a little? Relax. This is supposed to be fun. You make it sound like work."

"Relax, my butt, fishing is serious business."

Clarice shook her head and smiled at all the racket Bubba was making. Now awake, she picked up her book with the intention of reading. But, not so. Bubba continued his rant.

"Damn it, he's got the bait."

"How do you know it's a him catfish?"

"Because he got the bait. Female catfish are so much easier to catch. Bingo, they're caught and in the frying pan."

"Bubba, you sound so tough. If your friends only knew how much control I have over you, it'd be embarrassing. To Little Jimmy and the others, you're like a bull dog. To me, you're like a bull dog with no teeth." Clarice giggled. She thought it was so funny, comparing him to a bull dog with no teeth.

"You're crazy, girl," he replied to her assertion, while still holding his fishing rod. "You don't control me, you only think you do."

Clarice removed her halter top, letting her small, firm breasts, bathe in the sun.

Bubba, with his back to her, was still mumbling to himself about the catfish stealing his bait.

Lying back on the blanket, she said, "I wonder if this old blanket could catch me a fisherman who'd like to wiggle his worm—"

Bubba turned around and saw her reclining on the blanket, her hands behind her head and a big smile on her face.

"Hot damn," Bubba said, dropping his fishing rod to the ground . As he started toward her she said, "Bingo. The fish is in the pan and here comes my toothless bulldog."

"Call me what you want, just let me wiggle my worm in your pond for a while," he said as he slipped his blue jeans to the ground.

"What about Granny?" Clarice asked as he lay down next to her on the blanket.

"Granny who?"

After loading the truck, they climbed inside to head home. Clarice slid over next to Bubba and laid her head on his shoulder. Maude roared to life, with the tailpipes barking in unison.

"Love that sound," Clarice said softly.

"Yeah, those pipes do make beautiful music, don't they?" Bubba replied.

"Not the pipes, Bubba, the sounds we make when we do it."

Bubba smiled and said, "Do what, Clarice?"

Clarice, a little embarrassed, said, "Stop it, Bubba, you know what."

"Hot damn," Bubba said and let out a howl. "Beats fishing any day."

Clarice remembering the bulldog with no teeth, created her own little ditty and sang it for Bubba. "Girls rule and boys drool, so the story goes. I'm the boss and that's final, even if no one knows."

⤴⤴⤴

On Monday morning Bubba and Little Jimmy left for school early. Coach Henderson was in his office every morning by 6:30. They were hoping to talk to him before class. Bubba was sure it was a lost cause, but at least they would have made the attempt that should satisfy the double-dog dare. Coach Henderson's office was in the gym building. He heard their footsteps as they echoed in the empty gym and was surprised when the two young men opened the door and entered his office.

"Can I help you boys?" the coach said as he stood up behind his desk.

Extending his hand, Bubba introduced himself. "Sir, my name is Tom Preston and this is my friend, Jimmy Denton. We figured it's too late to try out for this year's football team, but we thought we'd ask."

After shaking their hands, he motioned for them to sit down in the chairs in front of his desk. He sat down but didn't say anything immediately. With his elbows on his desk and his chin resting on his hands, he studied the two boys for a few seconds. It was a very uncomfortable silence. His brow was wrinkled, but his face was expressionless. It made Bubba and Little Jimmy feel uneasy.

"I've seen both of you some time or the other in the hallways here or maybe in the parking lot. If you pay any attention at all to the announcements, you know we've already lost our first three games. And we started practicing four weeks before school started. So the boys playing on the team are already in their seventh week of football. Why now?"

Neither of the boys answered immediately so the coach continued with the grilling. "I can look at the two of you and tell both of you are in reasonably good physical condition. Have you ever played organized sports and, in particular, football?"

"Not with a school team or anything like that," Little Jimmy said, "but we play just about every Saturday behind Coosa Baptist Church and we usually play about two hours or so. And

Bubba—" Bubba elbowed Little Jimmy's arm discreetly, but the coach noticed it.

Bubba said, "We just play touch football at the church, nothing really special. We play, like Little Jimmy said, for a couple of hours most Saturdays before we have to go to work."

"Where do you work?"

"At McClain's," Little Jimmy answered before Bubba could respond.

"How many hours do you work each week, and what are the hours?"

"Counting Fridays and Saturdays, which are eight-hour shifts, and four hours a day Monday through Thursday, we usually get in around 32 hours a week."

"How do you manage that and go to school at the same time?" Coach Henderson asked.

"We make bad grades," Bubba said and smiled.

"No, we don't, Bubba, you know better than that," Little Jimmy countered. "I admit they could be better, but considering how much we work, we do pretty darn good, if you ask me."

Bubba shook his head at Little Jimmy's boldness, something he usually didn't display around strangers. It made him smile that million-dollar trademark smile. You couldn't help but like Bubba if you ever saw him smile. Little Jimmy's honesty and Bubba's smile had already captivated Coach Henderson.

"Sorry, boys. There's no way you can play. You're at least six weeks late, and we practice every afternoon after school and you have to work. I'm really sorry, but I can't use you."

"All right," Bubba said standing, and turning to leave. "Just thought we'd ask. Never hurts to ask."

Little Jimmy stood up also, but said, "Wait a minute. We chose that shift. We can change it to eight to twelve. That would make it work, Coach. If you'll give us a chance. I promise, you won't be sorry."

Little Jimmy sat back down, pulling Bubba back down with him.

"I don't know about this," Coach Henderson said, shaking his head and shrugging his shoulders at the same time. "Sounds like too much to me; school all day, practice each day after school and then a four-hour shift at McClain's. What about Fridays? That's game night."

Little Jimmy was quick with a response. "No problem, Coach, we'll cut our hours. Won't be a problem, I promise. That's an easy fix."

Bubba was baffled and amazed. Little Jimmy never took the lead in anything involving decisions or problems. He usually waited for someone else to sort it out or solve the issue. But not today.

The coach's brow was really wrinkled now. "Why?" he asked himself, "would anyone want to play ball this bad and yet come out after the summer practice and three weeks into the season. Why? Must be special boys sitting in front of me, or maybe it's an apparition. Maybe this isn't happening at all. We need help so bad, I must be imagining all of this."

But Little Jimmy was no apparition. He moved to the edge of his chair and put his arms on Coach Henderson's desk. Looking eye to eye with the coach, he said, "If you'll only give us a chance, I promise you won't be sorry. I give you my word on that. Bubba can—"

Bubba cleared his throat to get Little Jimmy's attention and he stopped with whatever he was about to say to him. Bubba was both frustrated and impressed with his friend. Frustrated, because Little Jimmy was going to keep pushing until he made this happen. And impressed because of the confidence he was showing.

"How are your grades? You joked about them being bad. What kind of grades do you really have?"

"Okay. Not the greatest, but okay. It's hard to study and work every night at McClain's. I have B's and one C right now."

"How about yours?" Coach Henderson addressed Bubba.

"Right now I have one A and the rest B's."

"Wow, I'm impressed, especially as much as the two of you are working. But can you add football and maintain these grades? That's the real question."

"The football season doesn't last but a few weeks," Little Jimmy interjected. "We'll just have to make it happen, that's all."

Who is this guy sitting next to me, Bubba wondered to himself. He's said more in the last twenty minutes than he's said in the past two months.

"I don't know about this," Coach Henderson said. "I just don't know."

"Just give us a chance. That's all we're asking for, is a chance. And you won't be sorry."

"What the hell," the coach said. "Y'all can't hurt us, that's for sure. You'll both have to get a physical. Old Doc Matthews will work you in. I'll give him a call. Do you know where his office is?"

"Sure do," Little Jimmy said with a smile on his face that would kill most people. "We'll go this morning, if that's okay with you."

"What about your classes?" the coach asked with concern in his voice.

Bubba finally decided to help Little Jimmy out. "They won't miss us. We sit at the back of the room. No one even knows we're there," Bubba responded, smiling at his own wit.

"You can take that to the bank," Little Jimmy added. "Believe us, they wouldn't miss us if we never came back."

Coach Henderson couldn't help but smile. "We do need some help," he said as if talking to himself and trying to justify letting them start so late.

"I don't know what I'll tell the team," he added, "but that's my problem. Do y'all know any of the players?"

"Know all of them," Little Jimmy answered.

"But only from the back of the room," Bubba added and laughed.

"Go on and get out of here. Doc Matthews opens at eight AM. Be there and then get back to school. Okay?"

"Okay," they answered in unison.

"Get to class as soon as possible, and this conversation never happened. Understand?"

"Yes, sir," they said as they hurried out of the coach's office.

They had no way of knowing it, but Coach Henderson was one of them. He didn't grow up living in a trailer, but he did grow up in a very small home, four rooms and a single bath, in a very small town in Alabama. His father, now retired, had been custodian for the main post office in Eufala. He had always told people he was just a janitor, but he was happy to have a federal job and the benefits that came with it.

After the boys left his office, the coach sat back down again and stared at the now empty chairs in front of his desk. "I can't believe I'm doing this," he said out loud, "but I know those guys. I've always known them."

Little Jimmy was excited and it was a bit contagious, despite Bubba pretending it didn't matter one way or the other to him. Several teachers were walking across the parking lot, so Little Jimmy didn't say anything until they were inside the truck. Maude looked a little out of place, parked in the teacher's parking area. She didn't seem intimidated as she roared to life, her tail pipes drawing attention as they pulled into the road headed over to Doc Matthews.

"Calm down, hoss," Bubba said, "you're gonna have a heart

attack before we get to the doctor. Like my old man says, 'you're rearing to go and can't go for rearing.' Do you realize what you just managed to do, all by your lonesome?"

"Yes, I know. Why wouldn't I know? You weren't much help in there."

"You didn't seem to need any help, the way you were going. You just landed us in seven weeks of hell, between school, football practice, Friday night games and McClain's."

"We're tough, and you know it. We're *trailer-park tough*. The dynamic-duo can handle anything. Can't we?"

The ship had already left port. Bubba had only one real option for an answer without hurting his best friend's feeling.

"Damn straight," Bubba said and smiled, "we're *trailer-park tough* and we can handle anything. But remember," he cautioned, "all we're gonna do is ride the bench. We'll never get in a game."

"Well, I'm hoping to get to play, but even if we don't, how about this? We can rest while sitting on the bench."

"Little Jimmy, you ain't got a lick of sense."

"*Hot damn*," Little Jimmy said, "wait till I tell Eula. Don't ever double-dog dare the dynamic-duo again."

Bubba couldn't help but feel the excitement his friend was creating.

"Notice anything about Coach Henderson?"

"Sure did. He's one of us."

"Bingo," Bubba said, as he wheeled Maude into the parking lot at Doc Matthews.

❦❧ ❦❧ ❦❧

Twenty-eight of Bubba's so-called *hootie tooties* sat in front of Eula in her second-period advanced chem class. She was very pretty, with long blonde hair falling over her shoulders and halfway to her waist.

Blue eyes weren't wasted here, either. And behind those baby-blues was a mind willing and able to excel academically. As a matter of fact, she believed her GPA would allow her to escape from poverty and help elevate those she loved to a better level as well. The previous year she had the second highest GPA of her school and had every intention of doing it again this year. This had to be maintained, in spite of working more than twenty-five hours a week behind the counter at the local DQ. She believed it would be her ticket to a better life for herself and her family.

Bubba ranted and raved about the perceived, or real, socioeconomic differences he felt impacted his life at school. He actually had very few classes with the kids who drove the BMWs, the Mercedes and the Corvettes. But Eula did. Because of her smarts, she lived in their world. While feeling at times uncomfortable and a little left out, she realized the kids were just that, kids like her. The only exception was that their parents, for whatever the reason, had more money than her parents. Not their fault, her fault, or anyone's fault. Just a fact. They were never ugly to her or anything of the sort. She simply couldn't run with them outside of school. Working at the DQ and studying took most of her spare time. "It is what it is" was one of her dad's favorite sayings.

She felt more comfortable sitting at the rear of the classroom. This Monday morning, sitting in her desk, she was running the weekend's events through her mind, worrying about what she had said to Bubba and LJ. She had no idea they were already on the team. She was lost in those thoughts as the buzzer sounded, ending class. It startled her and she rose quickly, causing her books and things to fall to the floor.

"Shit," she said under her breath, but still audible. Kneeling down on one knee, she began gathering up her belongings when she heard, "Amen to that."

Eyeballing a very nice pair of shoes, she looked up to see who was standing over her.

"Let me help you," he said softly, kneeling to give her a hand in gathering everything up. Second-period students had left and the next class was filing into the room.

"No, thanks, I can get this."

"No question about that. I know you don't need my help. You're Eula Johnson. You work a job and still manage to have the second highest GPA in the entire senior class. But, please. I want to help you. Please?"

Eula stood up, as the good-looking guy who sat toward the front of two of her classes gathered up her belongings.

"I'm—"

"I know who you are," she said hastily and a little sarcastically. After a short pause, she added, "I'm sorry, I didn't mean to sound so rude. Please forgive me," Eula said, as he placed her things back on her desk.

"It's okay, no harm done. I don't believe we've formally met before, so with your permission I'll try again." He flashed a beautiful smile, immediately reminding her of Bubba. She smiled as well and nodded okay.

Trying to be funny, he said, "After the last attempt, I almost forgot who I am." This broke the ice, and Eula laughed.

"I'm William Morgan, Jr. Some of my friends call me William and, of course, some just call me Junior. I'd be delighted to call you my friend, and it's up to you to call me whatever you want. Just don't reject my offer of friendship without at least giving me a chance."

Eula knew who he was. He was the son of the richest and most powerful man in Georgia. His father could make you or break you, his choice—or so the story went. He drove a brand new, or as Bubba would say, a brand damn new BMW. All of that didn't compute to be the person who had just picked her books up, and extended what seemed to be a serious attempt at friendship. It had only been a few seconds, as she processed what she knew about him, but it must have been an eternity for William. He turned to walk away.

With the entire incoming class watching and straining to hear what was being said between the richest boy in the school and probably one of the poorest girls in the school, she grabbed his arm before he took the second step.

"Wait, wait," she stammered. He stopped and turned to face her. His back was to the class and they couldn't see or hear anything. "My Mama didn't raise me like that. She'd be ashamed if she knew how I just treated you. I'm Eula Johnson, and I would very much enjoy your friendship, that is, if you still want to be friends."

She extended her hand and he took it immediately, covering it with his left hand. He held it a long time. "I've been trying to find the courage to do this for the last few weeks or so. Guess dropping your books opened the door. And the answer is yes. Yes, I very much want to be your friend."

As they started to leave, he literally wrestled her books from her and insisted on carrying them. She was flabbergasted, and so were the students who were still staring and trying to figure out what was happening.

On the way to calculus, not a word was said. He was beaming and she was perplexed. It had the appearance of a joke being told, and one person got it, and the other didn't. That's what it looked like to the other students they passed in the hallway.

No matter what the other students saw, or thought they saw, for the few minutes it took to walk to the next class, Eula Johnson was in Camelot. The shock was not over. It was about to intensify. As they entered the calculus class, he walked to the back of the room to the desk she always sat in. Placing her books on her desk, he took the empty seat next to her. "Mind if I sit next to you?" he asked politely.

"Of course not," she stammered, "I'd like that very much." She could feel her face turn red and flushed with embarrassment and couldn't believe her response to his question.

They both smiled at each other, a knowing smile having deep implications for both of them. And oddly enough, they both felt it. The rest of the students coming into the class stood and stared until the teacher said, "All right, please. Everyone turn around and take your seats." William and Eula were oblivious to the stares, each lost in their own thoughts.

❦❦❦

After school Bubba caught up with Eula in the student parking lot and told her about being on the team.

"You gotta be shittin' me," Eula said, leaving her mouth wide open in disbelief. "How you gonna work, study and play football?"

"Oh, no," Bubba responded, *"you gotta be shittin' ME.* You tell us how we're gonna do it. You caused it by that double-dog dare crap you laid on LJ. I know what you were trying to do, but he took it dead serious. Hope you're proud of yourself. Think about us when we leave practice headed for work. It's gonna be a great seven weeks."

"I was only trying to get you to lighten up on the *hootie tooties,* that's all. I never expected you to actually play on the high school football team."

"Should have convinced LJ of that. You lit a fuse under his butt, and he went berserk with Coach Henderson and pretty much single-handedly talked us onto the team."

"No way, not our Little Jimmy."

"Oh, hell yeah. You'd thought it was a good paying job the way he went after it."

Eula smiled. "Good for him. He needed that. It's not your fault, but he lives in your shadow."

"Yes he needed it bad. By the way, I've heard a few rumors, something about you trying to climb the social ladder. Perhaps that explains the *hootie tootie* endorsements of late."

"Call Granny Preston and ask her what she thinks of rumors. Told me, she did, that rumors come from the devil's workshop. And, besides, your few weeks of hell playing football and having to work—I actually study, Bubba Preston, and study a lot to make good grades in hopes of getting some scholarship money. And guess what, my man, I also work and some weeks I put in more hours than you and LJ. What do you think about that?"

"Not sure," he said and smiled. "Gotta check out these rumors with Granny. She's not gonna believe who I heard is apparently sweet on you. I'm telling you now, old moneybags won't approve."

"There's nothing that needs approving, Bubba. I just met William Morgan this morning in chem class. And you know people always gossip in this school and in this town. That's because they're bored silly and can't find anything worthwhile to do. Just because someone speaks to you in class doesn't mean there's anything to it other than being nice and as I've told you over and over, most of the kids with fancy cars and money are not as bad as you think they are."

"Remember what Mama always says, the proof's in the pudding." Bubba laughed. It was kinda fun getting Eula all riled up.

"Well there's no pudding here and nothing to put in the oven, so go on and leave me alone before you hack me off. And I know you don't want to do that."

"Just messin' with you," Bubba said.

❧❧❧

After meeting with Bubba and Little Jimmy about joining the team, Coach Henderson went to see the principal about his new players. Juanita Fisher was far more interested in academics than sports, but she realized their athletic program, and especially football, was a disaster. It wasn't Coach Henderson's fault; it was his first season as head coach.

"As long as they check out physically, I personally don't see a problem. But it's your call," Juanita told him.

"How are their grades?" he asked. "They claim they're pretty good, but they sure do have a hectic schedule ahead of them with football, studying and working."

"Some of these kids have it rather hard," Juanita said. "They come from families who struggle financially and they have to work to buy their own clothes and help out with the family's bills. I know one girl who has all advanced classes, plus works a job. Last year she had the second highest GPA score in the entire school and is off to a great start to do it again this year. How does that happen?"

Neither Juanita Fisher nor Coach Henderson had the faintest idea that the girl they were talking about was also the person who had issued the double-dog dare to the dynamic-duo in question.

"After getting your call, I pulled the grades of Tom Preston and Jimmy Denton, and they're actually better than those of most of the guys you already have on the team. Amazing! I'm sure it'll be hard, but the season isn't that long. Why now, or better yet, what do you see in these two students that makes you want to give them a chance?"

"Not sure, Juanita. Just a hunch. They appear to be in great shape, but that's not it. There's something in their faces that reminds me of someone else I once knew."

"It's not a mirror thing, is it?" she asked and smiled at the coach.

"I'm not telling. But thanks for approving this."

As he walked down the hallway on the way to the gym, he thought about what she had asked him. It was definitely a mirror thing. Assuming all went well at Doc Matthews, he had to tell the team immediately and wondered what their reaction would be to him letting two players start so late. When he got back to his office, he had a message from Doc Matthews' nurse that both boys passed their physicals with flying colors. He sent a message to Bubba and Little Jimmy in class telling them they were on the team and to come out tomorrow immediately after school for practice.

"Wonder why we can't practice today," Little Jimmy asked Bubba between fifth and sixth period classes.

"Well, first of all, we have to go and get our hours changed at McClain's. I know they'll do it, but we still have to tell them and get it cleared. Tomorrow will be soon enough to sit on the bench for three hours, watching what's his name try and throw the football."

Coach Henderson always met the guys in the gym as they made their way to the locker room with instructions for the day's practice. Sometimes, they would dress-out and go straight to the field. But other times, they would go over the previous week's game and discuss what happened and what they could do better next time, or go over new plays they would practice after dressing out and getting on the field.

"Have a seat," Coach Henderson instructed them as they

entered the gym on the way to the locker room. In a few minutes, the entire team was sitting, waiting on the coach to start practice.

"First of all, let me acknowledge how hard all of you have worked. It's been extremely hot, and you have practiced really hard. I hate the fact we're O-3 for the season, but I plan on changing that quickly. Tomorrow, we will have two new players joining the team. They have already had their physicals and have been cleared to play by Dr. Matthews and by the principal. I know they're a little late, but we could use a couple of more bodies so some of you might get a breather for a down or two. They haven't played organized football before, but they play every weekend with their friends. Their names are Tom Preston and Jimmy Denton."

From the back row came, "Oh, shit, not them two. They're trailer-park—"

A murmur went through the whole team.

"Knock it off," Coach Henderson said in a voice they hadn't heard before. "Judging someone by where they live, or what they have or don't have, isn't a fair evaluation of the person in question." The insight was wasted on most everyone, but the coach was pissed off.

"Dress out, give me five laps and meet me on the fifty-yard line," the coach said as he left the gym.

Johnny Kitchens, the quarterback, turned to the guy who had made the trailer-park remark and said, "That was about smart. Now we have to run five laps because of your big mouth."

"But that's what they are, they're nothing but trailer-park trash," someone else said. "They can't help this team."

"It's no big deal," Johnny said. "All they'll do is ride the bench. They'll quit inside of two weeks, I guarantee it. Those two won't ever amount to anything, on or off the field."

Another player interjected, "I hope you know what you're

talking about. I saw them playing one Saturday behind the Baptist church and stopped at the far end of the parking lot and watched for a few minutes. That Preston kid can throw the hell out of a football, and Jimmy Denton ain't no slouch when it comes to hauling in passes."

"That's bullshit," Johnny replied. "They'll never play here except to give someone a break for a down or two. Wait and see. I know what I'm talking about. In two weeks, they'll be gone."

After dressing out, the team was pounding the track for the five laps. It was very hot and sweat was pouring off them.

"Trailer-park trash, my ass," Coach Henderson said to himself as he sat watching the team run laps. "Should have made it ten laps. Y'all had better find out what the two new kids have and get some of it, because Mommy and Daddy won't always be around to bail you out and pay for your fancy lifestyle."

That evening at home the coach's phone rang off the hook. Johnny Kitchens' father called first. He owned the largest hardware store in the town. "Hey, coach, what's this I hear about letting anyone and everyone join the team whenever the hell they want to?"

Coach Henderson assured Mr. Kitchens he had the blessings of the principal to allow these two boys to join the team, albeit a little late. "Mr. Kitchens, I know you came to the first three games, but I don't know if you have paid any attention to the depth of our bench. It's basically non-existent. There are only nine extra players, which means most of the boys, with your son being the exception, have to play both ways for the entire game. We keep Johnny out on defense because we can't afford for him to get hurt. But no one, I mean no one, can play both ways for four consecutive quarters and be expected to ever win. So I thought, here's two more guys and that'll give us eleven on the bench."

As soon as the coach had finished with Mr. Kitchens, Terry Flannigan called. He owned the largest construction company in the county. His son, Rodney, was their running back. Same conversation with him.

And last, but not least, Dr. Williams called. His son, Jason, was a wide receiver. He hammered Coach Henderson harder than anyone. "Are you stupid, or what?" he began. Coach Henderson had him on speaker phone and his wife was listening. The coach slid up to the edge of his chair and started to rain down on the doc's private parade. But Cindi, his wife, laid a hand on his knee and smiled. She whispered, "Let them rant and rave, you're bigger than that."

Coach Henderson took a deep breath, but still unloaded a little. "I may actually be stupid," he said in agreement with Dr. Williams. "I knew when I came here that the school hadn't had a winning season in more years than I care to count. But I came anyway and, for your information, I'm glad I came. I view this a little differently than you do. Maybe these two kids, coming out late, is a sign that a little interest is being generated for the sports program here. I wish they had come out when everyone else did, but they both work a ton of hours every week and maybe they just didn't think about it. But they're here, and I'm damn glad they are." There was a click on the other end of the phone.

"The bastard hung up on me."

"It's okay, honey. Football is a very stressful thing for parents to deal with. Look at it this way. If you hack off enough of the right people the first year, we might get to move again, sooner than we expected. It could be an adventure. We just got unpacked, so it won't be hard to repack. I still have some of the boxes."

Coach Henderson laughed. He had a great relationship with Cindi. She was his anchor when the storms raged, as they frequently did around athletic programs. "You're right, we were looking for a job when we found this one, and we damn sure can find another one."

"That's my boy," Cindi said. "You should apologize for calling the doctor a bastard. That was ugly and your Mama would be ashamed of such language."

"He'll never know, unless you tell him. It's a good thing Mama didn't hear him call her pride and joy, stupid."

"That's for sure. She wouldn't call him ugly names, but she'd open up a can of whoop-ass and rub it all over him for calling you stupid."

They both laughed. "If the phone rings again, don't answer it."

"Amen to that."

⌘⌘⌘

William and Eula's interest in each other was nothing new for Union High. Twenty years earlier, a different William Morgan had fallen in love with another student who attended the same high school. Sue Ellen Thornton was beautiful and very smart. She had been valedictorian of her graduating class. She worked during the summer breaks at City Bank & Trust, where Mr. Morgan was president and principal stockholder. Her beauty attracted him and, unfortunately, she liked older men. In the early stages of wealth accumulation, Morgan paid little or no attention to the fact she was from a lower middle-class family. Earning a four-year degree in Business Administration in three years, Sue Ellen had numerous offers from top companies around the state. But she did what other kids from this town seldom did. She came back to Blairsville. Mr. Morgan had also made her an offer; one she couldn't refuse. He hired her as his executive secretary and moved her into a posh office next to his.

The bank was ablaze with gossip, as was the town. He was twenty years her senior, but it made no difference to Sue Ellen. He was rich, handsome and physically fit. Sue Ellen's parents, hearing all the nasty rumors, tried to talk some sense into their daughter, but it was like adding fuel to the fire. He was paying her a huge salary and her office had the ultimate décor, from furniture to window treatments. She loved the attention he paid her and seemingly enjoyed aggravating the other bank employees with what was obvious to everyone. Mr. Morgan was getting his money's worth, on all fronts.

William Morgan had no children. His first wife had died from cancer, and he was going through a divorce from his second wife. It had turned nasty and he couldn't care less what anyone said about him and Sue Ellen. Nor could Sue Ellen, for that matter.

Mr. Morgan had no intention of marrying her. He had his hands in every profitable venture in the Southeast. He had taken a multi-million dollar inheritance from his father and parleyed it into a fortune. He had only one question when it came to his involvement with anything or anybody—"What's in it for me?" It was clear to the whole town what was in it for him with regards to his executive secretary. As scandalous as this arrangement seemed to be, it would get a whole lot worse in short order.

The divorce from his second wife was finalized and since she had signed a prenuptial agreement, it severely limited the settlement she walked away with.

Sue Ellen had rented a very nice apartment, but after the second wife vacated the Morgan mansion, she spent more time there than at her own place. She sported around town in a Mercedes convertible, and no one could tell when she was staying at his place because the mansion had a six-car garage and was located on a hillside, hidden from passing traffic. A Mercedes convertible could easily hide there, and did so about five nights a week. After a couple of years had passed, the gossip settled down, as gossip will, and the affair he and Sue Ellen were having became somewhat of the norm and hardly noticed or commented on by the town folk.

One Friday night, as they were coming home from the country club, a terrible accident occured. A teenage boy, waiting to cross the street to go to a friend's house, was struck and killed by Morgan, who was intoxicated, but sober enough to convince Sue Ellen to take the blame. Mr. Morgan told the investigating officers the boy darted right out into her path, and she did all she could to avoid hitting him. Supposedly, there were no witnesses to the accident.

She was devastated. The boy killed had a sister who had been a friend of Sue Ellen's when they were in high school. There was a lot of gossip in town regarding the wreck. The skid marks didn't start until the car had passed the point where the body was lying. The car, for some reason, had also left the road, and tire marks were on the sidewalk and the ground next to the roadway. Mr. Morgan told Sue Ellen not to worry because the Chief of Police owed him a lot of favors, and he'd just call one in and make the questions go away and get the accident settled and put behind her. He was as good as his word.

Six months later, something strange happened, giving the townsfolk new fodder for their gossip mill. Sue Ellen Thornton went away, presumably on an extended European vacation. In the year she was gone, Morgan visited her several times. He didn't fill her position, and she returned and went back to work as if nothing had happened. But she no longer visited the mansion, and their relationship had clearly changed. It was now strictly professional, and she was as good at that as she had been when she was multitasking.

❧❧❧

Bubba was right about the shift change at McClain's. It really didn't matter what shift they worked. It was, for the most part, manual labor, usually loading trucks or moving inventory around in the warehouse. They only needed strong backs. The next day, after getting their work schedule changed, they would begin practice.

Bubba could feel the excitement, not his, but LJ's. It was a short walk from the main building to the gym. "Here goes nothing," Bubba said, raining on Little Jimmy's parade.

"You don't know that for sure, Bubba. We might have more fun than a one-legged man in a butt-kicking contest."

"Sure, and my Granny's passed out on her couch, stoned out of her mind."

"You know that ain't gonna happen," LJ said quickly, defending Bubba's Granny.

"And neither is this gonna be fun."

"Don't make bad jokes about her. She might be your Granny, but that woman's a saint, and you know it."

"You're right. Bad choice of an example. Granny, I'm sorry," Bubba said and patted LJ on the back.

As they approached the entrance to the gym, Johnny Kitchens, the quarterback, pulled up in his Corvette and parked in front of the gym door.

"Well, lookee here," he said sneeringly as he got out of his car, "It's our two latecomers."

"Sorry about coming out late," LJ said, offering an apology.

But not Bubba. "Yeah, we got here as quick as we could. Heard another disastrous season was taking place, and we thought we might offer a little help. How you doing this year, Johnny, 0-3, I believe, isn't it?"

They glared at each other for a few seconds. Seemed like an eternity to Little Jimmy. Clearing his throat and opening the door to break the ice, he said, "Let's do it."

Coach Henderson was in the gym, waiting on the team to assemble on the bleachers. He could feel the tension in the air. "Boys," he said and nodded toward Bubba, LJ and Johnny. "Have a seat."

"Afternoon, sir," Bubba replied. LJ smiled and nodded toward the coach. Johnny took a seat with a scowl on his face.

You could cut the air with a knife. Soon, the whole team was assembled on the bleachers. There was a definite space between Bubba, LJ and the rest of the team, even though they had sat down directly in front of the coach. From a distance, one would have thought the newcomers had some sort of plague.

"All right, guys. Everyone dress out and give me five laps. That is, everyone except Tom and Jimmy." A loud groan went through the team. They remembered the last time these two were mentioned got them five laps. It was normal to do laps after practice, but to do five laps before practice was a killer. "Buddy, get with Tom and Jimmy and issue them their practice uniforms." The team started toward the locker room, and Buddy Ferguson, the equipment manager, walked over to the new players to introduce himself.

"After Buddy gets your practice uniforms, dress out and meet me on the practice field behind the gym," the coach said.

"Yes, sir," they both replied in unison.

"Amazing," Coach Henderson thought to himself, "they even come with manners."

Buddy Ferguson loved sports. He was born with a birth defect and had undergone multiple surgeries in an attempt to correct it. He still walked with a limp on his right side. Equipment manager suited him just fine. He was a Eula person, with his glass half full. At least, he was still close to sports, whether he could actually play or not. His family owned the local Ford dealership and were prominent members of the community. There wasn't an arrogant, *hootie tootie* bone in Buddy's body, or in any member of the Ferguson family, for that matter. Eddie Ferguson, Buddy's father, worried more about the spiritual condition of his community than he worried about how many cars or trucks he could sell them.

Granny Preston would explain it this way. "Honor God with the first fruits of your labor and He'll bless you real good. Might not always be with things you want, but He'll bless you with things you need."

Buddy's birth defect was humbling. God showed up big time, bringing peace, understanding and joy to the Ferguson household. Buddy was the happiest member of the entire family. Bubba and LJ had not previously met him, but were impressed with the attention he gave them, making sure their uniforms fit and were in good shape. He literally beamed when he found two new helmets in their size.

Dressed out and headed to the practice field, LJ asked, "Now what do you think about Buddy?"

"Granny Preston would love him," Bubba replied.

"Bingo," LJ said and smiled. "Granny Preston loves everybody and we should at least try. What do you say?"

Bubba liked to aggravate LJ. "It'll be hard loving them from the bench, but I'll try real hard for you and Granny."

Eula was puzzled. What did William Morgan see in her? He could have any girl in the school, any girl in the state, for that matter. Standing in front of the mirror, she took stock. "I don't look half bad," she said to herself. Quoting one of her Grandpa's sayings, she added, "I clean up pretty good."

Two weeks had passed since she had officially met William Morgan, Jr. He continued to sit at the rear of the classroom next to her, and he waited and walked her to their next class, which was calculus. She insisted on carrying her own books, and he consented. He had a load of his own to carry. After calculus, they had separate classes and she didn't see him any more until the end of the day. Every day, he hurried from his last class and was waiting outside her English class. Their lives were so different, there really wasn't much to talk about, but they managed somehow to carry on enough of a conversation to keep the whole school abuzz with gossip. The *hootie tooties* were trying their best to figure out what was up with William taking up time with someone like Eula. Their conclusions, for the most part, weren't kind to her character or to her reputation. Even her friends were getting in on the gossip.

"How does that BMW ride?" Bubba asked her one day.

"Wouldn't have the foggiest," was her response, "and don't plan on finding out." Her raised eyebrows told Bubba he needed to be going somewhere, going there fast, and going there now.

"Sorry," he said, "didn't mean to rattle you."

"He's just a friend, Bubba, that's all. I told you a thousand times, everyone needs friends, even the son of old man Morgan."

After school, William would walk her to her truck, a homely looking thing compared to his shiny new BMW. It didn't seem to be a problem for him. He would open the truck door for her, and close it with a clunk and rattle sound after she climbed in. The upholstery was the pits, and Eula had covered the seat with an old beach towel. There weren't any power windows in the old truck, and she couldn't help but wonder if William had ever rolled a car window up and down manually.

It didn't have air conditioning, and she would always lower the window to let some of the heat out and to tell him goodbye. She liked the attention and he had been nothing but saintly in their relationship. One day, as she put her arm on the ledge of the truck window, he placed his hand on her forearm. "Thanks for being my friend. It means more than you'll ever know. I'd like to ask you out, but I don't feel like being rejected, and I sure don't want to damage our friendship."

She didn't try and move her arm. As a matter of fact, it felt good. It was the first time he had even touched her since their initial meeting and it sent signals throughout her body he had to pick up on. She flushed with embarrassment and smiled, which showed her approval for his actions. "I don't mind," she said and covered his hand with her right hand. It seemed like an eternity before he lifted his hand and told her good-bye. "Maybe soon," he said and smiled as he started toward where he was parked.

"Maybe soon," Eula responded, but she knew he was too far away to hear her.

⦿⦿⦿

The high school had a ten-game season. Three of them were already in the books, disasters on both offense and defense. Coach Henderson seemed to be inheriting the same curse his predecessors had to deal with. He went to the office to talk to the principal and get her thoughts on it.

"I don't understand it, Juanita. The community comes out to support them. Their families and friends yell and scream and you'd think, by the noise level, their team was in the Super Bowl and was three touchdowns ahead. But the team plays like it couldn't care less. The worse they do, the louder the fans cheer for them. Or at least it sounds that way and it almost seems to enable their lack of effort. And after every game, there's a get-together at the country club to celebrate. Celebrate what is the question that begs to be answered."

"So what's your take on it?" Juanita asked. "Surely you have some idea as to what's causing such lackluster performances in our athletic department. Nobody likes to lose all the time, and this has been going on for years and years. This attitude may be new for you, but having losing seasons has been a way of life for this school for the last fifteen years. Just the same old same old to me. Pep rallies on Fridays, rah-rahs and more losing games."

"Well, actually, I do have an idea about it, but I don't think you'll like it."

"Try it out on me. I'm just the principal, not even very athletic, but I'm sick and tired of our school losing all the time."

"Here goes. With over nine hundred students walking these hallways, and over four hundred of them male, surely there's better talent in the school, in general, than what's taking the field on game day. I went back to some old annuals and did some digging. It's amazing what a high school yearbook will tell you ten years after the fact."

"And?"

"And the key players seem to inherit their positions. They're the best ones on the team for their positions—quarterback, running backs and wide-receivers. Perhaps the best on the field, but not the best in the school. For the last ten years, all key positions, in all sports, not just football, have been filled by the kids of the most elite, richest families in town."

"Be careful with this analysis," Juanita said. "They give a ton of money to the booster clubs. All the beautiful campus landscaping was paid for by them. Most of those elites you're referencing graduated from Union High before heading off to their Ivy League destinations."

"I'm not saying anything to anybody. You asked me what I thought and I told you. It stays in this room."

"If we took your findings to a conclusion, where would they lead or what do you think they would tell you?" she asked.

"I believe the team as a whole is a reflection of the parents. The team is like an elite club. The parents played sports here, hell, their grandparents probably played sports here. So membership in the club continues. I think the regular, run-of-the-mill kids walking up and down the hallways don't even consider coming out for the team. They think, what's the use? All we'll do is just ride the bench and watch what's his name continue to make a fool of himself. The rich kids get to pretend to be jocks, the parents remember their time as jocks at Union High and support the charade, and the rest of the students and surrounding teams we play laugh their butts off every season."

"Wow, why don't you tell me how you really feel about this?" she said and laughed.

Coach Henderson stood up to leave. "Gotta run. Thanks for listening. My wife appreciates it, too. I talk to her about it so much she's about ready to shoot me."

Juanita smiled and said, "Anytime. The door is always open."

The dynamic-duo had mixed feelings as they left the locker room and headed for the field. Coach Henderson was address-ing the team as a few stragglers were finishing their last lap. LJ was like a kid at Christmas. The practice uniform and the sound of the cleats on the asphalt lit him up. The corners of his smile were hid somewhere in each side of his helmet. Bubba felt awkward, a little bit embarrassed, and out of his element. "If you don't relax, LJ, you're gonna wet your pants," Bubba kidded him.

"It could happen," LJ responded.

Coach Henderson saw them coming down the hill and motioned them over. The last player finished his fifth lap and also came over and joined the team.

"Uniforms okay?"

"Fine, sir," LJ answered and Bubba nodded in agreement.

"Give me five laps, and then rejoin the team."

"Yes, sir," Bubba said.

As they left the team and started out on the track, Bubba said, "This oughta take that smile off your face."

"Piece of cake, Bubba, and you know it. We should give the coach ten laps and show old what's his name how it's done."

"That would do it. Then they'll all think we're both stupid and that neither one of us can count to five."

The idea the team would think they were so stupid they couldn't count to five tickled LJ. At the end of the field where the team was scrimmaging, all the players heard him laughing his ass off.

Someone said, "Just listen to those two laughing fools. They think this is supposed to be funny."

Overhearing the remark gave the coach an opportunity to make a comment. "I don't know what they're laughing at or what they find so funny, but this game is actually supposed to be fun." He could see Buddy slowly making his way down to the field to watch the boys scrimmage, which he did every day after he made sure all the equipment was clean and in its proper place. He was limping, favoring his right leg, and was still out of earshot of the group.

"You're all healthy and able to play the game. There are some who'd give anything to be able to run and play like you can. Take this home with you and remember it. Count your blessings. And as far as having fun, those two laughing fools just ran their first lap fifty five seconds faster than any of you did earlier. And they laughed the entire time about something."

Holding up his stopwatch, he poked them a little. "Being happy and glad to be here must make running a little easier."

As they started their last lap, Bubba asked LJ, "Are we running laps or racing?"

"Wanna race?"

"No, I don't, but if we did, I'd beat you and you know it."

"You know better. This uniform gives me speed, awesome speed. I'm football man and I can fly."

"You're not football man, you're a crazy man. And look, football man's done wet his pants."

LJ was having so much fun, he fell for it and broke stride to look down at the front of his uniform.

When he did, Bubba found another gear and was gone.

Realizing what had happened, LJ, who was considerably faster than Bubba, went into overdrive and caught up with him quickly. As he pulled up next to him, Bubba slowed and allowed LJ to blow by him. Getting back together, they were both laughing their butts off while still pacing well.

Looking over toward the team, they realized all eyes were on them. Bubba said, "I told you they thought we were crazy. Now they know we are."

"It'll just give old what's his name something else to bitch about," LJ noted.

Their antics on the track had not gone unnoticed by Coach Henderson. "Unbelievable," he said to himself. "Lap five, and they still have awesome speed. They must be in great physical shape. Where have you been all my life," he wondered, "or at least the past few weeks?"

Finishing the last lap, they joined the team. Coach Henderson put them on the defensive squad for the remainder of the practice. The offense was walking through some new plays at half-speed, trying to get them down for the next game. He had Bubba and LJ working with the secondary defensive players so they could get an idea of what he wanted on defense. Both of them had watched football their whole lives. It wasn't rocket science to them—mirror the pass receiver, don't interfere with his opportunity to catch the pass, just make sure it doesn't happen.

At the end of practice, Coach Henderson said, "Give me two more laps. Everyone on the track."

"Let's beat all of them," LJ said, so only Bubba could hear.

"Hell, no," he responded quickly. "They hate us already. That'd only put icing on the cake for them." Pulling back, they ran the entire two laps buried in the middle of the pack. The coach had wondered about the outcome of the final two laps. He had a new assessment. "They've also got some common sense," he thought. "At least one of them has."

Eula knew it was coming. Sooner or later, William would ask

her out. She couldn't imagine how two opposites could find common ground outside of the classroom or the walk through the parking lot. She felt ashamed of the mental process she used to evaluate the possibilities of their relationship.

Word on the street was that the Morgan's lived in a mansion. It was located on a hillside at the edge of town and was more like an estate than a home. Electronic gates monitored those going and coming, and the house was barely visible from the street. What would it be like to leave such a place and drive up a gravel driveway to their double-wide in a car that cost two or three times more than their home? She tried to imagine her dad greeting him at the door and inviting him into their humble abode. No telling what her father might say to him. He had a quick wit and was the life of any gathering, at home, work and even at church. But William lived in a different universe. The road the Morgan's traveled ran parallel with the one her father and the rest of her family and friends traveled. And parallel roads never intersect.

Eula considered her situation unique and it never occurred to her that William was facing similar issues. Without her knowing it, he had ridden by their double-wide numerous times in a van his father's bank used for deliveries. He could never find the courage to stop. He had never even been inside a mobile home and had no idea what to expect or how he would be received by her family. He wasn't blind to the same issues she addressed in her mind. These differences in their economic levels posed no issue for him. His problem was simple—somehow he needed to make two parallel roads come together.

Eula had no idea what kind of relationship the Morgan family had with each other. Except for the gossip always shadowing wealth and power, she had no inkling how complicated his relationship with his family really was. The whole town knew William, Jr. had been adopted at birth, but it was never brought up in conversations.

William had not told his parents about his interest in Eula. As a matter of fact, he hardly ever saw them. He would not have left the electronic gates at the mansion, as Eula had envisioned, in order to drive to her double-wide. He would have left Sue Ellen's place, which was one of the nicest homes in town, but without the gates. Her home was also a source of gossip. How does a single woman afford a place like that?

She seemingly had no interest in men and never dated. Except for the affair she had with Mr. Morgan when he first made her his executive secretary, she had stayed completely out of the gossip line of fire. Her affair with him had all but been forgotten. After all, it had happened over twenty years earlier. Old gossip always gives way to the latest and greatest.

Had William told his parents about Eula, they would have disapproved of his friendship with her. She would not make their top ten list of possible candidates to be his wife. They would be ashamed to have their country club friends find out their son would even consider dating someone who lived in a double-wide trailer.

When Mr. Morgan married Marsha, his third wife, neither one of them had ever had children. When they adopted a son, most of the people in town figured it was done more for appearance and acceptance than for anything else. Mr. Morgan and Marsha were both way past their prime for raising a son.

As one man in town asked, "What kind of nuts adopt a child when they're damned near fifty years old?" The answer most of the townsfolk came up with was "someone with enough money to hire someone else to do the raising for them." And that was exactly what happened. That someone was his executive secretary, Sue Ellen Thornton. She would be more like family to William, Jr. than his adopted parents ever were.

Mr. Morgan spent all of his time and energy in pursuit of just a little bit more. William's mother spent most of her time volunteering in the community and traveling abroad. Business kept Mr. Morgan from being a hands-on father, and community involvement and travel kept Marsha from being a doting mother. They were always there for their adopted son, but more in monetary ways than in nurturing ways. William's upbringing was more on Sue Ellen than anyone in town could imagine. When William fell down, Sue Ellen was there to pick him up. When he was hurt or crying, she was there to hug and comfort. Not only did Mr. Morgan pay Sue Ellen a handsome salary, he also paid for her to have an executive secretary, which accounted for the fact she could come and go as she pleased. William's parents seemingly had no time for him, but one has to give Mr. Morgan a little credit. He paid plenty to make sure William was loved and looked after, even if it was by someone else. William spent his summers with Sue Ellen and most Christmases would find Santa delivering his toys to her house. The gigantic, beautiful home and the very expensive cars Sue Ellen drove were what generated the gossip suggesting Sue Ellen Thornton must have some real dirt on old man Morgan.

⁂

Three practices aren't enough to make one efficient at anything. LJ was raring to go and Bubba was willing, but Coach

Henderson knew he needed to give them at least one more week on the practice field before putting them in a game situation. Friday nights meant football at most high schools in America. LJ really had high hopes and was convinced they would get to play a down or two. From the time of the opening kickoff until the end of the game, he stood on the sideline near Coach Henderson, expecting to get to play a couple of downs.

Bubba did what he said he would do, he rode the bench the entire game. Final score was 27-6. The Cougars would have been shut out, but Rodney, the running back, managed to stumble into the end zone from the three-yard line. The extra point was wide right.

Coach Henderson saw two things in his new players. Extreme disappointment was written all over LJ's face. It was almost pitiful to look at him. Bubba, on the other hand, sat on the bench, smug and accepting of the fact they didn't play a single down.

With three minutes to go in the game, Coach Henderson walked over to where LJ was standing and said quietly, "I give you my word, you'll play in next week's game. I promise."

Eula, Clarice and several of their friends had come to the game in hopes Bubba and LJ would get some playing time. They could see LJ was bummed just by the expression on his face. They saw what Coach Henderson saw. Bubba was downright embarrassed, dressed out in full football gear and sitting on a bench for four quarters. What a lousy way to spend a Friday night. As their friends sat in the stands, Bubba's words echoed in their minds. "They'll let us join the team, but they'll never let us play."

Clarice said to Eula, "I wish I hadn't come. This is so hard to watch."

"Life can be hard sometimes, but Bubba and LJ are tough, or as they like to say, *trailer-park tough*. They'll survive and live to see another game, and I believe Coach Henderson's a fair man and he's in no one's pocket. I actually have a real good feeling about this," Eula replied, trying to encourage Clarice.

"I'm glad someone has a good feeling about it. And I hope you're right. I can't stand to see Bubba this down over anything, especially over something he didn't really want to do in the first place."

"He'll be fine, I promise you," Eula told her. "Let's go over to the diner and get a table. They'll beat us over there if we don't watch it." Bill's Diner was a favorite hang-out for Eula and her friends. She hardly ever got to go with them because she worked so much. The *hootie tooties* wouldn't be caught dead at the diner. That suited Eula and her friends just fine.

The locker room was silent. The coach gave a brief analysis of why they lost, but withheld how he really felt about the loss. He wanted to say, "Y'all really stunk out there tonight. But what else is new? Y'all always play to lose." He gritted his teeth and held his tirade in check. He would share that with Cindi when he got home.

Since the dynamic-duo never touched the field or the ball, they had clean hands relating to the loss. Johnny quickly dressed and his Corvette could be heard screaming out of the parking lot.

Bubba commented to LJ, "Now he decides to move fast. Moved like dead lice was falling off him during the game." Several other players heard it, but no one took up for the quarterback.

Bubba was right. Johnny fumbled once on the exchange from center, threw two interceptions and was sacked three times. He exhibited no pocket mobility, costing them the game. The visiting team scored twice on the turnovers.

Bubba liked Buddy, the equipment manager. "Saved you a little work," he joked as he turned in his game uniform. "It's just as clean as it was when I put it on."

Buddy smiled at Bubba. He was very football savvy and heard what he had said about Johnny's lack of mobility in the pocket. "Just be patient," he said to Bubba, sounding like someone older than he was, giving advice to a younger person. "I have a good feeling things are about to change big time around here, and it's way past time."

∽✪∽✪∽✪∽

It was a nice, sit-down meal. Sue Ellen usually prepared a somewhat formal meal three to four times a week. This allowed them to converse about whatever was happening in each other's lives. Getting up from the dinner table and starting to clear away the dishes, William said to Sue Ellen, "I have a problem."

"You? You have a problem? Come on. What kind of problem do you have?" Sue Ellen joked with him. The look on his face told her this wasn't a time to kid around. "I'm sorry. I thought you were kidding. Hope I'm up to this. For heaven's sake, what is it?"

William smiled. "Oh, it's nothing bad. As a matter of fact, it's wonderful. I just don't know what to do next." He poured her some more wine and grabbed another Coke from the fridge and sat back down at the table.

"Let me guess," Sue Ellen said, "or maybe I should just ask you what her name is."

"How did you know what it was? I haven't said a thing about her or even indicated I was interested in anyone."

"You didn't have to say anything. You've been moping around here like you were about to die or something. I figured one of those frilly cheerleaders must be after a ride in your new car."

"Trust me, this girl makes the cheerleaders look bad," William said emphatically. "She's sweet and unassuming, not like the other girls in school. You've always told me that whenever I had a problem with anything, if I'd be patient and smart, I'd find a way or figure out the dilemma. Well, you were right. I found a way. The problem may or may not have existed, but I was scared silly to even speak to her, not wanting to ruin my chances of getting to know her. Several weeks ago, in chemistry class, she dropped all of her books, and I used the opportunity to help her and make her acquaintance at the same time."

"Wait, wait, wait a minute. Doesn't she know who you are? That your father owns half the town and has the other half in hock to his bank. Has she seen your set of wheels? Surely, she'd give her right arm for you to pay her any attention at all. I know I would have if I'd been in her place."

"She's not like that."

"What do you mean, not like that? What's wrong with recognizing a hunk, and a wealthy hunk at that, and wanting his attention? Who's her father and where do they live?"

"That's the catch. Her father is a factory worker at McClain's. They live in a double-wide trailer on Pine Ridge Road, a little county road that runs off of Upper Hightower. She spends most of her time studying and works evenings and weekends at the Dairy Queen. She drives a really old truck—and—and she has the second highest GPA in the entire school. Now what do you think about all of that?"

William hadn't noticed, but Sue Ellen's eyes had filled with tears.

"Hey, what's wrong? Did I make you cry? I'm so sorry."

"Oh, no, you didn't do anything, but I'm so proud of your choice. I'm overwhelmed at the depth of your understanding of life at your age. You shouldn't even be looking at someone who lives in a trailer, or who has a father that has never amounted to anything by your dad's standards. I am so proud of you, William. What you have, what kind of house you live in, and how much your car cost, has nothing to do with who you are. Sometimes things possess the people who have them. The jury has been out on you, William, but the verdict is now in. It reads: William Morgan, Jr. is bigger than the things he owns, and he sees things in the material world for what they're really worth. He sees beauty residing on the inside, not just superficial beauty that's only skin deep. Don't worry about what she doesn't own or what her family doesn't have. If you think this girl is right for you, then make it happen. If given a chance, things will always work themselves out. I'm so proud of you, William. And what is this beautiful young woman's name? I have to know."

William was all smiles. He knew his parents would have blown a gasket if he had shared the same information with them, and he hadn't been completely sure how Sue Ellen would respond.

"Her name is Eula Johnson, and she's beautiful, on the outside and on the inside."

⚜ ⚜ ⚜

Monday's practice seemed more like a funeral. Talk about a somber mood. Coach Henderson paced slowly back and forth for a full minute without uttering a word. The team knew they had disappointed him. The sound of his footsteps on the gym floor was deafening.

"Today is the first day of our new season. By new season, I mean winning season. We're starting over. Losing is something the team did last week and the three weeks before that, and only God knows how many games this school has lost over the past decade. This is day one of a new era at Union High. I personally don't like to lose, and I didn't come here to carry on what seems like a family tradition."

He hadn't meant to throw in the part about the family tradition. It just popped in his mind and out his mouth before he could check it. "Probably generate some more phone calls," he said to himself. He wasn't sure how he would pull this miracle off, but proclaiming it was at least a start. Then he stepped in it, his wife would later tell him, as he shared with her the speech he had given the team.

"This Friday night we will beat Milton High and it'll be so bad, they'll leave our stadium with their tails tucked between their legs. No prediction as to the final score, but it'll be lopsided and in our favor. This is our house, and we will not go back to the losing well again. Do I make myself clear?"

All the players were silent. They had been mesmerized by Coach Henderson's speech and delivery. He had been way more forceful than they were used to. He was, in fact pumped, and very articulate in his delivery and very convincing in his argument. There were at least three people who were also pumped after the pep talk— Bubba, LJ and Buddy.

Then came the bombshell as he wrapped up his diatribe.

"If there is anyone sitting here who doesn't believe what I just said, get up and leave now. I don't want you or need you on this team. If there is anyone here who is not willing to give me and your teammates one hundred percent, get up and leave now."

Most couldn't believe what they were hearing. The silence was overwhelming. Bubba would later swear he could hear his own heart beating. No one moved a muscle or said a word. They were spellbound and didn't really know how to respond or what to say. The one thing everyone knew for sure, he was dead serious about turning the season around.

"If you want to win, dress out and meet me on the practice field. If not, I say again, loud and clear, get up and leave."

Everyone stood up and headed for the locker room to dress out. Buddy was all smiles. Coach Henderson noticed something he hadn't seen before—a little hustle in their step.

⚜⚜⚜

Talking to Sue Ellen about Eula gave William hope and courage. He had been concerned Sue Ellen might have pushed back a little after hearing about the double-wide, the old truck and Eula's background. Her response caught him off guard, and he was pleasantly surprised.

He knew he was adopted and also knew his father had a nasty reputation for forcing his will on people around him and the community in general. His father, a mover and shaker, did a lot of good for the town and county, even though he had a bad habit of riding roughshod over his friends and business associates. Though his dad wasn't a saint, William still loved him and was thankful for all the nice things he had, and especially thankful for the fact his parents were always busy or traveling and allowed him to spend all the time he wanted with Sue Ellen. Some folks in town referred to Sue Ellen as the Morgan's nanny.

What William hadn't heard about was the affair his father had indulged himself in with a very young Sue Ellen Thornton. Many years had passed, many things had changed and a few things were swept under the rug. Their affair was old news and had been replaced by juicier tidbits of information to fuel the gossip mill. Even more important, was the fact that the Sue Ellen who went on an extended European vacation was not the same person who returned. She had not given them anything to talk about. Actually, some residents commended her among themselves for being such a dear to raise someone else's child.

The Sue Ellen Mr. Morgan had hired as his executive secretary/lover would have never entertained being associated with someone on Eula's socioeconomic level. While she might not have openly criticized anyone with less than she had, she was far too concerned with amassing her own fortune to be aware they even existed. There were two parallel worlds, one where the Sue Ellen's lived and one where the Eula's lived.

The radical change in Sue Ellen's thinking didn't happen in Blairsville. The experience reducing her world to one of reality without parallels happened eighteen years before William's conversation with her regarding Eula. She owned a beautiful home, fancy cars and had a substantial income, but they no longer owned her completely as they had when she was young and just starting her career. The life-changing experience happened on her extended trip abroad. Sister Francis and Sister Cass, at Saint Mary's Hospital in England, were by her bedside when the radical transformation occurred. The broken cry of one desperately needing a miracle from the Almighty forever changed who Sue Ellen Thornton was. Granny Preston would say it this way, "Sometimes, the Lord has to box us into a corner in order to get our attention."

꩜꩜꩜

Union High had already lost their first three games before Bubba and LJ joined the team. They had three days of practice, Tuesday, Wednesday and Thursday, and then the fourth game was at home with rival Macon High. LJ watched from the sidelines and Bubba from the bench as Union High was handed its fourth consecutive loss.

Coach Henderson had been very disappointed with the loss to Macon High. He had hoped for a better showing, or at least a little improvement. It didn't happen and their lackluster effort had generated his "If you don't want to win, then leave now" speech.

Johnny Kitchens, the quarterback, was spoiled rotten. His performance on the field was no more than his father's had been when he played the quarterback position for Union High. The speech the coach delivered after their loss had pissed Johnny off, causing him to scream out of the parking lot in his Corvette.

He had driven around for about an hour before heading home. He didn't go to the country club as he usually did. Neither did his father. When he walked into their home, his dad was sitting in the den, waiting to pounce on him for his poor performance in the game.

"What the hell happened out there tonight?" was his first question. Johnny didn't give him an answer, only shrugged his shoulders. "Do you even want to play football?" was the second question, and Mr. Kitchens answered it before Johnny could even attempt an answer. "I don't think so, or at least it sure as hell looks that way to me and to anyone else with half a brain."

Johnny knew the best thing he could do was to say nothing and listen while his father ranted and raved about the loss.

"When I was quarterback at Union High, we stunk, just like the team does this year. And, truth be told, I probably wasn't any better or any more concerned than you are. However, you have a problem I didn't have back then."

Knowing he had to engage at some point to keep from aggravating his dad even more, he asked cautiously, "I don't know what problem you're talking about."

"Well, they're actually two problems, and they would be evident to you if you could get your head out of your butt long enough to recognize them."

"Two problems? I hope you're not talking about the trailer-park trash that's riding the bench. Surely not," Johnny said incredulously. "They didn't play a single down tonight and they'll be gone in two weeks. Trust me on that."

"Trust me on this!" his dad shot back hotly. "I know people and I read faces. The kid standing on the sidelines didn't play a single down tonight, but he's so fired up to play, he can't even stand still. And the one who sat on the bench the entire four quarters is dangerous to you and your kind. He's cool and calculating and exudes self-confidence. He'll kick your ass, on and off the field. He wasn't born with a silver spoon in his mouth, and the world will be a hard place for him. But he'll manage and manage well. Trust me on that, too."

"Are we talking about the same two pieces of shit? I don't think so."

"Oh, believe me, we're talking about the same two guys. You can call them pieces of shit if you want to, but if I were you, I'd see them as hungry, fierce competitors. I threw something else out there and you didn't pick up on it either," his dad said.

"Oh, I caught it, your kind. So what's my kind, Dad? Enlighten me."

"In reality, just like I was when I was your age. Pampered, petted and pooh-poohed — whatever you want to call it. Every-thing is given to you on a silver platter and nothing, or very little, is expected in return. Take your Corvette, for example. I saw the old truck those two came to the game in. Those two pieces of shit, as you call them, can dismantle that old truck and reassemble it faster than you can figure out how to raise the hood on your Vette. You better hope I have enough pull with Juanita Fisher and the new coach to keep them on the bench or you'll find yourself in deep shit. Get yourself a cushion, because that bench will be a bitch to sit on and your party will be over."

⚬⚬⚬⚬⚬⚬⚬

It was Sunday night and twenty minutes till closing at the Dairy Queen. A few customers sat around, chatting and no new customers had come in for Eula to wait on at the counter. As she wiped down tables, a pair of headlights caught her eye as a car pulled in and parked next to her truck.

"Oh, shit," Eula said, recognizing the car.

"Anything wrong?" Sam asked, having overheard her colorful exclamation.

"Oh, no, sir," she responded. "Just remembered something I have to take care of. That's all."

Sam nodded his head, smiled and said, "You let old Sam know if you need help with anything. All you have to do is let me know, okay?"

"Yes, sir, I will. I promise and I sure do appreciate it."

Sam Kerr, owner of the Dairy Queen, thought the sun rose and set in Eula Johnson. He had never had a high school kid as dependable and as hard working as she was.

As she continued to wipe down the tables and counters, her mind was spinning a hundred miles an hour. She wished Sam could help her with her problem, but he couldn't. Her problem had just got out of his BMW and was leaning up against the fender of her truck. "Oh, my God," she thought, "what does he want and what am I going to do?"

As he let Eula out of the store, Sam saw William standing next to her truck. Touching her arm, he asked, "Do you know that guy?"

"Yes, sir," she answered, "he's a friend."

"Nice wheels!" he commented.

"Yes, sir," she said, "nice wheels."

As she walked down to where her truck was parked, she tried to imagine why he was there, especially as late as it was. It didn't take but a few seconds to get the answer.

"Good evening, Eula. I know it's late and you're probably very tired, but I thought I'd stop by and see if you'd like to go somewhere for a Coke, a sandwich or whatever you might want. We won't stay long and I'll bring you back here to get your truck. Do you think your parents would mind?"

"I can't," Eula responded all too quickly.

"And why not?" he asked. "It's still early and we won't stay out long, I promise. Do you think your folks would mind?"

"I just can't," she said again, shrugging her shoulders and extending her hands out with the palms upward. She inadvertently looked at his BMW and the pickup truck, parked side by side. William was a quick study.

"Oh," he said. "You're one of them. I had you figured differently."

"One of who?" she asked, showing displeasure with his remark.

"One of those we have classes with. Always looking at and evaluating everyone, deciding whether or not to allow the person into their little world, letting only who's acceptable to them inside their circle. I'm sorry, Eula. I don't fit in their circle. For that matter, I don't even have a circle. Sorry I bothered you. It won't happen again, I promise. Good night."

Nodding to her, he got in his car and drove off, leaving Eula, the furniture worker's daughter, standing alone beside her dad's old Chevy truck.

Eula had trouble falling asleep. What had she done? Waking up Monday morning, she had the same problem she had when she went to bed Sunday night—William Morgan. She felt awful for the way she had treated him. There was one of Bubba's *hootie tooties* in the Dairy Queen parking lot Sunday night, and it wasn't William Morgan, Jr., the son of the richest man in the state. It was Eula Johnson, and she hated the way she had responded to him.

Skipping school crossed her mind, but that wouldn't solve the problem of facing him again. That was inevitable. As she put on her makeup, she had to acknowledge the person in the mirror needed to apologize. Whether he accepted it or not was of little consequence. Her parents had raised her better than she had behaved, and it needed fixing.

As she entered chem class, he was already seated close to the front, in his old desk. There was an empty desk behind him. Marching by the empty desk, she went straight to the rear of the classroom where she normally sat.

Turning quickly, she reversed her steps and took the desk directly behind him. After sitting down, she leaned forward and said three words, very softly, so no one else could hear. "I'm so sorry."

She wasn't sure he had heard her apology. There was no response, no acknowledgment of any kind, not even a nod of his head.

About five minutes before the class was over, while Mrs. Spangler was writing an assignment on the board, he discreetly passed her a note. It was even shorter than her three-word apology. There were only two words written on a scrap of paper.

The students behind them started whispering immediately, having seen him pass her the note. It was folded over, and when she opened it, she read, "You're forgiven."

She smiled and read it several more times before the bell ended the class time. She remained seated as the whispering classmates filed out. At last, he stood up and turned around to face her. Extending his hand to help her up, he said, "May I walk you to your next class?"

Looking directly into his eyes, something clicked. She didn't see William Morgan, Jr., bank president's son who lived in a mansion and drove a new BMW. She saw the man she very likely would spend the rest of her life with.

He would later tell her, "When you took my hand, my whole world changed. I knew, in that instant, we'd always be together."

༺❀༻ ༺❀༻ ༺❀༻

After school, football practice was about to yield another happening equivalent to the William and Eula event in the morning chem class. The coach had the team doing some offensive drills. Bubba and LJ were playing defense. There seemed to be a little more spirit than in previous practices. His play or quit speech seemed to have done some good.

Changing up, the team began to practice some two-minute offensive drills. Bubba and LJ, along with the other extra players, were standing on the sideline.

Coach Henderson, while watching the team practice the drill, meandered over to where Bubba and LJ were standing and commented quietly so that only they could hear. "I'm disappointed," he said, "not in you, but in my judgment. I hate being wrong about a gut feeling, but apparently I missed this one by a country mile." He walked away without saying anything more.

LJ wanted to jump up and down and scream. He had wanted this so badly—a chance to participate and the coach wasn't the only one disappointed. Looking directly at Bubba, he asked, "So when are we going to show the coach what his gut feeling told him about us?"

Bubba, acknowledging what LJ had just asked, let that famous Bubba smile creep across his face. "Now," was all he said.

"Hot damn," LJ said, loud enough for the coach and several players to hear. Coach Henderson looked over at them to see what was going on. Bubba was smiling and LJ was about to go nuts, with excitement written all over his face. He smiled and nodded in their direction. He hadn't been wrong, and the *hot damn* had just confirmed it.

Next on the agenda was to practice kick-off returns. Bubba and LJ were lined up on defense. "Make it count, LJ," Bubba said as they lined up waiting for the kickoff.

"You know I will," LJ said and nodded.

The sound of the kicker's foot hitting the ball sent Bubba and LJ on a dead run down field, quickly out in front of the pack. The receiving team had set up their blockers and the punt returner was waiting for the ball.

"Go get him, LJ," Bubba yelled as he took out a lead blocker. Shooting through the gap Bubba had opened up for him, he sidestepped two would-be blockers who weren't fast enough to stop him. As the punt returner caught the ball, he also caught something else—the full fury of a young man with pent-up frustrations. As LJ nailed him, the ball was knocked loose. Bubba, right on LJ's heels, recovered the fumble and easily scampered into the end zone.

"Hot damn," Coach Henderson said, quoting LJ. "I'm still batting a thousand on gut feelings."

⚬❈⚬ ⚬❈⚬ ⚬❈⚬

Granny Preston knew the Scriptures and knew they applied to every aspect of one's life. She often told Bubba, "Son, a worker should be worthy of his hire. Give McClain's the best you have. God will reward you, even if McClain's don't."

Sometimes, when moving heavy boxes in the warehouse, he thought about her saying and wondered exactly how it fit in his life at McClain's. Granny Preston trusted the Lord to put someone or some job in Bubba's path where his work or dedication would not only be recognized but rewarded as well. If Bubba did a great job and McClain's failed to recognize it, then ultimately it would be their loss.

Bubba's mother worked from sun up to bedtime every day—at McClain's for eight to ten hours, then home to cook, do laundry and clean the house. She had a garden every summer and canned vegetables and fruit, which the family ate during the winter.

Bubba's father was a minimalist. Eight hours at McClain's or ten if they required it, and he was done. He was a good father and husband, but he gave only a minimum effort in life, which was always rewarded in kind.

Wall Street, as in the world of the stock market, was as foreign to most of the folks who worked at McClain's as tuxedos and caviar. Most of the families inside of Bubba's circle of friends barely made ends meet. They lived from paycheck to paycheck. Their clothes were dried on clothes lines, not in dryers. The same sun that hardens cement also dries clothes.

The difference between clothes drying on a line versus being dried in a clothes dryer is minimal, yet monumental. What's a little coarseness in a T-shirt? Not much, really. But when you consider the lives of these families versus the lives of the *hootie tooties,* coarse would be a good, descriptive term. And coarse shifts from minimal to monumental when it applies to everything in one's life— what one eats, wears and even sleeps on. Run your hand down a rough-cut piece of lumber. Do it one time and get a splinter or two. That's painful. But every day, when the coarseness of one's life slaps them down, over and over, they develop a Bubba personality.

Bubba had his mama's work ethic, which she inherited from her father. Bubba went to school, worked at McClain's, kept Granny Preston's place up, took her to church every Sunday, played hard with his friends and even harder with Clarice. Adding football, he still functioned at an acceptable level. And just like Granny Preston had predicted, his hard work and ability would pay off, and it was about to be recognized on the athletic field at Union High.

∞∞∞

Monday's practice confirmed what the coach felt regarding the abilities of Bubba and LJ. Overall, the team practiced with a little more get up and go. The kick-off and fumble recovery seemed to soften some of the alienation the dynamic-duo felt coming from their teammates. Everyone but Johnny. He told Jason it was a fluke, just plain dumb luck. He told another player, "Even a blind rat finds a crumb every once in a while." Good thing LJ didn't hear his comments.

Tuesday's practice was a good one with nothing unusual happening.

On Wednesday, LJ had to do something for a teacher after

school and was a little late getting to the locker room. Bubba felt his absence as he dressed out. The other players talked among themselves, excluding Bubba from the conversations, which was fine with him.

Coach Henderson was still looking for a place to put them where they could make the greatest contribution to the team. LJ showed up, dressed out and practiced defensive drills with Bubba and the rest of the defense.

Whenever Coach Henderson had a new play, he would insert it near the end of the practice session.

"All right, boys," he said. "We have a new twist to an old play. Pay attention, Rodney. You'll fake a run off left tackle. Jason, you'll run fifteen yards up field, cut hard right at the hash mark, and Johnny will hit you over your right shoulder as you reach the sideline. That will protect the ball from being intercepted. As long as Johnny keeps it on your right shoulder, you'll be the only one to have a shot at it. Not a lot of yardage, but a good solid play. If y'all connect, it'll move the chains every time. Let's walk through it a couple of times and then we'll run it a couple of times at half-speed."

After three practice plays, Johnny still hadn't connected with Jason. He was all over the place. If it had been a real game, there would definitely have been an interception. He was either throwing it behind Jason or over his head.

"Concentrate, Johnny. You can make this throw. It's an easy pass. Just relax. You can do it."

Another snap, and another miss. Johnny was feeling the heat and was also a little embarrassed. "Damn, Jason, run the route right and you can catch the frigging ball," Johnny yelled, berating his receiver and friend. Jason didn't say anything, just sorta hung his head, feeling more sorry for Johnny than anything else.

LJ had heard and seen enough. "Damn, Johnny." Bubba knew what the next line would be.

"You couldn't hit a bull in the ass with a handful of rice. It wasn't Jason's fault. The pass missed him by a country mile. Hell, winged Pegasus couldn't have caught those passes."

The visual image of Johnny trying to hit a bull in the ass with a handful of rice was too much for everyone. Even his closest friends laughed out loud. Coach Henderson had heard Johnny berate Jason and had heard the bull in the ass remark as well. He smiled, but didn't enter the fray. He purposely waited to see how it would play out.

"I guess you think you could do better," Johnny sneered at LJ.

"Oh, not me," LJ said quickly and smiled at Johnny, "but he sure as hell can," he said, pointing to Bubba.

Tossing the ball to Bubba, Johnny said real smart-mouthed. "Show time, latecomer. Can you hit a bull in the ass with a handful of rice?" The whole team was silent, waiting for Bubba's response.

"Probably not," Bubba said, "but I can hit LJ in full stride as he crosses the fifty-yard line."

"That's bullshit."

LJ didn't hear Johnny's remark because he was gone, heading for the fifty. Bubba simulated taking a snap, and dropped back to pass. As LJ crossed the thirty-five, he let the ball fly and hit LJ in full stride as he stepped across the fifty-yard line.

"Pure damn luck," Johnny said as LJ came trotting back with the ball. Coach Henderson's lower jaw was still dropped in disbelief at what he had just witnessed.

"Pure damn luck," LJ said, getting up in Johnny's face. "Wanna see it again?" he said tossing the ball back to Bubba. "At the forty, over my right shoulder, as I step out of bounds. Color me gone." LJ was having a grand old time at the expense of the *hootie tooties.*

Bubba again simulated taking a snap from center. Dropping back, he hurled a perfect strike. LJ didn't even look for it until he crossed the thirty-five-yard line. Looking up, he took two more steps, hauled it in and stepped out of bounds.

LJ, trotting back, tossed the ball back to Johnny, who angrily batted it away. Instantly, he remembered what his dad had said about Bubba, "He'll kick your ass, on or off the field."

Taunting him, LJ said, "Just pure damn luck. Lightning striking twice in the same place? Imagine that."

Coach Henderson knew it was about to get physical. Bubba had already stepped between LJ and Johnny. Johnny was half again the size of LJ, but he had to look up at Bubba to read the message in his eyes that said, "Don't even think about laying a hand on LJ."

"All right, boys. That's enough. Gather around and give me your attention. Practice is over. Maybe we just witnessed a couple of lucky tosses but something tells me not so. Tomorrow, we'll offer Lady Luck an opportunity to visit us again. If she does, we'll insert a couple of Hail Mary passes for LJ in Friday night's game against Milton High. Not knowing about our two new players will give us a chance to go nuclear on them. They won't expect anything like that, and we'll do it immediately, on our first possession and probably on first down as well. If all goes well, we should come away with six. That's all for now. Shower, get dressed and go home and study. I got a printout yesterday, and a few of you are getting a little close to the line with your grades. So study! Tom and Jimmy, see me in my office before you go home."

"Yes, sir," LJ said and Bubba nodded, both noting he called them by their given names instead of their nicknames.

In the dressing room there were no high-fives and no comments about a great pass or a great catch, no kiss my ass, no nothing. Bubba and LJ showered, dressed quickly and headed to the coach's office. On the way to his office, Bubba said, "Well, you stepped in it this time, LJ."

"Sorry about that, Bubba, but I couldn't let that blow-hard piece of shit who thinks he's a quarterback fuss Jason out like that. Jason may be a *hootie tootie*, but my grandpa always said, 'right is right if nobody's doing it, and wrong is wrong if everybody's doing it.' What Johnny was doing was just plain wrong, and you know it. And I called him on it, just like my grandpa would have wanted."

"Then you sure as hell made your grandpa proud."

That made LJ smile. "Those passes were a mile over Jason's head, and you know as well as I do, that nobody could have caught them without a net."

"I know that, but you forgot something."

"What did I forget?"

"You forgot that the trailer-park kids aren't supposed to show up the *hootie tooties.*"

"Well, we sure as hell did," LJ said and made Bubba high-five him.

"Great passes, Bubba."

"Great catches, LJ."

They could see the coach sitting at his desk as they walked across the gym. "If we'd never come here the first time, none of this would be happening."

"Oh, shut up and enjoy it," LJ said, grinning from ear to ear.

"Sit down," the coach said, as they entered his office. "Seems like we just did this the other day."

"We did," Bubba remarked, raising his eyebrows and smiling.

He saw the events that had just unfolded on the practice field as problematic, but not LJ. To him, it was the greatest thing since sliced bread.

"I need an honest answer from the two of you. Did I see Lady Luck strike twice today or are y'all the real deal?"

Bubba wasn't about to say anything that would get him in any deeper than he already was. The silence was deafening. The only sound being heard was the sound of three people breathing.

"Well?" Coach Henderson finally exclaimed. LJ was about to explode, and it was written all over his face. Bubba just sat there, trying to look stoic and unassuming.

"I don't think Bubba is going to participate in our conversation today, LJ. So how about you and me having a little talk without him? I'll ask the same question again. Did I see Lady Luck strike twice today or are y'all the real deal?"

Bubba knew it was coming. He could feel it, much like a tremor is felt before the earthquake starts to topple buildings.

"Oh, hell no, sir," LJ blurted out. "Excuse my language, but we can do that all day long and twice on Sunday."

Bubba rolled his eyes, and it made the coach smile. Reaching across the desk, Coach Henderson made LJ high-five him. "I thought you could. I knew there was something special about both of you the first time we met."

Bubba decided to join the party and throw LJ under the bus. "You should see LJ carry the ball. It'll blow your mind when you see him running the ball."

"Oh, really," Coach Henderson replied to Bubba's assessment of LJ's ability to run the football. "Just when I thought it couldn't get any better, it does. By chance, can either of you kick fifty-yard field goals?"

"No," they answered in unison.

"Just asking, that's all. Mama always told us, you'll never know unless you ask."

"That's good," LJ noted. "We both got good mamas too. They're always saying things like that."

That made Bubba and the coach smile. LJ was LJ. What you saw and what you got was always the same, pure LJ. And that was what endeared him to Bubba and the rest of their friends.

On the way home, Bubba tried to pretend to be a little put out by the events of the day.

"Come on, Bubba. Wouldn't you like the dynamic-duo to give Union High the first winning season since the War of Northern Aggression?"

That made Bubba smile, but he didn't respond for a minute just to aggravate LJ.

"Hell, yes," he finally yelled, pumping a fist into the air. LJ about went nuts in the truck. "I'll pick them apart through the air and you can run their butts in the ground."

"Now that sounds like a plan," LJ said. "That's what I'm talking about."

⚬✪⚬⚬✪⚬⚬✪⚬

Practice was over early. Bubba dropped a very happy LJ off at his place and headed for Clarice's. He had a couple of hours before he had to go to work, and he wanted to share the good news about what had just happened at practice.

He had only pretended to be upset. LJ was like a kid brother at Christmas, the only one in the room who still believes in Santa Claus, bringing infectious smiles and happiness to everyone gathered around the tree. If he'd be honest with himself, he was more excited about the possibility of playing quarterback for

81

Union High than any other thing that had happened in his life with only one exception. And he was headed to her house right now. But down deep, in his heart of hearts, he didn't really believe it would actually happen. "But who knows," he said to himself. "Santa always comes through for the kids who really believe. Maybe, if I try my best to believe it'll happen, then it will."

Maude's pipes, rumbling up the long drive to Clarice's, had announced their arrival. His beautiful Clarice was already out on the deck, all smiles. Bubba, out of the truck the minute it stopped, bounded up the steps and laid a monster kiss on Clarice, while squeezing her butt with both hands. Her parents were still at work and they often took liberties here they shouldn't be taking anywhere.

"So, how's my new quarterback?" she asked, flashing a huge smile.

"Damn, LJ's done told everybody. He called you before I could even get over here?"

"No, he didn't. Eula did. He called her. Now, don't be mad at LJ. Eula said he's nowhere near as excited about the possibility of him getting to play as he is about you becoming a star quarterback at Union High and delivering the first winning season in years. She said he sounded happier than a hog eating slop."

They had forty-five minutes before her folks got home from work. Bubba wanted to celebrate the possibility of getting to play football by practicing a little body contact with the girl he loved. Immediately he started to unzip her jeans.

"No, Bubba. We have to stop doing this so much before I get pregnant." As always, Bubba was persistent and persuasive. Clarice's nos weren't strong enough.

"Stop it, Bubba" tapered off and became the sounds he usually kidded her about making. They were once and done, and sitting on the deck like innocent grade school kids when her mom and dad drove up the driveway from work. Clarice immediately told her parents the good news about Bubba and LJ getting to play in the next game as quarterback and wide receiver.

"Congratulations, Bubba," Clarice's father said. "How did you manage to pull that one off? You must know something on someone. They never let any of us play."

"Thanks, Mr. Smith. They really need the help on offense, and . . ."

"And," Clarice interjected, "Bubba says our quarterback couldn't hit a bull in the rump with a handful of rice, and Bubba is good at what he does."

Bubba drew up a little inside and hoped her dad didn't ask for details on how good he was at whatever it was he did that Clarice made reference to.

Telling her parents goodbye, Bubba headed for his truck. He had to pick LJ up and go to work in a little while. Clarice walked out to the driveway with him.

"Pick you up in the morning," he told her as he climbed into Maude. "You oughta sleep good tonight since I—"

"Get out of here, Bubba Preston, before I call Granny and tell her what you just did to me."

"I love you, Clarice."

"I know you do," she said as she watched him turn around in the driveway.

"In the morning," he reminded her again—"7:15. Be ready to go."

"I'm always ready to go, Bubba. You should know that by now."

As he drove off, she heard him yelling back to her. "I'm calling Granny right now."

McClain's was abuzz with chatter about two of their own. Bubba and LJ had achieved celebrity status and hadn't even played a single down in their new positions. LJ was on cloud nine, but Bubba felt the shadow of a storm cloud gathering on the horizon. He knew the *hootie tootie* infrastructure would not stand idly by while their own kids were removed from the spotlight. And he was right.

Johnny's father, bent out of shape, had already made an appointment with Juanita Fisher, the school principal. He told his wife, "No one is going to replace our son with somebody named Bubba who drives a two-hundred dollar truck and lives in a trailer. It's not going to happen, plain and simple."

Mrs. Kitchens, trying to calm the situation, said, "Johnny told me they're only going to use these two new players in some kind of Hail Mary play or something like that. Johnny's not going to lose his position at quarterback. The other two boys will just get to do the Hail Mary thing."

The Hail Mary thing his wife referred to would quickly turn into a disaster for his son, establishing Bubba Preston as a much more efficient passer. Johnny had shared the bull in the ass with a handful of rice statement with his dad and it was all Mr. Kitchens could do to refrain from agreeing with the remark. He did indeed have the gift of reading faces, and he could see how much Bubba Preston wanted the quarterback's position and could also see how little interest his own son had in keeping it. He followed through with his appointment with the principal, but to no avail. She told him the football program was in the hands of Coach Henderson and that she wouldn't interfere with his decisions regarding the team.

"Are you going to go see the coach?" Mrs. Kitchens asked her husband, after finding out the principal wouldn't do anything to help.

"Wouldn't do any good," he told her. "Henderson wants to win football games and unfortunately for Johnny, he's about to lose his starting job at quarterback and there's not a thing I can do." But he knew he would probably try, regardless of what he told his wife. His nature had always been and would always be to throw his weight around in order to get what he wanted.

cXoɔcXoɔcXoɔ

Thursday's practice was the last one before game day on Friday. Coach Henderson considered his two new players a gift from God and told his wife they were his secret weapons.

Gathering in the gym before dressing out, the coach went over the Hail Mary pass play. "We're referring to this play as a Hail Mary, but we all know a Hail Mary is when the ball is thrown up for grabs and someone just gets lucky. Hopefully, LJ will be the only one who'll have a chance to catch this one. I'll have Johnny throwing to Bubba on the sidelines. Bubba will throw the ball back to LJ. Everyone will think Johnny's just warming up. We don't want the other team to suspect anything until it's too late. On our first set of downs and on the very first play, we'll do the deep pass to LJ. It should take them by complete surprise, and if we're lucky, we'll come away with six. He could sense the resentment from the other players. They had been friends with Johnny for most of their lives, on and off the field. What Coach Henderson didn't realize was the length Johnny's friends would go to make Bubba and LJ look bad.

"Dress out and meet me on the field. No laps today."

Silence had apparently been ordered by someone for the locker room. No one spoke a word. Bubba and LJ noticed it, dressed quickly and got out of there. LJ winked at Bubba as they were walking down to the practice field. He pointed at him and mouthed, "This is all your fault." LJ winked a second time and smiled his signature winning smile. Bubba shook his head as they walked out on the field.

After they left the locker room, chatter erupted like small-arms fire on a battlefield. Buddy couldn't believe what he was hearing. Rodney, their running back, was apparently the designer of the push back.

"Our new whiz kid can't hit his friend with a pass if the defense is in his face. So, make it happen. Everyone half-ass block so the defense can get into the backfield. But make it look good. If Henderson figures this out, he'll be pissed off and we'll be running laps for the rest of our lives."

"This was your idea, Rodney," Johnny said, "and I'm not having anything to do with it. I won't be on the field, so it'll fall on you if Henderson figures it out. I can't stand these two pricks, but I think they'll self-destruct on their own, without any interference on our part. My old man sees something in these two that ain't there, but if he thinks I'm involved with a fix, he'll raise holy hell with me."

"No problem, Johnny, this one's on me. Everybody in?" Rodney asked the other teammates. They all nodded their heads as they started for the field.

Buddy wanted to tell the coach what they were planning, but decided to let it play out on the field. Mr. Kitchens wasn't the only one who could read faces. Buddy knew there was something special in these two and figured they were quite capable of handling whatever Rodney had planned.

After warming up and getting loose, the team took the field, with Johnny remaining on the sidelines. Bubba was under center and LJ was lined up as a wide receiver.

"Play tough, defense," Coach Henderson yelled from the side line. "Milton High will be all over our offense Friday night. Make it hard on the offensive line, and get pressure on the quarterback. Offensive line, keep them out. LJ needs time to get down field."

When Bubba took the snap from center, the defense crushed the offensive line and was in his face so fast he had to take the sack. LJ, trotting back to the huddle, asked Bubba, "What's up with that?"

"Good job, defense. Looking good. Hold that line, offense. The play has to have time to materialize," Coach Henderson said.

Two more snaps rendered the same results with Bubba ending up on the bottom of the pile. One time he swore he felt a fist in his rib cage.

Catching LJ's attention, Bubba said softly, "Don't go out for the pass this time. Come inside and block for me. I'm gonna do an end-around."

"Hot damn," LJ said enthusiastically, as he headed for the line. Coach Henderson was alerted. *Hot damns* usually held promise.

The center snapped the ball to Bubba. Instead of going down field for the pass, LJ came inside to block for Bubba, who had started outside for the end-around. After three successive sacks, Coach Henderson, like Bubba and LJ, suspected foul. The end-around caught the defense completely by surprise. LJ flattened the closest threat, then got out front to block for Bubba as he scampered toward the end zone.

"Hot damn, indeed," Coach Henderson said.

After a couple of minutes to catch their breath, they lined up again to try the Hail Mary. This time the defense was baffled. All eyes turned to Rodney, who had no clue what to expect. LJ was again lined up as wide receiver.

Bubba took the snap from center, and LJ took two steps inside. The defense bought in and thought Bubba was going to run the ball again. But LJ only made two steps inside, then back outside and flew down the sideline. The pass was already in the air. LJ looked over his right shoulder, hauled the pass in and was dancing in the end zone before Rodney and crew even knew what had happened.

"Hot damn," Coach Henderson said on the sideline.

"Hot damn," LJ said as he spiked the ball in the end zone.

"Just damn," Johnny said to himself. "Better find myself a cushion. This bench is a bitch."

Someone once said, "You have to play the hand you're dealt." Eula Johnson, if she had to, would play out the hand life had given her. But her work ethic was looking for a do-over. She studied so she could not only lift herself out of near-poverty, but help her family as well. She had received two scholarship offers from two in-state schools and was trying to decide between a degree in business administration or a bachelor's degree in accounting.

She wanted as much for her friends, hence the warnings she was always dropping on Clarice and Bubba, trying to get them to stop acting like married folk. So far, the attempt had failed, and she was really concerned Clarice would end up pregnant and Bubba would never get a house that didn't have wheels.

She thought she had life figured out and now she had the same problem she had been warning her friends about. She had fallen in love with the Beamer, as she had nicknamed him. He was indeed beaming. Sue Ellen was ecstatic. She had never seen him so happy. He still hadn't told his parents, but concealing the new love of his life from them was easy. They were either gone or too busy to notice anything outside their sphere of interest.

Eula's mother knew something was up. Monday through Thursday, she was coming home later than usual, causing her to have to stay up in order to study. It was evident their daughter was very happy, and her mother told Eula's dad, "Our Eula has fallen in love."

"How do you know?" he asked. "Has she told you anything about it?"

"She doesn't have to tell me anything. It's written all over her face. And besides, it hasn't been that long ago. I still remember falling in love with you and how it felt."

Mr. Johnson got up from his recliner, walked over to his wife and kissed her on the forehead. "I remember, too. It was a special time. Guess what? I'm still in love with you."

"I know, and I love you as much today, maybe more, than back then. I hope Eula finds the same happiness we have."

So many things money and success can't buy. Love is just one of them.

ᑲᑯᑲᑯᑲᑯ

William Morgan, Sr., had just been chosen Man of the Year by the local country club. While not totally undeserved, most would say he bought it. But accolades usually find their way to the ones who are extra generous with either their time or their money. Mr. Morgan was in New York, closing a business deal, and Mrs. Morgan was in Italy for a fall festival.

No one was at the Morgan mansion except for Edward and his wife, Melba, the Morgan's long-time housekeepers. The main staff went home at six o'clock, but Edward and Melba had an apartment on the first floor, near the kitchen.

Knowing all this, William figured it was the perfect time to take Eula for a visit in the home he supposedly grew up in. He spent more time at Sue Ellen's than he ever did at his parent's home but he knew that, sooner or later, Eula would have to see both places. With his parents out of town, he thought it the perfect time to show her their home.

There was a huge disconnect between their two worlds. Both of them were aware of it, but neither wanted to address it for fear it might destroy their personal Camelot. William was more in favor of addressing the issue and letting it play out, regardless of the consequences. Eula, a little more conservative, preferred to move with caution, knowing the outcome could be less than favorable.

Bubba had often accused Eula of pretending the *hootie tootie* world didn't exist. Perhaps he was right. By ignoring the material differences, it allowed her to soar academically and to vacillate between two different social orders with ease. She could kick their butts in the field of scholarly endeavor and then drive her old truck out to Coosa Baptist Church and grill hot dogs in perfect harmony with her friends.

Falling in love with William was different. It was crossing lines with monumental contrasts. William's world came with fancy cars, a gated mansion, a complete staff and sheets with high thread counts. Eula imagined they had more real silverware at one place setting than her family had in their entire collection in the drawer of their tiny kitchen. In reality, no silverware was in the Johnson's kitchen, only stainless flatware.

Every Camelot comes with family history and baggage. This one was no exception. William knew they had to deal with all the differences, perceived or real, so he asked Eula to visit his Mom and Dad's home while they were away.

"What do you mean, you don't want to? It's the perfect time for me to show you around my home."

"Well, it just doesn't seem right to visit when your parents are not there," she said.

"Edward and Melba will be there. They would love to meet you."

"And this Edward guy will tell your Dad we came over when he wasn't home."

"No, he won't. Edward is probably my best friend, outside of Sue Ellen."

"Well, thanks a lot. So much for me!"

"We're not friends," the Beamer said, flashing a Bubba-like smile. Leaning over, he whispered in her ear, "I'd never marry my friend, and I'm going to marry you."

Eula felt a shudder run through her body she hoped he didn't notice.

"Thanks for telling me. Is this a proposal?"

"Actually, no. It's more like an alert."

"An alert?"

"Yes, an alert. Kinda like a weather forecast. I'm giving you notice of an upcoming event."

"Wow, does anyone else know?"

"Not yet, but soon. So now that you have the alert, you can be friends with Edward and his wife. They're wonderful people and special friends of mine. What do you say now? Wouldn't you like to go see where I was supposed to grow up?"

"I'd rather meet Sue Ellen first," Eula said. "I'd prefer your parents be home when I go to your place. Do you understand?"

"Sure, no problem. But it's got to happen, sooner or later."

In his heart William knew his parents would never accept Eula, not because of who she was, but because of what she, along with her parents, didn't have. Who she was as a person would never enter the equation. For his parents, it was like horses, and to them, bloodlines mattered.

cXos cXos cXos

Friday night found the Union High stadium with a full house. There were lots of new faces, some attending a high school football game for the first time. The coach had instructed the players not to talk about their surprise play. Secrecy was paramount for the sting to work. They would use the play on their first possession and on first down.

The Athletic Association, with Mr. Morgan's bank as a major sponsor, had been generous indeed. Landscaping the front of the campus had been a welcome gift. Both snack stands inside the stadium had been completely remodeled, furnishing them with all the amenities any restaurant would need in order to serve the public. And then, to finish off the project, one hundred new padded seats with backrests had been purchased and installed on the fifty-yard line on the home side of the field.

Of course, this area was open to anyone who wanted to sit there. But it was understood that the Athletic Association members and the school faculty had first shot at these comfortable seats. About midway through the first quarter, any seats remaining were fair game for the general public. No signs, no announcements, just one of those givens.

On this Friday night, givens didn't count for much. Those interested in seeing two of their own actually getting to play football came out early and in droves. Those padded seats with the comfortable backs, situated perfectly on the fifty-yard line, were filled quickly with family and friends from school and from work. They were, after all, the best seats in the house.

Although the Hail Mary was kept quiet, the school was abuzz with gossip and rumors about the two new players who had been recruited from the student body to turn Union High into a winner. There were far more students who identified with Bubba and LJ than there were who could relate to living in mansions and driving BMWs and Corvettes. The buzz brought the student body out in force. The parking lots filled quickly, requiring the sheriff's department to assist with parking along the highway.

Eula knew this was a special night for her friends, and she wanted to be there. She hardly ever missed work and asking off was no problem. It surprised her boss for her to ask, but she was such a hard worker there was no way he could have even thought about saying no to her request.

She had bought tickets in advance for the game. There were two thoughts in her mind. First and foremost, support Bubba and LJ. Secondly, knowing her family would be there, it would be a golden opportunity to introduce William to her mother and father outside of mansions and double-wides. She would also have an opportunity to show him off to her friends, many of whom were already gossiping about their relationship behind her back.

Eula had no way of knowing the future, but this night, or at least this date to the ball game, would become family lore. It would be told and retold many times how their mother had asked their father William out on their first official date.

Eula said, "I'll pick you up at Sue Ellen's around five. We'll grab a bite to eat, my treat and your choice, and then we'll take in the ball game, root for my two special friends and I'll introduce you to my folks. All I need is Sue Ellen's address and all you have to do, Beamer, is be ready." Her calling him Beamer always made him smile.

Taking a piece of paper from his wallet, he wrote something on it and handed it to her. It read, "I love you."

"I already know that, Beamer, but I need the address if I'm gonna pick you up. The address, Beamer," she said smiling.

As he wrote it down, he did it with a little angst, knowing it would be the first time she would see his world up close and the first time she would meet Sue Ellen.

"Come on, come on," Eula kidded him. "Surely you know Sue Ellen's address."

When he handed the piece of paper back to her, she looked to make sure it had an address this time. It did, but at the bottom he had written, "I will always love you, and I promise to be ready."

That evening, as she drove the old pickup to the address he had given her, she felt queasy and nervous. "Get over it, Eula," she told herself. "It was your idea. You could have met him at the mall." There was really no way to clean up the old truck. It was twenty years old, and it was her ride. As her father often said, "It is what it is." She had swept out the old rubber floor mats, wiped off the dash, cleaned the windshield and put a fresh beach towel on the seat.

William was just as nervous. He had purposely not taken her anywhere near Sue Ellen's. She didn't even want to go to his actual home, and seeing Sue Ellen's would be no better. It was a mansion, just no gated entry.

"Try and relax," Sue Ellen said, watching him pace the floor. "It's going to be fine. Things always work themselves out if you give them enough time."

"But you don't understand the differences in who we are and who they are, how we live compared to how they live."

"There was a time," Sue Ellen replied, "when I wouldn't have understood what you're talking about and what you're dealing with. People with less ambition than I had weren't even on my radar. I know the almighty dollar can deal a heavy hand on relationships. However, we have to remember all people, regardless of their position in life, are or can be connected by heart and soul. That choice is as individual as the people making it. You said Eula is beautiful, on the inside and on the outside. Houses, cars and things will never change that. You reached across a great chasm and found her, everything you want in a companion. Guess what?"

"What?" William asked.

"That perfect someone you told me about just turned into our drive in a beat-up old pickup truck."

Trying to lighten the tension for William, she said, "Scratch that! News Flash. It's not a beat-up old pickup truck. It's a beautiful white charger and the driver is galloping her steed up the driveway, looking for her knight in shining armor."

"Oh, shit!" William said, looking out the window.

Laying a hand on his shoulder, and looking directly at him, she said, "You already know something your folks and the elitists of our community don't know. It's not about the old truck. It's about who's driving that old truck and about the heart that beats inside the driver. It's not about and never should be about the ride. William, I believe I just heard our doorbell."

"Oh, shit!" he said again as he went to answer the door.

Sue Ellen smiled. "Just get the door, William. I've been wanting to meet this young woman."

Eula waited patiently at the door. The drive up to the house had been intimidating enough and she had no intention of going in. Not this evening anyway. She had left the truck running on purpose.

William opened the door, and Eula could see Sue Ellen standing close behind him.

"Please come in, Eula, and let me introduce you to someone very special in my life."

Sue Ellen stepped forward and said, "So nice to meet you. I've heard nothing but wonderful things about you. Please come in. And if I might say so, you're even more beautiful than William led me to believe."

"Thank you, ma'am, for your kind words. William has told me so much about you. I wish I had longer to stay and talk, but we have to get a bite to eat before we go to the game. Maybe I can come over again sometime and we can spend more time getting to know each other."

William was in a tight spot. All he wanted to do was get out of the house and back to the Camelot he had grown to love. "Well, Eula's right, we'd better get going or we'll be late for what's supposed to be the game of all games for Union High."

"I understand completely," Sue Ellen said as William and Eula turned to leave.

"Be back after the game," he said as they headed for the truck, patiently running and dripping oil on Sue Ellen's spotless driveway.

William tried to open the passenger side door. Eula, who had started around the back of the truck, realized he was having trouble with the door and came back to help him. Sue Ellen, upon seeing the truck door causing problems, immediately and quietly closed the front door.

"You have to do it like this," Eula said, grabbing the door handle and snatching it hard enough to make the whole truck move.

"Oh, I see," he said as he climbed into the cab. Eula had hurried around to the driver's side, got in quickly and slammed her door. You could hear things rattle inside the door as it shut. "The old truck is a bit cantankerous," she said, a little embarrassed. "Shut your door as hard as I shut mine."

William, not wanting to fail at shutting his door, slammed it hard enough to break the door glass. Luckily, it didn't. "Good job, Beamer," she said and smiled. "Let's go get something to eat. Your choice, of course. What would you like?"

Sue Ellen watched as they drove down the drive and could see the large oil spot the truck had left in her driveway.

⚬⚬⚬⚬⚬⚬

Milton High was a fierce rival and Union High hadn't beaten them in five seasons. The distance between the two schools was only thirty miles, so Milton's huge fan base had turned out for this game. They had already filled the visitor's side. The stadium was rocking, adrenaline was flowing, and Friday night football was in the air.

Inside the locker room, Coach Henderson went over the scouting report. It was his first time, as head coach, to face the Milton High team. "Their strong point is their passing game. We have to get into their backfield and disrupt the quarterback. If we give him time in the pocket, he'll eat our lunch. I'm expecting to draw blood first with our surprise Hail Mary. If it works the first time, they'll be looking for it the next time they see Bubba and LJ in the offensive line-up. And let's be sure we make the extra point," Coach Henderson said, addressing the kicker.

"All right, guys, huddle up. Buddy's going to lead us in a team prayer."

"Lord, we thank you for healthy bodies and sharp minds. Give us wisdom and courage and protect us from injuries as we play here tonight. Help us represent You by playing fairly and giving You our best. We don't have to win all the time, but if You'll help us win tonight, we'll lay the victory at Your feet. In Thy name we pray. Amen."

There was definitely electricity in the air. Coach Henderson could feel it and so could the players. Bubba and LJ were the most excited. They knew they would see action, at least for a couple of downs on offense, and get some playing time on defense as well.

They heard the crowd erupt as Milton took the field. "All right, guys, your fans are waiting for you. Make them proud."

As the players took the field, a deafening roar went up from the home stands. The cheerleaders might as well have not been there because the fans didn't need anyone to lead them. They were loud, raucous and intimidating. Coach Henderson wondered if Milton High noticed the difference in the crowd and their enthusiasm. Normally, the stands and bleachers would have been half full and the enthusiasm minuscule at best. But not tonight. Excitement was in the air and change was coming to town. Tonight was destined to alter more than a few lives.

Unfortunately for Union High, Milton won the toss and elected to receive the ball. Coach Henderson gathered the team around him on the sidelines and said, "Do not let them score. It's imperative we draw first blood." Looking directly at Bubba and LJ, he said, "Make it happen. Today is a new beginning. Remember, this is our house and we will bow to no one."

LJ could feel the hair on the back of his neck stand up. He wasn't the only one. Coach Henderson had done a good job firing up the team and putting a little pride and swagger back into their game. The kick-off team sprinted onto the field, with Bubba and LJ lining up on each side of the ball.

"You know what to do, LJ," Bubba said. LJ responded, but the crowd noise drowned out his *hot damn*. Didn't make any difference though. Coach Henderson heard it in his mind.

It looked like an instant replay of the practice where LJ hit the punt returner, causing the fumble Bubba picked up and ran in for a score. Only this time, they had help. LJ was trying to get to the punt return man, but Bubba got to him first. He laid a hit on him, and the contact could be heard in the stands. Jason, picking up the fumble that had been jarred loose, scampered into the end zone. The extra point was good.

Hot damn was fast becoming the team's buzz word. "Good job, defense. Way to go, Jason," Coach Henderson shouted as Union High got ready to kick off again.

The stands were rocking and the roar was deafening. The Cougars had the lead and less than a minute had been run off the clock.

Union High kicked off a second time. This time, Milton held onto the ball and kept it for awhile, making two first downs before having to punt it away. Bubba, LJ and Johnny were already warming up on the sidelines for the Hail Mary.

Milton punted and Donnie, Union's punt returner, signaled for a fair catch at the twenty-five-yard line. "Make it count," the coach said, as Bubba and the offense took the field.

Milton's head coach noticed someone different in at quarterback, but hesitated calling a time out. Union broke huddle and came to the line with Bubba under center. The ball was snapped, and LJ ran his pattern down the left sideline. Bubba scrambled around for a second or two, giving LJ time to break free of the linebacker that was tailing him. The defensive player covering LJ was blown away with LJ's speed. He had five steps on him when the perfect spiral thrown by Bubba was hauled in and carried into the end zone for six more. Just like that, it was 13-0. The extra point was good.

Milton High was in shock. Union High's fans were so loud they became their twelfth man on the field. Everyone, except Johnny, was playing great. Rodney was running hard and moving the ball. At the beginning of the fourth quarter, he scored from eight yards out, making the score Union, 21, and Milton, 7. Then the expected happened. Johnny threw an interception, resulting in another touchdown for Milton High. Now the score was 21-14.

Before the Cougars went on offense, Coach Henderson told their return man to call for a fair catch. "Don't run it back, just turn it over to the offense." This was a little strange, but he acknowledged the instruction and ran out on the field to receive the kick.

Walking over to where Bubba was standing, Coach Henderson asked, "Do you think you can run our offense with LJ and Jason as receivers and Rodney as your running back."

"What about Johnny?" Bubba asked.

"Let me worry about Johnny," the coach responded quickly. "Can you run the offense?"

"Yes, sir. I can run it. Mostly the same thing we do on the weekends behind the church. I don't know all the plays by number or name, but if Rodney and Jason could help me, I can get the job done."

The coach called a timeout. Catching Johnny before he took the field, he said, "I'm making a change, Johnny. Bubba's going in at quarterback."

Johnny was shocked. Something he seemingly didn't care about was suddenly gone. Without saying another word, he walked over to the bench and sat down. Coach Henderson called another receiver over to the sideline and sent LJ and Bubba back to the huddle. Before they left, he told them, "Make this count, Bubba. For yourself, for LJ and for the school. We need this one."

"Will do, sir."

Mr. Kitchens and his wife weren't sitting in the nice seats he had purchased at mid-field. They were standing up with a bunch of students near the thirty-yard line on the home side. When he saw the coach pull his son, he threw the coke he was holding to the ground and stomped off. His wife followed.

Bubba knelt down in the huddle, not knowing the plays by name or number, and not knowing how Johnny's friends were going to react to him taking over at quarterback. Something was different. He didn't feel the resentment he figured would be there. "Rodney, call a running play." Rodney quickly called a number and a different team went to the line of scrimmage.

"Hot damns" were uttered by more than LJ, and Bubba knew all was well with him taking Johnny's place. The Union High fans went nuts, and all of Bubba's and LJ's friends from McClain's added to the noise level considerably.

The ball was snapped and Bubba handed off to Rodney, who ran for seven punishing yards. Bubba called a pass play, and hit Jason coming across the middle for fifteen more yards. Milton High was stunned with this fast-paced offense. Bubba made moving the ball look easy. Clarice and Janice weren't screaming for LJ and Bubba. They had no voice left to scream with.

In the huddle, Bubba said, "Great catch, Jason. LJ, the next one's yours. Right corner of the end zone."

"Hot damn," Rodney said, grinning. "Make it happen, LJ."

Before the defense knew what had happened, LJ was spiking

the ball in the end zone. The score now Union High, 28 and Milton, 14.

It turned ugly from there for Milton. A fired-up defense kept them scoreless. Bubba completed six more passes to LJ and four to Jason, and Rodney ran his heart out on the ground. The ball was on the eight-yard line and fourth down was coming up. There was less than two minutes left in the game. Instead of calling for the usual field goal attempt, Coach Henderson decided to let Bubba have a shot at the end zone and called their last time out.

When Bubba got over to the sideline, Coach Henderson put his hand on Bubba's shoulder and said, "Awesome job, son. I'm proud of you. I have one more thing for you to do."

"And what's that, sir?"

"This one is yours. Keep it, and run it in."

A huge smile came across Bubba's face. "Yes, sir," he said and then rejoined the team.

Milton, who figured they would kick a field goal, had to scramble to make adjustments for a run or pass to the end zone when the kicker didn't come out on the field.

In the huddle, Bubba knelt down and said, "Coach called a keeper. I'm running off right tackle. I need help. Open me a hole. *Hot damns* went around the huddle. A snap, a hole big enough to drive Eula's truck through, and Union High had six more points. LJ ran over to Bubba in the end zone and he tossed the ball to LJ and said, "Spike it for me." LJ got to spike two that night.

The extra point was missed, but the final score was Union, 34 and Milton, 14.

Milton High had always been a power house in Region IV. Losing was not something they did well, especially to a school like Union High. But Coach Henderson had been clairvoyant during his play to win or quit speech when he said the visiting team would leave the field with their tails tucked between their legs. On that day, Coach Henderson wasn't completely sure he believed it would happen. But tonight, Union High delivered, and Coach Henderson was proud of how the boys rallied around Bubba and played as a team.

The locker room was loud; they weren't used to winning, especially by twenty points. And it had seemed so easy. Bubba and LJ finally felt accepted and it seemed like it had always been so. Coach Henderson took it all in for a few minutes before finally addressing the team.

"Boys," he said in a booming voice. "Do you know what you just did? You beat the best team in our region, and you made it look easy." *Hot damns* reverberated around the locker room. "Most importantly, you played as a team, and I'm very proud of every one of you."

Rodney, the instigator of the plan to make Bubba and LJ look bad with the Hail Mary pass play, raised his hand and Coach Henderson recognized him. The coach had the game ball and had been tossing it up and down while talking to the team. "May I," he said, gesturing toward the game ball with his hands. The coach tossed him the ball.

The coach would later tell his wife, "It was such an emotional moment. I knew he had caused the problem with the Hail Mary play during practice, but I also felt like I knew why he wanted the game ball."

"As most of you know," Rodney began, fumbling for words, "I'm no expert on this game." A ripple of laughter made its way around the room. "Like most of you, I watch way too much football on TV, and just like you, I have my favorite players. And, like you, I can recognize natural talent when I see it. It's easy to spot those who have it, love the game, and make playing the game look easy."

Turning, he walked to the outer edge of the circle where Bubba and LJ were standing. All eyes followed him, and Coach Henderson swallowed hard, figuring he knew what was coming next. Stopping in front of Bubba, Rodney stood for what seemed like an eternity before speaking. You could have heard a pin drop.

"I'm sorry," he said to Bubba, clearly choked with emotion. "As I said earlier, I'm no expert on the game of football, but you have more talent in your little finger than the rest of us have combined. And on behalf of the coach and all the players, this win belongs to you and so does this game ball."

A wave of *hot damns* went around the room and then the players all clapped and cheered. Coach Henderson had to fight back tears of joy. A young player had not only seen the error of his ways, but was man enough to apologize and laud praise on someone deserving of it. To the coach, this was way more important than the win.

Now, it was Bubba's turn to be speechless and emotional. It took forever for him to find his voice. "It was a great game, but I don't deserve it any more than anyone else on the team. But thank you. I will always remember this night."

As he took the game ball, everyone cheered again. Johnny, who had already dressed, slipped quietly out the side door and drove his Corvette into the night. He had a lot to think about.

It took forever for the stands to empty and the people to get out of the parking lots and to their cars lined up and down the highway. Rodney and some others had invited Bubba and LJ to the country club to celebrate the win, but they graciously declined the invite. They wanted to be with Clarice and Janice to share the victory with them. When Bubba and LJ left the locker room, there were fifty-plus friends, some from school and some from McClain's, waiting to congratulate them. They were all headed to

Bill's Diner to grab a bite to eat and continue the celebration. Neither Clarice nor Janice could talk above a whisper.

"Look what Bubba's got," LJ told everyone.

"What's he got?" Clarice asked in a whisper, not seeing anything but a football in his hand.

"He's got the game ball," LJ said proudly, "for his outstanding play tonight."

Clarice got a little closer and whispered in Bubba's ear, "I've got something for you better than that old game ball."

"I'm calling Granny Preston right now," he said, smiling at the possibility the night might get better still. "If she only knew!"

A *"hot damn,"* uttered by LJ when Janice got close to him, made Bubba think both of them might score again.

⁓⁕⁓⁕⁓

William and Eula never saw a single play of the game. The parking lot was full, and cars and trucks were parked on both sides of the road for a quarter mile in all directions. In the dark, the old truck truly became the White Charger Sue Ellen had dubbed it.

Both occupants of the White Charger were in uncharted territory. For the first time, Eula realized what Bubba and Clarice had been dealing with, and she had no one offering her words of caution.

As she drove around a second time looking for a parking space, it became evident that if they were to see the game, they would have to park a long ways from the stadium and walk back. Pulling out to the highway, she turned right and headed out of town.

"Where are we going?" William asked.

"Slide over here next to me, Beamer." She didn't have to ask a second time.

William laid his left hand on Eula's leg and that became the catalyst for a violent explosion of emotion and teenage hormones, which had been raging inside both of them, desperately trying to find a way out.

Eula turned right onto a dirt road about a half mile from the stadium. The BMW would have prevented them from acting like married folk, but not her old truck. The White Charger was more than happy to accommodate them. Privately, in the future, both would remember this night differently. Each one, jokingly, would blame the other for stealing his/her virginity.

Had they listened, they could have faintly heard the Union High fans in delirious celebration as their team continued to play well. But they didn't. The only sounds they heard were sounds similar to the ones Bubba always accused Clarice of making every time they did it.

On this night, Camelot became real, unbridled passion won out, and the old Chevy truck, now known as the White Charger, secured itself a place in the future Mr. and Mrs. William Morgan, Jr's garage forever.

⁓⊗⁓⊗⁓⊗⁓

While Bubba and LJ were on their way to becoming local icons, and William and Eula were acting like married folk, Sue Ellen was alone. Her house on Georgia Avenue could be warm and cozy or sometimes downright sad and lonely. Tonight, it was the latter.

Sue Ellen, with a glass of wine from dinner, went into her library to find something to read. Seeing William and Eula together made her very happy. She wondered how their first date was going and who had won the ball game.

Picking out a John Grisham novel, she went to the den to wait for their return. After pouring herself a second glass of wine, she settled into her favorite chair to read. But tonight she would not read; she would remember. Her fingers did not turn the pages of the book. Instead, her mind turned the pages of her memories. Laying the book in her lap, she reclined in her chair, galloping into the past as the White Charger was galloping in the present, carrying two passengers who would spend the rest of their lives together.

Seeing Eula, so beautiful, vibrant and full of life reminded her of herself. But there was a big difference. Eula seemed content to drive the old truck and go to a local football game with her friends. Even when she was Eula's age, Sue Ellen had big plans and ideas on how to get fancy clothes, expensive cars and a job with an awesome salary. And she had made it all happen.

Taking another sip of wine, she thought about Saint Mary's in Oxford, England. Hospitals are where you go when you're sick and she was definitely sick. Being pregnant with her boss's baby and refusing to get an abortion had brought her there. Morally, she was opposed to abortion and considered it wrong. Saint Mary's opposed abortion and had a program that specialized in helping unwed mothers, quietly and discreetly, find good homes for their unwanted babies. And, most importantly, it was thousands of miles away from home.

There was already enough talk at the bank and around town concerning the affair William Morgan was having with his twenty-three-year-old executive secretary, who was living with him in his mansion. However, having a baby tied to him was not something he wanted to happen. So, he sent her away, supposedly on a well-deserved, extended vacation in Europe. Maybe someday she'd want children, but now was not the time to have a baby. For now, she was only interested in climbing the corporate ladder to success.

Granny Preston would have quoted Scripture here. "And we

know that all things work together for good, to them that love God, to them who are called according to His purpose." A very pregnant Sue Ellen would have argued that point with Granny, because she had long since forgotten the spiritual things taught to her as a child.

Saint Mary's was selected because it had a history of confidentiality, securely guarding the birth mother's identity and the placement of the babies with the adoptive parents. Mr. Morgan made a sizable contribution to their unwed mothers' program to add emphasis that the non-disclosure policies were to be strictly observed. It would not look good if the community found out he had knocked up Sue Ellen, especially considering the difference in their ages.

Sue Ellen's mind turned to Sister Cass and Sister Francis, two angels of mercy, both working at Saint Mary's. She had kept in touch over the years, and when Sister Cass passed away, she had flown back to England to attend the service. It was on this return trip for the funeral that Sister Francis told Sue Ellen the whole story about the night she gave birth to her son and the two days following when her son's life was hanging in the balance.

As Sue Ellen remembered the past, her eyes filled with tears. "Too much wine," she said out loud. The baby boy she delivered had multiple problems with his heart and lungs. His kidneys weren't functioning as well as they should. Saint Mary's had determined he probably wouldn't make it and didn't put him up for adoption.

Sister Cass, a prayer warrior, had immediately lifted the baby in prayer to the Almighty. Whenever God spoke to Sister Cass, she always listened and obeyed.

"You know she doesn't want this baby and doesn't care anything about it," Sister Francis said to Sister Cass.

"It's not this baby," Sister Cass said, "It's her baby."

"I understand how you feel, but our only job here is to save babies and place them with people who want to adopt them, people who really want them."

"Our first priority is to listen to the Lord, and He told me to take this baby to see his birth mother. Without a miracle, this little fellow will not survive. Surely, he deserves to see his mother and perhaps, just maybe, she'll hold him for a few minutes before he dies."

"It's your decision," Sister Francis said. "I'm only reminding you of the hospital's policies and part of it requires us to honor the request made by the mother."

"Would you go with me to see Miss Thornton?" Sister Cass asked.

"You know I will," she responded, "but I don't know how Father Rodriguez will react if Miss Thornton tells the administration. But how could Father Rodriguez get upset, especially if it's a God-thing. You did say it's a God-thing, right?"

"Trust me, it's a God-thing. I don't know why, but the woman in Room 14 is special, and so is this baby. We're not to judge the whys and what ifs, we're just to do what the Lord tells us to do. And He told me to take this sick little baby boy to see his mother."

Sister Cass picked up the baby and Sister Francis pushed the IV pole holding the much-needed meds, dripping slowly into the infant's tiny leg.

Stopping abruptly as they were about to leave the nursery ICU, Sister Francis said, "Oh, Lord."

"What? What's wrong?" Sister Cass asked, seeing the emotion in Sister Francis' face.

"It is a God-thing," she said, with tears running down her cheeks. "He just spoke to me as well."

"And what did He say? Tell me now!" Sister Cass implored.

Sister Francis, turning to face her friend, said, "Behold, I am the Lord. All things are possible, if you only believe."

Both Sisters were now crying. As they started a second time to leave the nursery, they ran headlong into Father Rodriguez. Still crying, both Sisters were speechless.

"And where are you going with the baby?" he asked. Not wanting them to get anxious, he continued, "I already know. You're taking the baby to see his birth mother, even though she requested not to see the child. That's against her rights as a patient and against all hospital rules. But it's okay. It's a God-thing. He just spoke to me and told me what was happening and to accompany you on your errand of obedience. May I go with you?"

"Please do," both Sisters said in unison.

"But we must pray first," Father Rodriguez said. Everyone bowed their head. The infant, awake but not crying, seemed to be watching the three of them.

"Lord, we're thankful You've chosen us, weak vessels that we are, to do Your will. While we don't understand what's happening here, we ask You to walk with us down this hallway. Bless this child and heal it of all infirmities and bless the birth mother and make her heart receptive to Your will. Make Yourself known to her, even now, Lord Jesus. And Lord, help our unbelief. *Amen and Amen.*"

Boldly, Sister Cass asked Father Rodriquiz what the Lord told him.

"This is a special child and the birth mother is special, too."

A lot of years had passed since the story had been told to Sue Ellen. She was suddenly brought back to reality when she heard the White Charger galloping up her drive, delivering the sickly infant, now a healthy young man, back to his friend named Sue Ellen Thornton, who was, without his knowledge, his mother.

Before Sue Ellen could get out of her recliner, William had already come inside and was making his way to the den.

"And where's Miss Eula," she asked, looking around William as if she expected to see her coming down the hallway.

"Oh, she has to work in the morning and needed to get home to get some shut-eye. She said to tell you she'd come by real soon for a visit. Just let her know when it's convenient for you."

Sue Ellen could tell William was a little out of sorts. He seemed nervous and immediately said, "I think I'll turn in early myself. It's been a long week."

"Is everything okay?" she asked him as he turned to go to his bedroom.

"Sure, I'm just a little tired. It's been a long week."

"Well, at least tell me who won the game. Did Eula's friends get to play any?"

Luckily for William, he had a few answers that would lead Sue Ellen to assume they actually went to the game. They had stopped to gas the White Charger, and some of Eula's friends were also there fueling their cars and they told her the final score and how well Bubba and LJ had played in the game. Also, they had learned Johnny Kitchens had been benched and Bubba had finished the game at quarterback. He turned and went into the den area and sat down to convey this information to her.

She noticed his shirt was buttoned up wrong, with one side of the collar higher than the other. She decided to let it pass and didn't mention it to him. After telling her about the game, via the gas station informers, he excused himself and went up to his room. Upon looking in the mirror, he said, "Oh, shit," when he saw the way he had buttoned his shirt. "I hope she didn't notice it," he muttered to himself.

Sue Ellen poured herself another glass of wine and sat back

down in her recliner. Shrugging her shoulders and shaking her head from side to side, she thought about the way his shirt was buttoned, and then said a prayer, "It's a special time in his life, Lord. Let him be young and enjoy it, but please look after him for me, and keep him safe and out of harm's way."

⚬❀⚬⚬❀⚬⚬❀⚬

In the Kitchens household, things didn't go quite as smoothly for Johnny as they had for the Beamer. Johnny had ridden around for an hour or so and had stopped by a lake house his family owned. He considered spending the night there, but knew it would worry his mom and only create more tension with his father for not coming home after being benched in the game.

His mother was already in bed, but Johnny knew his father would be waiting up for him. Johnny hoped for the best and entered the house as quietly as he could. His father was waiting for him in the den. "And where have you been?" he asked.

"Riding around, mostly, thinking about the game. Rode by the lake house for a few minutes. Hadn't been by there in a while. Everything looked okay."

"And what were you thinking about, the fact I was dead on with my prediction? I told you what would happen. You let some piece of shit from a trailer park take your quarterback position away from you."

Johnny handled it well. He didn't get upset, raise his voice or create a situation that would only escalate into a shouting match with his father. "Dad, you were right. Tom Preston does, in fact, live in a trailer park. And you were right when you compared my ability to his. He's a much better quarterback than I am. One last thing. It was nice to beat Milton for a change, even if I was sitting on the bench."

That immediately stopped the conversation from escalating into a shouting match. His dad couldn't say another thing because Johnny had totally diffused the situation by agreeing with him. Johnny Kitchens had grown up quite a bit in the space of one quarter of football.

"Dad, I know you're disappointed in me and I'm sorry I let you down. I'm going to bed now. It's been a tough night." With that said, he turned and went upstairs, leaving his father with a lot to think about.

◦◦◦◦◦◦◦◦◦

Saturday morning found Eula in panic mode. "What if I'm pregnant?" she asked herself. "We didn't use anything. How stupid was that? Surely I'm not—not after doing it just one time." Remembering Bubba and Clarice, and all the advice she had given them regarding acting like married folk, she said out loud, "I'm not going down that road."

"What did you say, honey?" her mother asked from the kitchen.

"Oh, nothing, Mom. Just talking to myself. Guess I'm getting old."

"Oh, not yet, Eula. At least you're not answering yourself like I do."

"Oh, Mom, stop it, you're not old," Eula said, as she came into the kitchen where her mother was cooking breakfast.

"You're up early," her mom noted inquiringly.

"Got a couple of errands to run before work. Thought I'd get an early start. I'll grab a biscuit at McDonald's or somewhere. Gotta go, Mom."

"Be careful and make sure you get enough rest. We worry about all the work and studying you do."

"I'm fine. Have to get it all done while the sun's shining. Speaking of which, daylight's burning. See you this afternoon."

After kissing her mother on the forehead, she went out to her truck. When she got in, she could smell the Beamer's cologne and the memories came flooding back. "Oh, what have we done?" she asked herself, but then smiled, remembering the moment for what it had been.

She knew a lot of her friends were sexually active, but she had chosen the old-fashioned way of don't do it until you're married. Firing up the Chevy truck, she shook her head and said aloud, "So much for saving myself."

She was headed to meet William at the mall. "He probably won't show," she thought. "He's already got what he was after." She knew better, but was beating herself up for giving in to her desires. As she wheeled the White Charger into the parking lot, there he was, already out of his car. Before she could stop in the parking place next to his car, he was at her door. The look on his face told her he was thinking the same thing she was.

He was standing between his car and her truck door, and she couldn't get out. As she started to roll the window down, he placed both hands on the top of the glass and said, "I'm so sorry about last night. Please forgive me. It was all my fault, and I should have stopped us from doing that. That's not how I wanted it to happen. I should have been stronger and made us wait. Now I've ruined everything."

Eula, being who she was, rushed to the rescue of her beloved. "Was it that bad?" she asked jokingly.

"No, that's the problem. It was wonderful, and I can't stop thinking about it. But that doesn't make it right."

"Get in," Eula said, "and let's talk about it."

Going around to the passenger side, William jerked the old truck door hard enough to get it open and got in. Eula smiled and placed a hand on his knee.

"Oh, no. Don't do that. That's how it started last night."

That made both of them laugh.

"I don't think we'll do a repeat performance in broad open daylight in the mall parking lot, do you?"

"I don't know," the Beamer joked, "it's like pie and ice cream. It's hard to leave good stuff alone."

Leaning over, she kissed him and said, "I love you."

"And God only knows how much I love you," he said. "We won't do that again until we're married, okay?"

"Absolutely," she agreed, "not until we're married."

It was Monday morning and the school was abuzz about their new powerhouse football team who had crushed Milton High the previous Friday night. Juanita Fisher was excited because the sports reporter from their local paper had made an appointment for 2 PM to interview her and Coach Henderson regarding the Friday night game. The whole town was talking, saying it was nothing short of a miracle. Clarice and Janice knew better. It was Bubba and LJ, pure and simple.

Coach Henderson walked into the principal's office about twenty minutes before the reporter was scheduled to arrive. "Winning may be more trouble than it's worth," Juanita said jokingly. "Close the door and have a seat," she said, motioning to a large conference table where the interview would take place.

"What's wrong with winning for a change?" he asked, as she sat down at the head of the table.

"I think you were right about that dynasty thing and the upper-crust expecting all the important roles to be handed to them."

"But everyone's not like that," Coach Henderson said. "I know some mighty rich and powerful people who look like they don't have a pot to pee in or a window to throw it out of."

Juanita sat for a few seconds trying to visualize the old saying the coach had just painted with words on her mind screen. A smile crept across her face as the image materialized. "Wow!" she said, laughing out loud, "That's a new one on me. How descriptive. Gets to the point without wasting time."

"For sure," he responded. "I'm surprised you've never heard it. It's as old as Methuselah in my neck of the woods."

"But I'm not from your neck of the woods. I'm sure our friendship will probably cost me my job some day when I drop one of your barbs of wisdom on the wrong person at an inopportune time."

"Don't worry about it. Use them as teaching aids for the unenlightened you have to associate with at work. Now tell me, what's happened to make you see and agree with my analysis about big money securing the key positions in our school?"

"Frank Kitchens came in early this morning, raising hell, excuse my language, because you benched his son Friday night. He was mad as an old wet hen and named all the projects on campus his company had paid for, and get this—he railed against people who don't have a lot of money and never contribute anything at all to the school. He called them lazy takers. He then reminded me of the padded seats the Athletic Association put in the stadium and I quote, 'My wife and I couldn't even sit in the seats I helped pay for because they were filled with a bunch of rednecks, whooping and hollering like the trailer-park trash they are.' He made me sick to my stomach."

"Why did he bring poor people into this?"

"I guess because Tom Preston's family works at McClain's and they live in a trailer. No one who lives in a trailer should replace his son as quarterback is my take on his ranting and raving. This is Vegas. Do you know what that means?" Juanita asked.

"Sure," Coach Henderson said, "what happens here, stays here."

"Or to be perfectly sure you understand, what's said here also stays here. Do I have your word on that?"

"Now you're starting to scare me." Holding up three fingers, he added, "Scouts honor, I promise."

"Just listen to the crap that he said to me. When he left, I wrote it down so I could remember all of it." Getting a notepad out of a locked drawer, she continued her tirade. She was so mad her face was red and her voice was trembling as she spoke. Coach Henderson had never seen this side of her.

"Listen, and I quote, 'No poor, white-trash kid living in a trailer and driving a piece of shit old truck is going to take the quarterback job away from my son. Hell, his Corvette is worth more than the shit-hole the Preston kid calls home.' Now, what would you have said to that?" Juanita asked the coach.

Coach Henderson took a deep breath and then said, "You have no idea what I would like to say about that but, more importantly, what did you say back to him?"

"I was so mad and infuriated, I stood up. He remained seated. I told him his son Johnny was a good student who unfortunately was not a good quarterback and the word on campus was that Johnny couldn't hit a bull in the ass with a handful of rice. I told him it was also unfortunate for Johnny he had an elitist piece of shit for a father. With that said, he immediately stood up and started to say something. But I finished my rant before he could get started. I told him people like him, who measure the value of others by what they possess, are a blight on mankind. And then I told him to get the hell out of my office and that if I ever saw him on campus again, I would tell the whole town about the conversation we had just had. I finished it by telling him not to let my door hit him in the butt."

Coach Henderson was all smiles. "I'm proud of you, girl. Put the old bastard in his place. What did he do then?"

"Nothing. Just stomped out of my office and slammed the door hard."

There was a knock at the door. Before acknowledging it, Juanita said, "Remember your promise and where you're at."

"I'm in Vegas and having a ball," Coach Henderson said and smiled.

Juanita went over and opened her door. "The reporter from the *Herald* is here," her secretary informed her.

"Send him in, please." She turned and took her seat back at the conference table. A nice-looking young man entered her office. Juanita and Coach Henderson both stood to greet him. "I'm Tony Adkins, sports reporter for the *Herald*. After introducing the coach and herself, she gestured for Tony to take a seat at the conference table.

"And what can we do for you today?" Juanita asked, as if she had no idea why he was there. Coach Henderson smiled, comparing the greeting just given the reporter to the bashing he had just heard her give Kitchens in Vegas.

"I won't take up much of your time, and I appreciate you allowing me to see both of you this afternoon. I have only one question. I've heard it asked, seems like a thousand times, since Friday night's game. What happened here Friday night and how did Union High pull off that upset?"

"That's actually two questions," Juanita said and smiled at Tony.

"Sorry about that," he said, finding the humor in her remark. "But to flesh out the question, let me tell you what I saw. I attended the game, expecting the usual blow-out, with Milton High winning by a huge margin. Union is not known for its football prowess, and Milton High is a powerhouse in AAAA football. And, if I might add, y'all made it look easy." Flashing a smile at Juanita, he said, "And a third question, where did Tom Preston and Jimmy Denton come from? And a fourth question, if I might. Who, excuse the language, lit a fire under Rodney Flannigan's butt? He ran like he had been energized by the Almighty."

"I may have to get my calculator to keep up with the number of questions you've asked. You might have a future in politics," Juanita said and laughed. "You started out with only one question and we're at four or five, I think, and still counting."

"Sorry about that, ma'am, I didn't mean to mislead you. I guess I'm like everyone else in town and just excited to have something like this happening in our community."

"Just kidding you, Tony. I'll let Coach Henderson answer all your questions. After all, he's the architect of this renewal or revival or whatever you call it when you finally stop losing and win one for a change. Coach—"

"Mama always told me to tell the truth, and if I did, I'd never have to try and remember what I had told someone," Coach Henderson interjected.

Tony immediately said, "My mama's always saying stuff like that to me."

"Seems like good mamas are plentiful in this area," Coach Henderson noted. "I'd like to take the credit for the fabulous win last Friday night, but truth is I can't. We got lucky, plain and simple. There's no supersonic football savvy salve I

119

rubbed on the players, or any special playbook I found with magic plays. Truth is, those two boys you mentioned, Tom and Jimmy, stepped forward and joined the team. They had never played a single down of organized ball before coming out, only sand-lot football. When a player has God-given talent, and in this case it's two players who are gifted, the coach will always look good. They've brought new life into a lifeless program, one that has always taken losing for granted. But not any longer. Case in point, Rodney Flannigan. You already noted how he racked up yardage carrying the ball in the last game. Why? Tom, we call him Bubba, and Jimmy, better known as LJ, have energized the team, and I predict we'll win the rest of our games this year."

"Easy, Coach," Juanita said jokingly, "that's quite a prediction."

"Can I quote you on that one?" Tony asked quickly. Juanita raised her eyebrows, but the coach was already nodding his head.

"Absolutely, you can quote me. Seeing my faith in this team in the newspaper will only increase their determination to make it happen. Absolutely, quote me. We'll win the rest of our games this year and . . ."

Juanita cut him off. "And that's probably enough predictions for today. Any more questions, Tony?"

"Just a couple more," he said quickly. "And what about Johnny Kitchens? Will he get any more playing time?"

"Sure he will," Coach Henderson replied with sincerity, "Johnny's a good athlete and a good student."

"One last question and I'll let y'all get back to work. Mrs. Juanita, how does it feel to have your school's team listed in the win column for a change and to have an article written about it in our paper?"

"Awesome," she said. "I love it. And you heard it from the

horse's mouth, we're going to win the rest of our games this year. Right, Coach?"

"Every one of them. You can take it to the bank."

"This will make a great story. I'll send a copy over before I run it. Thanks a million. Both of you have been very helpful."

Juanita and Coach Henderson stood, shook Tony's hand, and Juanita walked him to the door. Closing it behind her, she returned to the conference table.

"What was all that prediction stuff about?" she asked grinning with her hands out and palms up. "Are you sure you can win the rest of the games this season? That's a pretty tall order."

"Damn straight we will, if I can get out of Vegas and back to the gym. Let me know if I need to deal with Mr. High and Mighty Kitchens."

"No problem," she said, "I've got him by the balls."

"By the what?" Coach Henderson asked.

"Look how you're corrupting me," Juanita said, and smiled sheepishly.

"I think you were corrupted a long time before I got here. I've got to get out of Vegas before my reputation gets tarnished. I'm heading for the gym."

Sitting on the bleachers in the gym, Coach Henderson pondered the events of the day. He couldn't help but smile, thinking about what Juanita had said about Mr. Kitchens. What a shame she couldn't squeeze them just enough to make him tear up. She definitely knew what she had on him, because the entire town would be enraged if his comments to her were made public. He had to get serious. Any minute, the entire team would be sitting on these bleachers and he had to praise them, encourage them and tell them he had publicly claimed they would win the rest of this season's games.

"Tall order," he thought to himself.

"Show time," he whispered as the door opened and a mob of excited football players made their way into the gym. "Good afternoon, boys," he said, as they took seats on the bleachers. "How does it feel to be winners?"

"It's awesome," Rodney yelled out from the back row. "Beats losing any day."

"Jason, how many passes are you going to catch Friday night?" Coach Henderson asked.

"Everyone Bubba throws to me," was the answer and the one the coach wanted to hear. Bubba and LJ had taken places on the front row. Bubba smiled and LJ said loud enough for all to hear, "*Hot damn,* Jason. Let's do it again this Friday night and make it two in a row. That ought to be a record for Union High."

Johnny sat on the back row next to Rodney and exhibited no animosity about losing his starting quarterback position. Coach Henderson sensed he was troubled, but also felt like he was looking at the loss of his position in a positive light. Time would tell.

Coach Henderson liked the way the players were opening up. They were bringing their own pep rally, and he didn't seem to be needed as a cheerleader after all. When the players settled down, he asked them a question. "Guess what I did today."

"Asked for a raise," someone on the back row yelled out. Everyone laughed.

"No, that's not it, but I like your way of thinking. When we win the rest of our games this season, I may try that asking-for-a-raise thing." No one commented on his statement about winning the rest of the games.

There was silence as the team waited to find out what their coach had done. Rodney, who could never be accused of being bashful, asked point blank, "Well, if you didn't ask for a raise, what did you do, Coach?"

"The principal and I had the privilege of being interviewed by Tony Adkins, sports reporter for the newspaper. And guess what he wanted to talk about?"

"The miracle that took place Friday night?" Josh Hogan shouted out.

"Sort of," Coach Henderson said. "The reporter almost called it a miracle himself. He wanted to know what happened and how did we pull off such an upset against Milton. I told him we'd gotten tired of losing, especially in our house, and we weren't going to lose another game this season. What do you say, boys, can we deliver on that prediction? Well, can we?" he asked a second time before they even had time to consider what he had said to them . "Can we win the rest of our games?"

LJ was pure LJ, and what you saw was always what you got. Jumping to his feet, and thrusting his right fist in the air, he said, "Damned straight, we can. Every one of them, in our house, and in their house, too."

Following LJ's lead, the entire team stood up. The sound of *hot damns* filled the gym. Coach Henderson usually didn't say much about the colorful language the boys often threw around. He knew it was just their way of communicating and didn't see it as something he should weigh in on. If a little profanity was their only moral slip in high school, they'd be fine for sure.

"I just want to tell all of you how proud I am of the whole team. And, if we're through blowing smoke up everyone's noses, let's dress out and hit the track and run three laps. What do you say to that, Cougars?"

Someone shouted, "Let's do five."

"Five it is," someone else shouted out. A number of *hot damns* circulated through the team as they headed for the locker room.

Bubba paused long enough to give the Coach a good laugh. "I liked the way you cleaned that old saying up."

"What old saying?"

"The one about blowing smoke up everyone's noses. First time I heard it that way. Not bad."

"I try hard," Coach Henderson said and smiled at Bubba. Our mamas wouldn't want us talking trash all the time, now would they?"

LJ, listening to the whole conversation, chimed in. "Oh, no, sir. Our mamas are old-fashioned and would send us out to cut a limb if they heard half of what we say. Mama says she's part Irish, and in Ireland they call a switch a weapon of arse destruction. And believe me, my mama can flat lay into one of us kids when it's called for."

As they started to head for the locker room, Coach Henderson stopped Bubba and LJ and said, "Wait a second. I need to say something without the rest of the team here. You are both gifted, and I knew it the first time y'all came into my office. Good, hard-working families produce great kids, at least most of the time. And both of you are exceptionally talented young men and just plain good folk. I'm proud to know both of you. And, if you repeat any of this, I'll deny it."

⁓✸⁓✸⁓✸⁓

Clarice was a part-time cashier at Ingle's grocery store, and she cleaned houses for three elderly couples. A strong work ethic ran deep in their community. As a matter of fact, most of the kids from the trailer park had at least one job and some had two. That's what it took, if they wanted wheels and insurance and a few dollars of their own. Their parents didn't have enough to make ends meet, let alone finance extras for their kids. Eula, while aware of what her dad's old pickup looked like, was thankful to have the use of it. It had never seemed to be a problem until she started associating with the Beamer.

Clarice walked into Brock's Hardware and went directly to Sporting Goods. "Hello, Mr. Mike," she said as she walked up to the counter. "I've come to make a payment on my layaway."

"Bubba is one lucky young man," he said responding to Clarice's greeting. "Wish I'd had a girlfriend who would have bought me a gun like you bought him. You're something special, for sure, and I hope Bubba appreciates you."

Clarice blushed. "I think he does," she said sheepishly. "He'd better, anyway, because it's breaking me every week, paying for this thing."

"Well, it's top of the line for deer rifles, no doubt about that," Mike said, assuring her she'd made a good choice. "He'll keep this one for the rest of his life, and something tells me he's gonna keep you, too."

Clarice smiled and said, "I hope so, on both accounts." He took her twenty dollar payment and gave her a receipt. "Only three more payments and it's all mine."

"I thought it was his," Mike joked.

"Well, if we're staying together, it can be mine, too, can't it?"

"Absolutely. Sounds like you got this thing all figured out."

"See you next week, Mr. Mike," she said and left the sporting goods section. She wanted to run by the mall and look at some jeans for herself, but had to pass. She put the gun on layaway early because of the price and all her extra money was going on Bubba's Christmas present. The jeans would have to wait until later.

⁂

Monday, after practice, Bubba and LJ headed for McClain's. They had been in the warehouse for only about ten minutes when their boss sent for them to come to his office. They were both scared, fearing a layoff. McClain's, rumor had it, was really struggling to keep operating at full capacity. Even their parents were a little concerned. It was, for all intents and purposes, the only place to work without driving to Gainesville or Atlanta.

As they walked into Mr. Solenberger's office, he greeted them with a friendly, "Good evening, boys. How was practice today?"

"Fine, sir," LJ said, and Bubba nodded in agreement.

Feeling their angst, Mr. Solenberger immediately set their minds at ease. "Congratulations on that win Friday night. That was some game. I was one of the last to leave the parking lot. The two of you made McClain's proud. You've got the whole town talking. I had no idea we had such talented ball players in our warehouse shuffling boxes."

"Well, thank you, sir," LJ said quickly. "We appreciate you letting us shuffle those boxes for you. It really helps us and helps out at home, too."

"Mr. McClain wanted to congratulate you both personally, but he had to take Mrs. McClain to the doctor. They were at the game and were very impressed with the way the two of you played. That's really what this is all about."

Bubba and LJ were afraid this was the beginning of

something bad about to happen and so neither one could think of anything to say.

"Starting tomorrow, both of you come in one hour later than normal."

"But, sir, we need the—"

Mr. Solenberger held up his hand and LJ stopped in mid-sentence.

Mrs. McClain is responsible for this change. She said anyone who works as hard as the two of you and plays football at the level they witnessed last Friday night needs a break, and she insisted Mr. McClain change your schedule so you'd have an extra hour between the end of practice and the time you have to be at work."

LJ started again, "But, sir, we can—"

Mr. Solenberger smiled. "LJ, don't worry about the money."

It was Bubba's turn. "But, sir, if you knew how much—"

"I guess I'd better get to the good part before one of you has a heart attack and Union High starts losing again. The good part is this. Your pay will not be docked for the hour off and starting today, you both get a raise of seventy-five-cents an hour."

Both boys were speechless. Bubba felt his eyes water. Granny Preston had always claimed he had a sensitive spirit, just like hers, and he did. Their boss, realizing emotions were filling the room faster than the good news was soaking in, said, "That's all, boys." And to bring them back to the reality of who he was, he said again, "Congratulations. Now, get out there and shuffle those boxes for me."

"Yes, sir," they responded, leaving his office quickly.

"Wow," Bubba said, as they walked toward the warehouse.

"That's not a wow," LJ replied, "that's a triple wow."

Football had moved to center stage at Union High. Friday morning pep rallies were main events. Friday night games, formerly of little interest to anyone in the town, were now major sporting events, with the school stadium packed with family, friends, and students. Games six, seven, eight and nine were easy wins. Bubba, LJ, Rodney and Jason had quickly synchronized on offense and were virtually unstoppable. They made it look too easy, with Bubba racking up all kinds of passing yardage and also running for forty-plus yards in every game. Whenever they chased him out of the pocket, he would take off and run as efficiently as any high school running back in the region. LJ and Jason seemingly had glue on their hands and seldom missed a pass.

Bubba, in five games, had become a sensation. Rumor had it, even though he was only a junior, that scouts were starting to show interest in this very talented young man who had appeared out of nowhere to set school and regional records. If he continued playing at the same level as he had done so far, he would own the high school record for single-season passing and rushing for a high school quarterback. And he would have accomplished this feat in only six games. LJ, likewise, was likely to break the high school record for receptions. Rodney and Jason had become stars in their own right.

❧❧❧

Eula could no longer be concerned about what Bubba and Clarice were doing. She was in over her head and had no business making observations about them acting like married folk.

Clarice continued to try and slow their escapades down. "We can't do it every time you complete a pass or win a game," she told him. "We just can't, Bubba."

"But we have to celebrate," he countered, flashing his million-dollar smile, "and doing it is what makes me a good quarterback."

"Bubba Preston, we were doing it before you started playing football and sooner or later, we're gonna do it one too many times. Then what?"

"You worry too much, Clarice. Everything's gonna be fine. Besides, we'll be seniors next year and just try and imagine this," he teased her.

"Imagine what?"

"Try and imagine a Big Bubba and a Little Bubba. Now, that would be something special, and guess what else?"

"I'm almost scared to ask. What else?"

"And you, the love of my life, will get to take care of both of us. Now, what do you have to say about that, Mrs. Preston?"

"Imagine is not the word. It'll be reality long before we finish school if we don't slow down. I'm just saying, Bubba, we have to stop acting like married folk."

⌀⌀⌀⌀⌀⌀

Sue Ellen's office at the bank was just as plush as Mr. Morgan's. The only noticeable difference was the plaque on the door. His read *President* and Sue Ellen's read *Vice-President*. But make no mistake, she ran the bank and everyone knew it. Even when he was there, she made the majority of the decisions without even consulting him. He was always wheeling and dealing, trying to make just a little more money. She had an excellent rapport with the bank personnel and everyone loved her. She was the face of the bank and involved in all community activities.

In an entire lifetime, Mr. Morgan had allowed only one weak

spot in his armor—Sue Ellen Thornton. During the long-ago affair, it would have seemed like a rich and powerful older man was taking advantage of a sweet, innocent young woman. Not so. The sexual aspect of their relationship was just that, sexual. But the drunk-driving incident, where she took the rap for an intoxicated William Morgan, followed by a refusal to terminate her pregnancy, turned that innocent young girl into his worst nightmare.

At Saint Mary's Hospital, eighteen years earlier, two things happened the morning Sister Cass, Sister Francis and Father Rodriquez paid a visit to Sue Ellen's room with the sick newborn. The hospital's grounds were immaculately kept and Sue Ellen was admiring them from her hospital room window. A life-changing event was headed her way.

Sister Cass, carrying the infant, Sister Francis pushing the IV pole, and Father Rodriquez in tow raised more than a few eyebrows as they walked down the hallway. A fly on the wall would have been mesmerized by the event. Entering Sue Ellen's room, the entourage stopped just inside the door. No one spoke. Sue Ellen would remember the moment, and she would call it life changing.

Later that evening, she would tell Mr. Morgan, who had flown over for a business deal and to check on her, what had happened and he would scoff at her analysis, blaming the medications for the experience.

"I didn't expect you to believe me, because you've always scoffed at spiritual things, believing only in yourself," she would tell him. "I know it, because I was guilty of the same foolish, self-centered thought process."

From the fly's perspective, it seemed like a stalemate on a battlefield. A Father and two Sisters, with one holding a baby, standing at the door and Sue Ellen, seemingly frozen in time, looking out at the hospital grounds.

And then the baby cried out, almost like he was in pain or anguish at being rejected by his mother. Sue Ellen Thornton, bank executive, world-by-the-tail Sue Ellen Thornton, turned from the window and cried out in her own pain and anguish. She saw the two Sisters, the baby and the Father. But she also saw another person, standing behind them, and He had the appearance of shepherding them into the room.

Sue Ellen's worldly heart melted, as she found forgiveness and acceptance from her heavenly Father. The baby, not wanting to be rejected any longer, cried out again and instantly found himself in his mother's arms.

It was indeed a joyous moment. Father Rodriguez fell to his knees, both hands raised in thanksgiving and praise. Sister Francis wept, holding tightly to the IV pole. Sister Cass hugged Sue Ellen and whispered in her ear. "Welcome home. You'll make a wonderful mother because He's a wonderful Savior."

"How did you know?" a puzzled Sue Ellen asked.

"I saw Him, too. It's an awesome experience to be in the presence of the living Christ. Praise the Lord."

The re-birth of Sue Ellen Thornton wasn't the only miracle happening that day. A second miracle would be announced later that morning. Father Rodriquez and Sister Francis didn't see what Sue Ellen and Sister Cass saw. The infant wasn't given to the mother by Sister Cass. Jesus took the child from her and placed it in Sue Ellen's arms, healing it of all its infirmities and forgiving Sue Ellen at the same time. The medical staff announced a miraculous healing had taken place. The front office announced the baby was not up for adoption.

Saint Mary's was in a tizzy. Two miracles in one day. God is an awesome God.

William Morgan was also in a tizzy. The whole purpose of

Sue Ellen's vacation in Europe and coming to Saint Mary's was to remedy an untenable situation and make provisions for an unwanted child.

"You have to decide," he told Sue Ellen, "do you want to keep this child or do you want to keep your job, salary, expensive cars and mansion? You have three days to make up your mind. I'll wait three days, and no longer. I have to get back to work, just like you need to, as well. If you can't make a rational decision, then I'll decide for you. I can't imagine what's come over you. Keeping this child is going to ruin your life. It's lunacy, and you know it."

Sue Ellen asked Sister Cass to make arrangements for the baby and for her to stay an additional three days. Mr. Morgan had given so much to Saint Mary's, there was no way they would not accommodate her request. She needed help with the baby and time to decide how to negotiate with William Morgan.

The next morning she rose early and went outside to the garden area. She needed time to think, not like the new Sue Ellen, but like the old one. That's what it would take to handle Mr. William Morgan and his ultimatums. It didn't take her long to come up with a foolproof plan that, short of having her killed, would forever keep him at bay with his threats.

Sue Ellen needed a little help and information on being a mother. She hadn't even considered keeping her baby, so she hadn't thought much about taking care of him. She was nursing him and spending most of the time with him in her room. He hadn't been named yet, because she had to get a commitment from Mr. Morgan. It was the third day, ultimatum day. She had already nursed the baby, nicknamed Junior by her and Sister Cass, and had left a note for Morgan at the desk, directing him to the garden area outside her room.

At ten sharp, as she sat in the garden area, she heard his footsteps on the sidewalk. He was always punctual and she could tell by the brisk steps on the cement, it was him. Almost immediately, he rounded the corner and was face to face with what would turn out to be his nemesis.

No formalities, no nothing, just straight to the point. "Have you made a decision yet?" he asked in a business-like manner. One would have thought they had never enjoyed intimate moments together. When she didn't reply immediately, he said, "Well, what is it? I have a plane to catch. Are you going to continue your career or are you going to throw it all away for a mistake and a baby someone else could easily raise?"

"Have a seat, Bill," she said, gesturing to a chair across from her. "Let me tell you how this is going to work. You're a good teacher, and I'm sure you'll agree, I'm an excellent student."

Immediately, he asked her, "Who the hell do you think you're talking to? You're not in charge here, I am, and I call the shots. Do you understand that, or are you still on some whacked-out, drug-induced spiritual odyssey?"

"Sit down, Mr. Morgan, and let me tell you exactly how this is going to play out."

Mentally, he noted the name change from Bill to Mr. Morgan, but stood there defiantly for a second and then turned to walk away.

"Mr. Morgan, does the name Lewis Padgett mean anything to you?"

One would have thought he had stepped in some serious glue on the sidewalk. He never even completed his second step, but froze, as it seemed, in place, after the name had registered with him.

"And how, might I ask, did you get that name?"

"Well, sir, I was taught by the best and as you know, I'm very smart. Did you think I was going to take a rap for vehicular homicide and not look for cover or a way out? Surely, you didn't think there was any love between us. You were using me and I was using you. And a beautiful baby boy was the result of our sexual indulgence. Sister Cass told me God takes mistakes and turns them into beautiful things. And He did. But that's beside the point. Sit down, Mr. Morgan. I have a way out of this for both of us, and I think you'll find it agreeable."

He stood motionless for so long, she wasn't sure he was going to buy in. But then he turned, gave her a long, hard look and took the seat across from her.

"Before you tell me something I know I don't want to hear, let me make a statement first. Of all the people I have encountered in the business world, you are, without a doubt, the smartest. That's why I hate this so bad. I can use your talent at the bank, allowing me to expand and grow my other business interests. I won't ever pretend our affair was about love, but it was good for both of us, and I know it. So, how much more am I going to have to pay you to give up this idea of being the world's best mother?"

"Money doesn't even enter into the picture here, and I'm not trying to become the world's best mother. It's about the baby. You were seeing Marsha McMillan and having an affair with me at the same time. I knew about her and didn't care. Whether she knew about us is none of my concern at this juncture. I was never interested in marrying you, and I know you felt the same way. In the time I've been over here, you've married Marsha and I'm sure both of you will be happy. Our affair is over, and I know you realize that as well. I'll do a better job for you because we will no longer be sexually involved with each other. All of this actually works well together. Marsha seems like a fine woman, and I know she'll make a good mother for the baby."

Standing abruptly, he said, "Have you lost your mind? What the hell kinda garbage have they fed you in this piece-of-shit place?"

"I beg to differ with your opinion concerning Saint Mary's. It's a wonderful place and we, that's you and me, are going to continue to support their ministry of saving babies and finding good homes for them. As a matter of fact, I've already told them you would be leaving a donation of ten thousand dollars for their new prenatal facility scheduled to open soon."

There were two Sisters having tea across the garden, requiring both Sue Ellen and Mr. Morgan to keep a lid on their rapidly escalating war of words.

"Now, I know you've lost it. I'm not giving another damn cent to this pretend-to-care hospital, not now, not tomorrow and not ever. Do I make myself clear, Miss Thornton?"

He had set his briefcase down on the table and once again picked it up to leave.

"I love that phrase," Sue Ellen said, smiling, as if all was right with the world. It was such a cocky, self-confident smile, it begged to be questioned by Mr. Morgan. And he bit, hook, line and sinker.

"And what phrase might that be?" he asked, taking a couple of steps away from the table.

"The do I make myself clear, Miss Thornton? Mind if I use it?" she asked, as she glared at him and his arrogance. "I will, however, modify the subject of the question. Here's my version. 'Sit down, William, and sit down now, before I change my mind and take your offer of salvation off the table.'"

It was a powerful scene. One power-hungry man being taken down by an old version of Sue Ellen Thornton.

"Humor me a bit, for old times' sake, if you don't mind. It'll only take a few minutes if you'll sit there and keep your mouth shut. Can you manage that, William, for maybe five minutes, while I tell you exactly how this will play out. And then, if you don't have any questions, and if you'll be a good boy and write the check for Saint Mary's, you can leave in peace, knowing your world is intact and protected by me, the mother of your son, who, by the way, would be dead, if God hadn't healed him. That's a fact. Ask any doctor here and they will tell you that it's an absolute miracle your son is still alive."

William Morgan had the gift of reading faces and situations. Something told him he didn't have a leg to stand on and he knew Sue Ellen too well to ever think she'd try and run a bluff, especially against him. He had indeed taught her too much and now he felt like he was about to pay for his mistake.

She pointed to the seat he had recently vacated. He stared, long and hard. It was only for a few seconds, but it seemed like an eternity to Sue Ellen. She had all the aces, and she knew it. But she also knew how hard the business world had made him and wouldn't have bet money he would take the chair again. Finally, setting the briefcase back on the table, he sat down across from her. That was the key, and she knew she had him.

"I will tell you enough to let you know I have the ability to break you and to ruin you, if I so desire. But I won't. If you'll work with me and do what I ask, I promise to keep your dirty little secrets and my evidence to myself and take them to my grave. You know I'll keep my word, just like I know you'll keep yours." She paused as if reflecting for a moment.

"First, I was young and infatuated with William Morgan, bank president, and while it wasn't a good thing, our affair at the time was wonderful for both of us. I know you'll agree with that."

Morgan sat with his elbows on the table and his chin in his hands. He looked like a statue, cold and emotionless.

"And I watched and learned from the best; the best of the money-hungry power brokers in the banking business. And I took notes and put your lessons into practice. I wasn't about to trust you with my future regarding the drunk-driving accident you had. I let you use me, and you kept your word. You called in some God-awful thing you had on the Chief of Police and he got me out of the charge by saying little Billy Brown was at fault because he ran out in front of my car. Unavoidable, I believe, was the term he used. Even though I knew about your involvement with Marsha, our affair continued until I became pregnant with your son."

"I know all of that," he said, still sitting as stoic as a stone statue.

"Here's what you don't know," Sue Ellen continued. "I saw the only witness that night. He was standing about a half block away from where you ran off the road and killed little Billy Brown, who was standing on the sidewalk, waiting for us to pass. I recognized the witness as Lewis Padgett, because he comes into the bank on a regular basis. So, I figured you probably saw him as well. But I wasn't sure, as drunk as you were, if you'd remember him standing up the street. He immediately left the area before the police and ambulance arrived. I started watching his account very closely, figuring if you had recognized him, I might find a little protection for myself. And, guess what. A hundred and fifty thousand dollars found its way into old Lewis' savings account. I couldn't find any paper trail, so I called him into my office on one of his visits to the bank and played a long shot. I asked him if he recognized me and he nodded his head yes. I asked him where from, and he said, 'I see you most times I come into the bank.' And then, I pushed the envelope a little farther, asking him if he'd ever seen me outside the bank. He hesitated, and I gave him that you'd better tell me the truth look.

I think being in my office and sitting across from me intimidated him. 'Yes, ma'am,' he finally said. 'I saw you the night that Brown boy was killed.'"

"Bingo. I was in. Then I played a bluff you'd been proud of. I told him how much you appreciated his silence and you wanted to give him another twenty-five thousand. He was very surprised and happy, and told me to tell you thank you and he would never tell anyone he saw you run over little Billy Brown. And then I took the recorder from my desk drawer and played it all back to him. He was so frightened, I thought he would pass out. I told him there wasn't another payoff, and I was just verifying the first one had indeed happened. I told him the hundred and fifty thousand was his to keep, and if he ever opened his mouth to anyone, I would turn the recording over to the police department and he would be in serious trouble. He swore, on his mother's grave, he would keep our dirty little secret. I even found out what you had on Chief Clark at the police department. Shame, shame, shame on you for telling him you'd ruin his career with another one of your dirty little secrets."

William Morgan knew when to throw in the towel. "So, what happens now?" he asked quietly, with a totally different attitude and tone.

"Well, it can go one of two ways. You can help me get our baby back home, so I can be sure he's cared for and loved. Or you can play hardball and I promise I'll ruin your reputation and you might even get a little rest and relaxation in a confined space somewhere. Perhaps the police chief could also join you there, and the two of you could curse me for the duration of your sentence and protect each other in the shower. And, if by some miracle of hanky panky on your part, you escape the drunk-driving, vehicular-homicide charge, I've found quite a few banking irregularities, hidden very neatly out of sight from the regulators, tied directly to you. So, what do you say to your best student, former lover, mother of your son, and holder of the keys to your kingdom?"

"I guess, at this junction, there's only one question to ask. But before I ask it, let me compliment you on your work. You left no stone unturned. I like that. Resourceful, beautiful and conniving, all rolled into one neat little package, who now wants to be a mother. Imagine that. So, how do we get the baby home and, better yet, how do we explain it so the world won't know I'm the father?"

"That's the beautiful part. I have it all figured out," Sue Ellen said, smiling.

"Somehow, I knew you would. So, how's this thing going down?"

"You'll go back home, just as planned. Your business trip abroad is over, you simply go home. I'll stay here until I've placed our son in a proper environment, and then I'll come home from my vacation and go back to work, giving the whisperers more fodder for their break room gossip. I have arranged for Saint Mary's to monitor the baby's well-being until you and Marsha can finalize the adoption of William Morgan, Jr. Adopting a son, at your age, and with your sweet, new wife, will probably get you a Father of the Year Award. The whole town has always wondered who would inherit all your money. Think about it. You and I would be the only ones to ever know, but you'll actually be adopting your own son. How incredible is that?"

She wasn't sure how well he was processing all of this, but then, he asked, "And how do you fit into this picture? What's your role going to look like?"

"It's really very simple and easy. I believe Marsha likes to travel, and you're always away on some business trip. You know I can easily run the bank and guess what? From all appearances, the town will think you have a twofer."

"And what's a twofer?" he asked cautiously.

"Two for the price of one. I'll continue to run the bank for you and I'll be young William's nanny. A win-win for all. You get the son you need to inherit your money and estate, your new wife gets to travel, and I get to raise my son. And no one will ever know you're his real father and I'm his mother. Not even Marsha. Agreed? Isn't this a lot better than me having to raise our son on a shoestring budget and you possibly ending up in jail for drunk driving and vehicular homicide or money laundering?"

In a gesture that Sue Ellen didn't think would happen so easily, he opened his briefcase, took out his checkbook and wrote the check to Saint Mary's. Walking over to her, he took her hand, leaned over and kissed her on the forehead. It caught her by surprise and the tenderness of the kiss surprised her even more. She felt herself blushing and memories came flooding back.

"See you back home," he said as he released her hand. "I'll get my attorney to contact Saint Mary's and get the adoption process in motion. I'll tell Marsha something. She won't care as long as the baby doesn't interfere with her travels. I'll tell her I'm going to hire you another assistant and that you'll be a nanny for the boy and assure her it won't interfere with our busy lives. She'll be fine with it as long as you raise him. Almost makes me sad we didn't make it."

With that said, he was gone. Sue Ellen looked at the check and was shocked. It wasn't for the ten thousand she had tried to make him donate. It was for fifty thousand dollars. Sue Ellen felt tears well up in her eyes. Had William Morgan—a powerful man and a mover and shaker—just been taken down, or had he reached deep inside and found the good man still lurking around in the shadows of greed and, for once, the good man surfaced of his own accord?

⸙⸙⸙

Sue Ellen had been correct. Mr. Morgan, when he arrived home and started talking about adoption and becoming a father, became an overnight sensation.

Saint Mary's was well known the world over for its efforts in preventing abortions and helping to find good, loving homes for the unwanted babies they were able to save. He told his wife and friends he had visited Saint Mary's Hospital while he was in England and was moved not only to help financially but to fill a void in his life and adopt a son. He explained it so well that the local newspaper ran a story about the upcoming adoption and the newest member in the Morgan household. Marsha, who had also been childless, was super excited about the baby coming to live with them, having been promised a full staff to assist her. To further convince his peers he had decided this on his own, he held a Saturday golfing event, inviting some serious money people, and raised a hundred thousand dollars for Saint Mary's new prenatal facility. The hospital was ecstatic with the news of the donation, and the gesture on Morgan's part solidified his sincerity regarding becoming a father, albeit a little late in life.

Sister Cass was also very smart and read between the lines. Mr. Morgan wasn't just Sue Ellen's boss, he was also the father of her baby. She kept her analysis to herself. Sue Ellen, with Sister Cass advising her, interviewed prospective couples who, in times past, had helped out in the role of foster parents. After two weeks, she decided on a couple to take care of little Junior for about three months. This would allow her to go home and get back in the saddle again, running the bank and getting her house ready for some serious nannying. Out of gratitude for the fundraising effort by Mr. Morgan when everything was set up, Saint Mary's flew little William, Jr. home, accompanied by a pediatric nurse and assistant.

He would never admit it, but Mr. Morgan was excited about having an heir who was actually his son. And that heir was now a grown man. Time is a fleeting thing.

Sue Ellen would often remember the happenings of so long ago. It had been hard to keep the secret for so many years of who William Morgan, Jr.'s real father and mother were. But she had kept her word, Mr. Morgan had kept his and so had Lewis Padgett, who had recently passed away. Police Chief Clark, up in years, had retired and suffered from dementia. The dark secret was now held in a two-way trust, and neither party would benefit from breaking the code of silence.

∞∞∞

Clarice had made it to the big day—final payment on her layaway. Walking into the hardware store, she went straight back to the hunting and fishing section and the layaway department. "Well, here comes my favorite customer," Mike said with a grin. "Guess what payment this one is?" he asked and smiled again.

"It's the last one, and only God knows how thankful I am. I didn't believe I was ever going to get this gun paid off. Maybe now I can buy some Christmas presents for other people. I'm not sure Bubba Preston is worth as much as this gun cost." Several old guys, who always hung out in the hunting and fishing section, laughed.

One of them walked over to Clarice and said, "Honey, my wife ain't never bought me a gun and we've been married for fifty-two years. Your fella is one lucky guy, and I hope he knows it."

Mike had brought the gun out of the layaway department and laid it on the counter. It was a bolt-action Remington 700, chambered for 30-06 rounds and had a scope already mounted. He opened the factory box for Clarice to see it again, and all the old guys gathered around and carried on over what a nice gun it was.

Always the salesman, Mike asked, "Would you like to buy Bubba some ammo and a carrying case for his new gun?"

"No way," Clarice said, with an expression that was more shock than anything else. "I bought the gun and that's it. If he wants to shoot it, he can buy the ammo himself, and if he wants to carry it somewhere, he can use the box it came in."

That about tickled the old guys to death. "You tell him, girl," one of them said in support of her refusal to spend another dime on her boyfriend.

Mike walked her out to her car and placed the gun in the trunk. "You did a good thing," he said as he closed the trunk. "I hope he keeps both you and the gun for the rest of his life, and I hope God blesses both of you real good."

"Thank you, Mr. Mike, for all your help. After he gets the gun at Christmas, I'll send him back to buy the ammo and case from you. Okay?"

"That'll be fine," Mike said. "Look forward to hearing what he gives you for Christmas. Hope it's as nice or better than this old gun you bought him."

As she left the parking lot, she said to herself, "Bubba's always trying to give me something. Trouble is, I don't know how to stop him."

Clarice drove home, took the gun out of the trunk, and put it under her bed. Christmas was still a few weeks away and she had plenty of time to wrap it up for Bubba's big surprise gift.

It had been a Cinderella season for the football team. It seemed like an eternity had come and gone since Coach Henderson told the reporter with the *Herald* newspaper that the Union High Cougars would win all of their remaining games. Nine were in the books and they had five consecutive wins under their belt.

Monday after school, the team gathered, as usual, on the gym bleachers. Coach Henderson waited a moment for them to settle down and then said, "Five straight wins, can we get one more?"

"No problem," several yelled out. "It's in the bag." Coach Henderson didn't want to be cocky, but he actually felt the same way. The offense was a machine, moving so quickly off the line that most of the other teams couldn't stay balanced enough to stop it. The defense had matured and wanted to share the spotlight with the offense. Johnny Kitchens had become a big-time contributor to the team effort. He was still the back-up quarterback, but he had talked Coach Henderson into letting him play linebacker. Here, he proved quite efficient, and the coach told his wife that he believed the new position allowed Johnny to vent some of the frustration he felt because of losing the starting quarterback position. He had made some big-time stops and had two interceptions, one he ran back for a touchdown.

Mr. Kitchens was coming to the games and had told his son how proud he was of him making the switch from quarterback to linebacker and staying focused on being a good team member.

Not only had football helped Johnny grow up, it seemed his father, experiencing a teachable moment, had taken it to heart. He called the principal, Juanita, and apologized for his bad behavior, telling her he had been out of line and that it wouldn't happen again. This shocked Juanita, but Coach Henderson told her the transformation had been so powerful with Johnny, he automatically assumed it had carried over to some extent with his dad. "Everyone wins here," he told her.

"Next team we face is Rabun High," Coach Henderson told the team. "They have a running back that's the best in the state. Their strength is in their offense. Their defense has a lot to be desired and our offense should literally run over them. But we have to contain their running back and not let him get loose in open ground. Johnny, I'm giving him to you."

"Thanks, Coach, how nice of you to think of me." The whole team laughed.

"You're welcome. Glad to be able to make you happy. On a serious note, if we win, it won't be because of our offense, it'll be because you keep Speedball contained. When he runs outside, and he does that a lot, he's a bear to haul down because he's big and fast. Once he gets going, he's hard to stop."

"I'll stop him, Coach, I promise." *Hot damns* went around the bleachers.

"Couldn't ask for more," the coach said in response to Johnny's assurance of getting the job done. "Dress out, and meet me on the practice field. No laps until after practice."

◦◦◦◦◦◦◦◦◦

Eula, getting ready for work at the Dairy Queen, chastised herself in the mirror. Her parents weren't home, so she had her say to herself, loud and clear. She seemingly had no control over her and the Beamer acting like married folk and she was terrified she would end up pregnant, locking her into a job at the DQ or Walmart or some other minimum wage position. "Just how dumb are you, Eula Johnson? You've fussed and fumed at poor ole Clarice and you're following in her footsteps. Hell, Eula, you're probably doing it two times more than Bubba and Clarice. When the test shows up positive, and the shit hits the fan, don't blame the Beamer. God knows he tries to get us to date in the BMW. But, oh no, you insist on taking the White Charger, and every time, you end up driving out to the old country road, the same one you've parked on way too many times. Eula Johnson, are you stupid or what?"

Finishing putting on her makeup, she headed out to the White Charger. He was waiting patiently for her, right where she had parked him the night before. Getting in and smelling the expensive cologne the Beamer always had on made her forget her warnings to herself five minutes earlier.

"God, how I love this guy," she said out loud. Firing up the White Charger, she headed to the DQ for her eight-hour shift, followed by an hour or so with the Beamer. "I swear," she said, "we're not doing anything tonight, even if it means standing out in the middle of the mall parking lot. I think that should control both of us."

Eula had already missed three Friday night shifts at the DQ in order to attend and support Bubba and LJ. She talked to them, explaining how much she needed to work in order to have enough money to go to college and would have to miss the last game. "That's okay with us," they both told her. Bubba continued and prodded her a little. "Yeah, I could be working somewhere, too, on Friday nights, but some blonde broad talked me into playing football. How much does football pay? Not a damn thing, but that's okay. What are friends for, if not to screw up a fellow's life?"

Eula gave him that look and then added, "Poor, pitiful Bubba. He has to play ball on Friday nights and have everyone whoop and holler and cheer him on and pat him on the back and brag on him. Should be against the law to complain about being worshiped by the locals. I'm sure it is somewhere. And then he takes poor Clarice and—"

"Whoa, whoa there," Bubba said excitedly. Eula smiled and replied, "Gotcha! I gotta go to work now. Maybe I'll get lucky and score a six-point blizzard and get an extra point for good onion rings, but I doubt if anyone will cheer and hoot and holler and idolize me as DQ Queen. You go and win yourself another game."

Leaning over and whispering in Eula's ear, he said, "I'm not positive, but I believe that old truck of yours will hear a lot of whooping and hollering after you get off work." He stepped back and raised his eyebrows, waiting for her response.

"If I break both your legs, Bubba, then you won't have to play tonight, will you?"

"Hey, now, let's keep this thing civil here. Don't you know a joke when you hear one?"

"Yes, I do, and that was a poor effort at trying to be funny."

Getting in the White Charger, she slammed the door harder than usual, and drove off, headed to work.

The game with Rabun High was an away game. Eula loved her friends, especially Bubba, LJ, Clarice and Janice. They were like family. As game time approached, she thought about them and hoped they would win, keeping their streak alive.

Coach Henderson always rode the team bus to the away games. His wife Cindi usually attended the games, but she drove their car. Sometimes, Juanita Fisher, the principal, would carpool with her.

In the visitors' locker room, Coach Henderson went over the game plan a final time. "I'm proud of every one of you," he said as it got close to time to leave the locker room. "I want this game really bad, but not for me, like some may think. This is your team, the one you'll remember the rest of your lives. The good and the bad games will replay in your mind for decades to come. Every caught pass, every pass dropped, the interceptions, the missed opportunities, the whole game, will replay time and time again. This is your team. I'm a paid professional, and I can only instruct and teach. The actual drama, unfolding and playing out here during this game, is all yours, tonight and forever. So, let's make good memories. Johnny, you've got Speedball. He's all yours. Jason and LJ, no dropped passes, okay? Rodney, run tough, and show their running back how it's supposed to be done. Gather around, boys. Buddy will lead our team prayer."

After huddling up, Buddy began, "Lord, we have seen miraculous things happen this year, on and off the playing field. We hope You don't think it's arrogant and snooty but, Lord, we're trying to keep our winning streak alive. Bless us and help us to play fair, but play to win. Nothing wrong with winning, Lord. You made each of us winners with Your sacrifice on the cross. And, Lord, help Johnny tonight. He has a tough assignment and needs a little extra help. Protect us from injuries. Thank you, Lord."

And everybody said, *"Amen and Amen."*

Buddy, highlighting Johnny in his prayer, was special. No hot damns circulated through the locker room. Later, hopefully, but not right now.

The game got off to a terrible start. Doug Pullin, Rabun's running back, did his thing. Johnny tried really hard, but after realizing he had been assigned to take their running back out, Rabun's coach put blockers on Johnny. On two separate plays, they had Johnny tied up and Doug did an end-around and was gone for six points. One point after was missed, but Rabun led 13-0.

Coach Henderson walked over to the bench where Bubba was sitting. "I assume you know that sometimes we have to come from behind to win. They've stung us twice, but it shouldn't affect the way we play the rest of the game. You'll never be a great quarterback unless you can come from behind. You won't always have the lead, in football or in life. Do you understand what I'm trying to say?"

"Yes, sir," Bubba responded. "Can I say it to you the way I'd say it to the team?"

"I have a better idea. Why don't you tell the team what's on your mind? They're looking to you, and only you, to fix this half-hearted start. You're the team leader, so lead."

Rabun, having just scored, was teeing up the ball for a kickoff. The receiving team was on the field and most of the offense was on the sideline. Coach Henderson nodded for Bubba to take his best shot at rallying the troops.

"All right, guys. We look like shit out there. Coach told us they have a weak defense, and we should run all over them. Come on, it's thirteen to zip and we stink. Their defensive line is pushing our line back in my face and I can't even get a completion to one of our receivers. We're fixing to lose this game, ending our winning streak. Is that what y'all want?"

"Hell, no," two or three players said in unison.

"Then let's get back out there and kick some serious ass. How bout it? Give me a few seconds and I'll hit LJ or Jason and establish our passing game, taking some of the heat off Rodney so he can get our running game going. And, if I have to, I'll play defense and give Johnny a hand. They're ganging up on him and he can't even get a shot at stopping Speedball."

There were so many *hot damns* Coach Henderson was afraid Juanita, or some of the school board members in attendance, might hear and question who was in charge of the team. "Hold it down a little," he said, drawing nods and laughter from his team.

LJ, excited as usual, said, "Let's clean it up for the coach. Let's go back out and mop the field with their sorry asses, shoot the wounded, and leave the dead to rot on top of the ground."

"Not exactly how I would have cleaned it up," Coach Henderson said to the team. "But I like the message. Now, get your butts out there and deliver it."

Three consecutive first downs and then six points followed by an extra point.   Now it was 13-7 and the weak defense of Rabun was finally on the radar.

Union High was fired up and on a mission. Coach Henderson was right. This was their game to win or lose. It was totally up to them, and if LJ had anything to say about it, it would go down in the win column when all was said and done.

Bubba was far too valuable at quarterback to chance him getting injured playing defense. The team didn't have a lot of depth on defense or offense. Johnny now lined up on kickoffs in Bubba's old slot, opposite LJ. The sound of the kicker's foot, making contact with the football, sent the defense on a tear down the field. LJ got double-teamed and couldn't get to the punt returner. But Rodney did, and held the punt returner to two yards.

As LJ came off the field, he went straight to Coach Henderson. "Coach, let me go in and help Johnny with Speedball. We can't afford to let them score again."

"I can't. I need you to stay healthy and make receptions and hopefully score points. I can't risk it."

"But, Coach, if we don't win, what's the point? I promise you I won't get hurt. I'm tough and you know it. Bubba and I like to say we can handle anything, because we're *trailer-park tough.* Truth is we are and we can. Send me in so we can win this game. I promise I can play both ways and I won't get hurt."

As the conversation was taking place on the sidelines, Rabun had taken the first snap, double-teamed Johnny, and that had allowed their running back to pick up twelve yards and a first down before they could haul him down. He had almost broken another run for a touchdown.

"Sir," LJ said pleadingly.

"Get in there, LJ, but don't get hurt. Without you on offense, we'll lose anyway."

"I promise I won't get hurt," LJ said, as he ran onto the field.

LJ was by far the fastest player on the team. On the next play, they tried the run again, double teaming Johnny and trying to spring Speedball for another six. LJ was in their backfield about the same time the ball was handed off. He nailed Speedball, and he never even saw him coming. There was a two-yard loss on the play. LJ was pumped and so was the rest of the defense. Now, Rabun High had another problem, and this time they had no solution. They could double team one defensive player, but not two. LJ's speed made it almost impossible to double team him. Johnny had a great feel for the defense, and between him and LJ they shut Rabun High's offense completely down.

Bubba was having a great night, completing most of his passes. The offensive line had stiffened and was allowing him all the time in the world to find open receivers. He was rotating between Jason and LJ and even hit Rodney for a short pass play over the middle. It tickled Rodney to death. He always had to run the ball and they never even tried to connect with him on a passing play. The offense was going so well, it was like storybook football. Union High could do no wrong. Rabun managed a field goal in the fourth quarter, adding three to their original thirteen points. The final score was 41 to 16.

When it was over, and the team gathered in the locker room, the celebration was more like pandemonium than anything else. Tony Adkins, sportswriter for the *Herald*, had asked for permission and was allowed to come into the locker room to take pictures for the newspaper. Six wins in a row, just like Coach Henderson had promised. No one was more elated than Coach Henderson.

Getting them to quieten down enough so he could congratulate them, he said, "Tonight will be remembered by each of you for the rest of your lives. I told you that before the game, and it's true. And the memories will be good ones. A powerhouse invited us to their house, and you shut them down. You held the region's best running back to the fewest number of yards he's gained in a single game in three years. Great job, guys. And you helped make some good memories for me as well. We won the last six, and I won't have to eat a lot of crow because of failing to make my prediction come true. It really wasn't so much a prediction, as much as faith in my team. That's you, boys, and

I'm very proud of all of you. I wish I had enough game balls for everyone to get one. Since we only give one, I think this one should go to Johnny."

Hot damns went up around the locker room.

Johnny seemed a little embarrassed over the recognition and looked down at the floor. "Coach, I didn't stop Speedball nowhere near as many times as LJ did. He should get the game ball."

Coach Henderson had to wait a moment before speaking. The Johnny Kitchens he was about to address was light years away from the Johnny Kitchens who began the season.

"That's right," Coach Henderson said in agreement, "you didn't. But it took two of their offensive players to keep you in check. Not on one or two plays, Johnny, but on every play. That's why LJ was able to get to Speedball. It was a complete team win, but believe me, you are the most valuable player in this game and well deserving of the recognition."

Taking the ball, Johnny lifted it up over his head and said, "I will always remember this day and this team. I can't begin to tell you what I've learned this season, and the most important lessons weren't about football. They were about life. I thank all of you for putting up with me. Hopefully, I've got it together now. If y'all will, I'd like to get each of you to sign the ball. I want Bubba and LJ to sign it first. They brought a lot more to this team than most will ever realize."

Coach Henderson found a permanent marker in his travel bag.

When Johnny gave the ball to Bubba, they exchanged a long look. A lot was said with no words being spoken. They had no way of knowing it, but their paths crossing opened up new worlds for both these young men. Johnny got a first-hand look at someone who had few of the world's material things, but was gifted in many areas where money held no sway. And Bubba saw a *hootie tootie*, up close and personal, and had to admit what Eula had been trying to tell him. "They're people, just like us. Their folks just have more money than our folks."

Later that evening, after they returned home, Coach Henderson would tell his wife he had reached the pinnacle of his coaching career. "Nothing will ever top today. Wins and championships can't hold a candle to watching a young man mature and grow in grace and stature. It's a long trip from a spoiled-brat rich kid to a well-rounded, mature young adult. Johnny Kitchens made the journey in six weeks. That's a win for life, and he'll keep on giving to others and winning in whatever he decides to do. I'm so proud of him."

Cindi gave her husband a hug and said, "There was more than one Bubba on the team this year. Bubbas can do amazing things."

⠀⠀⠀⠀⠀⠀⠀⠀⠀⠀⠀⠀⠀⠀⠀⠀⠀⠀⠀⠀⠀⠀⠀⠀⠀⠀⠀⠀⠀⠀⠀

Coach Henderson and the Union High Cougars had made their town proud. They had won six in a row and their last game with Rabun High was a must-see for everyone. Even though it was an away game, it seemed like most of the town had shown up. Bubba's entire family was there, including Granny Preston. Eula was the only close friend of Bubba's that didn't make the last game of the season. William had decided to go by himself. Eula had not introduced him to anyone in her family or to any of her close friends. And likewise, William had not introduced Eula to anyone in his family.

William and Eula's relationship, though obvious to most of their friends at school, still operated out of the mall parking lot, with frequent jaunts to the dirt road close to the high school. She had not been back to Sue Ellen's, even though Sue Ellen had asked William multiple times to have her over. Camelot couldn't include anyone who might threaten it.

William saw a number of people who could have been Eula's parents, and several older women there who could have easily been Bubba's grandmother. William had heard about everyone in her circle of family and friends, but way too many fans were on hand who could have easily fit the image of her parents he had in his mind. He could have asked someone, but didn't. Meeting her parents, without her being there, would be too intimidating. Like Eula declining Sue Ellen's invitations, he would put it off for as long as possible. Love had bridged the chasm between their two worlds, but that bridge might be more difficult to cross over for others. Neither was willing to risk Camelot for the sake of family, friends or anything else. Soon, because it had to be, but not now.

⋘⋙⋘⋙⋘⋙

Mr. Kitchens, like his son Johnny, had learned a lot in a few short weeks. He had seen monumental changes in his son and had eye-opening experiences in his own life. Johnny had not only matured as a young man, he had become quite the football player. Mr. Kitchens wanted to do something special for the whole team, and while they were having lunch, the day after the close of the season, he ran his idea by Johnny.

"Son, how would you like to invite the whole team over to the country club for a celebration dinner?"

"That would be great, but it would cost a small fortune."

"Don't worry about the cost, Johnny. I'll let the business pick up most of it. The club will also give us a deep discount because all the members are very proud of our high school. What do you say?"

Johnny went from excited to apprehensive, and it showed in his countenance.

"What's wrong, son?"

"Dad, I'm not sure Bubba and LJ have suits to wear to the club. If I had to guess, I'd say they probably don't."

"It's amazing what you've done for both of us in a single season of football," Mr. Kitchens said. "Three months ago, I wouldn't have given a rip about something like that and, believe it or not, it had already crossed my mind as well. Here's what we'll do. Why don't I approach the club with the suggestion that we have an informal celebration for the team. I'll make sure the club okays jeans and jerseys for the evening's attire. Do you think that will work?"

"That would fix everything. I'm so proud of you."

"No, Johnny, it's me who's so proud of you. You've changed both of us for the good."

"It wasn't me, Dad. Bubba Preston should get all the credit. He's quite a gifted person regardless of how poor his family might be. And like you said, Bubba and LJ will do well in whatever they decide to do in life."

Spotting his dad's car, William parked next to it. His father had invited him to have lunch with him at the country club. William hadn't spent any time with him, one on one, in a while and looked forward to catching up on what his father and mother were doing. Living for the most part at Sue Ellen's created a huge disconnect between his world and that of his parents.

The club served an excellent buffet, and William loved eating there. After getting their food, they took a table by a window overlooking the golf course. Mr. Morgan told his son about a few pending business deals and about a piece of property he was looking at in England.

"If your mother and I were to buy a home in England, you could go to Oxford or Cambridge. Of course, that would be up to you. But a European education looks good on a resume."

Knowing that wouldn't happen, William still responded positively. "That might be an option. It would be fun to live in England for a while and Oxford is a great school."

Shifting gears, Mr. Morgan brought it back to William's level. "What's happening at school? I hear Union High's had a terrific football season. I've been too busy to make it to a game, but I've heard good things about the new coach. Henderson, I believe his name is. Do you know either one of those two new kids playing ball for Union High?"

"Not really. They're the talk of the town though. Someone said they started playing several weeks into the season, and then literally turned the year around for Union High."

"A friend said they come out of the trailer park near McClain's. The Preston kid, and I believe the other boy's name is Denton, both seem to have a lot of athletic ability, based on what I hear."

"I don't have any classes with either of them, but I have a friend, Eula Johnson, who is good friends with both of them, and . . ."

His father interrupted with a warning. "Be careful who you spend time with. It may seem judgmental, but the vast majority of people cycle within the same circle they were born in. It would be nigh impossible for you to be friends with either one of those students. They may have talent on the gridiron, and every once in a while one will rise above the poverty they were born into, but not often. Nothing good ever comes out of a trailer park. I'm sorry for interrupting, what were you about to say?"

Everything Sue Ellen had said about his father embracing his relationship with Eula had just played out in that conversation about Bubba and LJ. Realizing the futility of the situation, William said, "I was going to say that I'm looking forward to Christmas this year. Maybe we'll get lucky and have a little snow."

⚬⚬⚬⚬⚬⚬

Mr. Kitchens and his son weren't the only ones who wanted to honor the phenomenal season the football team had just completed. Bill Watson was sitting in his cramped office, thinking about the past year. Christmas was just a few weeks away, and he had paid a local artist to paint Christmas scenes and characters on the diner's windows as he did every Christmas season. He usually had the windows painted and the decorations up the week before Thanksgiving. Wise men, traveling by camels, were painted on one window and a Nativity scene was painted on the center window. Santa and Rudolph, along with some elves and toys, were painted on the remaining windows. The children loved to come and see Santa and Rudolph. The local artist did an excellent job. The spirit of Christmas could be felt by all who passed by the diner, regardless of whether they patronized it or not.

Susanna, a waitress who had worked for Bill since the diner opened nineteen years earlier, appeared in the doorway to his office.

"Well?" she said, with her right shoulder leaning against the doorway, left hand propped on her hip.

"Well, what?" Bill asked, looking up from his desk, pretending he didn't know what she was talking about.

"Well, what, my ass! You know what. Are we having a team Christmas party or not?"

Bill Watson, like Bubba, was a *hooti tootie warrior.* His clientele was mainly McClain's Furniture employees. To the best of his knowledge, not one person who was upper crust had ever darkened the door to his diner. And the same feelings of inferiority that Bubba felt, because of lack of money and social status, also applied to him. Real or imagined, it could be consuming.

"Yes," he responded. "What the hell? They can come or not, it's their choice."

"Atta boy," Susanna said, walking two steps to his desk and making Bill high-five her. "It's damn time they realized what they're missing. Country club, my ass. We'll show them country club, Bubba style."

Bubba Preston was Susanna's nephew, and she was one of his biggest fans. She even had an apron with his jersey number embroidered on it. Like Bubba and Bill, she also suffered from *hootie tootie* syndrome.

Bill had wanted to do something nice for the football team. The diner's location had a lot to do with the clientele. It was on the south side of town and had a huge mobile home park directly behind it. Great for Bill's business, but a little defining in the customer base. He wouldn't even admit it to himself, but he was afraid to make the offer to Coach Henderson. Fear of rejection is a powerful thing. The decision, thanks to Susanna, had been made. Bill Watson, without knowing it, had taken a quantum leap forward, stepping gingerly out onto the bridge the Beamer and Eula had crossed. The bridge connecting humanity can be reached from both sides. One only has to step out in faith.

Headlines in the local paper read, "Union High Wins Six In A

Row." The whole town was excited about the season. They had been losing for so long, winning had solidified everyone, regardless of their stature in the community. Old and young, rich and not so rich, were talking about the team. Bubba Preston had almost acquired rock star status. Little Jimmy was right up there next to him. When the townsfolk weren't talking about them, they were talking about Johnny, Rodney or Jason. It had been so long since the high school had produced a winning season, the people were euphoric.

Unfortunately, because their first four games were losses, they wouldn't be in the playoffs. It was still a storybook year with a Cinderella ending. Everyone said, "Wait until next year. We'll win the whole shebang next time." The teams that did make the playoffs were thankful Union High had not made the cut.

It was the first week in November, and word was out the country club was having the entire team over for a celebration dinner. Bill's Diner, not taking a back seat to the country club, announced they would treat the team to a Christmas dinner and each player would be allowed to bring one guest. Everyone in Bubba's circle of friends really appreciated Bill having the team over. You had two ends of the spectrum, both tiptoeing out on the bridge connecting humanity, both reaching out in faith. For the country club, most of the players dined there often, except Bubba and LJ. Bubba and LJ frequented Bill's Diner weekly, but the rest of the team had no idea what to expect.

The country club contacted Coach Henderson and set the team celebration dinner for the last Saturday evening in November. As per the arrangement Mr. Kitchens had worked out, team jerseys and jeans were to be worn, and a photographer would be there to take pictures.

Bill Watson and Coach Henderson set the party at the diner

for the second Saturday evening in December. Bill had suggested to the coach that some of the upper-crust team members might not show up, the diner being located in the wrong part of town.

"Believe me when I tell you this," Coach Henderson told Bill. "I know exactly how you feel and what you're talking about here. But trust me on this one. Something happened this year. Something that ought to make everyone, people like you and me, people like the Morgans and the Kitchens, take notes and learn from these players. A miracle of sorts took place on the field and in the locker room, making social order and pecking order disappear. I wish I could take the credit, but I can't. I only witnessed the transformation, but it was, and still is, real. Believe me, Bill, they'll all come and they'll all enjoy themselves."

"Hope you're right, Coach."

"I know I'm right, Bill. You'll see for yourself and be as amazed as I am at the changes. When we become one on a team, barriers and social orders disappear, and the whole solidifies behind the dream. And, Bill, thanks for the invite."

Henderson dreamed of next year and the playoffs, not realizing the team was going back to pumpkin status and Cinderella was about to fly the coop.

⚬✖⚬✖⚬✖⚬

The country club and Bill's Diner didn't have a lock on feeling the Christmas spirit. The Beamer, also in the Christmas spirit, desperately wanted to take Eula to meet his dad and mom.

"I know you're probably right," William said to Sue Ellen's assertion that his father would never accept the idea of Eula being his daughter-in-law. "But I have to try."

"Do you have any idea what your father's net worth is? Do

you have any idea how far-reaching his connections are? I need some time to think this through. You have to give me some time. This is very complicated, more so than you'll ever know."

"All I want to do is take her to my home and introduce her to my parents. How complicated could that possibly be?"

"Your father isn't a bad person; he's a mover and a shaker. He doesn't see people as we see them. He sees them as part of a deal or not. What can they do for me, or what will I profit by being their friend? His world isn't necessarily a bad place, it just excludes the people with less of the world's goods and financial resources."

William was quiet for a few seconds. He remembered the conversation he had with his father at the country club and his remark, "Nothing good ever comes out of a trailer park."

"You're right, Sue Ellen. I don't know what his net worth is, or who his real friends are. But I know what I want in life, and it isn't centered around the almighty dollar. Eula makes me happy and that's all I really need to know. He'll either accept her and her family or else."

Sue Ellen quickly countered his assertion.

"Never, ever, say or else to your dad. That's a hill you'll both die on. Don't doubt me on this. Give me a little time to think this through. Please? I know William Morgan, Sr. better than anyone on the planet. Let me work on this."

"Okay," William said, "but soon. It has to happen sooner or later and sooner suits me better. I don't think time will ever soften my father's opinion to the point he'll accept Eula and her family."

Bubba's dad was hard of hearing. His mother was a sound

sleeper and neither heard the phone ringing. Bubba, exhausted from his shift at McClain's, finally put the noise he was hearing together with the device making it and jumped out of bed to answer the phone. Looking at his watch, he had a bad feeling about the call. It was 3 AM.

"Preston residence," he said into the receiver, feeling the fear that accompanies every 3 AM call.

"This is Union Regional Hospital," the voice on the other end said. "We have a Mollie Preston here in the ER, and she gave us this number to call. Is there anyone named Bubba at this number?"

"Yes, ma'am, I'm Bubba. I'm her grandson. What's wrong with my Granny?"

"She apparently called 911 herself and was transported to the ER. She's complaining of severe chest pains and is undergoing diagnostic testing to determine the cause."

"Tell her I'm on my way," and with that he hung up the phone. Quickly slipping into some jeans and a T-shirt, he woke his mom and dad and told them what had happened and that he was headed to the ER.

They immediately got up and were getting dressed when they heard Maude fire up and race out of the driveway.

Parking in the first available space, Bubba sprinted to the ER. Quickly addressing the first available nurse, he found out Granny was in Treatment Room 2. Not asking or waiting for permission, he went directly into the room. Granny, hooked up to an IV and heart monitor, broke into a feeble smile. Lifting a very weak hand, Bubba quickly took it, leaned over and kissed her on the forehead.

"My Bubba. Thanks for coming. I was waiting for you to get here."

"Stop talking like that," Bubba said, gently squeezing her hand. "We'll have you out of here in no time. How can I go to church if I don't come by your house and pick you up? Maude wouldn't even go without you."

Bubba, with questioning eyes, looked up at the doctor who had come back into the room. He had a solemn look on his face, and moved his head slightly to the left and right.

Bubba's eyes immediately filled with tears.

"Do something for her," Bubba said directly to the doctor. Before the doctor could respond, Granny squeezed Bubba's hand so feebly, he barely felt it.

"Bubba, it's gonna be all right. I'm ninety-two years old and I'm tired. My old body is plumb tuckered out. The only thing I live for is going to church with you and Maude. Promise me, Bubba, you'll keep going. I'll be there, sitting right next to you, every Sunday."

Her voice was so weak Bubba had to lean close to hear what she was saying.

She saw his tears and managed to lift her other hand and wipe them away.

"Don't cry, Bubba. This is a good thing. I'm fixing to take a trip I've been wanting to take for a long time. You can't come with me now. Ain't your time. Remember all the things I told you about the Lord. Love Him with all your heart and always do good to your neighbor. That's the way you'll get to see me again. I gotta go, now, Bubba. I see Jesus—"

Her voice trailed off and he felt her hand let go of his. The doctor said, "She's gone, son. She must have been a fine lady."

"Sir, you have no idea."

Bubba didn't tell the doctor, but when Granny said, "I see Jesus," he was sure he saw him as well, with outstretched arms, standing and smiling at her.

The doctor put his arm around Bubba's shoulders and walked

him out of the room. It was over just that quick. Bubba's mom and dad were walking through the door as well as two of Granny's other children. They could tell by the expression on Bubba's face that Granny was gone.

⚬∞⚬ ⚬∞⚬ ⚬∞⚬

Maude was first in line behind the hearse. Clarice rode with Bubba, Granny Preston's Bible between them. The ride from the funeral home to Coosa Baptist Church was less than ten minutes. Bubba had tears in his eyes as he focused on the casket in the hearse. He would never see his Granny again, at least not in this life.

This was an old school town. At every intersection and red light, officers stopped traffic and stood at attention, hat in hand, placed over their heart. "What a great place to live," Bubba thought, as he passed the uniformed officers.

Tears trickled slowly down his cheeks. As they turned into the driveway of the church, the nearby tent, chairs and fresh mound of earth marked what would be Granny Preston's final resting place.

Clarice remembered the kids joking about the people buried in the cemetery watching them grill-out and play ball on Saturdays behind the church. Granny's gravesite was like having a seat on the fifty-yard line. Bubba had no way of knowing it, but he wouldn't play ball here again. Choices have consequences, and the scenes in one's life have a way of shifting and moving on.

Pastor Baker, knowing how close Bubba was to Granny Preston, had asked him to say a few words at the graveside service. Clarice wondered how he would handle it and what he would have to say.

The funeral procession, snaking slowly through the cemetery, finally stopped in front of the freshly dug grave site. Bubba was four years old when Papa Preston was buried here and had little or no recollection of it. He barely remembered his grandfather, but he often brought Granny Preston here to visit and place flowers on his grave.

The pallbearers assembled behind the hearse, and the family and friends began to get out of their vehicles. The sound of the car doors shutting made an eerie sound that reverberated across the hillside.

LJ, realizing Bubba's pain, stood beside his door, waiting patiently for his best friend. Bubba made no move to get out. He was gripping the steering wheel so hard his knuckles were white. "We have to get out," Clarice finally said. Janice was standing by her door.

"I know," Bubba said, "but getting out somehow makes it seem so final."

In what was a bold move for LJ, he opened Bubba's door, leaned inside and hugged his best friend. Pastor Baker, standing at the gravesite, saw the beautiful act of love and compassion, one friend consoling another.

"She's not here," LJ whispered in Bubba's ear. "She's with Jesus."

"I know," Bubba said, "but I wasn't ready for her to go, not yet, anyway."

LJ walked Bubba to the gravesite, with his arm around his waist. Clarice and Janice followed.

After the family members and friends had gathered around the casket, Pastor Baker spoke for a few minutes and everyone repeated the 23rd Psalm together. The pastor said, in his most solemn voice, "As a final tribute to Mollie Rush Preston, Tom

Preston, her grandson, known to most of you as Bubba, will close our service. I have had the privilege of watching this young man walk his Granny to her pew every Sunday morning, an act of love and devotion for all to see. It made Jesus smile, and most of us as well. Granny Preston had the pleasure of watching her grandson play football last Friday evening. Sunday morning, just like clockwork, he brought her to church and she went to be with her Lord and Savior on Thursday. It's only fitting Bubba has the final tribute to his beloved grandmother."

Bubba, holding Clarice's hand, stepped forward and laid his left hand on the casket. It seemed like forever before he found his voice. Pastor Baker prayed silently for the Holy Spirit to give him strength.

"Granny, I just want you to know Maude cried when I told her of your passing. Maude said she wasn't coming to your funeral, Granny, but I told her it was something we both had to do. More than anything, I'll miss taking you to church and listening to all your stories. Maude will miss them, too. I promise I'll keep going to church and Clarice has promised to go with me."

"Praise the Lord," Granny Preston whispered in his ear.

There wasn't a dry eye within hearing distance of a special grandson telling his special Granny goodbye for the last time.

"Now, go on, and get out of here. All y'all gotta lot of living to do, and I gotta lot of praising the Lord to do. And Bubba, tell Maude I said thanks for taking us to church all those times."

Bubba would swear till his dying day that Granny Preston talked to him at her funeral.

Pastor Baker said a closing prayer, spoke to each family member, and the service was over.

When Bubba and Clarice got back to the truck and opened Maude's door, there was a single red rose lying on the seat.

Granny Preston's funeral had been on Saturday. Lots of family members and friends came over to Bubba's house for a get-together after the funeral. Coosa Baptist Church had coordinated the meal and everyone's love for Granny Preston had spilled over to the grieving family, giving them the much needed support. After the meal, most family members went back over to the cemetery to see her grave. The grave had been filled in and flowers covered the fresh mound of earth.

Pastor Baker had gone over to the Preston trailer and accompanied the family back to the gravesite.

Bubba and Clarice drove over in Maude. Bubba couldn't help but remember all the joking and conversations he and his Granny had together concerning Maude and Maude's feelings being hurt. He could still hear her say, "Bubba, you and Maude are both full of it."

Pastor Baker walked over to where Bubba parked and waited for him to get out of the truck. He then walked with him and Clarice to the gravesite. "Bubba, your Granny Preston was a simple believer," Pastor Baker said. "And that's the best way to be. Not only could she quote Scripture, she lived it as well. For her, God said it, she believed it, and that settled it. She never worried about theological issues, didn't care who Martin Luther was or what he nailed to some door, or what contribution the Council of Nicea made to Christianity. Her beloved King James Bible was all she needed. She didn't beat anyone over the head with it, but used it for her daily walk with the Lord. It was her road map, and she just took a one-way vacation of a lifetime."

Bubba listened to Pastor Baker. He felt the greatest loss he had experienced in his young life to date. This type of loss was hard to accept. He had tears in his eyes when he extended his hand to his pastor. "Thanks for all you've done for our family. Granny loved you like you were one of her own, and I'll keep my word to her and to God. I'll see you in the morning."

"I never doubted that for a second," Pastor Baker responded. After shaking hands and visiting with the rest of the family, he excused himself and walked away.

Bubba and Clarice left and went to one of their favorite parking places. This evening would be different. Bubba cried softly while Clarice held him. He loved his grandmother and the only things capable of overcoming the void she left were the teachings she had passed on to him. They would last a lifetime.

Sunday morning dawned with a cloud of despair hanging over it. Bubba was awakened by the sun, creeping around the patched shade, where the duct tape, which he jokingly called Alabama Chrome, had lost its adhesion. Granny Preston's death was like a bad dream that wasn't. Keeping his eyes closed seemed to hold reality at bay. But it was Sunday morning, and he had made a promise to his Granny.

Dressing for church in clean jeans and a Polo, he went outside and walked over to where he had parked Maude. "Well, old girl, it's just you and me this morning. Clarice will go with us most Sundays, but she's out of town today. Say what? You want to ride by Granny's anyway? Sounds good to me. She'd like that, too."

Maude's tailpipes rumbled up Granny Preston's driveway. Bubba and Maude both knew it wouldn't bring her to the door, but somehow it felt good just stopping by. As he sat there in silence, he could feel her presence and her love. Out of habit and remembrance, he got out, went around to the passenger door, opened it, and then closed it back. "Let's go, Granny, the pastor's waiting."

Time can be both our friend and our foe. For Bubba, the football season had ended on a high note and then bottomed out with the passing of Granny Preston.

William had yet to fulfill Sue Ellen's wishes and bring Eula to dinner. With him wanting to take Eula to meet his parents and see his home, Sue Ellen insisted he honor her first with a visit. This also gave Sue Ellen a little more time to figure out how, or if, the Beamer could introduce the love of his life to his parents.

Eula or William never wanted to exclude their respective families. They knew the huge differences in lifestyles and living standards would be problematic. They were in protective mode, trying to preserve Camelot. The only reason William wanted to take Eula to meet his parents was because he wanted to announce their engagement. He had to get past William, Sr. before he could think about meeting her parents. They could always do it without family blessings, but he wanted Eula to be accepted and loved by his family.

Sue Ellen said, "Ask her over for dinner, have her meet me at the mall for lunch, or we could go out for dinner. It doesn't matter to me. But I want to get to know the woman you say you're going to marry before it takes place. Is that too much to ask?"

This made him sad, because in reality, he lived with her. She was right, and he knew it. The only time Sue Ellen had seen Eula was the evening she picked him up for the football game. Few words were exchanged that night, and she didn't even set foot in Sue Ellen's home. Nor did he bring her in after the game.

"You're right, Sue Ellen. I should have already brought her over. Eula will be my wife, and you're more of a mother to me than the woman I actually call mother. I'll make it happen this week. You'll love Eula as much as I do. Well, maybe not that much, but you'll quickly see in her what I saw from the beginning. Let's make it a lunch date at the mall, and without me.

The two of you will get along famously. I'll get her to check her schedule and give you a call, and the two of you can work out the details. How does that sound?"

"Couldn't have planned it any better myself," Sue Ellen replied. "Tell her I'm looking forward to spending some time with her. When she calls, we'll figure out where to meet and decide where we'll have lunch. Thanks, Junior."

Calling him Junior made him smile. He immediately thought about Eula calling him Beamer and wondered how these two women, who were such an important part of his life, would find common ground. Eula was easy to get along with and easier to love. But so was Sue Ellen. The meeting had to take place and the relationship between all parties established. End of story.

"I'll see her tonight when she gets off at the DQ. She'll call you tomorrow. Be back in a little while."

⁕⁕⁕

Sue Ellen could see the excitement on Mr. Morgan's face as he came into her office. Closing the door, he turned to her and said, "Guess what?"

"What?" Sue Ellen asked, smiling.

"I just closed the deal on the property in England."

"Terrific," Sue Ellen said. "That was a tough one. I wasn't sure you'd be able to make it happen. Congratulations! I know Marsha will be thrilled to finally have her own home in England. When are you flying out?"

"Probably Friday. Final drafts of the deed and paperwork are being completed and as soon as my lawyer looks them over, we'll be on our way. Possession of the property will be immediate."

"That's awesome. Can't wait to visit and see your new getaway."

"It's absolutely beautiful. The two-person staff has been tak-ing care of the place for over twenty years and have agreed to stay on. It's like home to them. They have a lovely apartment over the garage, and it has direct access to the house. Couldn't have set that up better myself."

"I know Marsha's excited and looking forward to having her own place there."

"Excited is an understatement. She's always wanted a home in Europe, and now she has one. I'm sure she'll probably stay there, at least for a while. But that's all right. What do the locals say? When mama's happy, everybody's happy."

"That's what they say. You might fit in yet," she added and laughed.

"Don't put money on that one," Mr. Morgan said as he started to leave. "The locals are a different breed."

"Tell Marsha I'm happy for her and am expecting an invitation in the near future."

"We'll make it happen," he assured her as he headed back to his office.

Sue Ellen, sitting behind her expensive desk mused to herself. "I own you," she thought, "and if that's not enough to worry you, Eula Johnson is about to have a piece of you as well. By the time this story is over, you'll have more local flavor running through your bloodlines than you can imagine. And as far as the locals being a different breed, you have no idea what you're missing. Different breed, my ass. I'll show you a different breed if you interfere with William and Eula's plans for their future."

Sue Ellen never used foul language, even to herself, but the different breed comment made the hair on the back of her neck stand up. He had gotten wealthy loaning money to these poor, local people at high interest rates, and he never showed compassion. If they couldn't meet the obligations of the loan, he'd fore-close at the first opportunity.

⚬∞⚬∞⚬∞⚬

Though available to give Bubba advice at the drop of a hat, Eula actually failed to take her own. At school she excelled in the advanced classes with the rich kids, but the association ended there. She had stalled her visit with Sue Ellen for as long as possible and had declined William's request to let him take her to see his home or meet his parents. Eula explained it this way to the Beamer. "For the sake of argument and explanation, let's swap places. Nothing wrong with you or me. We just live in two different worlds. Suppose you live in my double-wide and I live in Sue Ellen's home or in yours, the one somewhere up on the hillside behind those fancy gates."

William shook his head. "They're not really fancy gates. They just look that way."

"Had me fooled," Eula replied and laughed. Taking his hand in hers, she said, "Just hear me out." She paused for a few seconds. "We are both in the sixth or seventh grade and go to the same school. You'll have to stretch a little here, imagining you, William Morgan, Jr., riding a big, old yellow school bus."

"Stop it, Eula, that's not funny."

"I know it's not funny. I rode one of those monsters for ten years—to grammar school, middle school, and then the first two years of high school. If it wasn't for the White Charger, I'd still be riding the thing. Here we go. Pay attention." She smiled at him and he squeezed her hand. "The big, old yellow bus picks you up first every morning. You stand out in front of your home, the double-wide trailer. You're okay with it. It's home and those you

173

love are living there with you. You climb aboard and the driver starts up the street to my house. Let's say, for the sake of argument, it's Sue Ellen's house. You can see her house from the road. The driver stops in front of my house, aka Sue Ellen's, and I climb aboard. Don't tell me, Beamer, for one second, that you wouldn't look at my house and compare it to the double-wide trailer you live in. You couldn't help but feel the difference and wonder what it must look like inside, and what kind of furniture is in such a fancy place. You'd wonder, Beamer, trust me, you'd wonder, because I always have and still do. There's nothing wrong with either home. However, the kids that live in the trailers will always marvel at homes like yours and wonder what it must be like to live there. You have a very compassionate heart, and if truth be told, and if you'd admit to it, you've passed trailer homes many times and felt sorry for the people living there. Right?"

She had driven the point home, hard and straight to his heart. "I'm so sorry, Eula, I never looked at it that way before. But you're right. I've often wondered about the trailers, how small they seem and how poor so many of the people living in them must be. I'm sorry."

Pulling him over to her side of the White Charger, she said, "Oh, William, I love you so much. I'm just trying to give you a real perspective of who I am, where I come from, and what you say you want to marry into. Make sure, Beamer, because most of my friends and family live in trailers, just like the one I live in."

"I'll love them just like I love you, I promise. And if there's any way possible, together we'll try and make their lives better."

"Love you, Beamer," she said.

It was six-thirty. The alarm sounded and Bubba was on his feet faster than Little Jimmy could go through the two hole on a good night of football. Getting out of bed was a chore unto itself. The old mattress had a horrific hole worn in it from years of use. Bubba had to climb into it to sleep, and out of it to get up.

He had a huge history test in second period and had done little preparation for it. That was classic Bubba. "Rearing to go and can't go for rearing" was one of his favorite sayings. He had intended to study last evening but decided instead to spend time with Clarice immediately after school and then had to go to work. Exhausted, he came home, took a shower, and collapsed in his bed. The history test didn't cross his mind.

In less than fifteen minutes, Bubba was dressed, had a cup of coffee in his hand and was headed outside to fire up Maude and hightail it to Clarice's.

"Good morning, honeybuns," he said as she climbed into the cab of his truck. "Slide yourself over here next to the hoss," he said, smiling that winsome Bubba smile. Those big blue eyes and that smile, where the right side of his lip curled up like Elvis', made him irresistible on most days—but not today.

"Listen to these questions and let me help you while we have a few minutes. You're going to flunk history if you don't start studying. Do you understand me, Bubba Preston? I don't want the father of my children to be ignorant and flunk out of school. Here we go. Answer the questions correctly and we might see about a little reward after school."

Clarice, all petite at 116 pounds, had a smile of her own, blonde hair, and a figure Bubba said would stop a Mack truck on a dime.

"Hot damn, history teacher, fire away."

"What year was the Louisiana Purchase and from whom did we buy it?"

Bubba knew the answer, but thinking about what she said about not wanting the father of her kids to be ignorant did what a cold shower is supposed to do.

"Well, come on. You either know the answer or you don't."

He had great dreams of escaping the world of single-wides and a mundane job at the factory, making just enough to get by and too much to leave.

Perspiration had popped out on Bubba's forehead. "1800...1803 and we bought it from the French. We paid fifteen million dollars for it and Thomas Jefferson was president."

"I'm impressed," Clarice said. Noticing the sweat, she asked, "Are you okay, Bubba?"

"I'm fine," he said, but visions and dreams of a better life were suddenly closeted by his past family history. "What's the next question?"

⚜⚜⚜

"It's time," Eula said, looking at her watch. "I've got ten minutes and Sam is already covered up."

"I know," William responded, squeezing her hand and then letting it go. "I hate you having to work so much. You should let me help out a little."

"I'm fine. I don't mind working at the DQ. Sam's always been good to me and, besides, it's not your place to keep me up, not yet anyway."

That made the Beamer smile.

"Love you," he said, as he started to get in his car. He had wanted to tell her earlier about the lunch date with Sue Ellen but thought it better to tell her as he was leaving. That way, she could process it better by herself and decide what she wanted to do. "Oh, by the way, I almost forgot something very important. Sue Ellen wants you to call her tomorrow and set a lunch date at the mall. She's dying to meet you and spend some time with you. I know it's not the favorite thing on your to-do list, but we have a laundry list of such things to do, and we had better start checking them off. The sooner, the better."

He had gotten her attention. She was speechless, something that usually didn't happen to her. Finally, she managed to speak. "Thanks a lot, Beamer. How long have you known about this lunch date?"

"Don't worry about it. You'll love Sue Ellen and she's gonna love you, too. I'll give you her number tonight when you get off and you can call her tomorrow and arrange the details. She's so excited, and rightly so. After your story about double-wides and mansions, it'll be a whole lot better to meet at the mall for the first time than to have to go to her house. That will come later."

Eula was just standing there on the sidewalk, in shock.

"William smiled and pointed to the DQ. "Go to work, Eula. It's time and Sam needs your help."

"I'm gonna get you for this," she said and smiled. Blowing him a kiss, she turned and went inside.

His BMW was parked next to the White Charger. He remembered the first time he parked next to her truck, seemingly so long ago. Looking at them parked side by side, he imagined them friends. And they were indeed. The White Charger admired the BMW's paint and the BMW held the White Charger in high regard for his stamina and endurance. The BMW was also a little jealous. He was always getting left in the mall parking lot, watching the White Charger take William and Eula off again and again. He couldn't figure out what the White Charger had that he didn't. It was simple: more room.

Remembering their first meeting here, the Beamer thought

about how many things had changed in the space of a few short months. Turning to look back at the DQ, Eula was still standing inside, looking out toward the parking lot. He waved and she blew him another kiss. As he drove out of the parking lot, she had a weak moment. "How can this be?" she thought. Looking back at the White Charger, she swore he smiled at her, reminding her Camelot was indeed real.

Sam could see Eula was worried about something. "You okay, Eula?" he asked her early in her shift.

"Sure, Sam, just got a lot on my mind. Everything's fine."

Everything wasn't fine. She couldn't believe she had to be the first one to meet someone outside of Camelot. What would she say to someone as rich and powerful as Sue Ellen Thornton?

"Hell," Eula thought, "she's almost as big a *hootie tootie* as old man Morgan himself. What am I going to do?"

Ten o'clock came none too soon for Eula. About fifteen minutes till ten, she saw the Beamer drive back into the parking lot and park next to the White Charger. There would be no hanky-panky tonight. There was a serious conversation to be had and some explaining to do. "Get ready, Beamer, here I come," she thought as she clocked out and told Sam good night.

Sunday morning, over coffee, William shared with Sue Ellen the story of the poor kid and the rich kid, riding the same school bus. "I actually agree and understand where Eula, and all her friends, for that matter, are coming from, or at least how they must feel. I've ridden past those trailer homes and felt sorry for the people living inside. No telling how many times I rode by her home and never even realized what a wonderful person lived there. She's so apprehensive about spending time with you. I know how caring you are, but again, all she sees are the fancy cars and the big house you live in."

"Trust me with this one, William. I used to think like your father, but I had a life-changing event that I hope to tell you about someday. Eula and I will be fine. We'll have lunch and, who knows, I might tell her about that life-changing experience. That will put her at ease, I assure you."

"Let's see if I have this correct. You won't tell me about this mystery experience you had sometime in your past, but you'll share it with Eula on your first outing. How fair is that?"

"Women don't have to be fair. They just have to stick together."

William smiled at that one. "I bet I can get her to tell me whatever you tell her."

"And I know better. Women also keep each other's secrets."

∞∞∞

The notice everyone had feared was finally posted on the bulletin board at work. McClain's, due to a decrease in orders over the upcoming Christmas holidays, was going on a four-day workweek. Even though football season was over, Mr. McClain honored the increase in wages for Bubba and LJ. He took pride in knowing a couple of his employees had done so well in the Union High athletic program. It was sort of like bragging rights for the company.

This slowdown happened every Christmas season and wasn't really a surprise to anyone. Most employees had adjusted to it, buying presents early and planning on having less money to spend. But it still made it hard on everyone to take a pay cut during the wintertime. The heating bills were higher, and the employees and their children usually had to fight bouts of sickness brought on by winter weather. The term *trailer-park tough* would once again prevail, and they would get through it together.

Cold weather had definitely arrived, and the first snow of the new winter season covered the ground. It was early morning, and almost everyone was trying to catch a few extra winks. Bubba, the first up in his family, made coffee and looked out the kitchen window. The fresh fallen snow made him smile because Granny Preston always loved to see things covered by the white magic, as she called it.

One day, a year or so earlier, Bubba was visiting Granny and it had snowed the night before. He had stopped by to bring her a few things she needed from the grocery store. "Bubba, don't you just love this white magic?" she asked him when he brought the groceries in the house and set them on the kitchen table.

"And why do you call it white magic, Granny?" he asked.

"I call it that because it makes everything seem clean and pure. Old rusted-out cars and trucks, sitting out next to old barns and houses for years and years, look like new ones. The old houses, long ago abandoned and occupied by ghosts from the past, look like they're lived in. Fence posts don white hats and the grass bows down to the beautiful handiwork of the Lord. Now, ain't that magic, Bubba?"

"Can't argue with that," he had told her.

Taking a sip of his Maxwell House coffee, he decided to wake up the rest of the family.

"Get up, everyone. Granny Preston said to come see the white magic."

Immediately upon hearing white magic, his mother said to Bubba's dad, "Wake up, old man, we got snow." She slipped on her housecoat and was in the kitchen in a flash. Looking through the sliding glass doors out on the back porch, she said, "Granny always loved to see it snow. Said it covered the bad and ugly things in life. It's beautiful, no doubt about that."

"That's what she told me, too," Bubba said, taking another sip of his coffee. "I sure do miss her. It'll be our first Christmas without her here."

"Don't know so much about that. Your Granny's got connections. We may not see her in the flesh, but I have a feeling we'll feel her presence. Lord, how she loved you, Bubba. Thought the sun rose and set in you. Don't be surprised if she brings you another red rose or something. Would you like that, son?"

"Yes, ma'am, Granny was special, and I'll take a visit from her any way I can get it."

After a moment, Bubba said, "I've been thinking about something, Mom."

"And what might that be?"

"Granny Preston had a lot of Christmas decorations. A ton of them. Would you and Dad care if I decorated the trailer with her ornaments, lights and garlands? I used to put them up at her house, and I sure would like to put them up one more time."

"Sounds like a good idea to me, and I know your dad won't mind, one way or the other. You know him. He loves Christmas but doesn't give a hoot about helping trim the tree or anything else for that matter when it comes to decorating."

"And I was thinking," Bubba said, "would you and Dad mind if I invited a few friends over for a little Christmas party in Granny's memory? Just a few, like Eula and her boyfriend, LJ and Janice, and maybe one guy from the football team. Not sure about the last one, but I know Granny loved Eula, LJ and Janice."

"You left out Clarice. You and her still good?"

"Yes, ma'am, we're good. 'Fine as frog's hair', as the old guys like to say. That reminds me, I have to get her something for Christmas."

"You're just like your dad, always waiting till the last minute to buy cards or gifts."

"That's because we don't like to shop. We go in, pick it out on the first trip, and it's done."

"I like your idea about the Christmas party. We always have friends over anyway, and a few more won't hurt anything. I heard Eula's dating that Morgan kid. Ain't he kinda rich and snobbish?"

"Well, the only thing I know for sure is he rides around a lot in her old truck. You've seen her truck a thousand times and you know it's nothing fancy. So, to answer your question, if he's good enough for Eula, he's okay with me."

⚬⚬⚬⚬⚬⚬

The die had been cast, and Eula reluctantly placed a call to Sue Ellen.

"Hello," Sue Ellen said, not recognizing the number on the screen.

"Miss Sue Ellen," Eula said, "I'm calling to set up our lunch date. Is this a good time, or should I call back later?" Eula fervently hoped she would say call back later.

"Oh, no, this is great timing. I was just thinking about you and wondering if William told you I issued him an ultimatum. How have you been doing? It's been a long time since our brief encounter the night of the ball game. And, by the way, it's Sue Ellen, no Miss, please."

"I've been doing well, thank you. Just going to school and

working. That takes up most of my time. I work three evenings a week at the Dairy Queen and help close on Saturday and Sunday evenings. Between studying and working, I have very little free time."

"I understand," Sue Ellen said sympathetically, "but lunch won't take long and I promise not to keep you. What day looks good for you?"

"What about next Saturday, say around eleven? I don't have to be at work until four. That should give us plenty of time, don't you think?"

"Sounds good to me," Sue Ellen said. "What about Cracker Barrel? They're right across from the mall and after we eat, if you want to, we could walk around and shop some at the mall. They've got some great sales going on."

"I'll see you there at the Cracker Barrel next Saturday morning, at eleven."

"I'll put it on my calendar. Can't wait to get to know you better. I've heard so much about you from William. See you Saturday."

❧❧❧

Frank Kitchens was on the board of the Green Valley Country Club. Even board members had noticed a change in his demeanor. He had started back to church, something he used to do on a regular basis but had stopped several years earlier. His wife, Alice, was astonished at the changes and couldn't believe her husband had ceased being so aggressive and driven. He was helping out at the food pantry, a private organization set up to assist needy families in the area. On Thursday, he would be there at 7:30 AM to box the food for the recipients who would come by on Friday to pick it up.

Johnny had undergone a similar conversion—from a *hootie tootie* to a caring, sympathetic young man, viewing the world not through rose-colored glasses but through bifocals. He could see the world he lived in and the world Bubba and LJ lived in as well. Johnny, growing up and learning the real values of life, had reminded his dad of things his father had forgotten. It should have been the other way around. Granny Preston would say, "God works in mysterious ways, His wonders to perform."

Mr. Kitchens asked the board at the country club about the football team wearing jeans and their jerseys to the celebration dinner. They voted unanimously for his idea. Johnny was happy for his friends. His experiences during the football season had taught him that a level playing field and open dialogue was the beginning of good relationships and enduring friendships.

The celebration party at the country club would be the last Saturday in November. Mr. Kitchens had heard that Bill Watson had invited all the guys over to his diner the second Saturday in December and he wanted both celebration dinners to be a success. This would be great, back-to-back parties celebrating a spectacular football season.

◦◦◦◦◦◦◦◦◦

The Christmas party to honor Granny Preston's memory was set for five o'clock on Christmas Eve. Bubba's mom agreed with his choice of dates. "If we're gonna honor Granny's memory, then it has to be on Christmas Eve. She always insisted on decorating her tree Christmas Eve night."

Bubba took a long walk in the woods behind their home and found the perfect cedar tree for the occasion. He would cut it the day before Christmas Eve and have it ready to decorate at the party. Granny Preston loved the smell of cedar trees. She said it was good for what ails you. He would wait until the last week in November to actually start decorating, but he was going to go ahead and invite his friends. He wasn't sure about Johnny, but he knew for certain he had to invite William. Eula would be offended if he didn't.

Monday morning at school, he told LJ about the party to honor Granny. "First Christmas she's missed in ninety-two years."

LJ replied, "You know me and Janice will be there. Wouldn't miss it for the world. Your Granny was special to us, and we would count it an honor to come. Do you need us to bring anything?"

"Not a thing. Just come hungry. I've got it all covered."

The next person he would invite would have an anxiety attack.

Catching Eula between classes, he put his arm around her and said, "Eula, we're having a special get-together to honor Granny Preston's memory. First Christmas she's missed in ninety-two years." Whispering in her ear, he said, "You can come alone if you'd like, or you can bring your phantom significant other. The choice is yours. But know this—any friend of yours is welcome in our humble home."

His words had caused such a shocked expression, he immediately asked, "Eula, are you okay?"

"Yes, yes, of course I'm okay, why wouldn't I be?" But she was visibly shaken over the invitation and the implications it carried with it.

Pulling away abruptly, she said over her shoulder as she hurried away, "I'll get back with you. Gotta run. I'm gonna be late for class."

The bell rang and Eula knew she would be late for class, but she didn't care. Going into a stall in the restroom, she turned to face the commode and felt like she was going to throw up.

"This relationship is stupid," she told herself. "How could it ever work out? We have nothing in common. Even our friends are so different, they'll never be able to come together." Then the old Eula showed up and saved the day. "What the hell. Beamer's going to his first Christmas party in a house on wheels."

⚬⚬⚬⚬⚬⚬

Monday morning brought a very happy William Morgan, Sr. into Sue Ellen's office. "Just wanted to let you know, I'll be flying out to London on Thursday evening. I'm leaving at seven so I can get some shut-eye on the flight over. Marsha has our new home ready for inspection and wants me to come over to see what she's done with the place. I'm sure the staff is about ready to strangle her. It's probably a good thing for me to go and put their minds at ease, assuring them she'll settle in and stop all her shenanigans."

"How long will you be gone, and is there anything pending I need to know about?"

"I'll be back the following Wednesday. I've got everything taken care of except that stupid old Ernest Wilson. He's two months behind on his payments and asked me to let him have another month to get straightened out, whatever the hell that means. He's been avoiding my calls until today when he finally answered his phone. He was easy enough to get in touch with when he was wanting to borrow money from me. I shouldn't have taken his old trailer park for collateral. Nothing good ever comes out of a trailer park, end of story. If he contacts you, tell him to pay up, or get ready to move. See how he likes that answer."

"If he calls, I'll take care of it. Have a nice trip and tell Marsha hello for me."

⁗⁗⁗

Eula wished she lived closer to the mall. Seemed like she was always at the mall, on the way from the mall, or going to the mall. This Saturday would be a killer. She was meeting the Beamer at nine o'clock and then Sue Ellen at eleven for lunch. She had to be at the DQ by four. It would be a busy day. So far, she had avoided the Morgan mansion and Sue Ellen's fabulous home, which was also a mansion to her. "Just damn," she said out loud. "Am I lucky, or what? The Beamer gets a pass on having to take me to see his place, but not me. Imagine that."

Right on time, the Beamer turned into the mall parking lot. He was all smiles as he jerked the White Charger's door open, climbed in, leaned over and gave Eula a kiss. He had a bouquet of fresh flowers in his hand.

"God, how I love this guy," she thought, as she took the flowers and gave him a real kiss, one of those toe-curlers, he called them.

"Wow, I needed that," he said. "I can't get over how much I miss you. We need to get married, sooner than later. Think how wonderful it would be to wake up every morning next to each other for the rest of our lives."

Eula was one of those people who processed things to death until their conclusion, and meeting Sue Ellen at eleven and Bubba's Christmas Eve party was all she could process at one time.

Taking William by the hand, she said, "We have a problem."

187

"Oh, no," he said with fear in his eyes. "You're not pregnant, are you?"

She burst out laughing. "Oh, no! I could handle being pregnant easier than this problem."

"My God, Eula. What is it?"

Clearly she had his attention. "I've been thinking about how to break this to you, and I think I'll tell you some things about me you don't know. Okay? I think that may be the best way to handle this."

"If you're not pregnant and if you're not breaking up with me, I can't imagine anything else that could possibly be a problem."

"Just listen to me for a few minutes. It'll help me to get all of this out in the open. We've both had our heads in the sand and now something has come along and bit me in the butt."

"My God, honey, what is it?"

"Okay, okay, here we go. Let's do it like a little quiz. Do you know how many pieces of silverware my mom has?"

"You know I don't," the Beamer said.

"Play along," she said. "Just take a wild guess."

"Okay. One hundred pieces."

"Wrong. She has none. Not one. Nada. All of our silverware isn't. They're just assorted stainless steel forks, knives and spoons from Walmart. As a matter of fact, Dad gave her a new eight-piece setting last Christmas. Walmart had it on sale for $29.95. That should tell you the silver content."

William was quiet, absorbing the truth in the illustration she had given him.

"Next question. How many pieces of china do you think my mom has?"

"Let's see. If she has no real silverware, I'll assume she has no real china either, right?"

"Bingo," Eula said. "Not bad, Beamer. You're one for two. And for the record, she doesn't have a china cabinet either. And, in our home, there isn't a place to put a china cabinet."

She continued. "Do you know how much money my parents have in Wall Street investments?"

"Ten thousand!" he quickly answered.

Eula looked away and her eyes filled with tears. Turning back, he saw her crying and immediately pulled her close and said, "Stop this silly game. It's not fun anymore. What are you trying to tell me, honey? This is killing both of us."

"First, let me give you the last answer. If you mentioned Wall Street to my dad, he'd tell you it was a street on the south side of town, running off Broad Street. They don't have ten thousand, one thousand, or even ten dollars in Wall Street investments. They live paycheck to paycheck."

"Again, I ask you, what are you trying to tell me?"

"I'm trying to tell you we're going to a Christmas party at Bubba Preston's in memory of his Granny Preston—a very special person in all our lives. And all the questions I've asked you about my family, if I asked you the same questions about Bubba's family, the answers would be the same."

"Is that what's bothering you, Eula? Don't you know by now that I love you, your family I haven't yet had the privilege of meeting, your friends, your truck and everything about you. I even love your . . ."

"That's enough, Beamer. I get it," Eula said, smiling. "I know our hearts may be one, but the worlds we live in are a million miles apart."

"Eula, it's not about things and money. Never was, and never will be."

"I love you, Beamer."

"I know it, but we have to focus on the immediate issue, Sue Ellen's lunch date."

"Oh, shit," Eula said. "I got so caught up in my little quiz, I forgot about Sue Ellen. You're going with me to Cracker Barrel, Beamer. I'm not going by myself."

"No way," he said. "She told me it was a private luncheon and I wasn't invited."

"That's great. She's probably going to grill me for two hours. Just wait. It'll be your turn before you know it."

William was a glass-half-full person. "Let's try and be positive here. At least we're making the first step toward getting our families and friends involved in our relationship. Sue Ellen's really looking forward to this luncheon with you, and I hope you both enjoy getting to know each other. She's great, not at all like my old man. And you're great, too, so what could possibly go wrong?" William leaned over and gave her another kiss and smiled.

"I wish you were meeting my dad over at Bill's Diner this morning. I bet you'd have your underwear in a wad, too."

The underwear in a wad remark tickled William. He got a visual, and Eula was dumbfounded that he thought it so funny. "Haven't you ever heard that one before?" she asked.

"No, and I bet Sue Ellen hasn't either, so don't use it on her. She probably wouldn't even get it."

"I'm not completely sure you got it. Somehow, I think Sue Ellen is more savvy than you give her credit for. I believe she's been around the block more times than you might think."

"You could be right. And about that meeting with your dad at the diner, postpone that one as long as you can. Okay?"

"Yeah, right. Like you did this luncheon."

"I had no choice. She demanded she have an opportunity to meet the woman I'm going to marry."

"That's such a sweet way to put it," Eula said. "And guess what?"

"I'm almost afraid to ask," William replied.

"My dad is gonna expect the same thing. He's gonna want to meet the man of my dreams, to see if he's good enough for me."

"Don't remind me."

"Together, we'll find a way to make this work. We'll figure out a way to connect both worlds, and it begins today with this lunch date with Sue Ellen. And I promise, I won't say, *you gotta be shittin' me.* I'll be on my best behavior."

"What are you going to do with the flowers? I wasn't thinking about the lunch date when I picked them up."

"No problem. I'll have the waitress get me a glass of water to put them in. Remember, we're going to the Cracker Barrel, not the country club. It'll be fine."

The Beamer was quiet for a moment or two. "I have to come clean, Eula, and make a confession to you. A few weeks ago, when you were at work, I rode by your home and had every intention of stopping to introduce myself to your folks. And, oddly enough, they were outside, doing some yard work. They never noticed that I rode by several times. I'm ashamed to admit it, but you're right. I couldn't find the courage to stop. It should have been so simple, but oddly enough, I became aware of riding in the BMW and that's what's so stupid about all of this. It shouldn't matter what we drive or what kind of house we live in."

⚬◦⚬◦⚬

Eula drove across the street to the Cracker Barrel. William said Sue Ellen would probably drive her Mercedes, and sure enough, a beautiful Mercedes was parked in front of the restaurant. But no Sue Ellen.

"What the heck," Eula said out loud as she wheeled the White Charger into the empty place next to the Mercedes. "This is either going to work or it's not. End of story."

Having only met her one time, and briefly at that, Eula went into Cracker Barrel, fully expecting Sue Ellen to already be seated and waiting for her. But she wasn't. She was in the gift shop area, and looking at some of the merchandise. Glancing up and spotting Eula, she put the item she was holding back on the shelf, and immediately came to meet her.

"Finally," she said, as if it was an earth-shattering event. "I thought I would never get the opportunity to spend any time with you." She gave Eula a long hug and said, "Let's eat, I'm starving."

Fumbling for something to say, Eula asked, "Have you been waiting long?"

"Not really, only five or ten minutes. I love their gift shop and wasn't worried about the time. When I was a little girl, my mom and dad ate at Cracker Barrel all the time. Anytime we were traveling, it was always Cracker Barrel. I still have a bear I got from one of their restaurants when I was about ten years old."

The waitress picked up a couple of menus and took them to a table by the window. It wasn't crowded, which suited Eula just fine. "Eat and get out of here," she thought as she looked over the menu.

"What do you usually eat here?" she asked Sue Ellen.

"Their breakfast is my favorite, and I usually eat it no matter what time of day it is. To tell you the truth, this is like a flashback in time. There was a Cracker Barrel near the college I attended, and any time my folks came up to check on me, it was always where we ate. This is a special outing and so appropriate for our meeting."

Eula was taking mental notes and "so appropriate for our meeting" quickly registered with her.

The waitress came and took their order for two breakfasts. The prospect of eating made Eula feel like she would throw up. Nervous was not the word to describe how she felt.

Eula was smart and drop-dead beautiful. Sue Ellen, sensing how anxious she was, decided to go for the jugular and make Eula comfortable.

"Before you tell me about yourself and your family, I want to tell you about myself and my family. I think you'll be surprised and amazed at what I'm about to share with you. My father has been a truck driver his entire life, and my mother has worked in the lunchroom at Union High School for as long as I can remember. Dad still drives a truck, and she still prepares lunch for the students. They make a decent living, but it takes both of them working to do it. They pretty much live paycheck to paycheck. They drive older cars and live in a small, three-bedroom house. One of the bedrooms used to be mine, and the Cracker Barrel bear I mentioned is sitting on my old bed, even as we speak."

Eula felt the genuineness of the one-sided dialogue, and she started to relax a little. It was almost hard to believe, considering she had seen Sue Ellen's home and the Mercedes parked out front next to the White Charger. Feeling compelled to participate in the conversation she asked, "Do you ever help them, I mean, since you seem to be doing so well for yourself?"

Sue Ellen was caught a little off guard by such a direct question, but noted the legitimacy of such a thought.

"Great question. And the answer is yes I do, when they'll let me. Dad and Mom are old school and proud. Too proud sometimes, but growing up as they did made them tough— and I understand it."

Eula immediately ran *trailer-park tough* through her mind.

"I've offered many times to help them, even to buy them a new truck or car. The answer is always the same. Dad will tell me his truck is in great shape and Mom, remembering those tough times, will admonish me to be careful how much money I spend because one never knows what the future will hold. I've had their house painted, the roof replaced and central air and heat installed. They've complained with each project, telling me to hang onto my money because I might need it more than them."

"Sounds like my folks," Eula said. "They don't have a pot to pee in or a window to throw it out of, but they are God-awful proud. Too proud to accept handouts." The pot to pee in quip slipped out before she realized it, and, obviously, she couldn't call it back.

"I like that saying," Sue Ellen said. "It absolutely drives the point home. It could apply to my parents as well, and in their world they're completely happy and one can't argue with that."

Changing the subject, Eula asked, "What was your major in college and what made you so successful, if you don't mind me asking?"

"I don't mind you asking at all. But I'm not going to answer it here. We'll do that in private at my home, which, by the way, is always open to you. I want you to think about what I've told you about my parents and when we meet next week at my house, without William, I'll answer your questions and you can tell me all about your family. Fair enough?"

"Fair enough," Eula responded. "You tell me when and I'll be there."

"How about next Sunday morning, say eleven or eleven-thirty?"

"Sounds good," Eula said. "I'll definitely be there."

"My turn to ask a question," Sue Ellen said and smiled. "William tells me you're brilliant and have a work ethic second to none. What are your plans for college and what type of degree and career do you think you'll pursue?"

"I love to work with numbers, and as of right now, I'm looking at becoming a CPA, or something along those lines. Not sure exactly. Scholarship money and offers will play a huge part in my decision. I'm considering Young Harris College and the University of Georgia. I've made application to both and have sent them my transcripts. Hopefully, I'll hear soon and be able to start making plans. I also like the idea of becoming a lawyer. You know how it is. Students change their degree paths multiple times and often make wrong choices. I want to make the right choice and pick something I'll enjoy doing and something that pays well."

"They're hard decisions for sure. You only get one chance and it's very important to get it right the first time. Here comes our breakfast. This is going to be a treat for me. I shouldn't have waited so long between visits. Let's eat, and then we'll go over to the mall and see what's on sale."

"Good idea," Eula said. "I have a few hours before I have to be at the DQ."

❦❦❦

"Now what?" Juanita said, as Coach Henderson popped into her office. Smiling, she continued, "What have you done now, or maybe the better question would be, what do you want now?"

"Feel the love," Coach Henderson replied. "Gives me a warm, fuzzy feeling just seeing your name on the door."

"Stop the crap, Charlie, and sit down," Juanita said.

"You're the one who started it. I'm the innocent, abused employee here. All I wanted to ask you for was a raise, a new gym and a new scoreboard for next season. Guess the answer is no to all three."

"The answer isn't no, it's hell no. Now, what can I do for you, Charlie. You have to want something."

"Not really, I just wanted to let you know I'm having the team assemble in the gym tomorrow after school. I have two very nice invitations to extend to them, to honor them for their outstanding season this year. And I have come to extend an invitation to you and your Bob to the two upcoming events, if you think you can behave yourself in public and not embarrass me and the team."

"Me behave myself? Don't make me laugh, Charlie. It's you, not me, whose behavior might be questioned out in public. And where might these two invites take me?" she asked cautiously. "Surely not to a Christmas wrestling extravaganza," she quipped.

"No, no, I'm sure you'd like that better, but these are nice invitations. Frank Kitchens, representing the country club, and Bill Watson, from the diner, have both extended invitations. The country club is hosting the team the last Saturday evening in November and Bill's Diner on the second Saturday evening in December. Do you think this might be something you and Bob would want to attend?"

Juanita sat for a moment or two without responding.

"I learned a valuable lesson this year," she finally said. "The day I told Frank Kitchens not to let my door hit him in the butt, I figured I'd have trouble with him forever. But not so. That's what I learned and hope to remember. People can always change, even me. What happened with him?"

"An old hymn comes to mind when I think about Frank Kitchens and his son Johnny."

"What old hymn?" Juanita asked.

"*I Saw the Light,*" Coach Henderson said. "And I think he did. Can't tell you it was a God-thing, may have been. Maybe it was a humanity-thing. Who knows at this point? But the change is radical and genuine."

"A God-thing and a humanity-thing are so closely connected, they're almost inseparable," Juanita observed.

"Johnny had quite the conversion himself. He actually was the first one to cross the threshold separating the two worlds, the one he lived in and the one where Bubba Preston resided. It had a profound effect on his father. Losing the starting quarterback job humbled Johnny. Could have easily gone the other way. Could have made him mad and bitter, but it didn't. In my opinion, that's the God-part of the equation."

Juanita remembered a Bible verse and quoted part of it to the coach. "And a little child shall lead."

"Exactly, and if Johnny, the one who suffered the loss and prestige of being quarterback, could go on, how could his father not follow his son's example?"

"Are you our coach or preacher?" she asked.

"Both," Coach Henderson responded, "and I need to hold a serious revival in this office. Word has it an errant principal is in charge here."

"Oh, really," Juanita said, raising her eyebrows over her glasses. "Get out of here before I decide to put feelers out for a new coach."

"I'm gone. Let me know if you and Bob can attend either or both of the celebrations. Cindi's planning on going to both dinners."

"Will do, now git. Unlike you, I have work to do."

Coach Henderson had the office make an announcement for all football players to come to the gym immediately after the end of the school day. He was a little nervous, realizing he had to tippy-toe around some issues that shouldn't exist in the first place. "How could food be more palatable for some in a particular setting than for others?" he asked himself. The Green Valley Country Club and Bill's Diner had one thing in common—they both served excellent food that made both places a success in the community.

As the boys filed into the gym, they were laughing and joking with each other. Johnny said, "I can't wait for next year to get here. We'll win them all next time." *Hot damns* circled through the group. Bubba smiled and LJ was beside himself. The *hot damn* thing was all his, and he enjoyed hearing it.

"Have a seat, boys, I have a couple of things to run by you. Mr. Frank Kitchens, Johnny's father, has made arrangements for every one of you to come to the Green Valley Country Club at seven o'clock the last Saturday in November. They will feed you and pamper you, and it will be a very memorable experience."

An anxious thought had already gone through Bubba's mind. He envisioned a tux and all the trimmings. Neither he nor LJ owned a suit. He was fretting about it in his mind as the coach continued talking.

"As for what to wear, everyone should wear blue jeans and their jerseys. But make sure your jersey is clean!" Everyone laughed at that. "Tony Adkins from the *Herald* will be there covering the event and taking pictures for the paper."

"Can we bring our girlfriends?" someone asked.

"Not this time, boys. But you can take them there on your own some other time, and when you do just make sure you have a pocketful of money. The steaks are great and the prices reflect it. Mr. Kitchens has arranged a very nice dinner and evening out for the team. Be sure and thank him. Now, remember, it's the last Saturday evening in November at seven o'clock."

When the cheers had died down, the coach said, "Now for the second great announcement. Bill Watson, owner of Bill's Diner, has also extended a celebration invitation to all of you. It will be the second Saturday in December, two weeks before Christmas. It will also begin at seven o'clock. My wife and I eat there all the time, and Bill has the best food on the planet. He will probably have a buffet with a Christmas theme for the desserts. His banana pudding would win first place in any contest it was entered in. Banana pudding is always appropriate, regardless of the season. Again, wear your jeans and jerseys. Tony Adkins from the *Herald* will also be there, same as at the country club. The principal, her husband and my wife will also be in attendance. Mind your manners and act like civilized people. And remember to thank Bill for his hospitality."

Stomping went throughout the bleachers and someone started chanting, "We're civilized people, we're civilized people."

Coach Henderson smiled, gave them a moment to have fun, and then said, "All right, guys, knock it off. I want to finish this up and get out of here. Bill has graciously said each of you can bring one person to dinner. Bring your girlfriend or your mama. Bill doesn't care. I want to thank each of you for a great season and great memories. Mr. Kitchens and the country club and Bill Watson from the diner want to say thanks to each of you. Show your appreciation at each event and make your mama proud. Now, get out of here, go home and study."

∽∾∽∾∽∾

With McClain's on a four-day workweek, Bubba had Fridays off. He felt a chill in the air and wondered how much the temperature had dropped during the night. The last thing on his mind before he fell asleep was William Morgan, Jr. He had to stop thinking about it. The die was cast, and there was no way to call it off. "Eula would have come without him," he thought, "so why did I have to include him?" Once again, he found himself the *hootie tootie warrior*. He had lost a lot of his inferiority complex during the football season. Dressing quickly and quietly, he made coffee and looked out the kitchen window. A light dusting of snow covered the deck and yard, making it look cold and wintry.

The place was beautiful. Granny Preston would have been so proud. He had found a spot for every one of her Christmas decorations, either inside or outside. The only thing left to do was cut the tree the day before Christmas Eve. He was as ready as he could get. Granny always liked to put up her decorations several weeks before Christmas and save the decorating of the tree for Christmas Eve. Bubba would continue the tradition and hand it down to his children.

He had set aside some money for the party and planned to grill some venison steaks, hamburgers and baby back ribs. He was taking care of the meats and his mother, with Eula's mother volunteering to help, would take care of the sides and desserts. The older guys would probably drink a beer or two and the women a glass of wine. Sweet tea and hot cider would be available as well. Clarice's mom had promised to bring one of her soon to be famous banana puddings. She said it was just a simple recipe from the vanilla wafer box, but some magic took place somewhere, turning it into a wonderful favorite of everyone.

Putting on his coat, sock hat and gloves, Bubba quietly lifted his dad's deer rifle from the gun rack and slipped out the front door. Their property bordered U.S. Forestry property, and he and LJ often hunted behind their trailer. The brisk air was exhilarating and made him temporarily forget his issues, real or imagined, with his upcoming Christmas party. Walking to one of his deer stands, he climbed into the stand, dusted the snow off the boards, and sat down. "What a beautiful morning," he thought. About the time he settled in and got quiet, three does walked the ridgeline directly in front of him. He had brought his rifle but had no intention of taking a deer. They walked a step or two, stopped, sniffed the air, and then took another few steps. He was downwind from them, and they didn't pick up his scent. About the time they went over the ridge, an eight or nine-point buck stepped out of the woods and followed the ridgeline the does had taken.

"Coward," Bubba thought. "Sent them out first. Oughta shoot you for that, but I'm giving you an early Christmas present. Go catch up with the girls and enjoy another Christmas. But watch out. LJ will be hunting these woods, and he won't give you a pass. This one's for Granny Preston. She said to tell you, Go in Peace."

For some reason, he had started to process and compare what the differences must be between his home and William's home. Bubba didn't realize, that for the most part, William actually lived with Sue Ellen Thornton. That could have made it worse. Everyone knew Old Man Morgan lived up on top of the hill behind those fancy, electronic gates. But few of the townsfolk had ever seen his mansion. On the other hand, lots of people, including Bubba and Clarice, had driven by Sue Ellen's home to see her decorations at Christmas. It was a mansion in its own right. Had he known William lived there, the reality of having actually seen the home would have caused him even more angst.

The cedar tree he had picked out was about six feet tall. That was the maximum height you could have in the trailer and still put Granny Preston's angel on top. Bubba had no way of knowing it, but Mr. Morgan had the same company come out to his mansion every year and deliver and install his tree. The only requirement Mr. Morgan had was the height. He liked for it to reach the third floor, so when guests, either friends or business acquaintances, came out of their rooms, they would be looking at the tree topper. The tree was the focal point of his decorations. To accomplish this, the tree had to be thirty feet tall.

Mr. Morgan spent well over fifteen thousand dollars annually in decorating the main bank, the three bank branches and his private estate. Of course, he wrote it off as a business expense. That's why he had guests, aka business associates and customers, over to the mansion for Christmas parties. He would host two parties this Christmas, mainly for business associates, then he and Marsha would fly to London to spend their first Christmas in their new home there.

The same company also decorated Sue Ellen's tree and home, though she didn't want everything to be as lavish as it was at Mr. Morgan's. Her tree was only about ten feet tall, and the average expense was around two thousand dollars. She had the company place a beautiful Nativity scene on her lawn. Lots of townspeople drove by her house to see the Nativity scene. For her, it was a tribute to her two dear friends, Sister Cass and Sister Francis. Others in her neighborhood also put up elaborate Christmas decorations. A steady procession of vehicles came by every night during the Christmas season to see the homes. Mr. Morgan also picked up the tab for Sue Ellen's holiday decorations. After all, his son would spend Christmas, as usual, with Sue Ellen.

While Bubba was sitting in a deer stand worrying about William coming to the Christmas party in his humble home, he wasn't the only one fretting over it. William, lying in his king-size bed, and enjoying the comfort of expensive sheets, was thinking about the party as well. While he didn't know what to expect at his first party in a mobile home, he knew he had fallen in love with the driver of the White Charger. In his heart, he believed everything would work out okay. Sue Ellen's number-one rule would be in effect—"Everything will work itself out, if you give it time."

Bubba climbed down from the deer stand. He was cold but had a warm feeling in his heart. One of Granny Preston's favorite sayings from her Bible came to mind, giving him a little relief. "Love God with all your heart and love your neighbor as yourself." William Morgan, Jr. was his neighbor. Bubba smiled. "You're right, Granny, he's my neighbor, but you ain't seen his house."

It seemed like a running dialogue with someone on the other side. "I know, Bubba, but remember this. He puts his pants on just like you do."

That made him smile. "I know, Granny, one leg at a time."

✿✿✿

Christmas, a time to celebrate the birth of Christ, had taken on a whole different perspective in Blairsville.

From fretting over it lying between expensive sheets, to freezing to death worrying about it in a deer stand, neither William nor Bubba had anything on Bill Watson. This part of the Watson family had a work ethic to envy. He worked seven days a week and hadn't taken a vacation since he opened the restaurant.

Bill, a former employee of McClain's, had risked it all to start his restaurant. He built his business serving food the local people loved. Fried chicken, country fried steak, fresh mountain trout, hamburger steak and pork chops were his main entrees. Fresh local vegetables, when in season, were staples. His sweet tea, with a butt-load of sugar in it, was the favorite drink for most of his customers. In Bill's mind, a large hamburger steak, two sides of your choice, a homemade roll or cornbread, banana pudding and sweet tea was food for the gods. "Country club, my ass," he told his waitresses. "I'll show them country club."

But the Green Valley Country Club had first crack at the football team. Most of the team ate there on a regular basis with their parents. Very few had ever come to the diner.

Whenever he expressed his concern, his wife Sherry would say, "Honey, it's not a competition. You're not trying to outdo the country club. You're being generous and offering something really nice to the boys who played their hearts out this year. That's all. Just be yourself and let the diner do what it always does—serve some of the best food in the state. It's not about trying to one up the country club. They're doing something nice for the boys as well. And you're even letting the boys bring one guest with them. You've done good. Let it go at that."

The diner definitely had local flavor. The concrete floor had been painted, but hundreds of steps every day had created what looked like beaten pathways to the tables. The walls were covered with plaques customers had brought in from everywhere. Whenever someone went on vacation and saw some cute or sassy saying, they would buy it and give it to Bill. He would proudly hang it somewhere in the diner. You could sit for an hour and never finish reading all the plaques and signs; some philosophical, some borderline profane. Inside the diner, tiny white Christmas lights ran around the top of the walls and added atmosphere. They were left up year round and the customers seemed to like them.

Every Christmas, in addition to painting the windows with Christmas scenes and characters, Bill would remove a corner table and put up a Christmas tree. He headed up a huge annual toy drive in conjunction with the local sheriff's department. A twenty dollar toy would get you a one-time fifty-percent discount on a meal. Bubba and LJ always bought a toy and dropped it off at the restaurant. Several truckloads of toys would be collected, making Christmas memorable for the children in the impoverished areas of the county. It gave emphasis to community, people with little, giving to those who have even less.

The church crowd overwhelmed the diner staff on Sundays. Bill gave a fifteen-percent discount, per family, if they brought their church bulletin. He jokingly told customers some only went to church to get the bulletin, because he could tell church wasn't helping them a bit. Those churches with long-winded preachers would cause their members to arrive late, and they would have to take a number. The Methodists always got there first. Apparently, none of their pastors were long-winded. The Pentecostals were always late and claimed they had food to eat the Methodists and Baptists didn't know about. All in all, the customers were friendly and enjoyed sharing food and good times together.

Bill proudly displayed an American flag in one of the front windows. This particular window was never decorated by the local artist at Christmastime. It was there to honor his and Sherry's son, who had lost his life in Afghanistan, serving his country. A picture of their son, his family he left behind, and the medals he was awarded posthumously, for saving members of his platoon, were also on display.

There was a counter in front of the kitchen that could seat ten customers. These stools were occupied by seniors who came on a regular basis and who analyzed the daily news each morning. You might think you knew what was happening and why, but after hearing their analysis, you might leave the diner with a different perspective about what was really going on in your town, your country and the world. Bill loved every one of them like family and usually would not charge them for coffee in the mornings. The community loved Bill and his diner.

"You're right, Sherry," Bill said, as he walked into the diner's tiny office. God has blessed us with a good business and given us what we need with some to spare. It's not a competition, and I'll not make it one. I hope they enjoy the country club party." Smiling, he told her and one of the waitresses standing close by, "God's good. He's saving the best for last."

⋘⋙ ⋘⋙ ⋘⋙

Bubba, pulling into the Ingle's parking lot, saw Eula's truck. She was sitting in it and there was an empty parking space right next to her. Wheeling Maude in beside the White Charger, he got out and walked around to her door.

"What are you doing at Ingle's, Bubba?" she asked, as she let her window down. It was cold and she still had the truck running. "Come around and get in. It's too cold to stand outside." Hustling around the old pickup, he jerked the door open and climbed into the cab.

"Mama needed some baking stuff for some Thanksgiving goodies, and Dad has a bad cold. So, here I am, doing grocery shopping. I'm abused, what can I say?"

"Yeah, you look abused. Poor pitiful Bubba, having to do grocery shopping. Y'all doing anything big for Thanksgiving this year?"

"Not really. We've pretty much been focusing on Christmas and the party to remember Granny. I think Uncle Luke and his wife will probably eat Thanksgiving dinner with us, but that's about it. The pastor and his wife might drop in."

"But how about your family?" he asked.

"Same here," Eula said. "I've been so busy I haven't even bought Christmas presents yet for Mom and Dad. Gotta find time to get that done for sure. It seems like a long time until Christmas, but with working and going to school, the time will fly by quickly."

"I'm glad I ran into you. I have a question for you. I know more than you think, and from what I see and hear about you and William, it's quite a serious romantic fling. And that's okay with me. It's your business, and if it makes you happy, then I'm happy for you."

"Well, I'm relieved to know it's okay with you. If it's not, I'll stop seeing him immediately. I wouldn't want to do something my big Bubba doesn't approve of."

"Easy, easy, I'm just messing with you."

"Don't mess with that. It's a touchy subject at the moment. Why did you bring it up?"

"Well, I invited you and William to my Christmas Eve get-together, and though I'm trying hard not to worry about it, I have a hard time with the richest kid in three states coming to our party. I know you think it's just *hootie tootie* syndrome, but you can't tell me you don't feel it, too. I was wondering if it might help things if you and William arrived a little early, giving us time to get to know him and giving him some time to acclimate to the trailer before all the other guests arrive."

Trying to play devil's advocate, she said defensively, "I think you're worrying about nothing. My old truck is a far worse ride than his BMW, and William's perfectly at home in my truck."

A smile crept across Bubba's face.

Seeing it, Eula asked, "And what do you find so funny about that?"

"Your old truck, as you call it, has a perk his BMW doesn't have. What do you say to that, Eula Johnson?"

"I'll answer your question with a question, Bubba Preston. Do you want to walk away from this conversation or crawl away from it? Choice is yours."

"Easy, easy. Boy, you're touchy. Strike that last remark. You're not touchy, you're, you're . . ."

"Just put a cork in it, Bubba. You have no room to talk. At least we don't sneak into my mom and dad's home while they're working at McClain's."

Taking a deep breath, Bubba smiled and said, "Didn't think anyone had noticed that. Hmm?"

"Only a fool wouldn't have picked up on it. Leaving school at Mach I speed and heading to her house two and three times a week is a dead giveaway."

"For all you know, we're in a hurry so we can study together before I have to go to work."

"Study, my ass. Scratch that, wrong pronoun. Her ass, not mine. Now, there's an English lesson for you—pronouns."

A brief moment of silence followed the exchange, with each one seemingly lost in their respective thoughts.

"I gotta go," Eula said, breaking the silence. "The DQ's calling, and you have to pick up those things for your mama." In an unprecedented move, she extended her hand to him. When he took it, she pulled him close and gave him a long and much-needed hug. "Love you, Bubba," she whispered in his ear.

"I know," he responded, "and you know I love you." Bubba was a super-sensitive individual with a tough exterior. He hoped she didn't notice his eyes watering. Looking for an out, he said, "These damn allergies are killing me."

"Allergies, my ass," she replied and smiled. "You just ain't as tough as LJ and the rest of your friends think you are. You've got everyone fooled. That is, everyone but me."

"Another English lesson. Allergies, your ass is the correct choice of pronouns," he said and smiled that winsome smile. "I'm out of here. Bring the Beamer a little early to my Christmas party, if you don't mind. Do it for me, your semi-reformed, *hootie tootie warrior.*"

✺✺✺

Bubba's "Bring the Beamer a little early" request made sense. It was a world of difference they were all trying to embrace. Thinking about it could help make it easier. Eula already had Sunday morning scheduled. She would be going over to Sue Ellen's for brunch and the private conversation they couldn't have at Cracker Barrel. As she sat in the mall parking lot, waiting for the Beamer, she laid out her own plans for this Saturday morning.

"Here he comes," she noted, looking at her watch. "Right on time."

Parking next to the White Charger, he hurried around to the passenger door, jerked it open, and climbed in. "Good morning, sweet thing," Eula said as he leaned over and gave her a kiss. "Boy, do I have something special in mind for you today."

"All right," he responded enthusiastically.

"Sorry to burst your bubble, Beamer, that's not on the schedule for this morning."

"Shucks," he said, trying to be country. "Mother always said life would hold disappointments."

"Get out of here, Beamer. You wouldn't know a disappointment if one walked up and bit you on the butt."

"If something bit me on the butt, be it a disappointment or a bull moose, I think I'd know it, thank you very much."

"I'll give you the bull moose, maybe. This morning we're going up to Franklin."

"We do that almost every Saturday morning. What's special about breakfast in Franklin?"

"It's not the breakfast that's special, it's what we do after breakfast."

"Now, I'm almost afraid to ask what it is." He opened the door and pretended he was thinking about getting out of the White Charger.

"Get your butt back in my truck and shut the door. Okay, here goes. You're about to get an education regarding how the rest of us live in Blairsville. After breakfast, we're going to look at some mobile homes at Southern Mobile Home Sales in Franklin. They have single-wides and double-wides, both new and used. I really do think it's a good idea for you to educate yourself in this area— of what shall I call it—diminished living space. What say you to our Saturday morning outing, Mr. William Henry Morgan, Jr?"

"I think you're absolutely right, Miss Eula Alyson Johnson. I think I need to know what I'm walking into before I step through the door of Bubba's home. I was in the Boy Scouts, you know. Actually made Eagle Scout."

"What on earth does the Boy Scouts have to do with this?" she asked in amazement.

"Our motto, of course, *Be Prepared*. Believe me, I've run this party through my mind a thousand times. We, that's you and me, in case you're wondering, have to pull this one off, so that everyone accepts me the same way you do. They have to see in me what you saw. And me being caught off guard when I walk into Bubba's home will show in my face and expressions. I have to get this one right. And I will, I promise. So, it's to Southern Mobile Home Sales we go. But not until we have breakfast."

"You won't do, Beamer. I hope they see something in you. I'm starting to have second thoughts myself."

"I guess you could say that I'm practicing for an engagement with the other side. Guess what? You also need to be practicing for an engagement with the other side. Meeting Sue Ellen on neutral ground at Cracker Barrel was one thing. Her home is something else. Sue Ellen is your Bubba on steroids. And you can't walk in and say something like *holy shit,* how many bathrooms do you have?' You must promise me you won't use your favorite saying, *you gotta be shittin' me.* I also had a plan to help you deal with your upcoming visit. But, oh no, y'all went and scheduled it for tomorrow, and I can't get you over to my parents' home for a walk-through. Perhaps we could call up some real estate people in Franklin and ask them to show us some multimillion-dollar homes. But that call would pose a problem."

"And what might the problem be? Please enlighten me."

"Well, to tell you the truth, we're sitting in it. Can you imagine a real estate person taking the two of us out to some mansion in the White Charger?"

"Good point. We would need to be in your car to pull that one off."

⤜∞⤏ ⤜∞⤏ ⤜∞⤏

Sue Ellen had become accustomed to spending Saturday mornings alone. William was up and gone by 8:30 every Saturday morning and it would be after lunch before he returned. Because of past experience, she knew the signs and to echo Eula's sentiments regarding Bubba and Clarice, she was afraid William and Eula might be taking liberties they shouldn't.

Considering her own behavior when she was young, how could she possibly criticize anyone?

It had turned cold early for November, and Old Man Winter had already delivered a couple of light dustings of snow. Sitting in her den, Sue Ellen had a clear view of the landscape behind her home. Several deer were crossing the back of the property and squirrels were already out, scampering around, feverishly looking for nuts and frequenting her bird feeders way too often.

"You wanted this, and it's coming like a freight train," she said to herself. "Eula will be here tomorrow and just what am I going to tell her about myself, my mistakes, my conversion at Saint Mary's, and about William, her betrothed and my son? Maybe I'll tell her all of it, or none of it. I don't know how much is enough or too much."

Taking another sip of her coffee, she sighed. "How did life get so complicated?" Her den had twelve-foot ceilings, and expensive paintings, once valued highly by her, peered down at a woman in crisis. Looking at the people in the portraits gave her no consolation. On her desk, across the room, were some photographs that would. Taking her coffee with her, she moved from her recliner to the desk.

On her desk were pictures of Sister Cass, Sister Francis and Father Rodriquez. A picture of Saint Mary's was centered on the wall above the desk. William had inquired many times about the photos. "Who are these people? What is that building?" Her answer was always the same. "Someday, when the time is right, I may tell you about these people. Or I may not." She would always smile when she said it.

On the corner of her desk was a picture of Jesus. Sister Cass had given it to her as a keepsake when she left Saint Mary's. Bowing her head, she prayed, "Lord, I have a problem and need

Your help. Let me find the words to convey to Eula what would be pleasing to You and helpful to her. Thank you for loving me and for changing my life and for helping me to see others and situations as You see them. For Your forgiveness and blessings, I give You thanks. *Amen and Amen."*

Across town, behind some very fancy gates, Mr. Morgan was also sitting at his desk. He continued to support Saint Mary's because Sue Ellen insisted on it. For him, it was a tax deduction, pure and simple. If it helped the hospital, fine. He needed deductions and this worked for him and kept Sue Ellen happy.

His only real tie to Saint Mary's was their son, of whom he saw very little. He still valued having a flesh-and-blood heir, knowing he wouldn't be around forever. The same Jesus who healed little William and forgave his mother at the same time was still waiting on Mr. William Morgan, Sr. to come to the foot of the Cross. But that wasn't on Mr. Morgan's mind this morning. He was going through some financial statements. "How much is enough?" someone might ask. For Mr. Morgan, "Just a little bit more" was always his reply to that question. It was the mantra he lived by.

But just a little bit more doesn't buy companionship. It buys expensive paintings and mansions to put them in. It buys fancy gates and electronic security systems to hide behind. It buys European vacation homes. But the thing it buys the most is loneliness and isolation.

The ride to Franklin had become their standard Saturday

morning excursion. It was about a fifty-mile drive and repre-sented a safe zone for their outings. They had two favorite break-fast places, the Country Kitchen and Louise's Family Restaurant. Southern Mobile Home Sales was directly in front of Louise's. So, this Saturday, they would eat at Louise's and peruse the sales lot from their table by the window.

"Good morning," the waitress said as the Beamer and Eula walked through the door. "Good to see you again."

"Good morning, Lisa," William responded and smiled. "Could we have the table by the center window, please ma'am?"

"Sure thing. Just follow me, please." While the waitress stood by their table, they both ordered coffee and their usual breakfast. They had eaten there so many times, a menu wasn't necessary. As soon as the waitress walked away, the introduction to mobile homes began by Eula Johnson, narrator and unpaid sales rep for Southern Mobile Home Sales.

"I'm gonna keep this simple, Beamer, and assume you know nothing about mobile homes. So, while it might sound elementary, it is in fact just that. See those narrow, skinny ones? They're called single-wides. Those twice as large are called—jump right in here, Beamer."

"Double-wides," he added.

"Wow, a fast study in mobile homes. I'm impressed."

"No, you're not. You're being sarcastic and you need to do better. Remember, this is for both of us, and don't forget, your time's coming. Introductory Mansion Studies 101."

"Don't remind me," Eula said. "Now, pay attention. Notice the different lengths. Obviously, the double-wides and the longer ones cost more money. Also, some come with a list of upgrades you can choose from, like nicer furnishings and a better grade of building materials."

"The furniture comes with them?" William asked with a surprised look on his face.

"Right. Most of them are completely furnished. The more you pay, the better the quality of furniture, appliances and construction overall. They're like anything else. You can get them with bells and whistles or plain Jane models. The choice is yours and depends on your bank account. Notice the big sign out front. *Nothing Down with Approved Credit*. The average person shopping for a mobile home may have decent credit, but little or no cash on hand. They finance for up to twenty years and trust me on this one, they haven't made a trailer yet that will outlast a twenty year mortgage."

"Then why would anyone go in debt for one if they know it's a bad choice?" he asked.

"You just used the key word—choice. The average person stopping in to look around the lot doesn't usually have much choice in the matter. It's the best they can do and, quite honestly, they are usually very happy and excited with their purchase and delivery."

"They deliver?"

"How else do you think the customer could get something that large to the lot they're going to put it on? Of course, they deliver and set them up. They have to place blocks under them, level them, and tie them down with strapping and restraint rods to help them withstand storms."

"Wow," William said. "You sure you haven't worked at Southern before?"

"No, but I have lived in one and seen many bought and delivered to family members and friends over my short lifetime."

She glanced up. "Here comes our food, which ends your lesson for now. I'm starving. We'll eat and then drive over. I'll tell the sales rep, who will attack us the minute we drive up, that we're graduating this spring and are getting married and that we just want to look around at what they have and see what we might be able to afford. That's a surefire way to get you the grand tour."

"And, if I had my way," the Beamer said, "that's exactly what would happen. We'd get married, go to work and school, and make a lot of hard, but great, memories to share with our kids."

"Sounds like a plan, but right now we have to eat, go mobile home shopping, and then ride back to Blairsville so I can be at the DQ by four this afternoon. And I haven't told you this, but I have to go straight home after work because . . ."

"You have to be over at Sue Ellen's at eleven tomorrow, right?"

"Right. Now eat, so we can go over to Southern and pretend to be future mobile home customers."

⟡⟡⟡

When Eula and the Beamer first started meeting in the mall parking lot, the news spread like wildfire. Most people assumed the worst—just a young rich boy taking advantage of an impoverished young girl. They had no idea what had really happened or how serious the relationship actually was.

Sue Ellen had also experienced a tainted reputation years earlier, especially after she moved in with William Morgan. Her affair with a man almost twice her age was now a generation-plus removed, and all but forgotten. Her parents had bitterly disapproved, but to no avail. She had set her goal for success and didn't care what anyone said about her, not even her mom and dad. And the fatality she was accused of was never mentioned.

Mr. Morgan lived in Blairsville, but his financial empire prevented community participation. Sue Ellen was very efficient and professional when it came to running the bank. Over time, she had gathered a staff around her who was highly efficient and loyal, allowing her all the free time she could have ever wanted or needed. Mr. Morgan gave her flexibility, and he had a short list of only two things that required her to notify him immediately. One was any banking inquiries from the regulators, and the second one revolved around any pending foreclosures because of failure to make payments. He knew she was soft on people experiencing financial difficulties, and he viewed repossessions as opportunities to sell property again and again.

"Remember," he would always say, "they agreed to the terms and were happy to get them. They should pay on time as agreed or realize there are consequences to being sorry and good-for-nothing." She couldn't dispute the basic tenets of his argument. If the bank was run on compassion, it would fail quickly. She disagreed with his analysis that those who made late payments were sorry and good-for-nothing. But that was classic Morgan.

Even at the country club, he usually reserved private seating, either for himself or for Marsha, if she happened to be in town. He rarely took time to enjoy a round of golf, and even when he did, most of the people he called friends wouldn't have brought up his son's apparent involvement with a girl from the trailer park. He had heard tidbits of gossip regarding William's dilly-dallying around, but laughed it off privately, remembering his younger days when he thought himself a stud.

One evening at the club, over dinner, one of his oldest and closest business associates finally got up the courage to mention it to him. "I'm sure you've heard by now, or perhaps have seen for yourself, your young William is creating quite a bit of gossip over the girl he's seeing. I'm sure he's just sowing a few wild oats in an easy field."

"Got a name?" Morgan asked. "Or any idea who she is or where she comes from?"

"Yeah, I asked one of my kids about it, and he had all the info. Seems to be common knowledge, and William has been seeing her for quite a while. Her name is Eula Johnson and her folks are second-and third-generation workers down at McClain's. They live in a trailer in the mobile home park on Upper Hightower. Most of the time when I see her, she's driving a beat-up old Chevy truck, and for what it's worth, I've seen your son in it a number of times. I thought you'd like to know."

"Just damn," Mr. Morgan told his friend. "I appreciate the info. I'm sure William's having a ball with what's her name and playing a little grab-ass like we both used to do. Nothing to it, I assure you. He's not stupid, just young and dumb." They both had a good laugh, and the conversation went back to a business venture they were starting up.

After dinner, he went home but couldn't shake what his friend had shared with him. His son was not like him and he knew it. "Better look into this and make sure there's nothing more than sowing wild oats. The last thing I want is some slut getting her hooks into Junior and ultimately into me." He made a mental note to have Sue Ellen look into this Eula what's her name and give him an update.

✦✧✦✧✦✧

Eula was right in her assertion about the mobile home sales rep. Before they got out of her truck, a salesman was on his way to meet them.

"Good morning!" he said, smiling big. "My name is Tony, Tony Green. Would the two of you be interested in a new or a used modular home this morning?"

"Neither, this morning," the Beamer said on cue. "However,

in the spring, after we graduate, Mr. and Mrs. Morgan would very much be interested in a double-wide. Would you have a few minutes to show us around or could we look on our own?"

"Just call me Tony, and your first names are?"

"Henry and Alyson," William said, using their middle names.

"Here's my card, let me show you a couple of deals we have today, and then I'll let the two of you sorta wander around and browse on your own. How does that sound?"

"Perfect," Alyson said, "and in about five or six months, we'll be back to see you. Do you have another card so we both can have one? That way we'll be sure and ask for you when we come back."

"Yes, ma'am. Here's a card for you as well."

After showing them the single-wide and the double-wide specials of the week, he did as he said. Telling them all the modular homes were open, and they were welcome to look around as long or as short a time as they liked, he left to go greet another couple pulling into the sales lot.

Eula and William had both been spot on. She knew he had no idea how small a modular unit really was compared to his home or Sue Ellen's. But he was right as well. Spending an hour or so, going in and out of different models, would allow him to walk into Bubba Preston's home and look perfectly comfortable in that environment.

After looking at several single-wides and two double-wides, Eula asked, "So, what do you think?"

"They look very nice and smell like a new car," he responded. "But I have to admit, I'm shocked at how small they seem. Even the largest ones seem confining and a little cramped for space."

"They're definitely different from a regular home," Eula said. "I've spent my entire life living in one and to me it's as much home as your home is to you. Most of my family and friends live in them as well. Isn't it funny how that works?"

They exited one unit and were walking toward another. "I have to admit, I can't imagine living in a space as small as we've seen here today. But if I had grown up in one, I would probably be just as awe-struck walking into a large home with thirty-foot ceilings."

The comment about thirty-foot ceilings got Eula's attention. "What house do you know that has thirty-foot ceilings?" she asked in amazement.

"Our home has thirty-foot ceilings in the main entrance. There are three floors and each floor has ten-foot ceilings. The main entrance is open all the way up to the third floor. As a matter of fact, Dad insists on a thirty-foot-tall Christmas tree every year so his guests on the third floor can eyeball the angel on top of our tree."

"How do you get up to the third floor without being exhausted? I'd need an elevator," Eula said.

"Well, there's a spiral staircase wrapping around the entrance hall going to each floor. But there's also an elevator." William knew it was coming and it did.

"You gotta be shittin' me!" she said with utter disbelief on her face. "A thirty-foot Christmas tree? A spiral staircase and an elevator! *You gotta be—"*

"Enough," he said and laughed. "I get it—"

They had entered a double-wide and were in the master bedroom. William, looking at the king-size mattress, raised his eyebrows and said, "Now that would be an improvement over the White Charger."

"Surely you jest, Beamer. We can't do it here. Someone might walk in and how would we explain that?"

"We could tell them we're just trying out the mattress," he said and smiled. "We want to make sure it's a good one."

Still reeling over a thirty-foot Christmas tree, Eula had to ask, "Where does your dad get a tree that tall around here and how do you put it up and decorate it?"

"It's no big deal to my father. He has the same company come in every year and decorate the bank, the branches and our home. The tree comes from a specialty tree farm, and the crew delivering it also does the decorating. It takes them several days to complete the tree and the decorations. When Christmas is over, they come back and take it all down. It's not a traditional family trimming of the tree. It's not a Hallmark thing, it's a money thing and, sadly, not a good thing. The guests he invites over during Christmas are business related, and the thirty-foot Christmas tree does exactly what Dad wants it to do. The guests are impressed and wowed over the height of the tree. We have no family who comes to our home for Christmas, and for that reason I spend Christmas with Sue Ellen."

"Well, this Christmas will be different. Bubba will put up a small tree and we'll all take turns hanging decorations on it. Don't worry, just do what I do and you'll have a good time. Bubba's a good guy."

⤜∽⤛⤜∽⤛⤜∽⤛

Bill had worried and fretted over the upcoming Christmas party at his diner so much that his wife and staff were about ready to have him committed.

"I just want everything to be good and enjoyable for the team. We've never done anything like this before, and we don't even have a complete head count. What if we don't have enough food, or worse yet, what if no one shows up?"

Sherry, his wife, asked him a simple question. "Bill, can you give me just one reason why the boys wouldn't show up for a free meal and a good time? You're even allowing them to bring a girlfriend or a guest of their choosing. The country club isn't even allowing that. Come on, Bill, it'll be fine and you know it."

He posted a sign telling his regulars that the diner would be closing on the second Saturday in December at four o'clock and proudly hosting their own Union High Cougars for a dinner party at seven. The regulars thanked him for showing community spirit, especially during the busy Christmas season.

His staff would have to hustle, but he had already given them a liberal Christmas bonus and they'd make it happen. The stage was set, and in Bill's mind, the party was bearing down on them like a tornado on a trailer park.

⁕⁕⁕⁕⁕⁕

Eula tossed and turned all night. Modular Homes Introduction 101 had been good for the Beamer. Mansion Homes Introduction 101 would begin its first class at eleven AM. She was terrified at the prospect of having to spend three or four hours with Sue Ellen Thornton, executive assistant to William Morgan, Sr. She had no idea what to expect. It seemed a little bit like an interview to see if she could pass the test in order to proceed with the Beamer's proposal of marriage. Maybe so, maybe not.

As she put on her makeup, she looked into the mirror and said out loud, "Are you crazy, or what? How could someone with a father who has a company deliver and decorate a thirty-foot Christmas tree possibly think he could marry someone who can barely get a six-foot tree in their trailer? This is insane at best."

She had already told her parents she wouldn't be going to church with them. They were about to leave when her mom came into Eula's bedroom and gave her a hug.

"Everything okay?" she asked as she gave her a kiss on her cheek. "You seem a little stressed, and I thought I heard you talking to yourself again."

Eula laughed. "You did indeed, Mom. I'm taking after you and Dad. Sometimes the only conversation I have that makes any sense is the one I have with myself. You ever feel that way?"

"All the time, honey. Your father can't hear half of what I say to him. Might as well be talking to myself. Don't mean to be aggravating you, but your dad heard you had a boy friend, that Morgan boy, I think he said. I told him when you got ready for us to meet someone you were serious about you'd bring him home. You know anyone who's important to you is always welcome here. Anyway, gotta run. Your dad's in the truck and ready to go to church. Be careful, and we love you very much."

"I know, Mom. I've been seeing William Morgan, Jr., the son of the man who owns City Bank & Trust. It's serious, but not serious enough to be concerned at this time. I'm going over for lunch with Sue Ellen Thornton, Mr. Morgan's executive assistant at the bank. William is a wonderful person, and Sue Ellen seems to be the same way. She's different, somehow. If I had to compare her to someone, it would be Granny Preston. There's something special, maybe even spiritual, about her. Can't put my finger on it, but she's different in a good sort of way. Anyway, not to worry, Mom. Nothing's going to happen any time soon. I don't graduate until spring and he's off to college in the fall. We both have to finish school first. There's a good chance you'll meet him at Bubba's Christmas party. Are y'all going to his party to honor Granny Preston's memory?"

"I think so, or at least your father mentioned going. Maybe we'll meet him then. Gotta go. Your dad just blew the horn and we'll be late for church."

She hugged Eula again and hurried out the door.

Eula wasn't the only one in a lurch over the brunch. The young man in question, also known as the Beamer, had already been given his marching orders.

"Be out of here by ten o'clock and do not, I repeat, do not come back home before four o'clock."

"And just where do you want me to go?" he asked Sue Ellen.

"Go home and visit for six hours," she said and laughed, "and then get your butt back over here to our house."

"Go home" did sound funny. How long had it been since he spent six hours at his father's house?

"I'm sure Dad's off buying some distressed property some-where, and I know Mom's at the house in England."

"Then visit Edward and Melba for a little while. They love you like you're their own son and they'd really enjoy having you visit for a while, especially with your parents gone."

Sue Ellen had prayed about it several times and had definitely over thought it. Eula, with the White Charger tooling up Sue Ellen's driveway for the third time, could feel the tension coursing through her body.

Sue Ellen had come up with an ingenious plan to relieve some of the anxiety both of them were experiencing. Together, they would start at the beginning, where one had to wait their turn to use the bathroom, not choose from one of five.

Hearing the old truck rumbling up her drive, she took a deep breath and prayed. "Lord, I put this in your hands and I want Your will to be done. If it's Your will for these two young people to be together, then work out the vast social differences. Help us to relax and listen to the Holy Spirit. *Amen and Amen.*"

When Eula cut off the engine in her truck, a quiet settled over the place much like what a ceasefire would do on a battlefront. The silence was broken when she slammed the door on the White

Charger. Before she had rounded the front of the truck, two drops of black motor oil had fallen on the beautiful driveway.

Eula walked up the sidewalk through the bonsai garden. Sue Ellen was standing inside with her back to the door, looking more like a police officer expecting a breech in security. The doorbell rang and once again the portal between two worlds opened.

Sue Ellen stepped outside and greeted her warmly. "Good morning, Eula," she said, and gave her a hug. "So glad we're finally getting together at my house. It's been way too long in the making."

Eula, expecting to be invited in, was surprised when Sue Ellen turned and locked the door. Facing Eula, she said, "I've given this a lot of thought and also said a lot of prayers concerning our get-together. I know how you feel, because I feel it, too. And William, bless his heart, is counting on both of us to get this right."

"Yes, ma'am," Eula responded to her honesty, "I agree."

"There's no need for 'yes, ma'am.' It makes me feel old," she said and laughed. "This morning we will take a little trip down memory lane. Introducing you to my world from that perspective will answer a lot of questions you may have, help you relax, and also help you to view the two worlds on an equal footing. I'm going to walk you through a lifetime of mistakes. If I could have a do-over, I'd do things differently. I want to tell you about a miraculous transformation allowing me to see the world through a different lens. And, guess what? You have to look through that same lens. If we don't use the spiritual eyes given to us by the Lord, then we'll allow possessions and money to separate us forever. And that's what William and you are up against: worldly eyes looking at possessions instead of your hearts. Enough preaching. Are you ready for this? Let's get out of here. Do you mind if we go in your truck?"

"Oh, not at all, if you're sure that's what you want to do."

"Oh, I want to," Sue Ellen responded. "As a matter of fact, it's necessary to make this work."

Eula said, "You'll have to excuse my old truck. It's . . ."

"Stop that, Eula," she said, placing a hand on her shoulder. "Excuses and comparisons need to be left here in the driveway and not picked back up again. Consider your truck transportation. Good enough for you and absolutely good enough for me. And guess what? There are many in our community who would love to own the White Charger."

"How did you know his name?" Eula asked, laughing out loud. It sounded so funny to hear someone else call him the White Charger, other than herself or William.

"I named him the first night you came up our drive. I think he's the neatest thing, too."

Sue Ellen opened the passenger door and climbed inside the White Charger, while Eula hurried around to the driver's side door. Climbing in, she asked Sue Ellen, "Where to?"

"Let's take a little ride into the past. We'll start there and move forward. Go to the end of the driveway and turn right."

⌘⌘⌘

Blairsville was beautiful. Homes, large and small, were decorated for Thanksgiving, with some also decorated for the Christmas season. Fall decorations, including bales of hay, pumpkins and cornstalks adorned the entrances to driveways and subdivisions. The town had somewhat limited shopping opportunities. Walmart was the only big box-type store located there. The small mall was filled with local merchants, each one jockeying for the sale of his or her merchandise. Fall sales, Thanksgiving sales and Christmas sales all intermingled together, in an attempt to attract customers and separate them from their money.

A cold snap had brought out jackets and gloves, and hunters had taken to the woods in hopes of putting some venison in the freezer.

The town maintenance crew had started trimming the streetlight poles with lighted figures of Santa Claus, snowmen and angels. Several spruce trees on the lawn of the courthouse were already decorated and the lights were turned on each evening, making the hill and steps leading up to the courthouse mesmerizing.

With Sue Ellen as her passenger, Eula drove carefully. It made her nervous, feeling like Sue Ellen was critiquing every little thing she said or did. Her mind was racing, trying to figure out the meaning of all the things she had told her. Where on earth were they going, and what were they about to do?

"Aren't the decorations beautiful?" Sue Ellen said casually, as if she and Eula riding in the truck together was an everyday occurrence. "I just love the Christmas lights and the trees decorated on the courthouse lawn."

While they waited for the red light to change, Sue Ellen spotted a city maintenance man working on Sunday, putting up decorations. Struggling to get the window down, she yelled, "Hey, John, keep up the good work. It's beginning to look a lot like Christmas."

John turned to see who was shouting at him and his mouth literally fell open and stayed that way, as he watched the White Charger proceed through the intersection. Seeing Sue Ellen in the old truck had apparently short circuited something in his brain. As they drove away, Sue Ellen giggled like a school girl.

"John's never seen me in anything but my Mercedes or Jaguar. Don't you just love how we box everyone into a perceived role and make it almost impossible for them to operate in any capacity other than the one we mentally assign to them? When we come back by, if his mouth is still open, we'll stop and help him close it."

With that she started laughing all over again. Eula also started laughing and joined in the imaginary attempt to help John get over seeing Sue Ellen in the old truck. "I've got some duct tape under the seat. We could run a piece of it around his head and lower jaw to hold it together until he can regain control of it. Or we could take him for a ride. It'd be a little crowded, but the White Charger wouldn't mind."

Sue Ellen's light-spirited demeanor helped Eula relax. She had no way of knowing it, but Sue Ellen had ridden in a truck just like this for years—her dad's old Ford stepside pickup. Her dad would fall in love with Eula's truck and wouldn't even hold it against her for driving a Chevy.

Sue Ellen was giving directions, one turn at a time. "Where are we going this morning?" Eula finally asked.

Remembering her comment about the White Charger galloping up her driveway the first time she met Eula, she smiled and said, "We're galloping into the past, heading to where it all started for me. And this morning you'll get to meet Lilly."

"Who's Lilly?"

"Lilly is my very special friend from Cracker Barrel. Remember, I told you about her. I just didn't tell you her name. We're going to my mom and dad's. I want them to meet you and I want you to see my favorite place in all the world—the home I grew up in."

There was a small subdivision on the edge of town. Eula and her friends drove by it every day. As they approached it, Sue Ellen told her to turn right on Fieldstone Drive. Eula actually had a couple of friends who lived two streets over from where they had turned in. It was an older neighborhood, somewhat in disrepair, and all the homes were very small.

"Are they expecting us?" Eula asked.

"Sort of. I told Mom we'd probably drop in. I hope Dad's home, too. You'll love him. Everybody does."

She gave Eula more instructions. "Turn left on Brasstown, and their house will be the third one on the right."

"Wow," Eula said. "I like the truck."

"I thought you would," Sue Ellen said and smiled.

The house looked like it had been freshly painted, and the yard, unlike the yards of some of the neighbors, was immaculately kept. An older car was parked next to the old truck. The garage had apparently been closed in and made part of the house. It had been Sue Ellen's bedroom, and Lilly was sitting on the bed waiting to meet Eula.

Hearing the White Charger drive up, Mrs. Thornton opened the door and stepped out on the small front porch as Sue Ellen and Eula walked down the drive. "Hi, honey," she said, greeting them. "Is this your new friend?"

"Yes, ma'am," Sue Ellen responded, giving her mom a big hug. "Meet Eula Johnson. She's a special friend to me and even more special to William, if you know what I mean. I wanted her to meet you and Dad and especially Lilly."

"Well, Lilly will certainly be glad to see you. She asked me just the other day if you were ever coming back to see us."

"I'm sorry, Mom, just been . . ."

"I know, honey, you've been busy," her mother finished the sentence for her. "It's all right, you're here now and that's what counts. Y'all come on in and I'll get Rob up. He's taking one of his power naps, as he calls them."

As they entered the living room, Eula was stunned at the size. It was actually smaller than most living rooms in mobile homes. There was a small hallway with a bathroom, and two bedrooms opening from the hallway. The kitchen was to the left, and the closed-in garage was off the kitchen.

Sue Ellen, seeing the surprised look on Eula's face said to her, "A penny for your thoughts!"

Eula remembered visiting Southern Mobile Home Sales so the Beamer could avoid the type of jaw-dropping experience she was now having. "You'd be paying way too much," Eula said and smiled.

While her mom rescued her dad from his power nap, Sue Ellen said, "Let me show you my room and introduce you to Lilly." Eula followed her through the kitchen and into her old bedroom. There was Lilly, sitting on the bed, and Eula could sense the feelings of bygone years filling the room. Sue Ellen picked up Lilly and gave her a hug. "When bad storms used to come up, we'd both get scared and hide under the covers. Did you ever do that as a little girl?"

"Every time it thundered, as a matter of fact. But I didn't have a Lilly. I had a Fred. Fred was a small monkey I got one Christmas, and I think Fred was more afraid than I was."

"Do you still have Fred?" Sue Ellen inquired.

"No, I gave him to a cousin two or three years ago. I think she still has him. Maybe I need to go by and check on him. Couldn't do any harm."

Hugging Lilly one more time, she gave her to Eula and then said, "It doesn't do any harm to visit one's past as long as the person takes only good from it. Go see Fred. It'll do both of you a world of good."

Her mom walked into the bedroom with Rob close behind. He didn't look like he had experienced a power nap. As a matter of fact, he looked like he needed one. Playing to a full house, he extended his hand to Eula and said, "I don't believe I've had the honor of meeting you before, have I?"

"No, sir," Eula replied, "I don't think we've met."

Looking over at Sue Ellen, he asked Eula, "And who is this you've brought to visit us today?"

"Oh, stop it, Dad," Sue Ellen said, as she gave him a big hug. "Don't get dramatic on me. This is going to be a visit you'll love. Did you see what's parked in the driveway?"

"Yes, I did, and I'm on the way out there to look her over. Mighty fine looking set of wheels from what I saw through the doorway."

"Just so you'll know, Dad, it's a him, and his name is the White Charger."

"Must be a story there somewhere, but I'm afraid to ask. White Charger it is."

With that, her dad was on the way outside and the three women went into the kitchen and sat down at the table.

"Would y'all like some lunch?" her mother asked. "I could fix something in a jiffy."

"Not today, Mom. This whole day is already planned, and we have two more stops. Eula has to be at work at four this afternoon. But we may hook up with William someday real soon and all of us come over for dinner. How would that work for you and Dad?"

"It would make all three of us very happy."

"Three of us?"

"Your dad, Lilly and me. I think that's three of us," she said and smiled, raising her eyebrows and being devilish.

"Okay, we'll come see the three of you. I kinda like that idea anyway. Lilly needs to get out some. I may pick her up one day soon and let her stay at my house for a while."

Her mom couldn't resist taking a shot at the size of Sue Ellen's enormous home compared to theirs. "Be real careful if you take her home with you. She could get lost and you'd never be able to find her. May need to get one of those tracking things some people put on their dogs."

"Mom," Sue Ellen said. "One of our stops this afternoon is a first-time visit to my house for Eula. By the time she gets through listening to you, I may not be able to get her to come in."

Eula was enjoying the bantering between mother and daughter. She could tell it was harmless and the two of them were having a good time doing it.

Mrs. Thornton turned to Eula and pretended to whisper. "If you get lost, call 911. The rescue team is always having to go to Sue Ellen's to retrieve lost visitors. One time, it took three days — not to find the person who was initially lost, but to find one of the firefighters who had been looking for him."

"Mom, you're as bad as Dad. By the way, where is he?"

Looking out the kitchen window, she spotted her father sitting in the White Charger. "We'd better get out there before he decides to take your truck for a spin."

"Love your truck," he told Eula when they walked out on the front porch.

"Thank you, sir. I'm sorta partial to it myself. It's actually my father's old truck, but I've been the only one driving it for the last two years. Gets me there and back again."

"What more could you ask for?" Mr. Thornton replied.

Sue Ellen hugged her mom and then her Dad. "Gotta run, Dad. Mom will explain what we have going on today. We'll come back real soon, I promise."

"Don't be telling me. Tell Lilly. She's the one who's always fretting over you not coming to see her. Me and your mom, we're just sitting around here waiting to die."

Eula was eating this up. It was so funny to watch it from her perspective, not having a dog in the hunt. Sue Ellen hugged them again and told Eula to get them out of there before she fell for the tall tales they were running on her.

"Where to now?" Eula asked.

"Know where Veterans Memorial Park is?"

"I sure do."

"Let's make that our second stop, shall we? They have some nice benches and it's a great place for reminiscing."

As they parked and got out of the truck, they could hear the large American flag as it slapped in the gentle breeze coming over the hillside. Fallen heroes, with their names cut deep in marble, would forever be remembered here. Forever being the life expectancy of marble battling the elements.

Eula followed Sue Ellen to the far end of the black marble memorial. "Good morning, Tom," she said stopping near the end.

"Tom?" Eula said, and raised her eyebrows.

"Robert Thomas Thornton, but everyone called him Tom. He died in Afghanistan at the age of twenty-seven. Just about killed Mom and Dad. Dad suffered from depression for several years before he could move on with his life. I had just graduated from college and was too self-centered and too focused on climbing the ladder to success to even realize how devastating the loss of a son was to them." Walking closer to the memorial, she ran her fingers over her brother's name, cut deep in the stone.

"Let's walk down to the lake," Sue Ellen said. "It's all downhill from here," she quipped, "and downhill is appropriate for the part of my story I'm about to share with you. The only reason I'm telling you any of this is because I think your relationship with William is serious and will lead to marriage sometime in the future. Because of that, I'm going to share some things I haven't even shared with him. Some things are better left untold, and some of this fits in that bucket."

There was a walking track around the lake and many of the town's residents used it for daily exercise, weather permitting. Few were out today because the temperature had fallen.

Finding a bench in the sun, Sue Ellen told Eula to have a seat. "I'm going to pace and talk and all I ask of you is two things. Number one, listen closely to what I tell you. Number two, be Christ-like and don't be judgmental. Okay?"

"Okay," Eula responded.

Sue Ellen just nodded. "It's hard for William to understand my concern regarding his future and the impact his father can have on it. And you, not having been in the same circle, will definitely fail to see the implications of an irate William Morgan, Sr. The Beamer has no idea the cards I hold, keeping the world in check for all of us. Sounds a little conspiratorial, and it is."

Eula replied, "I understand why William cares so much about you. What's not to love? I feel your genuine concern for me even though we barely know each other. And, no doubt, you want only what's best for William and me, especially for him. For that, I'm grateful. There seems to be a missing piece here, but that's not for me to figure out and probably none of my business."

"Well, Eula, I can see that you're smart as well as beautiful. Now, listen. We're running out of time if you're going to get to the DQ by four. Here goes. Have you ever heard any rumors or gossip concerning me?"

Eula had heard innuendos about Mr. Morgan and Sue Ellen, but the gossip was so old it failed to generate interest. Kind of like dated milk. You just get rid of it.

"I'm smart, too," Sue Ellen said, "and you hesitated way too long and still haven't answered the question. If we're to be friends, and who knows, maybe family someday, it has to be based on honesty. This sounds like a game show on television. Can you answer the question for two dozen Twinkies?"

Eula laughed out loud. "How did you know I love Twinkies?"

"William told me."

"Okay, but remember that you asked the question and insisted on me answering it. I haven't heard much, just gossip about you when you were very young. I guess it was the time in your life you referenced earlier, when it was all about you climbing the ladder of success. Gossip has it that you have what you have—home, job and cars— because of, how can I say this, special time spent when you were very young with Mr. Morgan. Sorry."

"Oh, don't be sorry. I'm the one who's sorry, but God has forgiven me. The stories are true, probably all of them. There are some things that never even got out. To be completely honest, I slept with him during my summer internships at the bank, and when I graduated from college, it escalated. I literally moved in with him in his mansion. I was going places, and he was punching my ticket along with other things. I broke Mom and Dad's heart. Back then, twenty-plus years ago, the whole town was talking. And I didn't care."

"Sue Ellen, you don't have to share this stuff. The only thing that matters is today. If God has forgiven you, then it's in the past and forgotten as far as I'm concerned. And, besides, it's old news. The good news is who you are now, not who you were then."

"Amen and Amen," Sue Ellen said. "Maybe you should become a minister." She was silent for a few seconds before asking, "Have you and William ever discussed my past or my involvement with his dad?"

"Absolutely not. There's never been a word said connecting you with his father in any way that's not work related. There's a chance he hasn't heard the old gossip. It's hard to talk about someone in a negative light who has such a positive influence as you have on the Beamer. I can't imagine anyone doing it. And, like I said, it's so far in the past, it's no longer juicy gossip."

"Well, I may have climbed the success ladder in an inappropriate manner, but trust me on this one, I run the bank and I look after William Morgan, Sr. in business-related matters only. I earn the salary he pays me because I keep the bank operating successfully, and I keep his butt out of a sling. That's the only thing important to him. It allows him to create more wealth outside of his banking business. Because of things I won't ever share with you, or anyone else for that matter, he told me I was the only mistake he'd ever made."

"Now there's a deep statement if I ever heard one. The only mistake he'd ever made. It's loaded with conspiratorial darkness. There's not a story here, it's a novel."

"You're too much, Eula Johnson. You're more like me than you realize, because you actually get it."

"I consider that a compliment. But the question that needs answering here is where is all this going, and why are you telling me all of these things? What bearing does it have on my relationship with William?"

"My reason for telling you some of my personal past is to establish, at least in your mind, the fact I have more control over City Bank & Trust and Mr. William Morgan, Sr. than most would ever believe. Junior loves you very much and it's only natural to want to introduce the girl you want to marry someday to your parents. That won't fly here."

"Is his father that controlling?"

"You have no idea or conception of what level of control he demands. I'm the only one he doesn't control and the only one on the planet who can not only go toe to toe with him, but win, and win every time."

"This novel has to be written. It would become a best seller, for sure," Eula noted. "Why would he be so opposed to his son marrying me?"

"In his mind, he lives, like the Kennedys, in Camelot. In his mind, you and your family aren't good enough to marry into his family. Forget the fact Junior is adopted. He's the only heir his father will ever have, and he stands to inherit a fortune. I know you couldn't care less about the money, and I know it's a hard truth for you to accept that there are those who use people who have less as a means to make even more money. He sees the workers at McClain's and the people who live in trailers and houses like my mom and dad as interest he'll eventually make when they have to come to the bank to borrow money because of some crisis in their lives."

"What a terrible way to live," Eula commented. "He must be miserable all the time."

"As a matter of fact, he's not. I have firsthand experience living that way myself. There was a time, Eula Johnson, when I thought I was too good to speak to a maintenance man putting up decorations. And I would have never thought of spending one minute with you or anyone else who didn't want the very best of everything money could buy. My own family was so far beneath the rung of the ladder I was perched on, I couldn't even share their loss of my brother. And I sure didn't have any compassion for anyone else or care what happened to anyone other than myself."

"What changed your perspective, or a better question may be, how did you climb back down the ladder to where the maintenance man becomes important and you can have me as a friend?"

"That's for another outing, but I promise to tell you the story. It's a God-thing and He gets all the glory. We need to go check on the White Charger. He's about to take us to my house."

After walking back to the parking lot, Sue Ellen said, "So, what do you think, so far?"

"About what?" Eula replied.

"My humble, loving home and family, my unfortunate mistakes as a young woman, and my conversion by a gracious Savior."

"Wow," Eula said and smiled. "Surely you don't expect me to roll that into one answer. You've led an awesome life, one anyone could easily desire. Your mistakes were yours and you own them. Granny Preston would say, "Ain't that just like God. Forgave her, straightened out her life, and still allows her to be successful."

"Just like King David in the Old Testament. He messed up big time, just like I did. The God of David is also the God of today. He sent two angels, aka Sister Francis and Sister Cass, to rescue a foolish young woman from herself."

"You and Granny Preston would have been great friends. She's already in heaven, probably watching over all of us, even as we speak." Eula wondered who Sister Francis and Sister Cass were, but didn't ask.

"And what do you say, Eula Johnson? It's important to me to know what you think. When we get to my house, you'll see what

I no longer see. You'll see a house able to hold my parents' home, many times over. You'll see furniture and paintings. Things I fought for and would have died for when I was in my early twenties. And now, while they're nice things to have, they no longer own me. I see them as sort of on loan to me from the Lord, and they're no longer as important to me as speaking to John in town this morning. I think God blesses those whose faith and trust are placed in Him alone, and not in the things He may or may not allow them to have."

"Well put," Eula said. "That's exactly what I was going to tell you."

They both laughed and Sue Ellen said, "You're as full of it as William!"

"I doubt that," Eula said. "He can easily take that title from me, any day of the week and twice on Sunday."

A few minutes later, Sue Ellen unlocked the front door to her home, turned and said, "Do you want the fifty-cent tour or the premium tour?"

"If the front door is any indication of what's behind it, there's nothing fifty-cents about this place."

"Remember," Sue Ellen reminded her, "you're to take this all in as stuff, nothing more, nothing less." Opening the door, she turned to Eula and said, "Welcome to my home and, for the most part, William's, too."

When they walked through the front door, Eula couldn't help herself. Her eyes got really big, her mouth dropped open like John's did earlier, but she managed to close it enough to say, *"You gotta be shittin' me."*

"Stuff," Sue Ellen reminded Eula. "Just accumulated stuff."

"Look at your library. There must be a thousand books in there. How tall are the ceilings? Wow, what a fireplace. Look what a view. I've never seen a den this big before. The kitchen is unbelievable." And on and on with the exclamations over what a beautiful home Sue Ellen Thornton lived in.

When the tour was over, Sue Ellen asked, "So, what do you think about the day? About Dad and Mom's place, about my brother's memorial, and about my home? And what about my little Lilly?"

"I think I understand what you were trying to do. I think you wanted me to see where you came from and the fact it really isn't much different from where my friends and I come from. And you wanted me to know how you got all of the fine things you own and that the price you paid was way too high. And when your brother gave his life for our country, you weren't in any position to acknowledge the sacrifice or grieve for him, or willing to help your dad and mom get over such a tragedy." Eula hesitated, gathering her thoughts before continuing.

"And?"

"And you found forgiveness through some kind of transformation. Something happened, putting God in the driver's seat of your life, the bank and, apparently, Mr. Morgan, Sr., as well. I don't understand why William stays with you more than at his home, but that's really none of my business. And I don't understand what the Beamer sees in me. He knows everything about me and my family, and the fact that Mom's silverware isn't silver. It's Walmart wannabes. And he knows my family and most of my friend's families live pay check to pay check."

"Oh, your question about what the Beamer sees in you is an easy one to answer."

"Well, if you have the answer, fill me in. I've spent many sleepless nights trying to tell myself this isn't a dream and I'm not going to wake up and find him gone."

"Remember the night you picked him up for the ball game?"

"I do."

"That's the night I dubbed your truck the White Charger. Before you arrived, William was telling me all about you. He told me where you live and that your entire family has always worked at McClain's."

"And those facts didn't raise concern in your mind?"

"Oh, no. They made me proud of him, and I told him so. Want to know what I told him as you came up the driveway?"

"Absolutely," Eula responded.

"'William, it's not about the old truck. It's about the heart that beats inside the driver of the old truck.' And then I asked him, 'What is this young woman's name?' And he said, 'Her name is Eula Johnson, and she's beautiful on the outside and on the inside.'" Eula teared up and Sue Ellen gave her a hug.

"Here's your takeaway for the day," Sue Ellen said. "The Sue Ellen Thornton of yesterday would have done anything to have what you see here today. The new Sue Ellen Thornton, after meeting the Son of God and being forgiven, sees this stuff as nothing more, just stuff. God continues to bless me, allowing me to pass the blessings on to those in our community who are in need."

After a moment, she continued, "One last thing to see and then we have to eat, or you'll not make the DQ on time." Going to the kitchen, she opened the door into the garage. A Jaguar, a Mercedes and a Corvette sat side by side, with an empty space for the BMW William drove.

Eula's jaw dropped again, and Sue Ellen said, "Let me articulate the words you want to say, but can't at this moment. *You've gotta be shittin' me.*"

They both had a good laugh at Eula's favorite saying and then ate a quick lunch Sue Ellen had already prepared.

As she prepared to leave, Eula hugged and thanked Sue Ellen for a wonderful day. She said, "I see and understand, I really do. And you did a good job with a complicated presentation. It was like a seminar. Maybe we could call it *From Rags to Riches*."

"Not a bad idea. You gotta go. You have fifteen minutes to get across town to the DQ."

⊷∞⊷⊷∞⊷⊷∞⊷

The DQ was slammed all evening. Sam had run an ad in the paper, buy anything and get the second one for half price. It was his idea of giving back to his customers during the holiday season. And it worked. He was always glad to have Eula there whenever he did a promotional event like this one. She ran circles around the rest of the employees and just plain got it done.

"Hey, Sam," Eula said about thirty minutes before closing. "Next time you decide to give away the farm, let me know in advance."

"Why?" Sam asked.

"So I can come down with some twenty-four-hour bug, or maybe just leave town for a day or two. I didn't know we had this many people in the whole county."

"Who would've thought we would have sold this much ice cream this time of the year. I figured lots of chicken tenders, burgers and hot dogs, but I think we set some kind of record for blizzards tonight. I'm like you, if I have to fix another one, I think I'll have a screaming mimi fit."

Laughing, Eula said, "I'd like to see that."

Sam saw headlights turn into the parking lot and smiled. "Right on time," he remarked.

"He'd better be, if he knows what's good for him," Eula responded, looking out toward the parking lot.

"I hear good things about him and I believe them. I know you'd never have anything to do with him if he wasn't a good guy. Now, his father's a butthole. I cleaned that one up for you. I don't think old man Morgan has a friend in the world, and from what I hear on the street, that's exactly how he likes to live his life. Can't imagine living like that," Sam said, as he wiped down the counter where they were standing.

"Well, my William isn't like his father. I don't think I've ever heard anyone say anything bad about him. He'll go out of his way to help anyone, with anything. He's an awesome friend."

"Friend, my butt," Sam said and smiled. "I hear things and the bearer of the tales have you and him in a very serious relationship. Better not let the old butthole find out about it. People like you and me would have a hard time fitting in with old man Morgan. I hear your William lives with the Thornton woman more than he lives at home. Any truth to that?"

"For the most part, but I understand it. Sue Ellen Thornton is one of the nicest people I have ever had the pleasure of meeting."

"And one of the richest," Sam concluded. "Go on, get out of here. I've got this now. Thanks for all you do for me. I appreciate it more than you'll ever know. I put a bonus in your envelope and you deserve more. I'm blessed to have you working here, and I don't mind telling you so. Now, get out of here before your friend freezes to death."

"Thanks, Sam. Working for you is easy because you're a good man. We make a great team, no doubt about it. Thanks for the extra money. It'll come in handy for Christmas presents. I'm out of here. See you Monday evening."

Sam watched her leave. When she got to where the Beamer was leaning against the White Charger, she gave him a long, and much needed, kiss.

"Friends, my butt," Sam said to himself and smiled.

∞∞∞

"You impressed Eula with your trip down memory lane," William told Sue Ellen over dinner the next evening. "I have to hand it to you. I was wondering how you would introduce Eula to your world without frightening her to death."

"She's an amazing young woman, and it's easy to understand why you might want to spend the rest of your life with someone like her."

"Yes, she's amazing, no doubt about it. Her background causes her to have some hangups we'll have to work through. But look at my family. There's more issues in my family than you'd ever find in a single-wide mobile home. I was worried about the shock effect she would get with the brunch. You really bridged the gap between who you are now and who you were when you were growing up. She loved your dad and mom, but, then, what's not to love about them? She even told me things about you and your family I didn't know. Now, how did that happen?" William asked, raising his eyebrows.

"Oh, stop it. You don't have to know everything. A girl has to have some secrets, doesn't she? I hope she didn't tell you everything," Sue Ellen said.

"Knowing you two like I do, I'm sure I only got a sampling of the good stuff and none of the bad. Poor William was probably drawn and quartered, and he wasn't even there to defend himself."

"We actually had better things to talk about than you, and we had places to go and things to see. Lilly fell in love with your Eula."

"And who's Lilly?" the Beamer asked, wrinkling his brow.

"See, I told you we had better things to talk about, and Lilly's just one of them."

William, pretending to have a pen and paper, wrote an imaginary note and then pretended to fold it and place it in his pocket.

"And, young William Morgan, Jr., what have you written?" Sue Ellen asked.

"I've written two things in secret code on invisible paper. The first thing is a note to remind me to find out who this Lilly character is. The second thing is written in all caps and says, DO NOT LET THESE TWO WOMEN GET TOGETHER AGAIN."

"Let me help you out a little bit here," Sue Ellen said. "Lilly is my best kept secret." Suddenly, she realized she had made an incorrect statement. Her best kept secret wasn't Lilly. Her best kept secret was sitting across the table from her. "Scratch that, Lilly is my second best kept secret."

"And what is your best kept secret?" he asked.

"You know what they say in the movies. If I tell you, I'll have to kill you and we don't want to do that, do we?"

"One visit with Eula and you're a totally different person. How did this happen?"

She ignored his question. "Now let me address your second note, the silly one about not letting us get together again. It's just as well it's written on imaginary paper with an imaginary pen because it ain't gonna happen. These two old girls have teamed up and bonded, and we have come up with a plan to keep your butt in line."

"You're not a bit of help. Forget it. I'll just ask the White Charger. He's my friend and he'll tell me everything, like who this Lilly character is and what kind of devious plans you and Eula have cooked up for me."

"You've lost again. The White Charger is with us, especially since I told him it was okay if he leaked oil on my driveway. That made him smile so big I thought his grill was going to fall out."

Having finished dinner, William stood up and thanked her for the meal. "Leave the dishes for me. I'll do them in a little while. They say insanity is contagious, and I feel like I may be coming down with it."

"And where might you be off to, as if I didn't know?"

"To hire a detective to find this Lilly character, and to threaten the White Charger with a rubber hammer for being in cahoots with the two of you."

"I don't think another dent will get him to talk. Maybe a new oil pan gasket, but not an additional dent. Get out of here, Eula's waiting."

"I know," William said, "love you."

"Love you, too. Drive carefully, and I'll do the dishes. I don't have anything else to do. Tell Eula to call me. We have to schedule our next outing."

"No way," William said as he closed the door behind him.

Early on Monday morning, Marie, Sue Ellen's executive secretary, came into her office and closed the door. "Sorry to bother you, but Mr. Wilson is out in the lobby and wants to know if you can see him this morning. He's such a nice man."

"No, you're not sorry," Sue Ellen said and smiled. "You like Mr. Wilson as much as I do." They worked together as a team, and they both knew Mr. Morgan was chomping at the bit for Mr. Wilson to default on his loan so he could repossess the trailer park and put it back on the market.

Marie Adams had been hired as her executive secretary fifteen years earlier and had become an amazing asset to Sue Ellen and the bank. She knew everything except the dirt, and had little or no respect for Mr. Morgan.

"Bring me the files on Whispering Pines," Sue Ellen told her. "I'm sure he's behind again."

Opening the files, the first thing that jumped out at Sue Ellen was the note Mr. Morgan had attached to the inside of the file folder. The note read, "First available opportunity, foreclose on this guy."

"True to form," she said to herself.

Mr. Wilson had owned Whispering Pines Trailer Park for a number of years and had always struggled to keep the mortgage paid on time. The main reason for his financial difficulties was two-fold—all his tenants either worked at McClain's or were retired and had limited incomes. Compassion, a gift from her Lord and Savior, now made it more difficult for her to be hard-nosed and business only. "Pay up or get out" were words she tried hard not to resort to with the bank's customers.

She closed the file just as Marie buzzed her on the phone. "He wants to know if you can see him today or should he make an appointment for another time, but as soon as possible?"

"Send him in and close the door, please," she told Marie.

Ernest Wilson was in his late sixties, short, balding and slightly overweight. He attempted a comb-over, which failed miserably to cover his bald head. He had a contagious, bubbly personality and never seemed to meet a stranger. And he knew Jesus and wanted to tell everyone about Him. His affiliation with the Lord is what rendered him unable and unwilling to pull a Morgan, Sr. on his retired tenants and underemployed residents who lived at the trailer park.

As he was shown in, Sue Ellen immediately stood to greet him. "Good morning, Ernest. What brings you to my office today?"

"Thanks for seeing me on such short notice. And keep your seat. You don't have to stand for old Ernest."

He had already spied his file on the corner of her desk. "Come on, Sue Ellen, you're way too nice to be a banker. It's me, Ernest Wilson, the one who is always behind on his payments."

Smiling at him, she said, "This is true, but you're also the guy who has a heart as big as Texas and one who has compassion for others who are struggling to keep their heads above water. That's your problem, Ernest, as some financial wizards would see it."

"In other words," Ernest said, "I'm a sucker for a sob story." "Just like Jesus," she countered. "Almost every story in the New Testament where He healed or helped someone could be put in that category, 'sucker for a sob story'. Remember when Lazarus died, what did Jesus do? The Scriptures say, 'He wept.' Also remember the woman at the well, the Centurion's daughter, and let's not forget the ten lepers. So, Ernest Wilson, you're in good company, and I'm personally glad to know you and call you my friend."

"Thank you, Sue Ellen. Now tell me what to do. McClain's, at the worst possible time, just before Christmas, has cut everyone's work schedule to four days a week. Most everyone knows or believes they can let their trailer rent or lot rent go for a month or two and get by with it. Tell me how to throw a family out at Christmastime for choosing to buy toys for their kids or grandkids instead of paying old Ernest?"

"I couldn't do it either, Ernest," Sue Ellen said, "but you know I have a boss and a responsibility to the bank. You're three months behind, and in theory foreclosure could be started immediately.

Here's a suggestion. Go to the ones who are late and just be honest. Tell them if you lose Whispering Pines to foreclosure, then everyone will lose. Be upfront with your tenants and let's both pray they'll be able to come up with their rent. I'll note on your file that you came in and I'll personally sign off on it, keeping it out of foreclosure for the time being. But Mr. Morgan will override it in a heartbeat. And, in reality, the note calls for foreclosure after ninety days without payment."

"Thanks, Sue Ellen. I'll see all of the late tenants today. I know it's just a trailer park, but I see it as a ministry to those with less of life's goods."

"It's definitely a ministry because of who's running it. There are some fine people who live in Whispering Pines, and your love for them doesn't go unnoticed in my office or in His."

Smiling, Ernest said thank you again and left her office, quietly closing the door behind him.

Taking her checkbook out of her purse, Sue Ellen wrote a check to cash for three thousand dollars, which was one month's payment on his note. That would give him another month to collect the past due rent money. Cashing the check at a teller's window, she returned to her office and wrote up a payment coupon for the Whispering Pines payment. Then she buzzed Marie.

When Marie came into her office, she handed her the three thousand dollars along with the payment coupon. "Here's a payment from Mr. Wilson," she said.

Marie, raising her eyebrows, said, "You're a good woman, Sue Ellen Thornton, and God will bless you for it."

Before Sue Ellen could reply, Marie turned and quietly left her office.

The Beamer was ecstatic how the relationship between Eula and Sue Ellen had blossomed into a real friendship. Knowing this turn of events was important, he also knew the larger nut to crack was getting his father to accept the fact that he, William Morgan, Jr., had chosen someone from a mobile home and with no old money coursing through her family's history.

School was out for Thanksgiving holidays and a light dusting of snow had fallen in Blairsville. William and Sue Ellen were having coffee and a bagel on her glassed-in veranda. Gas logs kept them cozy as they both marveled at how beautiful a little snow can make a landscape.

"What do you have planned for today?" Sue Ellen asked, taking a sip of her coffee.

"Dad wants me to run by the bank. He said he has something to show me."

"I know what it is, and you'll really like it."

"Dad sounded very excited about whatever it is. I'm sure it's something neat and probably expensive. He's really a good father, but—"

"But what?" Sue Ellen asked.

"I know you're right about how he'll react to my choice of a girlfriend, because I know Dad, too. But I still wish I could take Eula to meet both of my parents and have them accept her the same way you have."

"I'm right about your father and I know how he'd react to Eula and the possibility of her ever being a part of his family. I know him better than anyone, and it would be a monumental mistake on your part to take her to meet him and your mother."

William took a sip of his coffee and sat quietly for several minutes before responding to Sue Ellen's warning.

"You always say things work themselves out if given enough time. I don't see how time will change how Dad views the world or those around him. It'll take more than time to soften his perspective and his heart. I wish it wasn't so, but it is."

Sue Ellen mentally noted the maturity in his sad but true assessment of his father. But a saying ran through her mind as well. "God can change bad things into good things." There was a spark of good inside her old lover. He still gave generous gifts to Saint Mary's, though never making it known publicly. She had access to financial records allowing her to see his gifts. Keying in on that, she told the Beamer, "I wouldn't completely give up on your father, but at this point, with college ahead for you and Eula, I think patience and time are the best avenues to pursue. Get some of your college completed and then revisit bringing your folks into the picture."

"Let's talk about something a little more positive. This is depressing," William said. "So how are the three of us doing Thanksgiving?"

"The three of us aren't," Sue Ellen said and grinned. "I'm going over to Dad and Mom's for lunch and Eula is doing the same with her folks. And then, the two of us, that's Eula and me, in case you're wondering, are going to a mall over in Asheville to do a little shopping. There's a couple of specialty shops that are running Thanksgiving Day specials. I assure you, nothing you'd be interested in. I told her we'd go in my Jag and she could drive. It'll be fun for her. What do you think about that?"

"It just got more depressing. Nothing like spending Thanksgiving by yourself," the Beamer said.

"Oh, here we go again. Poor pitiful William. Whatever will he do without the two women in his life?"

"I'll find something to do, I guess. Maybe I'll go over to Dad's and be alone there. They'll both be out of town. Poor, pitiful William. Nobody cares about him."

"We could go in another car and you could ride over to Asheville with us. How does that sound?" Sue Ellen asked. "Eula could drive the Jag some other time."

"No, thanks," William said quickly. "Being by myself isn't that bad."

"Yeah, you're right. Taking a man shopping with you is like taking the game warden hunting with you."

They both laughed and the Beamer said, "I'm really glad the two of you have hit it off so well. It means a lot to me. Thanks for taking Eula into your circle of friends."

"No need for thanks. She's an absolute joy to be around and smart as a whip. That girl's going places, with or without William Morgan, Jr. You'd better hold on to her with both hands. Trust me on this one, she's a keeper."

⚜ ⚜ ⚜

Thanksgiving Day dawned clear and extremely cold. Bubba didn't need someone on television to tell him how cold it was. Their older trailer, with very little insulation, allowed him an insight, from his bed, into outside conditions.

"Good morning, Granny," he thought as he pulled the cover up closer to his face. "First Thanksgiving without you. Hope you like what I did with your Christmas decorations. I think they look great. They'd look better if they were up at your place and you were still with us to enjoy them. I've picked out the perfect cedar Christmas tree for you, and as always, we'll decorate it Christmas Eve night. Pastor Baker and his wife, Marlene, are coming over for

Thanksgiving dinner today. Thought you'd like that. Maude told me to tell you she still misses picking you up on Sunday mornings. Maude has a favor to ask of you. Told me to ask you to put in a good word for her and to ask the Big Guy there if He'd consider letting a really nice old truck through the Pearly Gates. Know what they say, Maude reminded me, 'you have not because you ask not.' Can't argue with her on that one. The next time you see God, put in a good word for Maude and me. And don't forget Clarice, Dad and Mom. We need all the help we can get. Doesn't do any harm to have friends in high places. Love you still, Granny, and always will. Gotta get out of this bed and meet LJ at Bill's Diner for breakfast. I'm going hunting with him this afternoon."

❦❦❦

Eula was up early baking a sour cream pound cake for her mom for Thanksgiving dinner. She had to hurry because William had insisted on having breakfast with her at the Waffle House. She tried to put him off, telling him she'd just see him later that evening. Nothing would do but they meet for breakfast. Getting dressed in a hurry, she hopped in the White Charger and headed out. When she pulled into the parking lot, he was already there and outside, leaning against his car.

"Mercy," Eula exclaimed, getting out and hurrying toward the restaurant. "Aren't you freezing to death?"

"Not really," the Beamer replied quickly. "Just standing out here in the cold, contemplating a lifetime of loneliness."

"Now, that's bull and you know it," she said. "Question. Why the Waffle House?"

"Think about it. They're one of the few places open on major holidays," he said as they went inside.

"Guess you're right on that one. Why couldn't we just do something this evening after Sue Ellen and I get through shopping?"

"I hardly ever get to spend time with you anymore. Since you hooked up with her, you're either working, studying or going somewhere together. Usually shopping, like today. You'll eat with your folks and Sue Ellen will eat with her mom and dad and—I'll have to spend most of the day by myself."

"It's okay, Beamer. It's probably a good thing for us to spend a little less time together because it interferes with us acting like married folk. God knows we need to slow that down a little bit."

"Whoa, whoa," the Beamer quickly said while Eula was catching her breath. "Okay, I'll give you that one. I miss acting like married folk, and if you and Sue Ellen would listen to me, we'd be getting married really soon and we could act like married folk every day. Scratch that. Make it at least twice a day."

"That may be the sweetest thing you've ever told me," Eula said, leaning over and giving him a peck on the cheek. "Let's order and eat quickly. I've got to get back home and give Mom a hand with dinner. As soon as we eat, I'll head over to Sue Ellen's, and from there to Asheville. I can't wait to drive her Jag. Look out stores, here we come."

"So much for the sweetest thing I've ever told you. Maybe I'll get lucky and find some other restaurant open and get me some banana pudding. Make that two bowls of it. Mind if I take the White Charger on a quest for the pudding?"

"Be my guest. Don't tell the White Charger I'm driving the Jag or he'll be jealous."

Hughes Electrical Contractors had completely decorated the bank, the three bank branches, Sue Ellen's place and the Morgan mansion. Everything was finished, with the exception of the Christmas trees. They would be put up a few days after Thanksgiving so they would remain fresh and beautiful throughout the Christmas season.

A realistic looking stable was erected for the Nativity scene at the entrance to Sue Ellen's driveway. Joseph and Mary, the Wise Men, the shepherds and the animals were all lifelike. The manger would remain empty until Christmas Eve. Every year, after midnight, Sue Ellen, with William's help, placed the Christ child in the manger. This year, she'd ask Eula to help with the placing of baby Jesus.

After Thanksgiving, hundreds of cars would drive by to see the Nativity scene. Sometimes, the traffic would be so horrific the sheriff's office would dispatch a car to help with the congestion. For Sue Ellen, placing the Christ child in the manger was like revisiting Saint Mary's. She could feel the presence of the Holy Spirit and she believed with all her heart that Sister Cass and Sister Francis were looking on with approval. After placing baby Jesus in the manger, she always knelt and prayed before leaving.

⚬⚭⚬⚭⚬⚭⚬

The only day of the year Bill Watson closed the diner was Christmas. On Thanksgiving morning, Bubba and LJ and many of the locals were there early for some of his delicious pancakes and thick-sliced bacon.

"It'll be okay," Bubba told LJ. "You worry way too much. As Granny Preston used to say, 'we all put our pants on the same way.'" Bubba paused for LJ to finish the old saying he had also heard many times before.

255

"I know," LJ said, and the dynamic-duo said in unison, "one leg at a time."

"Well," LJ said, "it's only two days away from our big shindig at the country club. I've got my jersey clean and my best pair of jeans washed and ironed. The crease I put in them puppies is so sharp I could take them off and use them as a weapon."

The image of a naked LJ, using jeans as a weapon, tickled Bubba. "Now that would be something to see. You, in your underwear, slashing your way out of the country club."

"Yeah," LJ continued, "I could be the first naked ninja in history wielding lethal jeans. Now wouldn't that be something?"

They were laughing so much that Bill came over to see what was so funny. "Hey, guys, I need a good laugh. Make me laugh," he said, as he sat down next to Bubba.

This started the two laughing all over again. When Bubba regained his composure, he painted a verbal picture of a naked LJ using his super-creased jeans to slash his way out of the country club.

Bill, not crazy at all about his competitor, joined in the charade. "Knowing that bunch of highfalutin' snobs as well as I do, you might want to take a back-up pair of jeans. Or, you could call me and I'd be happy to come over and help."

It was fun to laugh and cut up with Bill, but when he left their table, it got quiet. LJ, always the worry wart, said again, "Only two days before the country club party, just damn."

An older couple came in and sat down behind Bubba and LJ. Lisa, one of waitresses, came over to take their order. You could tell by the couple's accent that they weren't from around Blairsville. They ordered breakfast and Lisa asked them if they wanted any homemade jam. The man asked, "What kind of jam do you have?"

Lisa had been working with Bill for years and had a great sense of humor. "Grape, strawberry, mixed fruit and toe jam." She intentionally ran the toe jam close together and the old man fell for it. "That last one you mentioned. What does it taste like?"

"Depends on which toe it comes from," she answered and died laughing. Bubba and LJ had heard it numerous times, but it was always funny when some new customer would bite on the old joke.

As Bubba and LJ got up to leave, Bubba told Lisa, "You ought to be ashamed of yourself. You're gonna be old too someday and all of this will come back to haunt you."

"Bubba Preston, you enjoyed it and you know it. It's always funny when someone asks how toe jam tastes."

"Granny Preston used to say laughter is the best medicine," Bubba said. "And it is. The old man's breakfast will taste a whole lot better with toe jam instead of grape jelly. I might try it myself next time I come in."

"We ought to ask for toe jam at the country club," LJ said, continuing the ruse.

"Just worry about the forks and spoons, LJ. That's enough for you to think about. Two days left."

"Just damn," LJ said. "Why did you have to go and remind me again?"

⚬⚭⚬⚭⚬⚭⚬

Maude purred as she cruised up Country Club Lane. Bubba and LJ weren't saying much. Both were apprehensive. LJ, thinking out loud, said, "You know they use real silverware here. That means more than one fork."

"More than one fork! Imagine that."

"Bubba, you can be cute out here all you want to, but inside, I may just wait and see which fork you pick up first."

"When in Rome, do as the Romans do," Bubba said. "I'm gonna keep my eye on Coach Henderson. I think he'll probably be as nervous as we are, and I'm not sure he knows which fork to use either. If you see him looking confused or not sure of himself, watch Mr. Kitchens and do whatever he does. I 'm sure he knows fork and spoon stuff. And, if all else fails, eat with your fingers."

That made LJ laugh. "Imagine what they would do if we both ate with our fingers. I bet we wouldn't ever have to worry about eating here again."

"Just damn," Bubba said as he wheeled Maude into a parking space. "Show time."

"Don't remind me. I was pretending we were going hunting."

"You're spot on, LJ. We are going hunting. Hunting for the right fork. Mama told me something about outside in or wrong side out or something like that. I hate to admit it, but Mama hasn't had any experience eating at country clubs."

"All Mama told me," LJ said, "was to mind my manners and thank them for inviting me."

"Can't go wrong with that advice. We both got good mamas, whether they know proper table manners or not. I'll have to be honest with you, LJ. I didn't want to come and actually started not to. But the boys on the team have really been nice to us, and Coach Henderson and Johnny would really be disappointed if we didn't show. I thought about something Granny Preston used to say whenever she was sick or was having a hard time with something. She'd always say, 'This too shall pass.'" Bubba made LJ high-five him, and then said, "We'll get through this because" —and they said in unison— *"we're trailer-park tough."*

The old truck that was Bubba's pride and joy definitely looked out of place parked in the lot with so many expensive cars. Johnny's Corvette was two places down.

"I'm glad we didn't have to wear a suit and tie," LJ said as they walked toward the entrance.

"Me, too," Bubba responded, "because I don't have one."

"How about our birthday suit," LJ said jokingly. "We could tie a ribbon around our . . ."

"Stop it, LJ. This is serious stuff here."

"I know, Bubba. This is so serious I'm about to wet my pants." They both started laughing and were surprised when the door opened and the doorman said, "Good evening, gentlemen. Welcome to Green Valley Country Club." Recognizing the jerseys, he continued, "Turn right and go to the second banquet hall on the left. You'll see a sign there that says, 'Welcome Cougars.' Y'all have a good evening."

"Thank you, sir," Bubba said, "and you as well."

When they walked into the banquet hall, they immediately relaxed. Everyone was talking and laughing and there was nothing formal or intimidating about it. LJ did, however, notice an excessive amount of silverware next to the plates on the nearby tables but was quickly engaged by Rodney, which helped him to put silverware hell out of his mind. Johnny saw them and immediately came over and started a conversation with Bubba.

"Nice place," Bubba said and smiled.

"Food's decent," Johnny replied. "Glad y'all could make it."

"Me, too," Bubba lied. "We've been looking forward to it."

With football season over, they didn't have a lot in common. They had bonded on the field and as a team, but it pretty much ended with the last game. They had classes together, but had nothing else in common.

Mr. Kitchens, noting their arrival, came over and welcomed both of them. He was wearing a shirt and tie, but no jacket. Across the room, Bubba could see Coach Henderson, and he wasn't wearing a tie. Team member's numbers were placed on the table, designating where the players were to sit.

Bubba, realizing the tables had their corresponding jersey numbers by the place settings, scanned the room for his. Coach Henderson and his wife were already seated at what appeared to be the head table. On one side of them, Bubba could see his number, as well as LJ's. Directly across from them were Johnny's and Rodney's numbers. Six to eight people would sit at each table.

Bubba breathed a little easier. Coach Henderson had a mama just like theirs. He was one of them and it would be all right. The banquet hall had been decorated with a sports theme and whatever they were cooking in the kitchen smelled delicious. A small podium with a microphone had been set up near the head table. Coach Henderson made his way to the microphone and said, "Good evening. Everyone look around, find your number, and please have a seat."

In a minute, everyone was seated and the noise level died down. Waiters and waitresses stood at the rear of the room, waiting to serve the guests. Mr. Kitchens walked over to the podium, shook hands with Coach Henderson and then turned to address the team.

"We want to thank Green Valley Country Club for having us this evening." He started to clap, and everyone followed suit. "They always do an outstanding job, and I know each of you will enjoy the dinner they've prepared for tonight's celebration. I also want to thank Coach Charlie Henderson for delivering a winning season for Union High this year. It's his first year, and we believe he'll do great things for our school.

It's the first winning season our football team has had in twenty years."

The room erupted with applause and *hot damns* got started spontaneously, even making Coach Henderson's wife smile. Juanita, the school principal who was sitting with her husband at Mr. Kitchens' table, wrinkled her brow at the *hot damns* and looked over at Coach Henderson, seeking an explanation for the language the team seemed accustomed to throwing around. Coach Henderson, realizing she was a little perplexed, mouthed Vegas. She got the message and smiled back.

The applause subsided and those who had stood sat back down. Mr. Kitchens thanked them for recognizing Coach Henderson, and added that he most definitely deserved it. "I promise we won't starve anyone to death tonight, but we have a couple of folks who need to say a few things. Coach Henderson," Mr. Kitchens said, gesturing toward him.

Rising from his seat, Coach Henderson came over to the podium to address the team and the special guests. Mr. Kitchens pointed toward the microphone, nodded his head, and then returned to his seat.

The team again rose and gave Coach Henderson another round of applause.

"I'll keep mine short, guys," he said as he winked and smiled at the players and the other guests. "Great job, team. You made your school and community proud of you. And you made me proud as well. Remember what I told you. The memories you made this year will replay a thousand times throughout your lifetime. And everything you do going forward will have the same effect. Always give it your best shot so the memories will be good ones, and your mamas will always be proud of you. Thank you," he said.

As he started over to his table, the team members gave him

another round of applause. Mr. Kitchens, stepping behind the podium again, said, "My turn. I'll keep it short and honest. Notice, boys, that I said short and honest, not short and sweet. Sometimes, honest can be a bitter pill to swallow, and anything but sweet. This year our school's athletic program had a major turnaround and I did as well. This may or may not be the right place for this, but I think it fits in with the coach's message, and I hope it will also help each of you with your journey through life."

Mr. Kitchens had a strong voice and didn't really need a microphone. He stepped out from behind the podium and got a little closer to where the team members were sitting.

"If there's anyone here tonight I have ever offended by my actions or by anything I may have said, please accept my apology. I am truly sorry. Perhaps the theme for this dinner should have been "you made your mama proud."

Everyone smiled, thinking about what Mr. Kitchens had proposed for the dinner theme.

"Going forward," he continued, "I've promised myself and my family to make my mama proud. She raised me better than I've acted of late and, with God's help, I'll make amends and do better. And that's the message I want to leave with you. God gives second chances. If anyone here tonight needs one, all you have to do is ask. If I can get a second chance, I'm sure it would be a piece of cake for you."

Coach Henderson was the first on his feet, and everyone else stood up also. Applause filled the room. Bubba couldn't help but notice a tear running down Johnny's cheek, and as they made eye contact, he smiled and nodded at Johnny.

Mr. Kitchens' honesty had been moving and emotional. Even the staff, waiting to serve the meal, was touched. Juanita was blown away with his sincerity.

Mr. Kitchens, taking a handkerchief from his pocket, wiped his eyes. "I'm done," he said, "and thank you for being so attentive. There's only one more speaker before we eat the delicious meal that's been prepared for us. And, I might add, the next speaker wasn't forewarned. This thing should have been the other way around, but God works in mysterious ways. In this case, the son instructed the father. Please welcome my son, Johnny, to the podium. Johnny, come up here and give a brief summary of what this season has meant to you and the team as a whole."

Johnny was momentarily stunned. Again, he looked across the table at Bubba who smiled and gave him two thumbs up. Standing to applause, Johnny made his way to the podium where his father gave him a big hug. As Mr. Kitchens returned to the head table, Coach Henderson stood and shook his hand. Juanita also stood up and gave him a hug. "I'm proud to know you," she said softly, "and even more proud to call you friend."

When Mr. Kitchens reached the table, his wife gave him a hug. Johnny, watching all of this unfold, had a death grip on the podium.

He finally found his voice and said, "What a great year. I don't know where to begin, but winning sure beats the heck out of losing!"

Everyone applauded and a softer wave of *hot damns* made its way around the room.

"Takeaways count in football, but I believe they count even more in life. This year has been life-changing for me. I found out quickly there are others who can hit a bull in the ass with a handful of rice. It's not the position you have on a team, and not who you might think you are. I learned it's not about me, it's about each of you, or in this case, it's about the team as a whole. When you put yourself first, everyone suffers. Putting others first is a win for everyone. We won six in a row and that makes us all proud. And, rightly so. God willing, we'll have another good season next year. If we play as a team, then we'll win as a team. To quote an old cliché, there's no *I* in team. Love you guys."

Everyone stood and applauded as Johnny made his way back to his table. Bubba winked and nodded approval and this time, LJ gave Johnny two thumbs up.

Coach Henderson called Buddy up to the podium to say grace. Buddy said, "Thank you, Jesus. *Amen and Amen.*"

When the party ended, everyone said their goodbyes and headed for the parking lot. Bubba and LJ slammed Maude's doors in unison. Bubba wheeled the truck out of the parking lot and onto the highway.

"I hate to admit it, LJ, but we were worried about nothing. Silverware doesn't matter if the people have good hearts and good intentions."

"You're sounding more and more like Granny Preston," LJ said and smiled. "About time you learned something. I told you it would be okay."

"You lying sucker. If memory serves me right, you're the one who was going to turn into a naked Ninja warrior and slash your way out of the country club. And the silverware issue was about to drive you nuts."

"Well, we made it through the first party and the one at Bill's Diner will be on home turf. No worries there. Hope he fixes plenty of banana pudding," LJ said.

"Don't worry, Bill will outdo himself. He's one of us and he will not want the other boys to think the country club did a better job than he did. Banana pudding is his crowning touch. Believe me, you'll have all the banana pudding you can eat."

Bill Watson sat in a booth in his diner. The cooks and waitresses had left and he was tallying the daily tickets against cash register receipts, something he did every night after closing. He thought about the country club Christmas party and wondered how it went. Soon, it would be his turn. Bill, without realizing it, was a *hootie tootie warrior*. He had been raised just like Bubba and LJ, and money, or lack of it, had always been the gorilla in the room for him. The restaurant, combined with his work ethic, had made him a very prosperous businessman in the community. The Christmas toy drive and the local food pantry were the only two things he supported and he did a fantastic job with both. Even though they had reached out to him, he had chosen not to join the Chamber of Commerce or the country club. He had traded in their double-wide for a modest brick home in a rural setting.

Looking across the restaurant, the placards on the walls caught his eye. They had been, and still were, welcome gifts from customers. They were cute sayings and quips, and he was sure Green Valley Country Club didn't have placards on the walls in its dining rooms, especially ones that read: "A balanced diet is two cookies, one in each hand" or "Fat dogs won't hunt." He looked at another, and it made him smile: "$5 charge for whining." And another, "Enter as strangers, leave as friends."

Most of his regular customers had a similar background to his. As surely as Bubba and LJ couldn't afford to frequent the country club, the other team players didn't come to Bill's Diner. What would the boys think of the waitresses in blue jeans, the old jukebox in the corner, and all the cute placards on the walls, he wondered. He would do his best to make everyone feel welcome, and he knew for a fact that his food was, hands down, better than anything the country club could ever serve. Bill

Watson, *hootie tootie warrior,* had broken the cycle of poverty but couldn't let go of the memories and the pain of his raising.

For whatever reason, Sue Ellen had fallen in love with the White Charger. She insisted on having her mechanic fix his oil leak, give him a complete tune-up and rebuild his carburetor. She told Eula it was her Christmas present to him. Inside her heart, she thought the attraction was rooted in memories from her childhood. Her parents couldn't afford two late-model vehicles, so her mom always kept the newer car and her father always drove an old truck, usually a Ford. She went everywhere with him. Somehow, whenever she was in the White Charger, it made her feel young again and memories flooded her mind. She had even borrowed it a couple of times when William, Sr. was out of town. Not only would his mouth fall open, his eyes would pop out of his head if he saw her driving the White Charger. Whenever she had the White Charger, Eula would drive her Jaguar. Both were in hog heaven, as the old-timers would say. Eula was amazed at how an expensive car handled, and Sue Ellen happily drove the old truck. Sue Ellen had gone from being a sweet and innocent young girl, going places with her father in his truck, to a college student, disappointing her parents with her shenanigans with Mr. Morgan. Somehow, driving the White Charger reconnected the now affluent Sue Ellen to the little girl hiding somewhere inside her.

Hughes Electrical Contractors came back out and put up the Christmas trees. There was one large one outside the bank and two smaller ones inside. The branches had one tree inside each location. Mr. Morgan's Christmas tree was next, and they made sure the tree topper almost reached the ceiling on the third-floor level. The trees at the bank and the Morgan mansion were the hard ones to put up and decorate. It took a small one-man lift to decorate the tree in the Morgan mansion. Sue Ellen's tree was last on the list and by far the easiest. It was usually about ten feet tall and nearly touched the ceiling. Hughes Electrical Contractors strung the lights and put the decorations up near the top, but they left the bottom part, up to about six feet from the floor, for Sue Ellen and William to decorate. Her parents had given her some ornaments that had been in their families for several generations. She also had some with pictures of Sister Cass and Sister Francis inset into ornaments. Decorating the Christmas tree with her son was a special time for Sue Ellen. This year, they had additional help with Eula joining the decorating team. Hundreds of cars were already coming by to see the manger scene at the end of Sue Ellen's driveway. Christmas was just a few weeks away, and the entire town had gotten into the Spirit of the Season.

֎֎֎֎֎

Saturday evening, near closing time, William arrived at the DQ. "He's here," Sam said, joking with Eula. "And what's this? He's heading up the sidewalk, and it looks like he's going to come in. Could I ask you a favor?" Sam said quickly.

"You know you can," Eula said, wondering why on earth the Beamer was coming in.

"Introduce me to him," Sam said softly, so the other employees couldn't hear. "I've never met anyone as rich as him before."

"Oh, stop it, Sam. His father has all the money, not William, Jr.

He's more like you and me than you could ever imagine. But I'd love to introduce you to him, the greatest boss a girl could ever have."

"Now, it's really getting deep in here," Sam said. "Introduce me anyway. I want to meet the guy my best employee ever is going to marry."

Eula blushed big time and wondered if their feelings were so easy to read, or if Sam was just trying to aggravate her.

There was no time to decide on the answer. Junior was coming through the door and had started for the counter. Eula came out from behind the counter and planted a kiss on his cheek. Sam, without thinking, had followed her out to where William was standing.

"William, I'd like for you to meet Sam Kerr, owner of this wonderful place to work and the best boss a girl could ever have."

William shook hands with Sam and said, "Pleased to meet you, sir. I've heard nothing but good things about you. Eula brags a lot and says she's the best employee you've ever had or ever will have. Is there a grain of truth to any of that or is she just blowing smoke?"

Her mouth fell open, but Sam picked right up where the Beamer left off. "She's blowing more than smoke," Sam said. "She's coming close to just out and out lying. What do you think we should do about it, William?"

"Maybe a pay cut would get her attention. If it doesn't, you might have to send her to Liars Anonymous. I hear they can really get to the root cause of lying. It's usually a security issue, I believe."

"That's enough," Eula said. "The two of you are more full of it than a Christmas turkey."

Sam moved closer and gave Eula a big hug. "Best damn

employee I've ever had or ever will have. That's the truth and the sad truth it is. When she leaves me, and I know it'll be soon, it'll just about kill me."

"Why are you so early?" Eula asked, with Sam still standing there. "It's about forty-five minutes until I clock out."

"Sue Ellen wants to ride around town and look at all the Christmas decorations. Didn't know for sure, but I thought you might could slip away a few minutes early so we could all go together."

Sam jumped right in on cue. "Go ahead. It's quiet and won't get busy again tonight. Have a good time."

"Are you sure, Sam?"

"Go on and get out of here before I cut your pay. Nice to meet you, William," Sam said.

"And nice to meet you as well, sir. Sorry you have to put up with all her nonsense. It about drives me crazy, but at least I don't have to pay her. Can't imagine paying her and having to listen to her carry on the way she does. Let me know if I can help. Not promising anything, you understand."

"Thanks, Sam," Eula said. "You're a good man. Be careful the Beamer doesn't corrupt you. He has a way of doing that. Seems harmless, but he's a troublemaker. Let me get my things before he convinces you to fire me."

Sam was enjoying the bantering back and forth with Eula and William. "William, would you like a Coke or a blizzard? Anything at all? It's on the house. I really appreciate you getting her out of here early tonight. I needed a break."

"No, thank you, Sam. I just had a bite before I drove over. But I appreciate the offer. Might take you up on it another time."

Eula, listening to the conversation while getting her coat and purse, put them both in their place.

"You two need a break, all right, and I'm just the one to give it to you. You're both so full of it I'm surprised your shoes don't slosh when you walk."

"Wow," Sam responded. "Now, was that being ugly or what?"

"And it's almost Christmas," William said. "How could anyone talk about someone that way at Christmas? We're leaving now, Sam. Let me get her out of here before she hurts your feelings again." Sam, pretending to wipe his eyes, said, "Thanks, William, I owe you one."

꙰ꙮ꙰ꙮ꙰ꙮ

Sue Ellen walked to the gazebo, half way down her driveway. It didn't feel like Christmas. It had turned a little warm for December and a lightweight jacket was all she needed to feel snug and comfortable. Cars were slowly driving by the Nativity scene, with some people getting out to take pictures. The few minutes she had, while waiting on the Beamer and Eula to pick her up, was long enough to travel down memory lane.

Mr. Morgan and Marsha were out of the country for the holiday season. Her workload had been horrific for the past two weeks, and she was near exhaustion. End of the year filings and paperwork were monumental at banking facilities. Regulators wanted all the i's dotted and the t's crossed, and the majority of closing out the year fell on her shoulders.

Thinking about the Morgans being in England stirred old memories. Her involvement with William, Sr. had given her an intense course and training program in what the world looks like from the top down. Had it not been for the drunk-driving fatality, he would have discarded her and moved on. She had been his one big screw-up and had turned out to be his nemesis.

She was, and would remain, a thorn in his side, one he couldn't remove.

From him, she had earned a PhD in top-down economics. But then, at Saint Mary's, courtesy of Sister Cass, Sister Francis and the Fourth Man Walking, she had earned another PhD. The second one trumped the first. It was in bottom-up economics and compassion.

Whether sitting in her office with banking regulators or shopping at Tiffany's, or Walmart, she could scan people and see with clarity the rich and powerful or the poor and downtrodden. When God forgave her, He not only gave her a new heart, but a new vision as well, allowing her to view the world through His eyes. She could now see both ends of the socioeconomic spectrum and have compassion for both.

A smile crept across her face as she saw the White Charger turning in her driveway. The occupants of the vehicles driving by the Nativity scene probably wondered why an old truck was heading up the driveway toward the biggest house in the neighborhood. Sue Ellen left the gazebo and stepped out into the headlights of the old truck.

"Ready to go look at some Christmas decorations?" Sue Ellen asked as she slid in next to William.

"Absolutely," Eula replied. "Thanks for suggesting it. I love to see all the lights and decorations. Sorry it's a little crowded in here, but it'll be fun."

"I can't tell you how many miles I have ridden squeezed in the cab of my Dad's old trucks over the years. Whether looking at Christmas lights or going shopping with Mom, he always insisted the three of us go in his truck. And, most of the time, Lilly was riding in my lap."

"I have a great idea," Eula said excitedly. "Why don't we go by and pick up Lilly and take her with us?"

"Super idea," Sue Ellen responded. "Lilly would love that and so would my mom and dad."

"Who's Lilly," the Beamer asked, "and how is she going to fit in this cab?"

"We're putting you in the back," Eula said and giggled.

"Getting the two of you together was a monumental mistake," William said, half under his breath.

Two weeks had flown by, and Bill Watson was anxious and excited about the party the diner was giving the team. The diner was decorated and ready. Bill's wife, Sherry, and Susanna, his head waitress, had both considered having Bill committed to stop him from fretting himself to death over the party. He had gone over everything imaginable a hundred times, or so it seemed to them, and still couldn't stop worrying. It was a first for the diner, but also a first in recent history for the football team—a winning season. The time had come and Bill surveyed a full house. Small talk among the players and their guests filled the diner with a soft ambience, highlighting the Christmas celebration. The stage was set and only needed someone to start the party in motion.

Coach Henderson touched Cindi's hand and whispered, "Here goes nothing. Wish me luck."

Smiling, she whispered back to him, "You'll do fine. I'm hungry, Coach, let's get this party going."

Coach Henderson and Bill Watson had something in common. They were both glass-half-empty people, and while worrying about everything, they usually excelled, filling their glasses to the brim.

Bill had set up a podium in front of the cedar Christmas tree.

Toys donated and delivered to the diner were piled high around the tree, creating a festive, holiday spirit of giving.

The coach stepped up to the microphone and said, "Ladies and gentlemen, if the food tastes anything like it smells, we're in for a treat. And I can tell you from experience, it tastes even better than it smells. Before we begin, Buddy Ferguson, our outstanding equipment manager, will ask God's blessings upon each of us and our celebration here tonight."

Buddy, coming up to the microphone, surveyed his friends for a moment. They were all quiet and reverent. "Let us pray," Buddy said. "Lord, we thank You for loving us and sending Your son Jesus to dwell among us. Born so long ago in Bethlehem, may He have relevance and priority in each and every life gathered here tonight. Thank you, Lord, for a successful football season, where growth of spirit surpassed all athletic endeavors. For that we are exceedingly thankful. May we love each other as You commanded and be Your witnesses to everyone, everywhere. Bless this food and our time together. *Amen and Amen.*"

"Thank you, Buddy, for the prayer and your insight into our most amazing season. Now, where to begin is the question at hand." Winking at his wife, Cindi, he said, "Let's see if I can fill up this glass."

A few eyebrows were raised regarding the glass he had mentioned. There wasn't one on the podium or anywhere near him for that matter.

"Does anyone know why we're here tonight?"

"To eat and have fun," Rodney shouted out from a corner table.

Coach Henderson feared *hot damns* would break out, but restraint prevailed.

"Two good reasons, Rodney," the coach said. "But there's another reason, and it's one we seldom acknowledge, or give due credit. It allows us to assemble here tonight, laugh, eat, sing or pray without fear of reprisal. It's a powerful force, centered around brave men and women, each one putting the other ahead of themselves. Tonight, around the globe, they have our backs. They make this celebration possible and keep our country safe. They're called patriots, and the father of one of those patriots happens to be your host tonight. Bill, please come up for a moment. Let's give Mr. Bill Watson a round of applause for his kindness and support of our team and our community."

Everyone clapped enthusiastically and the waitresses, standing at the back of the room, started a chant, *"Bill, Bill, Bill."*

Always gracious and engaging, Bill came up to the mic and said, "Thank you for coming tonight. We are pleased to welcome you to the diner, and we hope you enjoy our hospitality. Come back to see us real soon." With that, he nodded and returned to his seat.

Coach Henderson, returning to the podium, gave the guests a moment to settle down and as soon as the room was quiet, he continued. "Lieutenant John William Watson was Bill and Sherry's son. He's with us tonight in spirit and represents the very best of what America stands for. John served twelve years in the Marine Corps and did three tours in Afghanistan. On a hot July day, seven years ago, John William Watson paid the ultimate price, sacrificing his life for love of country and his band of brothers. He was awarded posthumously the Purple Heart and the Medal of Honor."

Not a sound was heard in the room as Coach Henderson continued.

"Coming under fire, his platoon was pinned down on a ridge, with several forward troops wounded. Over and over, John, en-countering heavy incoming fire, left cover to drag the wounded back to safety. He went out one time too many and died on that ridge, spilling a hero's blood in the sands of a foreign land. This Christmas season we celebrate the birth of our Savior, Jesus Christ, who sacrificed His life for our salvation. Let us also celebrate the life of Lieutenant John William Watson and extend our heartfelt thanks to Bill and Sherry for their son's sacrifice for his country."

Absolute silence had fallen over the room. Bill had closed his eyes and Coach Henderson wondered what he was thinking. The group was spellbound as the coach reached behind him and picked up a framed picture of Bill and Sherry's son in full dress blues. He held it up for the team to see.

"Lieutenant John William Watson would have been proud to honor you tonight. He, too, graduated from Union High and would have enjoyed seeing his beloved Cougars win six in a row. I'm proud of you and am honored to be your coach. Our school has bragging rights again. It's been a long time coming, but let's be thankful and let's be humble as well. Our community has rallied around us, and their support is greatly appreciated. When you pray, thank God for men and women like Bill and Sherry's son, who loved others and country more than they loved self."

The team, led by Buddy, stood as a group and clapped reverently for Bill and Sherry and for their son. It was a moving tribute and surprised Coach Henderson.

"I could say a lot more, but I know you want me to sit down and hush so we can eat some of the wonderful food our noses tell us is somewhere in the building. But before I sit down and we eat, I'd like to ask Bubba Preston to come to the podium and say a few words."

"Oh, shit," Bubba said softly, but still audibly.

"Not exactly what I had in mind," Coach Henderson said and laughed along with everyone else.

Clarice had to push him out of his chair.

"Go on, Bubba," LJ said. "Go tell us what really happened this year." There was no way out of this, short of leaving the party.

While he was standing, but still not moving forward, the team started a chant—Bubba, Bubba, Bubba. After a few seconds, Bubba finally began making his way toward the podium and Coach Henderson.

LJ said, "Hot damn, somebody lock the door so he can't run out." Bubba, smiling at LJ's remark, found himself behind the podium.

Coach Henderson introduced him. "I give you Mr. Tom Preston, aka Bubba Preston, a primary reason for this year's success on the playing field and, hopefully, next year as well." With that said, the coach sat down next to his wife, leaving Bubba by himself behind the podium.

Bubba had the gift of gab among his friends but had never spoken before to a group in a forum like this one. Grabbing the podium with both hands brought laughter from everyone throughout the restaurant.

"Hold on tight," someone yelled out from the back of the room.

Finding his voice, Bubba said, "What I'd like to do is pull a Coach Henderson and name someone else to share their thoughts about this year. But, somehow, I don't think it's an option. Two things come to my mind."

"Run and keep running," Johnny shouted out.

"Well, four things come to mind if I count Johnny's two." Laughter, said to be the best medicine, was working.

Nodding at Bill and Sherry, Bubba said, "I love this place. Eat here all the time, but tonight is different. I've seen Lieutenant John's picture time and time again. I've seen the American flag in the window and the medals and awards many times before tonight. But being so caught up in my own world, I've never even asked any questions or let the significance of the flag and medals register in my mind."

The room had grown reverently quiet.

"A question for me and for you as well is this— would I risk my life for any one of you? For LJ? For anyone? I hope so, but in reality, I'm not sure. I think they call it trial by fire. I'm humbled to be in the same room with Bill and Sherry. Not the owners of Bill's Diner and our gracious hosts tonight, but the father and mother of a true hero who gave his life for others. That's a sobering thought, when compared to a celebration for winning six consecutive games on a grassy field at some high school no one has ever heard of before. That's the first thing that comes to my mind."

The room was so quiet it seemed like a church service.

"Second thing and the most important. The Tom Preston who became part of the Union High Cougars football team and the Tom Preston who stands before you tonight is not the same person. My Granny Preston, who recently passed away, told me to always remember God's two greatest commandments. Number one. Love God with all your heart, mind, body and soul. Number two. Love your neighbor as you love yourself. What I've learned this year and hope to always remember is this. People live in different houses, drive different kinds of cars, wear different brands of clothes and even eat out in different restaurants. And, if there's a sliding scale of one to ten, it doesn't matter if you're a one, a ten, or somewhere in the middle. We're all still neighbors and commanded by God to love one another. With that said, God bless you, Merry Christmas, and I love every one of you."

The only sound heard was Bubba walking back to his seat and moving his chair on the cement floor of the restaurant.

Coach Henderson, standing again behind the podium, said, "Nothing more could be said, or needs to be said. Let's eat."

Everyone in the room had been to church. *Amen and Amen.*

⌘⌘⌘

It was 4:30 on Christmas Eve. Bubba had done a great job decorating and preparing for the party. His mom was impressed with his attention to detail regarding Granny Preston's decorations and the party in general. Walking out into the front yard for a final check of the lights left him satisfied with his effort. "Granny Preston would love this," he thought.

His dad and mom were inside entertaining Clarice's and Eula's parents. They had been friends from way back, even before Bubba, Clarice and Janice were born. LJ had taken Janice and Clarice to the mall for some last-minute shopping. Eula had promised to get there early, but they never discussed what early meant. He had cut the cedar tree the day before and it was inside, in a stand, waiting to be decorated.

As he started inside, someone pulled into the driveway. Turning, he saw Eula and William in her old truck. Meeting them as they parked, he walked around to the driver's side and opened the door for Eula. "Did you get an early Christmas present on manners?" she asked and poked Bubba in the ribs with her finger at the same time.

"I apologize for her," William said. "I've been trying to get her to act better, but so far, I haven't had any luck."

Shaking William's hand, Bubba said, "Glad you could come. As far as Eula Johnson is concerned, you can forget her ever doing any better. She's beyond hope."

"Guys, in case you haven't noticed, it's cold out here, and it's getting deeper by the second. And, for the record, it ain't snowing," Eula noted in response to their remarks.

"Sharp-tongued devil," Bubba said to William. "Y'all come inside and get warm."

As they entered the trailer, Mr. Johnson, Mr. Smith and Mr. Preston stood up. Eula gave each of them a hug and then introduced William to everyone there.

The visit to Southern Mobile Home Sales had paid off. The Beamer was totally at home, and everyone there could feel it. The Morgan name was synonymous with wealth and power, but the portal had opened again and William Morgan, Jr. had successfully crossed it one more time, displaying humility and love. Granny Preston would have enjoyed meeting him.

LJ, Janice and Clarice arrived, followed by LJ's parents. Eula quipped, "Old folks eight, young folks, six."

"Don't forget Granny," Bubba said, "she's coming to the party."

"Then it's old folks eight, and young folks seven," Eula said.

"Granny's an angel now and they're forever young," Clarice added.

Everyone had placed their presents near the tree. Clarice had intentionally left Bubba's surprise gift in the swing on the front porch. She wanted it to be the last gift he received and she knew the weight and shape of the box would give it away.

Mr. Johnson was impressed with William. "Not a bad choice," he thought to himself, "especially considering his old man is a horse's ass."

Bubba relaxed, realizing Eula was right again. Money doesn't have to be an enemy. William was not who Bubba had feared would show up at his party. As a matter of fact, everybody immediately liked him.

LJ talked William's head off. One would have thought they were long-lost friends.

Mrs. Preston had warned her husband, and told him to tell the other men, to keep jokes to a minimum and to absolutely keep them clean. "It's Christmastime," she reminded him. "Save your jokes for Bill's Diner." She had also asked Bubba to help her keep an ear out. "You know how these old men love to tell their jokes," she told her son.

"Good luck with that one, Mom. I'll try and keep them in line, but no promises."

All the guys were sitting in the living room and the women were in the kitchen. Mr. Preston said, "LJ, did you hear the one about the church organist who had played for the same church for thirty years and had never missed a service?"

Bubba perked up, but it sounded innocent enough. It had an organist and a church setting. Couldn't be that bad, he thought.

"No sir, I haven't heard that one," LJ said smiling. He loved good jokes.

"Well, one day the organist was practicing a song and the pastor came by and stopped to chat with her. 'Diane,' he said. 'I know you've been playing this organ faithfully for a long time and have never been out sick, not even once. Some of us were wondering, what's your secret for staying healthy?'

'Pastor, it's like this. I was walking across the parking lot the very first Sunday I played the organ for y'all. I saw a small box on the pavement. I picked it up and it had writing on it. It said, place on organ for the prevention of disease. I did, and I haven't been sick a single time.'" Mrs. Preston heard the laughter and knew someone had told a joke. She looked into the den. Everyone was laughing their butts off.

"Keep it down a little, guys," Bubba said softly. "Don't let Mama hear any of your jokes or we'll all be put in time-out."

"For sure," his father said. "Keep it down, boys."

Mr. Johnson, Eula's dad, was next. "Did y'all hear the one about the little boy and his teacher? He had his hand in his pocket and she asked him, 'David, what do you have in your pocket? Take your hand out of your pocket this instant.' The little boy didn't respond and she told him again. 'David, take your hand out of your pocket and show me what you have in it.'

'Teacher, if you can guess what I have in my pocket, I'll let you have it. I'll give you three clues.'

'Okay,' the teacher said. 'What are the clues?'

The little boy was all smiles. 'It's round and it's hard, and it's got a head on it.'

The teacher was beside herself. She grabbed him by the ear and marched him down to the principal's office. Before she could even start to explain what she thought the little boy had done, he pulled a quarter out of his pocket and said, 'Here it is, ma'am. You didn't guess it, but I'll give it to you anyway.'"

Again, the guys were hooting with laughter.

"My turn," LJ said. "Just heard this one today at the hardware store. A city slicker was lost. Seeing an old country store, he wheeled in to ask directions. Seven or eight old men were sitting on the porch in chairs, most of them on two legs as they leaned back against the wall. A huge old hound dog was lying next to the front door, licking himself. The salesman stopped on the top step and noticed the dog. 'Wish I could do that,' he said, trying to be funny. The old man closest to him said with a straight face. 'Wouldn't do that, if I were you. Old Blue will bite you.'"

William thought that was the funniest one of all. He got a visual of Old Blue biting the salesman and laughed for what seemed like forever.

Mrs. Preston knew they were telling bad jokes, but smiled anyway. They seemed to be having such fun. Maybe they weren't too bad and William wouldn't be too embarrassed by their shenanigans. She noted he was quite the willing participant and laughing as hard as the rest of the guys. Eula said, "I'm sure they're corrupting William in there."

The older women started to get the food together and Eula, Clarice and Janice set the table. It was not silverware, just Walmart's finest flatware. Mrs. Preston had been cooking all day. Bubba had grilled some hamburgers and hot dogs and also had some deer steaks and baby back ribs. There was a ton of food with delicious savory smells wafting through the trailer. Mrs. Preston had a reputation for making the best banana pudding in the free world. She had made two for the party.

The guys finally stopped telling jokes and were talking sports and politics. The Beamer seemed like he had always been one of the family. Eula kept an eye on him and an ear out, but it was soon apparent that he was okay and enjoying himself. Bubba was shell-shocked at how much he actually liked the guy.

When everything was ready, the food was placed on the counter in the kitchen. Everyone filled their plates and then found a seat at the table. The young people found a place on the floor in the living room. When the last guest was seated, Bubba stood to say grace.

"Lord, for Your blessings, we give You thanks. For your Grace, we gladly give ourselves. We thank You for family and friends, and for our beloved Granny Preston, who's celebrating her first Christmas with You. We thank You for letting us have her for such a long time. Our lives have all been shaped by You, through her example of how to live a Godly life. And now, Lord, bless the food and the hands that prepared it. Bless the banana pudding, Lord. May it be like the oil and meal that fed the widow and Elijah. May we eat our fill and have leftovers for tomorrow. Amen."

When everyone had opened their eyes, Bubba caught Eula's glance and she was shaking her head. "So eloquent, except for the part about the banana pudding," she said jokingly.

LJ chimed in. "I see it differently. I think the blessing on the banana pudding should have been first."

William, fitting right in, said, "I love banana pudding. Can't ever have too much banana pudding."

Eula shook her head and said, "Boys will be boys."

Mrs. Preston, ever vigilant for the Lord, said, "Now don't be sacrilegious, LJ."

"Oh, no, ma'am, I wasn't. God understands our weaknesses and provides grace to cover them. He knows how much I love banana pudding."

The meal was delicious. The Beamer went through the line twice. Eula was amazed. He fit into the group like an old worn out shoe easily slips onto one's foot. He was a messy eater and had pudding all over his shirt. Eula chastised him for missing his mouth.

After everyone finished eating, Bubba stood up again and said, "Before we decorate the tree and open presents, I think it would be appropriate to take a moment or two for reflection on what Granny Preston meant to those who knew her and loved her."

Eula couldn't resist. "Who is this young man who speaks so eloquently?"

Bubba raised his eyebrows and pointed a finger at her and then put it to his lips. Everyone smiled, most thinking how hard it would be, if not impossible, to get Eula to be quiet.

"I'll go first," Bubba said. "Words would fail me if I tried to tell you how much I miss her. Our Sunday morning ride to church was the highlight of my week. Though we had the same conversations every week for the last year or so, the stories she told made the people and times she remembered come alive again. And her words of wisdom, which were mostly God's words with her spin put on them, will stay with me for the rest of my life."

One by one, around the table, everyone shared a special memory of Granny Preston. LJ called her a saint in a print dress. Eula said on multiple occasions one of Granny's sayings or Bible verses had saved Bubba's life, and had kept her from killing him. Everyone laughed.

The last to stand was William Morgan, Jr., who never knew or met Granny Preston.

"May I say something?" he asked humbly.

"Absolutely," Bubba said, without hesitation. "You're part of the family."

Eula's eyes watered. "That's Granny Preston's Bubba," she thought.

William nodded and continued. "I can't claim any memories of this woman who is held in such high esteem by everyone gathered here tonight. And Eula is the only one I have spent time with up until now. But if the love each of you has extended to me is any reflection of Granny Preston's influence, then she was a saint long before she left this world."

"Amen," Bubba said under his breath.

"And, while I have the floor—and I might add, I didn't ask Eula's permission to speak tonight, I have an announcement of sorts to make."

Eula's eyes got big. "Oh shit. Beamer, be careful here," she said under her breath. Bubba, seeing the surprised look, pointed at her and smiled.

Turning to Bubba, William asked, "May I give Eula her present while the family is gathered around the table?"

"Sure thing," Bubba said, caught off guard by William's deference to him.

Addressing Mr. and Mrs. Johnson, he continued, "Both of you

should be very proud. Your daughter is a sweet, beautiful, kind, caring and thoughtful person. I'm sure Granny Preston is proud of her, too. I'm going to stop this short of a formal announcement and let everyone interpret it as they please."

Eula's hands felt clammy and she felt like perspiration was beading on her forehead. Bubba was all smiles. The men were seated on one side of the table, the women on the other and all the young people had gathered around the table. Turning to Eula, he extended his hand to her. She felt like her legs were about to buckle. Reaching into his pocket, he took out a ring box.

She couldn't contain it any longer. *"You gotta be . . ."* William quickly put a finger on her lips and smiled. The table erupted in laughter. Everyone knew what she was about to say had William not stopped her.

Opening the ring box, he removed a very simple, inexpensive ring. Taking her left hand, he slipped the ring on her finger, leaned over and kissed her. "Now, Eula Johnson, what do you think about that?"

Mrs. Johnson was crying. Mr. Johnson was all smiles. "Well, boys, I think she's brought him home."

Everyone clapped and Bubba said, "Nice touch, William. I might steal that one from you for a later date."

Clarice said to herself, "If you don't listen to me, Bubba Preston, later will be sooner than you think."

Eula, responding with a tight hug, followed by a long kiss, said, "I love you, Beamer."

"I know," he said.

After coffee, everyone moved to the living room and found places around the tree. The young people sat on the floor near the presents. Before sitting down, Clarice took a peek out on the porch to make sure Bubba's present was still in the swing.

"Why did you go outside?" Bubba asked her.

"To see if it was snowing."

"I don't think the weather forecast called for any snow," Eula said.

"It's Christmas Eve," Clarice said. "We can hope, can't we?"

Bubba let it go and Clarice said to herself, "You don't have to know everything. Mess with me, Big Boy, and I'll take that old gun back and go on a shopping spree that won't wait." She giggled, which made Bubba wrinkle his brow in question. She just smiled back and shrugged her shoulders in innocence.

After everyone was comfortable, Bubba placed Granny Preston's angel on the top of the cedar Christmas tree. "Granny Preston loved cedar Christmas trees. She told me many times that a cedar Christmas tree was good for your health, and if you were feeling puny, it would fix what ails you." Standing in front of the tree, with everyone listening, Bubba continued remembering good things about his Granny.

"Christmas was her favorite time of the year. Always told me about the birth of Jesus, and every Christmas season she made it sound brand new, like it had just happened. She scraped and saved all year so she could buy everyone a little something." Looking up, Bubba said, "This is your party, Granny. We feel your spirit, but wish you were here with us in person."

William, feeling the love the family and friends had for each other, was almost sad. Except for Sue Ellen, no one else in his family even acknowledged it was a special time of the year. He felt loved by everyone, and wished he could have had a chance to meet Granny Preston.

After Bubba had finished, Mrs. Johnson said, "There's plenty of coffee and Cokes in the kitchen. And there's a lot of banana pudding left. Please, everyone help yourself."

William, sitting next to Eula on the floor, looked at her and said, "Mind if I have a little more?"

"You could probably get a spoonful from your shirt. I couldn't get it all off. You made a huge mess with the pudding. I don't know if you need anymore. Can't take you anywhere."

Eula was just joking and playing around about the banana pudding, but it sounded bad to her dad. He got up from the couch and walked over to where they were sitting. "Come on, son. It's now or never. Give her an inch and she'll take a foot. Let's go get ourselves a huge bowl of that banana pudding. And, if you get more on your shirt, that's okay, too."

"Dad," Eula exclaimed. "Whose side are you on here?"

"His," Mr. Johnson said. "Can't believe you'd deny him another bowl of banana pudding."

LJ jumped up and followed Mr. Johnson. "Mighty good stuff, that pudding. Think I'll get myself another bowl, too."

"While y'all are attacking the banana pudding, I'll string the lights so we can get on with the rest of the decorations," Bubba told LJ. "Then we'll all take turns hanging the ornaments."

"Sounds like a plan," LJ said, as he disappeared into the kitchen.

In a few minutes, Mr. Johnson, William, and LJ were back, each with a huge portion of banana pudding.

"Might need to put some side rails on your bowl," Eula told the Beamer.

"No need to worry," he responded. "I got this under control."

Watching the three of them scarf down the banana pudding caused Janice to comment on what it looked and sounded like. "Hey, Eula, this is just like slopping hogs," she said and laughed at her own wit. "If we ever marry one of these guys, at least they'll be low maintenance. Just cook them a banana pudding once a month and they'll do anything we tell them."

"They do anything we tell them now, don't they?" Eula said softly so the guys couldn't hear.

Clarice and Janice both smiled at Eula's remark. "Got them trained already," Janice said, "and I don't even know how to make a banana pudding."

Bubba had placed the ornaments on the coffee table. "I'm stringing the lights, and when I get done, anyone who wants to can hang ornaments on the tree. Granny Preston used these ornaments for years. The ones with family photos will be last and we'll let Mom put them on."

"Great idea," LJ said. "Granny would like it." LJ's grandparents had all passed away years before, and he had loved Granny Preston as if she was his own grandmother.

While Bubba put the lights on the tree, the older generation talked about past Christmases and remembered family members who were no longer living. The younger generation, sitting on the floor around the base of the tree, talked about the here and now. Bubba heard Clarice tell Eula about a big after-Christmas sale at the mall. According to her, they were literally giving away their inventory. He couldn't pass up the opportunity to comment.

"Hey, William," Bubba said. "What do you think about the girls already planning a shopping spree? I don't think Clarice even bought me a Christmas present, but she's talking about buying herself more clothes and shoes. As if she needs them, poor thing. Imagine that, William."

"I know what you mean, Bubba. Eula just told them she'd go, too."

"Hard to keep good women down," Janice added. "I'm going with them."

"Look at this," LJ chimed in. "Now, they're corrupting Janice and dragging her into their scheme."

Janice smiled and poked LJ in the ribs. "No one is dragging me, LJ. I'm going because I can and because I want to."

When the lights were on the tree, everyone took turns hanging the ornaments. In no time, the tree was decorated except for the ornaments left for Bubba's mother to hang. There were ten, each a small, framed picture of family members. Most of them were older photographs, and Mrs. Preston shared the significance of each one.

When the last ornament was hung, Bubba put garland around the tree and plugged in the lights. It was beautiful. William was experiencing something new. People with less were having far more enjoyment decorating a six-foot Christmas tree than visitors exclaiming over the thirty-foot tree delivered and decorated by Hughes Electrical Contractors at the Morgan mansion.

LJ, forever the kid in the group, said excitedly. "Listen," in a serious tone. Everyone immediately got quiet. After a few seconds passed and no one heard anything, Bubba asked, "To what?"

"Reindeer," LJ said enthusiastically, "Santa just landed on the roof." He had caught Bubba in his ruse and everyone laughed.

"Got me," Bubba said. "Guess that means the kid in the bunch is in need of a present. Hope Janice got you something. If she did, maybe you'll share it with me because I looked as I put the presents around the tree, and my name wasn't on any of them."

"Poor Bubba," Eula said. "You've been naughty all year and that's why you're not going to get a present. Santa's been watching you with both eyes, and you're out of luck. Boy, I cleaned that one up. Santa's already been good to me," she said, holding up her ring for all to see.

Clarice, listening to all the bull, said, "Keep it up, Bubba, and I may just put you in time-out."

"Yeah," LJ chimed in. "I can just see Bubba standing in the corner."

Bubba passed all the presents out and a massive pile of paper had accumulated in the middle of the room. William made a mental note that the ribbons and bows were saved so they could be used again.

Santa Claus had been good to everyone. Everyone except Bubba. When Clarice thought she had punished him enough, she said in a very excited voice, "Listen, everybody."

"To what?" Bubba asked, rolling his eyes.

Clarice was having a ball, messing with his mind. "You'd better listen, Bubba Preston, or I'll tell Granny what you've been up to lately."

That made Clarice's parents take note.

"Listen," she said again. "Listen and mind me, Tom Preston. What you didn't hear was Santa making a special delivery to the front porch swing. You'd better get out there and see if he left you something."

Bubba hesitated as everyone watched to see what was unfolding.

"Go," Clarice said in a loud voice. "Go before Santa changes her mind."

That made the entire group laugh and wonder with Bubba what Santa had possibly left in the swing.

"If you don't go," LJ said, "I will. Might have left me something, too. I've been real good this year."

"Right," Janice remarked. "Sure, you have."

Bubba went outside and returned quickly, holding three wrapped presents. Clarice, against her better judgment, had gone back and bought the gun case and two boxes of ammo. The weight and shape of the presents obviously suggested a gun to Bubba. He couldn't help himself. He had kid written all over his face.

Clarice took over. "Open the small one first."

Ripping the paper off the heavy little present revealed two boxes of ammo. He quickly reached for the one that was obviously a gun of some kind.

"Whoa, whoa, whoa," Clarice said, with excitement in her voice. Everyone laughed. Bubba stopped and waited for further instructions.

"You have to learn patience, Bubba," she told him in a long, slow, drawn-out sentence.

"I'll show you patience," Bubba thought.

She was having too much fun to have it end. "Since it's Christmas, and we're honoring Granny's memory, let's all sing two verses of *Silent Night*. If you can't remember all the words, just hum along."

It was a nice touch for the party, and everyone was enjoying Clarice's humor and wit. When the singing and humming stopped, all eyes turned to her to see what was coming next. Bubba sat, as if suspended in a time warp.

"Now, Mr. Preston, you may open the one with the red bow." Bubba morphed back to a ten-year-old and unashamedly ripped the paper from the gun case she swore she wouldn't buy.

Looking up, he said, "Please don't make us sing again." Laughter filled the mobile home.

It was only a few seconds, but it seemed like an eternity.

"I sit here tonight, battered, abused, neglected, and only you know, Lord, how unappreciated I am by this young man known as Tom Preston." On the surface, it sounded reverent, but Clarice was having far too much fun for it to be a prayer.

"Go," she said.

Bubba tore off the paper covering the brown box holding the top-of-the-line deer rifle. When he opened the box and took the rifle out, Mr. Johnson, Mr. Preston and Mr. Smith couldn't believe their eyes. None of them had a deer rifle anywhere near as nice as this one.

A grateful Bubba lowered the rifle and asked, "How did . . ."

Clarice didn't wait for him to finish. "Took me six months to pay for it," she said and smiled. "I'm nearly naked for need of clothes I couldn't buy because every cent I made I had to take to Mike at the hardware store. Mike told me he wished he had someone to buy him a rifle like this. I told him not to look at me. One was my limit. He said he knew you'd appreciate it."

"I'll show you appreciation later," Bubba thought. Getting up, he went over to where she was sitting, helped her up and gave her a hug and a long kiss. This embrace was duly noted by her parents.

It was a very special party. Everyone was in a festive mood and, overall, it expressed the true meaning of Christmas—people loving one another and showing it.

William felt older than his years and was humbled by the love and happiness he had witnessed and felt between this family and their friends. As the party was coming to an end, he said a silent prayer. "Thank you, Lord, for opening my eyes to the truly important things in life."

"Amen and Amen."

Christmas had come and gone. Bubba had carefully stored Granny Preston's decorations away for the next Christmas. McClain's, getting additional orders, returned to a forty-hour workweek. This helped to ease the financial strain the short hours and the extra expenses the Christmas season had created.

Mr. Morgan was fast-tracking three mega business mergers. Hughes Electrical Contractors had taken down the giant Christmas tree at the Morgan mansion his guests had oohed and ahhed over and it was now in the landfill. The Morgan mansion had returned to normal, a lonely place. Hughes removed the Nativity stable and lifelike figures and Sue Ellen's tree as well. Sue Ellen kept baby Jesus in a spare bedroom year round.

The second week in January, Bubba killed a ten-point buck with the gun Clarice gave him for Christmas. He priced having it mounted by the local taxidermist but couldn't afford to spend the money. There would be other opportunities, and perhaps a deer with a larger rack.

Poor old Ernest was three months behind again on Whispering Pines, and this time Sue Ellen could not bail him out.

Eula and the Beamer continued to test the springs on the White Charger several times a week. Bubba and Clarice were still squeezing in several married folk sessions a week at her house, utilizing the forty-five-minutes to an hour window they had between the time school was out and her folks got home from work.

Time passes quickly, and twinkling Christmas lights and gifts were now a distant memory. Daffodils were starting to push their way up through the soil. Trees were getting new leaves, and life was coming back from the hiatus known as winter. Birds were singing in chorus, welcoming the coming season. It was time to build nests and prepare for new families, a time for renewal and a time for restoration.

For Bubba and LJ, it was school all day and work every evening until midnight. LJ called it balls to the wall. A pregnancy scare late in January gave Clarice the resolve once again to tell Bubba no. Valentine's Day, with flowers and candy, earned Bubba what Clarice called a week-end pass from no. As fate would have it, the accident she had so frequently referred to would take place with the tantalizing smell of roses filling the inside of Maude's cab. The die had been cast, and Bubba's future secured at McClain's. A home, with wheels had his name on the mailbox.

Though no formal announcement was made, the ring William gave Eula at Bubba's Christmas party paved the way for their future together. When he shared it with Sue Ellen, she understood and was okay with it. She only had one request. "Do not, I repeat, do not tell your parents or anyone close to them about Eula or the ring. I love Eula like my own daughter and you know how much I care for you. But your father will never stand for you marrying someone from a mobile home with generational attachments to a furniture manufacturing plant. That's sad, but it's just the way it is. He thinks like the ancients who tried to marry off their children to strengthen alliances and build kingdoms. He will disinherit you faster than you can say Jack Scat, and will never reconsider. Down deep, he's a good man. I've seen the good man surface on more than one occasion. However, he's stubborn and strong willed. He thinks he needs no one, and in his world, he doesn't. I want you and Eula to inherit his fortune, some of which is ill-gotten gain, but yours to inherit, and with clean hands on your part. The two of you could do a world of good with the inheritance, alleviating more problems than you could ever imagine. Please trust me on this one. I absolutely know what I'm talking about."

⁓⊷⁓⊷⁓⊷⁓

"Where to?" Eula asked as the Jaguar roared to life.

"How about Lou's inside the mall?" Sue Ellen suggested. "They have great soup and usually good tuna fish sandwiches. I need to eat healthy. I put on five pounds over the holidays, mostly because of eating too many sweets."

"Me, too," Eula said. "I ate too much cake and too many cookies and way too much banana pudding. Everywhere I went, someone had baked cookies or a cake, or made a banana pudding. It may not be a universal Christmas favorite, but banana pudding has first place for Christmas desserts in my circle of friends and family."

"William has put on a few pounds like we have," Sue Ellen said. "He denies it, but I tell him his belly has done lopped over his belt. It aggravates him a little, but the proof is in the pudding, no pun intended."

"That's funny," Eula said. The Jag was purring along and it ran so smoothly.

"Love this car," Eula told Sue Ellen.

"It does drive good, doesn't it?" she acknowledged. "One day, we'll take the Corvette on one of our outings. The only reason I bought the Corvette was because William thought I would look good driving it around town. Do I look that gullible? He really thought he would look good driving it around town. So, anyway, one day we'll both look good driving it up to Asheville."

"I'd like that. I might see if Sam will let the Beamer cover for me."

"I'd like to see the blizzard William would make," Sue Ellen said. They both were laughing as they pulled into the mall parking lot.

William watched from his upstairs bedroom window as the shopping duo drove away in the Jaguar. Sue Ellen and Eula were acting like high school friends. His mother was in England and his dad was scheduled to fly out in the afternoon to join her for some vacation downtime. She was spending more time at their home in England than she was at the Blairsville mansion.

Giving Eula the ring, with her family and friends sitting around the table, had left an indelible impression on him. The love he felt, and the warm, friendly relationships everyone seemed to have with one another, was something his family didn't have, and he wanted this in his life. Fueled by those thoughts, he remembered he had not yet gone by his father's office to see the surprise his dad had to show him. Dressing quickly, he headed to the bank in Sue Ellen's Corvette. His father would be there, making last-minute preparations for his short vacation in England.

Mr. Morgan had bought an original Norman Rockwell and couldn't wait to show it to his son. He collected art for financial gain, not for the love of art itself. Any distress sale or inside tip would bring him scrambling to pick up a piece below market value. He actually considered it a hedge against market fluctuations, and he only purchased rare or original pieces, knowing they would always bring a premium.

As surely as Mr. Morgan desired to share his good fortune with his son about his new art piece, the Beamer wanted to tell his father about the wonderful young woman he had given a ring to and had every intention of marrying one day. He would be throwing Sue Ellen's advice out the window regarding how his father would react to his announcement.

"Good morning, William," his father said as his son entered his office.

"Hi, Dad. Sue Ellen said you had a surprise you wanted to show me."

"You're not going to believe what I bought. Let me show you something so extraordinary, I can't believe my good fortune."

Getting up from behind his massive desk, he walked over to a huge safe, put in the combination and opened the door to what looked more like a large room than a safe. There were numerous pieces of art and other collectibles, hanging or on shelves. It was temperature controlled, and the humidity was also regulated to protect the works of art.

"What do you say to this, William?" his dad said, holding up a rare, original Norman Rockwell.

"Wow! Isn't that one of Rockwell's masterpieces? I wouldn't have thought anyone would have put it on the market."

"Well, in fact, it never hit the market. Your old man just happened to be in the right place at the right time when the grapevine was whispering about the financial misfortunes of my friend. He had made several market blunders and missteps and selling this original Rockwell made it possible for him to recover from those mistakes. A very reliable art dealer confirmed its value, and I called and offered him twenty-five percent less than market value. I offered him cash and told him I would keep the selling price confidential, to save him embarrassment. He hated to part with it because the whole world associates ownership of this painting with him, but no longer. Now, whenever it's brought up, the Morgan name will accompany the painting. Today, they will think of William Morgan, Sr. Someday, they will think of William Morgan, Jr. What have you got to say about that, son?"

"It's an awesome painting, dad, and a stroke of luck to buy it at any price. You know I'd consider it an honor and a privilege to own it someday, and I'd cherish it. Twenty-five percent below value was a steal," William told his Dad. "Steal is the right word," he thought.

"Would you like something to drink? I think I'll get Elaine to bring me a cup of coffee."

"Sure thing, Dad, I'll take a Coke."

When the refreshments were brought in, Mr. Morgan asked Elaine, his secretary, to close his office door.

"Have a seat, William, and stay a few minutes. I don't have to leave until three o'clock. What has Sue Ellen been up to lately?"

"Nothing much," he responded. "She's doing her usual routine of working, shopping and more work. She's still helping out at the local children's hospital on weekends. How about Mom? Is she still enjoying the new home in England?"

"You know she is. She spent a small fortune decorating for her first Christmas overseas. I'm sure many more will follow. She loves Europe and the people there love her back. Of course, they should, the way she throws my money around," he said and smiled. "But it's okay. She's a fine woman, a good wife and a good mother."

William was apprehensive, but the atmosphere seemed right for the conversation concerning Eula.

"Dad, I've met someone who has become really special to me. Obviously, it would be after college, but I have every intention of marrying her someday. Her name is—"

"Wait, wait, wait, hold on a second, son. You're thinking about marrying someone you haven't even introduced to your mother and me? I sure hope this girl you're about to tell me about isn't the one from the trailer park down on Upper

Hightower Road. Because if it is, it's not going to happen, not today, not tomorrow, not ever. Do I make myself clear? A friend of mine told me he had seen you fooling around with someone from that trailer park, and I assured him he was mistaken. Not my William, I told him. If anything, he's found a cheap thrill and is enjoying himself. I assured him that you knew better than to ever become serious about someone living there."

William couldn't believe what he was hearing. Sue Ellen had been right, one hundred percent right. He could feel his face flush and his palms getting sweaty. It had been only a couple of seconds, but it felt like an eternity since his father had stopped him in mid-sentence and began his tirade. How to respond to his father's bias was the question. Before he could decide whether to tell his dad to take a flying leap, Mr. Morgan continued his rant.

Rising behind his desk, William Morgan, Sr. leaned over and put both hands, palms down, on the desk. His son, sitting directly in front of him, had no idea what was about to happen.

"My father gave his entire life amassing a fortune that I inherited. Thirty-five years have passed since his death, and I've personally tripled the net worth of the Morgan family. I'm proud to call you my son, and have every intention of leaving you everything I own. I have no secrets, and just so you know, you're the only heir to the Morgan empire. Your mother signed a prenuptial agreement and won't get jack from my estate. She's financially secure in her own right."

Sue Ellen had been correct, making her analysis so many years ago at Saint Mary's. He knew his blood flowed through young William's veins—something he valued even more now than then. William was getting insight into the monster wealth had created, and the unhappiness in the life of the man he called father. He would later think about it and wonder how Sue Ellen managed to work with and control someone so biased and so consumed by power and wealth.

Mr. Morgan could tell his son was angry and knew he was treading on dangerous ground. He would do some soul searching on his flight to England, and would surmise that Sue Ellen's DNA was very strong in their son.

"Hear this, William. Any serious relationship with this girl or with any girl from any trailer park, anywhere, will get you nothing. I'll cut you so far out of my will you won't even be able to spell Morgan. Do I make myself clear? People who live in low-rent housing and trailer parks are beneath the Morgan family name. They serve a purpose to the bank because they're always desperate and needing money. I make money from their stupidity, but not a one of them will ever have the Morgan name with my blessing. Do you understand me, William?"

Standing to leave, William said, "I understand, Dad. Thanks for showing me your new painting." He walked out, leaving the door open, passing the secretary's desk without speaking. His father watched him go down the sidewalk to his car, somehow knowing he had just lost a war that moments earlier he had considered a victory.

Feeling like a jerk, Mr. Morgan sat down behind his desk. William had left his Coke setting on a coaster. He knew his son was special. He would never admit it to Sue Ellen, but he also knew he was more like his mother than he would ever be like his father. And just like Sue Ellen had told him so long ago, blood lines are important. What's the point of amassing wealth with no heirs? Somewhere down deep, really deep, was a good man who had simply placed too much emphasis on money and possessions. What he wanted for his son was a wife who was on the same playing field. He viewed the world in tiers, with the Morgan family being top tier. He simply couldn't imagine his son finding any common ground with someone who lived in a mobile home and whose family suffered from generational poverty. For him, there were no portals connecting such vastly different worlds.

⁂

William sat in the Corvette for a few minutes before cranking it up. Everything inside of him wanted to go back to his father's office and tell him where he could put his painting, his money, his real estate holdings and his family name he seemingly held so dear. "What just happened in there?" he asked himself. "How could he feel so biased against someone he doesn't even know?"

Leaving the bank, he drove out to Upper Hightower Road and by Eula's home. No cars were there, so he pulled in her driveway and sat there for a few minutes. It was a beautiful place. No comparison to the mansion he called home or to Sue Ellen's, but a fine place to live and raise a family. Backing out of the drive, he headed back to Sue Ellen's. Pulling up her driveway, he parked the Corvette next to the White Charger.

After he had walked about fifty feet from where he had parked, William turned around and looked at both vehicles. Posing a question he needed to answer, he asked himself, "If I had never met Eula and her family and friends, which one of these two vehicles would I want to own?" Being honest with himself, he said, "Without a doubt, the Corvette." Continuing the honest introspection, he asked himself another question. "If I had met Eula and her family and friends, had fallen in love with her and perhaps even married her and had the same choice, which vehicle would I choose to own?" Without hesitation, he said, "I'd still pick the Corvette over the White Charger."

Leaving the Corvette parked next to Eula's truck, he went inside. He asked himself, "If I had to choose between Bubba's mobile home and Sue Ellen's home, which one would it be?" Again, being honest, he chose Sue Ellen's over Bubba's. "What am I saying to myself here, and where is this going? Am I no better than my old man? Two vehicles and two places to live, and I choose only the best."

Then, from out of nowhere, he remembered the night Eula picked him up for the football game and something Sue Ellen had said. "It's not about the old truck. It's about the heart that beats inside the driver." A light came on. "That's it, that's it," he concluded. "It's not about possessions or the value of the possessions. Obviously, anyone, if given a choice, would choose the best. It's not the possessions, in and of themselves that make the difference, it's the heart inside the person who has the possessions that makes the difference. The largest mansion in town can be a lonely hellhole if the owner's heart is void of love and compassion. Likewise, the lowliest dwelling on earth can be a wonderful place to live, if those living there have love and respect for one another."

Kneeling down by the couch, he prayed, "Lord, please help my dad see the world through Your eyes and teach him to love others as You do. Fill him with the Holy Spirit and give him a new heart. And, Lord, fill my heart with divine love, so I can love my father as You love him."

෴ ෴ ෴

Crossing thresholds often opens eyes to alternative universes. Falling in love with Eula had done that very thing for William. Mobile homes had always been plentiful in North Georgia. They were everywhere. He had passed them daily and never even noticed them. It wasn't an intentional slight on his part, they just weren't part of the world he lived in.

But not anymore. He couldn't help but wonder how many beautiful, loving people and families lived in them. Some of the mobile homes were landscaped and looked very nice. And some were not so nice. Poverty, indeed, seemed to target mobile homes and take up residence in quite a few of them. Junk cars and tons of trash littered some of the yards. Before, he would have seen this as a flaw in the resident's character or work ethic. But not any longer. God had given him a super dose of compassion, and now, whenever he passed a mobile home, or any home that was in disrepair. he would ask himself, "I wonder what happened here? Mistakes made, sickness, missed opportunities, debt?" And, now, something totally new for the Beamer. "I wonder what I could do to help them. No one wants to live like that. They just need a hand up."

⌒◯◯୭ ⌒◯◯୭ ⌒◯◯୭

The Beamer and Eula had a lot in common with Granny's King David. Bubba and Clarice were in the same story line. Eula had driven down to a nearby town to pick up a pregnancy test kit, hoping it was far enough away from home that no one she knew would see her purchase it.

Great minds think alike and perhaps pregnant high school girls do the same. Clarice had gone the other way, over to Clayton, to pick up her kit. The results were the same. Both of them were pregnant and neither knew what to do about it.

Clarice broke first and called Eula on the phone. "Can you meet me in the parking lot at the diner?" a shaken voice asked. Recognizing that Clarice must have a significant problem, Eula told her she'd be there.

"When?" Clarice asked, now crying.

"You tell me," Eula quickly responded.

"How about now?"

"I'm on my way." Eula dropped everything, brushed through her hair, went out and fired up the White Charger.

While driving over, she tried to imagine what had upset Clarice so much. "Maybe Bubba's broke up with her," she thought. "No way that's happening. They're together for life. Then she's pregnant," was her next thought. Looking in the truck mirror, she said, "Must be contagious."

Pulling into Bill's, she saw Clarice's car toward the back of the parking lot. Clarice was sitting inside. Parking next to her, Eula got out of the White Charger and got into her car. Clarice broke down and started sobbing. Sliding over next to her, Eula asked, "What's happened, what's going on?"

"I'm pregnant," Clarice said between sobs. "I'm gonna ruin Bubba's life."

For whatever reason, Eula had always seemed more mature than her friends. She was supposed to have all the answers, all of the time. This morning, she was fresh out of answers.

Revisiting wisdom she had just discovered for herself, she said, "Now, now. This isn't the end of the world. It's simply the beginning of a new life. Are you one hundred percent sure you're pregnant?"

"Positive," she answered. "Went over to Clayton and bought three of those old test kits. The cashier looked at me like she thought I was crazy, or something."

"Yeah, the pharmacist down in Jasper looked at me the same way, and I only bought two of them."

Using one of Eula's favorite sayings, Clarice said, between sobs, *"You gotta be shittin' me."*

"I wish," Eula said. "Bill is looking out the front of the diner and thinks he sees two of us in your car. Boy, is he ever in for a surprise. There's four of us, at least, that is, if neither one of us is carrying twins. Two in the car and two in the oven."

What are we gonna do?" Clarice asked her dearest friend.

"Well, if I know Bubba Preston, he'll step right up to the plate, marry you, and work himself to death for you and Bubba, Jr. Have you told him yet?"

"No, and that's why I haven't told him. All he's ever talked about is someday having a home that doesn't have wheels. His dream is gone now, and it's my fault. Have you told William yet?" Clarice asked.

"No, not yet. I guess we're both carrying babies and bad news at the same time. Bad news from the standpoint of disrupting lives."

"At least you'll graduate," Clarice said, "Bubba and me won't even get to do that."

"There's all kinds of ways to get more education these days," Eula responded, "but getting smarter will have to wait for a little while. We should have been smarter earlier and said no to them and to ourselves as well."

"I tried to tell Bubba no. God only knows how many times I tried."

"Well, I can't blame the Beamer. I guess I'm more like Bubba. Couldn't tell myself no, and William just went along for the ride."

It took about three seconds, but just going along for the ride hit home and both the girls broke into peels of laughter at the same time.

"Well, we just proved one thing," Eula said.

"And what's that?" Clarice asked.

"Pregnant girls can still laugh and have a good time."

"Having a good time is what got us pregnant in the first place," Clarice added somberly. "Thanks for coming," she told Eula and gave her a hug.

"No problem. I'm always ready to go. That's why I'm pregnant, I guess."

"I told Bubba the same thing once."

"Told him what?" Eula asked.

"Told him I was always ready to go."

"And what did he say to that?"

"Said he was calling Granny Preston."

Perplexed, Eula asked, "And what does Granny Preston have to do with this?"

"It's a long story. I'll tell you about it sometime. Right now, I have to figure out what I'm gonna do."

"I already have your answer. You tell Bubba, and being Southern born and bred, no pun intended, he'll ride to the rescue with a ring, and in no time at all you'll be Mrs. Thomas Steven Preston. And it may not be easy, but you'll both be happy, whether your home has wheels or not."

"What about you?" Clarice asked.

"Well, my situation is a little different. It's very complicated. I may have little William on my own. At least that's what I'm considering at the moment."

"Why?" a puzzled Clarice asked.

"Like I said, it's complicated. I'll fill you in on the details when I know what I'm going to do."

Giving Clarice a much needed hug, Eula climbed into the White Charger and drove away, feeling nowhere near as safe and secure as Clarice.

"Are you sure? How accurate are those test kits, anyway?" Bubba asked, hoping to find a loophole in Clarice's announcement he was going to be a father.

"Well, I don't think three of them, all showing the same results, could be wrong. And, besides, I have the morning sickness, as Mama calls it."

"You done told your parents?"

"No, Bubba, I've only told you." She knew he'd get upset if he knew she had already told Eula. A little white lie seemed innocent enough considering the issue at hand.

He sat for a minute without saying a word.

"Say something, Bubba."

Flashing that big old smile, he did exactly what Eula said he would do. Southern born and bred, he rode to the rescue of a damsel in distress.

"Ma'am" —

"What, Bubba?" Clarice responded with tears running down her cheeks.

"Ma'am, will you marry me?" Bubba asked, wiping her tears with his shirtsleeve.

"Only if you want to. You don't have to, if you don't want to."

"Clarice, Granny Preston would call you and me a God-thing. We were made for each other and you know it. He's probably not been pleased with the things we've been doing, but me and God understand each other. He'll bless us, our home, and little Bubba, Jr."

"Are you sure, Bubba?"

"As sure about this as anything I've ever thought about. Imagine this," he said. Pretending to write words in the air, he asked, "Now what do you think about that?"

"Bubba, I don't know what you wrote."

Holding his hands up in the air, with the imaginary words he had written somewhere between them, he read it to her. Thomas Steven Preston, aka Bubba, Jr.

He was trying to be positive, but she broke down and cried again.

"Stop it," he said. "Everything's going to be fine, I promise you, and we're going to be happy."

As he comforted the young woman he would spend the rest of his life with, a Bubba thought ran through his mind: "We're tough, we're *trailer-park tough*. We can handle anything."

⧏∞⧐⧏∞⧐⧏∞⧐

Eula knew she had the harder of the two pregnancies to work through. No doubt, William would marry her. Obviously, she had to tell him. Abortion wasn't an option she'd ever think about, let alone do. She considered telling Sue Ellen first, but realized it wasn't her problem. "I'll do this on my own," she decided. "People will talk and point, but they always do. It'll give them something new to gossip about and maybe give someone else a break."

The Beamer had shared his visit to his dad's office with her and Sue Ellen. For Eula's sake, he had softened some of the language his father had used concerning residents of mobile homes and the less fortunate in general. He had shared the real tirade with Sue Ellen and had acknowledged to her she had called it perfectly. Remembering everything she had learned about William's father, Eula knew that if he'd disown his son for marrying her, no telling what kind of fit he'd pitch if he found out she was pregnant with a Morgan baby.

The school year was winding down. Good thing, too, because Clarice and Eula were both starting to show. Bubba had manned up, as he called it, and they told Clarice's mom and dad. Her mother cried, sitting on the couch, wiping tears. Mr. Smith eased the situation by assessing it a little differently than what Bubba and Clarice had expected. "Well," he said after a long, suspenseful pause, "everyone knew the two of you would get hitched, sooner or later. I guess it's sooner. Would have been nice if y'all could have waited. My grandma used to say, 'there's sunshine behind every cloud'. Look at it this way. You're getting a head start on life. Probably not a bad thing with times like they are. Life's hard at best and getting an early start might help out in the long run. Y'all both know we ain't got much ourselves, but we'll help out where we can."

Mrs. Smith hugged both of them. Mr. Smith shook hands with Bubba and said, "Welcome to our family."

Her mom, still in tears, hugged Clarice and whispered, "Things will be okay. We'll be here for you."

∽◌∽∽◌∽∽◌∽

Eula decided to tell the Beamer in the mall parking lot. After all, Camelot's foundation was asphalt. They had previously planned to meet there and then ride to Cracker Barrel for breakfast. "I have some good news and some bad news," she told him. "First, the good news. You will be going to your father's alma mater, and I'm sure you'll make Harvard proud."

William knew something was wrong and interrupted her before she got to the bad news. "What's this, you will be going to Harvard stuff? We haven't decided anything for certain yet."

"Hear me out, Beamer. I've decided for us. We will not be getting married, at least not until you're completely through with your education. You need that. You'd never survive at McClain's or any similar place requiring manual labor. After you finish your education, and if you're still interested in marrying me, we'll talk about it then."

"Wait a minute."

"No, you have to wait until I'm finished. This is hard enough, without starting and stopping a dozen times. Here's the bad news. Then again, maybe not so bad. It depends on who you are and how you look at it. I'm pregnant, about three months. I will be fine and my folks will be there for me. You don't have to worry, and there's no way I'm going to let you throw away your future. We both know your father will go ballistic and disown you, which would be far worse than me raising little Luke on my own. Do you like the name? I would have named him William, but I won't fuel the gossip mongers in town."

"So, you don't love me after all?" William said. "It was just a charade and now you're dumping me and going to cause yourself and our child a world of pain, being a single mother. I can't believe this. You know how much I want to marry you. To hell with my father and his precious money. You know that's not who I am. Does Sue Ellen know?"

"Of course not. I wouldn't tell her before I told you."

"Kiss me," the Beamer demanded.

She leaned over and gave him a long kiss. Her eyes filled with tears.

"You're lying to me and to yourself," he concluded. "You still love me and you know it."

"I never said I didn't love you, Beamer. I said I wouldn't marry you and ruin your life. That's precisely what love does. It does what's right, this time and every time."

"Do me one favor, Eula. Sue Ellen will find out sooner or later. Go with me to talk with her about this. If she agrees with you, I'll do what you ask. But you'll never convince me in a million years that Sue Ellen Thornton will agree it's better for you to raise our baby by yourself. I'd be willing to bet the farm on that one. Let's go right now. She's not working and was reading when I left the house. Let's agree to let her have the last word. She's smart and has been around a lot longer than the two of us."

Eula paused for a moment or two, thinking about what the Beamer was suggesting. "Okay, I'll agree to discussing it with her, but I can still do it my way if I choose to do so. Agreed?"

Eula was being so obstinate and William had no other choice but to agree to her terms. Firing up the White Charger, she followed him back home.

"Well, isn't this a nice surprise," Sue Ellen said as the Beamer walked in with Eula in tow. Sue Ellen could tell Eula had been crying. "What on earth is going on?" she asked before either one of them could say anything.

"You might want to sit down," Eula told her. "This is both complicated and involved."

Sue Ellen nodded her head and returned to her seat. Laying her book aside, she waited as Eula and William took seats opposite her on the sofa.

"Whoever said silence is golden was mistaken," Sue Ellen noted, after the pair was seated and no one immediately offered an explanation as to what was complicated and involved.

Sue Ellen's remark about silence made Eula smile, and gave her the courage to start the conversation.

"Daddy always said if you have something to say, just spit it out. A bad visual, to say the least, but true, nonetheless. William is not at fault here. I'm responsible for what's happened. I'm about three months pregnant."

Sue Ellen took a deep breath, but didn't say anything. The Beamer started to say something, but Eula lovingly pointed at him, smiled, and said, "Let me finish first, and then you can have the floor. We all know how Mr. Morgan feels about the Beamer's involvement with me, or with anyone not from a rich, notable family. I know for a fact that he'll never accept me or this baby I'm carrying, and I don't intend to try and force the issue with him. I've seen him from a distance but have never spoken to him and, frankly, have no desire to. The Beamer needs to get his education so he can have a decent future. I told him I never want to see him having to work at some place like McClain's for minimum wages, and therefore I refused his offer to marry me. Tell him I happen to be right here, and please assure him I will be fine. I told him after he finishes school at Harvard, we might possibly revisit our relationship."

"Sue Ellen, please tell Eula she's absolutely out of her mind if she thinks I shouldn't marry her immediately. I know for a fact it's my child and I have every right to be in its life. I'm prepared to do whatever is necessary to care for both of them, whether it's manual labor or whatever I have to do. Tell Miss Smarty Britches that no one, absolutely no one, will ever love her as much as I do."

"Both of you go to the kitchen and make us a pot of coffee. Give me a few minutes to absorb this and let me have some time to think it through."

William stood first, extended his hand to help Eula up and, together, they disappeared into the kitchen. Sue Ellen took another deep breath before she got out of her recliner. Going to her study, she took a key from her desk drawer, and went over to a file cabinet. Unlocking the top drawer, she took out a small box and opened it. Inside was the blanket her baby, William, had been wrapped in the day she held him for the first time. This little blanket had been touched by the Son of God, and the Beamer was wrapped in it when he received his miraculous healing. Closing the drawer, she took the blanket and went back to her recliner. The pair was still in the kitchen.

Holding the blanket near her heart, she prayed, "Jesus, Sue Ellen is in need of another miracle. I need Your love and wisdom. Give me the words I need to speak to William and Eula. I know You don't approve of what they did, but I know Your forgiveness covers all sin. Bless the three of us and forgive us when we've failed You. I don't know what to say or what to do, so I'm placing it in Your hands. *Amen and Amen."*

Eula brought Sue Ellen a fresh cup of coffee and also had one for herself. The Beamer had his usual, a Coke. Both sat down on the sofa and waited for Sue Ellen to speak. She sipped her coffee slowly, and one would have thought nothing of importance was on the table for discussion. The silence was almost frightening for Eula and William. Both of them noticed the blanket, but didn't say anything.

Standing, Sue Ellen walked over to them and extended a hand to Eula. She stood up, and so did William. Each of you take hold of this blanket, no questions asked. They each grasped a corner with their hands, with Sue Ellen holding it as well.

"Let's pray about this before any decisions are made. Lord, forgive us our sins and shortcomings. We have a problem and we need Your help and wisdom. Let us love one another, and may we always be family. Give us Your guidance and blessings. We pray for this unborn child and we dedicate it to You, even while it's in the womb. *Amen and Amen."*

The mood of everyone immediately changed. Eula reached over and took William's hand. They both had tears in their eyes. Sue Ellen was all smiles. The answers had just been downloaded from the Almighty to her heart. They poured in, much like a mighty river rushes through a canyon, on its way to the sea. She couldn't believe the simplicity of the plan and the results that would follow. "God is an awesome God," she said aloud. She couldn't be mad at either of the kids. She had done the same thing, which had resulted in her own pregnancy, and love wasn't even in the equation.

"Here's what we'll do this morning. How does Cracker Barrel sound to everyone for breakfast? I know how to handle this, and it will turn out fine for everyone. I have to work out the details, and we'll talk about it very soon, I promise. But for now, let's have a private celebration for the new mother and baby, and get both of them some nourishment. How does that sound?"

Eula didn't know why, but she felt an overwhelming peace about the whole thing. Sue Ellen had always looked out for William and he had absolute confidence in her abilities.

"Sounds good to me," Eula said, "and since we already have a majority consensus, it's a done deal."

The Beamer shook his head. "I think my life will be tough, hanging out with the two of you. Cracker Barrel it is."

Sue Ellen told them to go ahead, that she'd be there in a few minutes. The Beamer and Eula held hands as they headed for the White Charger.

Watching them drive away, Sue Ellen knelt by her recliner and offered a prayer of Thanksgiving.

"Lord, thank you for hearing your servant and for giving me a way to help these young people. They've made a mistake, but you specialize in second chances. Give me wisdom in dealing with William's father, and give me patience. Help me to love him as you do, realizing a good man resides somewhere deep inside, wanting very much to have a chance to surface. Give Eula and William wisdom and patience as well. I know what they can do if given an opportunity. Your will be done, Lord. *Amen and Amen.*"

She went back to her study and placed the blanket in its special box, locked the drawer and put the key away. She wished she had time to make some notes. Answers to her prayer were flooding her mind. It was truly a miraculous plan, with everyone learning and benefiting from God's wisdom and His love. Simply amazing. Getting in her Jag, she headed for Cracker Barrel.

⁂

Rumors and gossip can thrive in a vacuum. It was clear to everyone that both girls were pregnant. With two weeks to go in the school year, the rumor mill was running at full throttle.

Bubba had told his parents and, while concerned, they were excited to have Clarice as part of their family. He had also talked to Mr. Solenberger, his boss at McClain's, and would become a full-time employee on June 1st. He had talked to Pastor Baker and arranged for a small and simple wedding at his parents' home on the weekend following the last day of school.

Clarice was feeling a little better about the situation and had her first checkup at the doctor. Everything looked fine. Bubba, aka Tom Preston, aka *hootie tootie* warrior, put his hands to the plow and would never look back at what might have been.

Mr. and Mrs. Preston managed to scrape up $1,000 and gave it to Bubba and Clarice as a wedding gift. Thankful for it, he used it to rent a double-wide mobile home at Whispering Pines Trailer Park. It was fully furnished and was very clean and pretty. There was money left over to set up their kitchen and linen closets.

Clarice's parents gave them $1,500 for a wedding gift. For all intents and purposes, except for their age and disruption of their education, they were starting out as Mr. and Mrs. on a decent footing. It could have been much worse.

Though neither would have acknowledged it, the night of the graduation was a low point for Bubba and Clarice. Being a year older, Eula and William were graduating. Eula, in her fourth month, was showing, but the robe covered it well. The school was abuzz with discussions about who had gotten her pregnant. The consensus leaned toward William Morgan, Jr. but most students were trying to pin it on someone else.

"Are we going to the graduation?" Clarice asked Bubba.

"I don't really want to. What's the point in going?" Bubba replied.

"Well, I don't really want to go either, but Eula and William are our friends and they're both graduating tonight."

"I've already told Eula we probably wouldn't be coming," Bubba said. "She said it was fine and she understood."

"Well, what would you like to do? You don't have to work tonight. Got any ideas?"

"How about a Bubba burger? There's still some ground deer in Mom's freezer. We could go over to Coosa Baptist Church and grill out. Janice and LJ aren't going to the graduation either. We could invite them to tag along. I hear those Bubba burgers are special, or so I've been told."

Clarice had been depressed over her pregnancy and teared up. "I'm so sorry I got pregnant. I've ruined your life, Bubba."

Pulling her over next to him, he said, "No one, I mean no one, has ruined anyone's life here. Look at it this way. We're getting a head start on the others."

"In a rental trailer at Whispering Pines? How's that getting a head start?"

"Anytime I'm with you, Clarice, I'm miles ahead of whoever is in second place."

"I hope you're right, Bubba Preston. What about LJ and Janice? Think they'll be okay?"

"We're all tough, Clarice. Life has always been tough for any-one working an hourly job. LJ and Janice will graduate next year and they're just like us. They'll be together for the rest of their lives and love each other, in good times and in bad times. We'll find a way, or we'll make one. End of story. There's more to life than a high school diploma or a degree from some college. Granny Preston always said that common sense and a good work ethic were gifts from God. And, I'm ate up with both. So is LJ. At our fiftieth anniversary, I'll remind you of this conversa-tion and these big ole tears you're shedding for nothing."

Thinking about being married to Bubba for fifty years made Clarice smile and then laugh. "Fifty years is a long time to put up with you, Bubba Preston. Hope I'm up to it."

"Me, too. I'd hate to have to trade you in."

Clarice said, "What? If there's anyone trading anyone in, it'll probably be me, trading you in." They both laughed.

"What about those Bubba burgers?"

"Sounds good to me. Call LJ and invite them."

Pastor Baker preferred to do premarital counseling for couples who wanted him to perform their wedding ceremony. There were usually three or four sessions. When Bubba contacted Pastor Baker, he had to tell him Clarice was already pregnant. The pastor explained to Bubba he preferred to do counseling before the wedding and before the pregnancy, whenever possible. Granny Preston loved Pastor Baker's sense of humor. "Since the horse is already out of the pasture, we'll have to mend the fences as y'all go along. Just know I'm here if either one of you ever need me," he told Bubba.

The wedding was scheduled for the second Saturday after school was out. It would be marriage and redemption all rolled into a single, simple wedding ceremony. And instead of having it at Bubba's home, Pastor Baker insisted on having it in the church.

❧❦❧❦❧❦❧

"Ernest Wilson is on line one," Marie told Sue Ellen. "He said he got the foreclosure paperwork and wants to come in and talk to you."

"Tell him to come in after lunch. Block out some time for him, okay?"

"I'll take care of it," Marie responded.

Sue Ellen already had the Whispering Pines file on her desk. Oddly enough, as sad as it was for Ernest, it would be turned into a blessing for Eula Johnson, God willing, and with the cooperation of William Morgan, Sr. If Sue Ellen had her way, and she always did, he'd cooperate.

She couldn't blame the bank or Mr. Morgan for calling in the note. Without anyone knowing it, and using her own money, she had bailed Ernest out three different times. She knew God wasn't happy with Eula and William's behavior, but after the fact, she couldn't help but wonder if the foreclosure of the trailer park wasn't postponed until it fit into the grand scheme of things. Her financial help had staved off the foreclosure and now, if everything worked out, it would benefit Eula and William.

At two o'clock sharp, Marie buzzed Sue Ellen. "Ernest is here to see you."

"Send him in, please."

Ernest was clearly shaken and embarrassed, and Sue Ellen felt compassion for him. "I'm sorry I've caused you so much trouble," he began. "I know you've helped me a number of times and I

318

would've already lost the park had it not been for you. There's no hard feelings on my part. I guess I'm not cut out to be a landlord. So, tell me how this will work, and I'll cooperate and do whatever I need to do to make it smooth and simple."

"Ernest, you're a good man and not being able to be a landlord doesn't damage your character in the least. It simply means you can't meet your financial obligations to the bank because you can't throw tenants out in the street. You lose, but the tenants lose as well. I hate it for you, because you basically forfeit all the equity you have built up in the property. The legal proceedings have already been started and the only way to stop them now is to pay the note off in full. Can you do that, or borrow the money anywhere else to satisfy your indebtedness to the bank?"

"I have the means to make that happen. However, I would still be a lousy landlord and all my savings and retirement would be gone. I don't think I want to go down that road. I talked about it with my wife, and she agrees. It's time to cut our losses and move on."

"I agree with both of you. Keeping your savings and retirement intact is a smart move. Since the papers have already been served, all you have to do is the required paperwork and basically vacate the property. The bank will appoint someone to oversee the park and will try and find another buyer. I will miss you, Ernest Wilson."

Standing, with his ball cap in hand and tears in his eyes, he said, "I know you spent your own money to help me out. Had to be you. Old man Morgan wouldn't give the time of day to help anyone. I would have lost the property a long time ago had it not been for your kindness. God bless you."

"He already has," Sue Ellen said, as she stood to see him out. Walking over to Ernest, she gave him a big hug. As she walked him out of her office, they passed Marie's desk, where she sat, wiping tears from her eyes. When Sue Ellen came back in, Marie said, "That's the saddest thing I think I've ever heard. Breaks my heart."

"I know," Sue Ellen said, "but God has plans for Ernest and for Whispering Pines Trailer Park."

The die had been cast, and the timing was perfect. Sue Ellen told the Beamer to bring Eula over Wednesday evening for dinner. After dinner, they would make plans for the future and she would explain to both of them how she thought everything would happen. Of course, the options were always open, and both Eula and the Beamer could always reject her suggestions. She had instructed him to have her there by five o'clock and as they pulled up, the pizza delivery man pulled up behind them.

"Great timing," she told Eula and William, as she paid for the pizza. "Y'all get some paper plates and something to drink. I'll be in there in a minute."

As the pizza delivery man drove away, she closed her eyes and prayed a short prayer asking for wisdom, then turned and headed to the dining room.

As soon as she entered the dining room, she said, "The pizza smells wonderful."

"Sure does," Eula said, "I'm starving to death. Mom says I'm eating them out of house and home. Seems like I can't ever get enough to eat."

"You're eating for two now," Sue Ellen reminded her.

"Yeah," Eula replied with a laugh, "that's what they always say."

The Beamer was quiet. He wasn't sure what Sue Ellen had worked out, and he had mixed emotions about going away to school as if nothing had happened, leaving Eula and their child in a tough spot.

The three of them ate their fill of pizza and breadsticks and then retired to the living room to hear Sue Ellen's plan.

"Eula, I believe God has intervened in this situation and on your behalf. William, Eula is one hundred percent correct in her assessment of what your position should be in her life. I believe God has a plan for you, and it doesn't include marriage to Eula at this time. It will come later. Something has happened at the bank that will enable Eula to live comfortably while you get your education. After college, you can get a job in Atlanta, and you and Eula can work out details to continue your relationship, outside of marriage for the present time. Your father is so busy and travels so much, you'll never have to worry about him discovering the fact the two of you are still together. It may sound underhanded and sneaky, but I want both of you to inherit the fortune he has spent his life accumulating. You can give it back as God directs. William, after you go to work, you can buy a home in Atlanta. Eula, you can buy a home close to William. The baby must never know the Beamer is his father, not until Mr. Morgan either dies or changes his ways, whichever comes first. William, you can be friends with your child and maintain a relationship with Eula. It will work out fine, if you want it to."

"Where are we going to get money to buy these homes in Atlanta, or how are we going to make the payments on them?" Eula asked. "And I don't see how I'm going to live comfortably without working two jobs while my mom keeps the baby."

"Tell us how this will work," William said. He knew Sue Ellen had control of lots of resources and knowledge of things happening all over town. He had seen her do things he still had a hard time believing she pulled off.

"Do you know where Whispering Pines Trailer Park is located?"

"Sure, out on State Route 85, right before you get to the big bridge. I have a couple of friends who live there," Eula said.

"If you and your father will cooperate with me, that property will belong to you in about four weeks. You can live there, manage it and make a decent living. I'll help by giving you pointers on what to do and what not to do. I have personal experience with this property. When you finish school, William, I'll make sure your father gives you enough money to buy yourself a home. We'll call it a graduation present. If you excel at Harvard and get a good job in Atlanta, then you and Eula can maintain your relationship and you'll be a part of your child's life. It's only two hours or less to Atlanta, depending on where you buy your home."

Sue Ellen paused to see how they were absorbing all of it.

"Eula, I'll personally help you get a home in the Atlanta area close to William. You can get one of the residents at Whispering Pines to fill in for you on weekends, allowing you to spend lots of time at your home in Atlanta. The baby will grow up thinking the Beamer is your best friend and his as well. You can put him in a private boarding school when he's old enough and he'll get a head start on his education. I'm going to convince William's father that he has to pay off Eula's dad with the trailer park in order to stop a paternity suit, thereby freeing William to go to Harvard without a dark cloud hanging over his head. Notice, I'm assuming it's going to be a boy."

"Wow," Eula said. "How did you come up with all of this?"

"Call it inspired, I guess," she said. "Will your father help us with this? All he has to do is follow my instructions. I'll handle Mr. Morgan and shield your dad from any confrontations. I'll simply present the demands as if they're his, and Mr. Morgan will fall in line with the request."

"We can ask my dad, that's all I can tell you. He may, I just don't know. I'll let you explain it to him. How about that? He'll be more apt to understand it and help if it comes from you."

Sue Ellen's plan for the next four to six years of their lives seemed problematic and dysfunctional at best. The Beamer had some real concerns.

"How do you know my father will buy me a home in Atlanta as a graduation gift?" he asked.

"The why isn't important. Know this, William, he will buy you two homes if I ask him to."

"And my family has no extra money," Eula said. "How can I buy a home in Atlanta, and what will make Mr. Morgan just roll over and give me Whispering Pines Trailer Park? What if he challenges the paternity suit?"

"I understand your concerns and even your lack of confidence in my ability to make all of this happen. It does sound like a lot, and Mr. Morgan does indeed have a bad reputation when it comes to being congenial and caring," Sue Ellen said, and smiled at them. "Here's what you both need to know. I actually became the person in life I set out to be—fully equipped and functional, to devise, implement, to control, to help or destroy things and people who got in my way. God, through His Son, Jesus Christ, transformed the old Sue Ellen Thornton and gave me a new heart of love and compassion for everybody and everything. That even includes your father, William. All of my former acquired attributes went into an arsenal for the accomplishment of good in the world. I prayed and asked God for an answer to your problems and this is it."

"I thank you for all you've done for me, Sue Ellen," William said. "You've practically raised me. Dad and Mom have done very little for me, other than throw money my way. You've told me some stories of amazing things you have accomplished and huge obstacles you have overcome at the bank. But this seems a little over the top, considering my father will have such a vital role in making it happen."

"Good way to put it, William. It does seem a little over the top to me as well." Changing her tone and demeanor, and perhaps reverting to how the old Sue Ellen Thornton would have addressed this issue, she said, "Know this, son. If I tell him to buy you three houses, then the only problem you'll have is dividing your time between them. The why you'll never hear from me, and the how is a God-thing."

Eula took the Beamer's hand and said, "I love you enough to wait however long it takes to be Mrs. William Morgan. If she can pull this off, you, me and our child will be a complete family, with only the four of us in the know. I'll take that any day over not having you in our lives."

"Well said," Sue Ellen chimed in, "and what say you, Beamer?"

"Look out, Dad. Here comes Sue Ellen and apparently you've lost the battle before you even get started."

"My sentiments exactly," Eula said. The fact of Sue Ellen, addressing William as son was not lost on her.

"The Lord works in mysterious ways," Sue Ellen continued. "I believe with all my heart, this is His plan for right now. He can always change things and often does. However, any changes are always for the better. I say, follow this plan for now, and pray that God will work it out so the two of you can be husband and wife, sooner than later."

After staying for about thirty more minutes, Eula and William left Sue Ellen's and headed to the mall.

Sue Ellen, sitting in her recliner, couldn't help but compare her life with the one she was setting up for her son. She had raised him, loved him, and never one time had he ever called her "Mother." Of course, he didn't know she was his mother. He called William Morgan, Sr. father, but thought he was adopted. Ironically, William Morgan, Jr. was about to live the same kind of life she had lived for eighteen years. He would come and go, be active in his child's life and the child would call him friend, not father. Was it worth it? After a few minutes of reflection, she said aloud. "Absolutely, it was worth it. He may never call me mother, but I am his mother and I know he loves me. Is that not what it's about? Loving one another. At least William will have Eula and they will love each other and be together. They will raise their child, regardless of whether the world ever recognizes my son as the child's father. God is good, all the time. *Amen and Amen."*

⚬◇◦⚬◇◦⚬◇◦

It was Bubba's second week as a full-time employee at McClain's. On Saturday he would marry Clarice and they would begin their life together. Clarice had gotten a job, three days a week, at Walmart. McClain's had insurance for their employees, but there was a one-year probationary period before it would cover pregnancies. This one would be on them.

As Bubba and LJ loaded trucks in the warehouse, Mr. Solenberger's voice boomed over the intercom. "Tom Preston, please come to my office."

"Oh, shit," Bubba said to himself. "I hope there's nothing wrong with my working full time." He headed his forklift toward the office. LJ also heard the summons and wondered what was going on. Parking near dispatch, Bubba got off the lift and slowly walked toward Mr. Solenberger's office. Going in, he sat down across from his boss who was on the phone. Mr. Solenberger held up a finger, indicating the conversation would be short.

When he hung up, Bubba spoke up immediately. "Sir, I hope

325

this isn't about my full-time status. I really need this job, more than you'll ever know."

"Relax, Tom, this is a small town, and unfortunately most everyone talks and everybody else listens. I know why you need this job. It's not about you. You're one of the best workers I've ever had the privilege to work for me. This isn't about you. It's about LJ."

"You have no idea how happy it makes me to know my job isn't in jeopardy. But what about LJ? What's he done now?" Bubba said and smiled.

"He's followed your example and has come to work at McClain's full time. Actually, beginning today. I thought you'd want to know, and I figured he hadn't told you yet."

"Damn it," Bubba said before he caught himself. "Sorry, sir. He hasn't finished school yet. What's he thinking about? Why did y'all hire him?"

"Well, I guess the best explanation, and perhaps the only one, is he loves you like a brother. Everyone knows that. He literally worships the ground you walk on, so don't fuss at him. As to why we hired him, he's as good a worker as you are. I tried to talk him out of it, but he said if we didn't put him on full time, he'd find someone who would. And I believed him. He's too good an employee to lose."

"Just damn," Bubba said again. This time he didn't apologize.

"That's all I wanted with you. You can go back to work. Don't be mad at LJ. You're one lucky guy to have a friend like him. Wish I'd had an LJ in my life. Bubba, everyone here knows what's happened, and we're all proud of you. You've stepped up and done it the way it's supposed to be done. Even Mr. McClain told me he expected great things from you and knows you will make a great husband and a good father."

"Thank you, sir. I appreciate your confidence in me. I will do my best not to let anyone down. And I don't rightly know what I'll say to LJ, but I won't fuss at him, I promise."

After leaving the office, he drove his forklift back toward the warehouse. LJ was watching for him and was literally driving his forklift to meet him. They parked and both of them got off their lifts.

"What's wrong, Bubba," LJ asked, really concerned.

Bubba stood there for a moment, looking at his friend, not knowing what to say about him quitting school. Finally, not finding words, he stepped up and gave LJ a big hug. "Love you, man."

"Back at you," LJ said, wondering what had happened in Mr. Solenberger's office. There was nothing to say that would trump the hug.

"Let's get back to work," Bubba said. "Mr. Solenberger just told me we're the two best full-time employees he's ever had. Let's not disappoint him."

Firing up his forklift, a happy LJ said, "Absolutely, we wouldn't want to disappoint him, would we?"

ɔ◦ꝏ◦ꝏ◦ꝏ◦

Clarice and Bubba had gone shopping for wedding attire. Clarice bought a simple, but beautiful, light-blue dress. Bubba bought a nice blue sports coat and a pair of dark-blue trousers. It would be a small wedding. Clarice's parents, Bubba's parents and Eula's parents would be there. Eula had asked if she could bring the Beamer and Bubba said, "Absolutely, I'd be honored to have him there." Sue Ellen slipped Eula five hundred dollars as a gift to the bride and groom, with the stipulation no one would know, including William, where the money came from. She also decided, at the last moment, to go with Eula and William to the wedding.

"I have an idea," she told them as they drove to the church. "Listen as the pastor reads the vows to your friends, and as they say 'I do,' both of you participate, quietly, answering the appropriate questions as they're asked."

"That's a neat idea," William said. "We can have our own ceremony as Bubba and Clarice have theirs."

"And we won't even have to pay the pastor anything," Eula said and laughed.

"I was trying to suggest we make this a serious thing," Sue Ellen said and smiled.

"We are," William added. "We could get you to make Dad pay the preacher."

Sue Ellen was impressed with the ceremony. Pastor Baker hit a grand slam and covered all the bases. He began the ceremony with prayer.

"Lord, as this couple is joined in Holy Matrimony, we pray for unity of spirit, forgiveness of sins, and a melting of both their hearts into a single, vibrant heart, beating for You and for each other."

Though a very small wedding, the joining of these two young people in holy matrimony united those in attendance in heart and in spirit as well. The only feelings felt by anyone were joyous and loving.

"Do you, Clarice Smith, take Tom Preston to be your lawfully wedded husband, to have and to hold, until death do you part?"

"I do," Clarice said.

"Do you, Tom Preston, take Clarice Smith to be your lawfully wedded wife, to have and to hold, until death do you part?"

"I do," Tom said.

"If you both want God to be first in your marriage and, after that, for each of you to be first in each other's life, say I do."

"I do," they both said in unison.

"By the power vested in me by God in heaven and by the State of Georgia, I now pronounce you husband and wife. Tom, you may kiss your bride."

As Bubba kissed Clarice, William and Eula, who had also quietly participated in the ceremony, bestowed a kiss on each other.

"Praise the Lord," Sue Ellen said to herself. "Lord, bless the union of Tom and Clarice and bless the union of William and Eula. Thank you, Lord, for answered prayer."

William Morgan, Sr. had once again been bested by Sue Ellen Thornton, the smartest person he had ever hired. She had been a little concerned about getting the trailer park for Eula, but Eula's father turned out to be a quick study in how to threaten a paternity suit. Poor, old Ernest Wilson had already paid two thirds of the note on the trailer park. That's why Mr. Morgan wanted it back. But he wanted his son to go to Harvard, his alma mater, more than he wanted the trailer park, so he gave it up without a single objection. Mr. Morgan bought the story—hook, line and sinker—that the Morgan family was completely through with Eula Johnson and her family. He would, however, give William a piece of his mind regarding his indiscretion, and warn him about dilly-dallying around with someone beneath the Morgan name. He let him know how much it had cost to free the family's good name from the girl from the trailer park. William listened without objections, noting in his mind the equity Eula would automatically have in Whispering Pines. Sue Ellen was a genius.

Four years passed quickly and, as Sue Ellen had predicted, the Beamer graduated with honors from Harvard, and landed a job with a pharmaceutical company in Atlanta. Mr. Morgan was so proud of him he didn't even hesitate in following Sue Ellen's suggestion that he give William enough money for his graduation present to purchase a nice home in Atlanta. In his mind, it was more of an investment than a gift, but Sue Ellen made sure the property was titled in the Beamer's name.

Once that was completed, she found a nice home close to the Beamer and purchased it herself, putting the deed in Eula's name. The baby had been born healthy, and they had named him William Luke Johnson. Luke lived with Eula at Whispering Pines, but they visited their Atlanta home every weekend, where William was an active part of their lives as a friend. The Beamer would come home to Blairsville about once a month to see his parents, but he would always stay at Sue Ellen's house for those weekend visits.

Luke was growing like a weed, and the years went by way too fast for everyone. Sue Ellen felt like she finally had a complete family. She had a son, a daughter-in-law and a grandson. Her family was a secret, known only to her, but it was a good secret and made her very happy. She visited Atlanta often enough to feel like the mother and grandmother she really was. Mr. Morgan, intensifying his effort to accumulate more wealth, was gone most of the time. He hardly ever visited William in Atlanta, leaving the family there in peace. Marsha, William's adoptive mother, had just about taken up permanent residence in England and everything was working out for the good of everyone.

PART II

***

W hispering Pines Trailer Park, located six miles south of town, was nestled in a stand of longleaf pines and bordered by a creek on one side and U.S. Forestry land on the other. The double-wide trailer at the entrance served two purposes. It was the trailer park office and also Eula and Luke's home.

The park had fourteen mobile homes, eight single-wides and six double-wides. They were fully furnished for the most part, but were older units, showing their age. There were twenty-six rental lots, and most of them were occupied. Several of Eula's high school friends had moved into the park. Bubba had rented a furnished double-wide before Eula acquired the property. LJ, after marrying Janice, also moved in. They rented the single-wide next door to Bubba and Clarice.

In all, there was twenty acres. The park had asphalt streets and asphalt parking pads at each lot. A cookshed on the property served as a gathering place for the neighborhood. The cookshed had several grills and a fridge for everyone to use. A large fireplace, built at one end, allowed for limited use in cold weather. Horseshoe pits were nearby, as well as a playground for the small kids living in the park. All in all, it wasn't a bad place to live. Eula had a new car, but the White Charger had its own special parking place with a carport to protect it. Little Luke loved riding in the old truck and Eula would oftentimes drive it over to her folks' place, to keep the White Charger from feeling abandoned and unloved.

Ten years had come and gone. Bubba was twenty-seven years old and his fears have become reality. His home had wheels, and he was a permanent fixture at McClain's. He had worked his way up to foreman, but still has to worry about job security. Rumors had always circulated about the plant closing for good. His weekends went by too quickly, and the daily grind at McClain's seemed to stretch into infinity. Whispering Pines was home to many of Bubba's friends. LJ and Janice had two kids, a boy and a girl. Bubba and Clarice had two boys. Most of their friends, like them, had to work two jobs in order to make ends meet.

LJ was balding, Bubba's hair was receding, and his beard was sprinkled with gray. Life was good, but it was also hard. Being *trailer-park tough* had worn them thin, but remained the core of who they were.

It was Saturday morning, and there was a chill in the air. The smell of coffee, coming from the cookshed, greeted friends, most of them in their late twenties or early thirties. High school was a distant memory.

Another resident, Carl, also had a receding hairline. Bubba teased him, telling him his hairline was receding faster than a roach moved when someone turned on the kitchen light in the middle of the night. Little Jimmy blamed his balding on genetics, claiming his dad and grandfather were both bald by the time they were thirty years old.

They were not really that old, but the hard manual labor and the second jobs had taken a little spring out of their step and the zing out of everything else. Bubba used to brag that his sex life was better than hunting. No one believed him, but they were all wrong. When he saw the guys at the cookshed on Saturday mornings, he'd always say bingo and pretended to shoot a basket, with a follow-up swoosh, indicating he had left Clarice again with a smile on her face. Bubba hardly ever says bingo anymore and few baskets are shot, and the follow-up swoosh that used to be his standard Saturday morning greeting was seldom heard. Bubba, maturing, had cut out some of the foolishness and joking around with his friends.

The Saturday morning summit meeting at Whispering Pines had come to order. Christmas was just around the corner. The best of friends, in the not so best of times, met, laughed and complained together under the roof of the cookshed.

Across town, William Morgan, Sr. backed his new Mercedes out of the garage of his mansion. His wife, Marsha, was in Europe, and he was headed for a round of golf at the country club. On the surface, a round of golf was supposed to be fun. But Mr. Morgan was trying to close another business deal, sealing it with the golf outing. His health was excellent, he tried to eat healthy and he exercised daily. No one wished him harm, but it seemed like a long road ahead before Eula and William would be able to proclaim their love for each other in the public venue and in the presence of William Morgan, Sr.

Luke was ten years old. He spent his summers at Whispering Pines and went to a private prep school in Atlanta during the school year. Even in the summer, Eula and Luke left the trailer park around ten AM on Friday mornings and returned on Monday evenings. During the school year, Eula dropped Luke off at boarding school on Monday morning and picked him up on Friday afternoon. They spent their weekends at the Atlanta home. They had a good friend there, named Henry. Eula, Luke and Henry spent a lot of time together. It had been Sue Ellen's idea to use William's middle name in order to keep everything under wraps.

Someone once said, where there's smoke, there's fire. The rumors surrounding McClain's going out of business finally materialized into reality. An hour had passed, and Bubba, LJ and their friends were still in the parking lot at McClain's. Nobody wanted to leave, because leaving meant having to go home and tell their families they had just lost their jobs. And to make matters worse, if that were possible, it was just twenty-eight days until Christmas.

"What are we going to do?" Carl asked, expecting somebody in the group to have an answer.

"I don't have a clue," LJ said in response to Carl's question. "There's no business around here that's hiring. Hell, most everything is hanging on by a thread. The only place to find work is over the mountain in Atlanta."

"It's seventy-five miles to Atlanta, one way," someone said. "Most of our trucks couldn't make that run, day in and day out."

Bubba, who had been sitting on Maude's tailgate, jumped up and said, "I know what we can do. Let's go see Eula. She should be in her office today. She's smart and has a good business head on her shoulders. I bet she'll come up with something. She almost has to. Hell, most of us live there. If we don't get jobs, she won't get paid."

Everyone agreed, and one after the other, the pickups roared to life. It looked like a parade, as Chevys and Fords left the company parking lot, heading for Whispering Pines. The faint sound of country music could be heard over the sound of the barking tailpipes.

Eula was sitting at her desk when the entourage of pickups turned into the trailer park and stopped abruptly at the office. Recognizing something had happened, she hurried out on the deck to meet her tenants, who were also her friends. Bubba got to the deck first.

Seeing the stress and worry etched into his face, she asked, "What's wrong, Bubba?"

"We just lost our jobs and the plant's closing for good. We know we all have to find new jobs, but we also know Christmas is breathing down our necks. If it wasn't so bad, it'd be funny and we could sing Haggard's song about making it through December. But this ain't funny and we don't know what to do. Got any good ideas?"

By now, everyone was on the deck. Some leaned against the community hot tub and others against the deck railing. Taking a deep breath, Eula sat down in a deck chair. "Give me a few minutes to think," she said. "There's beer in the fridge. LJ, go get everyone a beer and we'll think this thing through together."

LJ went inside her trailer, and in a few minutes returned with an armful of beer.

The tabs were pulled in unison, all except Eula's. She sat, hands behind her head, mulling over the situation. She had a faraway look in her eyes the boys hadn't seen before. She was doing much better than she'd ever expected, and the trailer park was making her a decent living. The Beamer also insisted on helping her and Luke out financially, which was icing on the cake. Her second home in Atlanta, which no one knew about except the Beamer and Sue Ellen, was like a castle, compared to what most of her friends lived in. Bubba and a few of Eula's close friends talked among themselves about Eula and Luke being gone most weekends, but they had so much on their plates they could have cared less where she spent her time. They all knew Luke was in some kind of private boarding school in Atlanta so they figured Eula went there on weekends to spend time with her son. She usually got back to the park late Monday evenings. But, today, sitting in the midst of her lifelong friends, she remembered less fortunate times, and her heart ached for the men gathered around her, waiting for an answer to their serious situation.

"Life's not fair," she finally said.

"Tell us something we don't already know," LJ said, as he halfheartedly tried to smile.

"You already know what has to be done about the jobs." Eula said. "If McClain's has closed for good, then there's nowhere around here for any of you to work. Y'all will have to go over the mountain, hopefully finding jobs close together, so some of you can carpool. That'll help a little. But Christmas is the big problem we have to deal with immediately."

"It's just four weeks away and most of us haven't bought much of anything for our families and none of us have any money stashed away," Bubba said, with most of the guys nodding in agreement.

"Wait a minute," Eula said, with a smile creeping across her face. Jumping up from her deck chair, she disappeared into her trailer home, and in a few minutes returned with a brochure. "Here's the answer," she said as she handed the brochure to Bubba.

Bubba looked puzzled, and after looking at it, he passed it around to the rest of the guys to see. No one, looking at the brochure, seemed to get it. It was announcing the Christmas Tour of Homes the city of Blairsville held annually. No one from Whispering Pines had ever even thought about going.

Bubba was the first to question her sanity. "How is paying the *hootie tooties* to see inside their fancy homes in town going to help us with buying Christmas presents or paying our rent?"

"Yeah," LJ chimed in. "How's paying them gonna help us out?"

"Just hear me out, boys. Here's what we'll do. They charge twenty dollars for their tour of homes, and it generates a ton of money every year for charity. And that's a good thing. We'll charge thirty dollars for our tour of homes, and they'll pay because most of them have never been inside a trailer before. We'll make a killing, and the only charity it'll be going to is yours. This might be the best Christmas y'all have ever had."

"Have you been drinking this morning?" Bubba asked her. "It's awfully early to be hitting the hard stuff."

"Bubba, you know I don't drink hard stuff."

"The *hootie tooties* aren't going to pay us to come see our mobile homes," LJ said. "Hell, Eula, they're scared to drive inside the park. They sure ain't gonna get out and come inside."

"I agree with LJ," Carl said. "No way will they pay to look inside a trailer."

"Leave their coming to me," Eula said to the guys gathered on her deck. "They'll come, come gladly, and be happy to pay. I'll get them here, but y'all have a part to play in this also. Let's clean this place up. Check for litter, and if you find any decks or trailers needing pressure washing, get it taken care of quickly. The weather is unusually mild and there's no rain in the forecast. I'll furnish any supplies you need. Get everyone to get the inside of their homes spic and span. We'll figure out which ones to put on the tour later. We'll probably do six single-wides and six double-wides, preferably newer homes. That should be enough for a good tour. We need a few more decorations at the entrance, and I have garland and lights for the office deck and railings. We need a Christmas tree and lights put up at the cookshed. I want Whispering Pines to look like Vegas on a dark night. And, if the weather's good, we might even let them play trailer park horseshoes."

LJ piped up and asked, "What's trailer park horseshoes?"

Several of the guys laughed and Bubba gave LJ that *"you gotta be shittin' me"* look.

"And boys, we're going to have burgers, dogs and beer, compliments of Whispering Pines. I'll pick up the cost of the food and beer. But, most importantly, I want y'all to be to our visitors what you are to each other and to me— just good ole boys. Be yourself and tell your families to do the same. Everyone in Whispering Pines is a class act, and it's past time the people in town had a chance to realize it. Who knows, this could become an annual event. Holding both hands up as if to frame her statement, she said, "Christmas at Whispering Pines."

Eula had finished her declaration and no one was moving or saying anything. They were dumbfounded.

"Why is everyone standing around?" she asked as she started inside. "I'm headed to town to have the fliers printed. Let's get this place shipshape. We want the townsfolk to have a good experience on their first visit to Whispering Pines."

As she backed out of the parking place next to her double-wide, her friends and tenants were still just milling around at the back of their trucks. They looked more like little boys than unemployed fathers worrying about Christmas. Not only could she feel their pain, it was prominently displayed on their faces. To encourage them, she let down her car window, pumped her fist in the air, and yelled, "Yes" loud enough for them to hear her.

Eula had a friend that did banners, posters and printing. Parking outside his small shop, she decided to give Sue Ellen a call and feel her out on the trailer park tour of homes idea.

"Well, this is a nice surprise. When are we going to Cracker Barrel for lunch?" Sue Ellen asked.

"I'm ready whenever you are. Just pick a day and I'll set it aside. I called because I need your advice on something."

"As smart as you are, I'm flattered you would ask me for advice. What is it that's got you stumped?"

"Well, I'm not stumped. I've actually already jumped off the cliff. You know me, grab a bull by the horns, and then try and figure out how to get him in the stall. Here's the skinny of the situation. McClain's has closed its doors for good. All the guys at Whispering Pines are officially unemployed. The major problem for them now is Christmas. They have no savings to speak of and have bought little or, in most cases, nothing for their kids and wives for Christmas."

"I would be willing to help out as much as I can," Sue Ellen said quickly.

"I really appreciate the offer and I know you would in a heartbeat. But that's not why I called. They need to do this on their own. It's time they learned to work things out for themselves."

"I agree," Sue Ellen said. "There won't always be someone standing around to bail them out. What's your plan?"

"I know you're familiar with the Christmas Tour of Homes the city puts on every year for charity. I proposed to the guys we have a tour of homes of our own. Obviously, we will spit shine everything and put up lots of decorations. We'll have burgers, dogs and beer as well as games for the adults and kids. I'm not sure what all we'll do, but we plan to showcase six single-wides and six double-wides. I have just suggested this to the guys, but they're all nervous and doubtful about whether or not it will work. I consider it an opportunity to get the townsfolk and the people at Whispering Pines together. My main concern is how to get the people to come out to support our tour of homes. I'm sitting outside of Mike's Printing right now, about to get him to help me design a flier for the tour. Got any ideas or suggestions or tell me whether you think it will work."

There was a long silence on the other end of the line. "Sue Ellen, Sue Ellen, are you still there?"

"Oh, yes. I was just thinking about everything you just told me. It's actually ingenious, and there's no doubt in my mind it'll be a big success. Don't worry. I think I know how to get a huge turnout for your tour. Get your flier designed and printed and call me back tomorrow and I'll put your mind at ease with regards to the response of the townspeople."

"Boy, you sure do sound confident. What can I say except thanks? I'll call you tomorrow morning. Can't wait to hear this can't miss idea. I've got a feeling it'll be very interesting."

"You have no idea," Sue Ellen said and laughed. "Call me tomorrow morning."

Three hours later, when Eula returned to Whispering Pines, some of the guys were still standing around, feeling sorry for themselves. Even though they had brought their problem to her for help, her idea still sounded insane to them. No one, they thought, would pay for a tour of homes in a trailer park, not at Christmas, nor any other time for that matter.

Getting out of her car and walking over to where they were milling around, she gave them a "what's this" gesture with her hands. "Get all the other guys rounded up and meet me here in fifteen minutes," she told them. "Go get Bubba and LJ to help you."

The group mumbled a little bit, but scattered throughout the park, telling everyone what Eula had said.

Going into her office, she quickly typed up an announcement notifying the residents to be at her office in two hours. She printed enough copies for everyone to get the notice. Thankfully, because of the mild December weather, a large number of the residents gathered outside her office for the called meeting.

"Thanks for coming," she began. "I'm sure most of you know about McClain's closing for good. It's roughly four weeks until Christmas and I've come up with an idea. If everyone cooperates, it should make us enough money for each family to have a good Christmas. We are planning a Christmas Tour of Homes at Whispering Pines, much like the one they hold every year in town. They raise money for charity, and it's a good thing. We're going to raise money for us, and that's a good thing."

There was a small burst of applause and some hear, hears scattered throughout the group.

When they had all quieted down, Eula continued. "We want to showcase six single-wides and six double-wides. I need this place shining like new money. I want volunteers for showcasing your homes. All of you get together and get me a list of who's willing to do it. We only need twelve residents to participate. The homes on tour should be warm and charming, and decorated to the best of your ability."

She paused to let her message sink in. "Bubba, divide the guys into groups. Some to do the landscaping and lawn maintenance, some to take care of any pressure washing that might need doing, and some to help the elderly in the park with their homes. We'll all be old someday, and God will bless you for helping them. Designate someone to go down to High Shoals Creek and cut a large cedar tree for the front entrance and a small one for the cookshed. I'll call old man Riley and tell him someone's coming down. There's plenty of lights and decorations in the park workshop. Bubba has the key. See him or LJ for help. By the way, LJ, pick out some guys, and their wives can help, to be in charge of grilling the dogs and burgers. Also, get some wives to volunteer to make some desserts for the guests who will be eating with us. Several banana puddings would be nice."

Bubba smiled. Everyone liked banana pudding. LJ let out a *hot damn* for the puddings.

Bubba caught Eula looking directly at him. He smiled and she winked. She sounded like a drill sergeant, barking orders at new recruits.

"Tomorrow, I'll have the fliers back from the printer, and I'll also have complete details as to how this will work. Get the trailers picked out for showcasing on the tour of homes. I need that list no later than Friday. This is about the residents who live here. It's your Christmas and your kids. If you want them to have a good Christmas, cooperate with me, and together we'll make it happen."

⚬∞⚬ ⚬∞⚬ ⚬∞⚬

After a sleepless night, Eula got dressed and couldn't wait for Sue Ellen's call. "What if I can't deliver the townspeople," she thought over and over. "I know the residents will do their part, but . . ."

The phone ringing broke her concentration. It was Sue Ellen. Her instructions were short and to the point.

"Meet me at Cracker Barrel for breakfast. Be there in forty-five minutes. Is that okay?"

"I'll be there," Eula said. "I need to know about this miraculous plan you have to make this happen. I'm starting to unravel just thinking about it failing to materialize. I'm getting dressed now and will see you shortly."

Sue Ellen beat Eula there, went ahead and got a table, and

was on her second cup of coffee, when a very rattled Eula came in and literally flopped down across from her.

"Please tell me you know how to get these folks to our tour of homes."

"I know how to get these folks to your tour of homes! Did I say it correctly?" Sue Ellen asked and grinned.

"There's nothing funny about this not working," Eula said.

"It's in the bag. That is, if you can be a good actress and deliver a few choice lines. Can you do that?"

"Oh, my," Eula said exasperated, "what lines and to whom and where?"

"You will deliver your lines at City Bank & Trust, and the person you'll deliver them to in your Oscar winning performance will be none other than William Morgan, Sr. himself."

"You gotta be shittin' me," Eula said. "I'm sorry. I didn't mean to say that."

"Yes, you did," Sue Ellen said and laughed. "It's okay, and even appropriate."

"How can he help us? He hates the trailer park and the residents as well, doesn't he?"

"I think hate may be a little strong. He just has tunnel vision and can't see things that are important to others. This will be good for him. You are going to deliver a powerful message, and he will bow to your wishes. I guarantee it."

"Oh, God, help me," Eula said. "I don't know if I can do this or not."

"Sounds like you've put quite a burden and a high level of expectations on your friends. I think I remember someone saying, 'it's time they learned to work things out for themselves.' It's time for Eula Johnson, scratch that, Eula Morgan, to step up to the big time. You'll do fine and you'll make me proud."

Handing her a legal pad, Sue Ellen told her to take some notes.

"Write these instructions down. I will be at the bank when you come in, and I know he'll be in all day tomorrow. Here goes. You'll have a stack of fliers with you. You walk right past his secretary and directly into his office. This will take him aback, and he'll probably make some ugly remarks. But he'll remember who you are. Here are your opening lines."

Mr. Morgan, as you know, McClain's has closed its doors for good. A lot of the residents at Whispering Pines worked there and are now out of work. "He may or may not interrupt you anywhere along the way. He does that a lot. Just ignore the interruptions and keep delivering your message." *We are having a tour of homes at the trailer park, and we'd like for you to help us by promoting it at the bank and among your friends.*

"At this point, he'll probably stand up and threaten to have, you thrown out. Stay calm and continue with your message." *Sir if you'll help promote our Christmas Tour of Homes, I know it will be a huge success and will help our unemployed residents provide a nice Christmas for their kids.*

"He'll probably tell you he doesn't give a rats' butt about your trailer park, the residents or the kids. He'll say things that will make you mad and will tell you he wouldn't lift a finger to help any one of you. He may even throw in some derogatory remarks about your character and the character of the residents. Stay calm. Talk over him and keep to your message. He won't make too big of a scene, because it's in the bank and others would hear. Ask him nicely to make the fliers available at the tellers' windows and at the country club. At this point, he may use the Eula special and say, *'You gotta be shittin' me.'*"

Eula laughed.

"As you leave, tell him you expect him to be at your office, that's the office at Whispering Pines, at nine o'clock on Saturday morning. And, for good measure, tell him not to be late."

"Does he have a gun in his office?" Eula asked.

"He's a selfish, self-centered old fool, but he's not violent. Trust me on that. If he was, I would have been dead a long time ago. He's going to tell you no, and hell no, and it's not going to happen. Lay a stack of fliers on his desk, stand and start to leave. Stop, turn and say, *Does the name Lewis Padgett mean anything to you? We can keep this between ourselves or we can let the whole town know. The choice is yours. Be at my office at the trailer park at nine o'clock on Saturday morning and, Bank Daddy, don't be late.*"

"You want me to call him Bank Daddy? Sue Ellen, have you lost your mind? That'll make him mad enough to call the cops and have me thrown out for sure. And just mentioning the name Lewis Padgett will make him do this? Whoever is Lewis Padgett?" Eula asked.

"You don't need to know, and don't ever ask again," Sue Ellen said in a tone Eula wasn't used to hearing. "Use this name one time, and then erase it from your memory. You asked me to make this happen and this will. But, promise me, not a word of this to the Beamer or to anyone at Whispering Pines or to anyone period. You'll only have to use it once. It will stay forever in his office, between you and him. I trust you, Eula, and you mean the world to me. Do I have your word on this?"

"You have my word. I'll take it to my grave."

"That's exactly what I expect. Nothing less will be acceptable."

Eula took her time driving back to Whispering Pines. She had a lot to think about. "All you have to do is be a good actress and deliver a few choice lines," Eula remembered Sue Ellen saying to her. "Oh, yeah," Eula said to herself, "just deliver a few lines chocked full of demands to the richest, most powerful man in the entire state, and follow it up by uttering a single name, one that's supposed to make this bank mogul tremble in his boots and jump through any hoops I put in front of him. Right, and I'm supposed to swallow this hook, line and sinker?"

Turning into the trailer park, she wheeled into her parking place and sat there for a moment, wondering how she had gotten herself into this mess. "Get a grip, Eula. Sue Ellen's smart and she knows lots of things about our community and the folks living here," she reasoned to herself. "She wouldn't tell me these things if she didn't believe them."

When she looked around, she could tell things in the trailer park were beginning to happen. She could hear the pressure washer running somewhere in the park. A leaf blower was going on the other end, and guys were picking up litter and putting out mulch. Some of the women were out sweeping off decks and two or three were actually putting up more decorations.

Going into her office, she felt ashamed of herself. Like Sue Ellen had noted, she had placed a huge burden on her residents, expecting them to welcome the cream of society from town into their humble trailers, and be friendly and cordial to them. Most of the cars they would drive out to Whispering Pines would be more valuable than the homes they had come to visit. And who knows how many times they would have to open the door of their homes to total strangers.

"I should be ashamed," she said out loud. "I have to face only one man and deliver one message. They have a far greater challenge than I do. And I have a secret weapon. A single name that would make Superman soil his shorts." Smiling at her humorous thought, she began studying her notes, preparing for delivery the next morning. "Give me wisdom, Lord," she prayed "and help me complete the task lying ahead of me." It would be a long night.

The next morning, after picking up the fliers from the print shop, Eula headed straight to the bank. She had rehearsed her lines over and over and had them down to a tee. "Who knows, there might be an Oscar in the works," she thought and smiled. There were other places to bank in the town, but she had purposely kept her business and personal accounts at City Bank & Trust. She had seen Mr. Morgan many times while making deposits, but had never spoken to him. She never spoke to Sue Ellen either. That's the way Sue Ellen wanted it to be at the bank. "No need to go looking for trouble," she had said. Today would be a different type of visit, and she was scared.

Sue Ellen's office was walled in by glass and Eula could see her sitting at her desk. She looked up and smiled, discreetly giving her two thumbs up. Eula walked right past Mr. Morgan's secretary and straight into his office. He looked up as she closed the door. The door immediately opened again and his secretary flew in to extract Eula. With eyes and mouth wide open in disbelief, she apologized to her boss for allowing the intrusion.

Mr. Morgan waved her off. "It's all right," he said. "I'll call you if I need anything." He had stood abruptly behind his desk when Eula walked in. After his secretary went out, closing the door behind her, Mr. Morgan remained standing for a moment before sitting down again.

Eula had already taken a seat on the other side of his massive cherry wood desk. He recognized her, but had no idea why, after all these years, she had decided to confront him in person, and enter his office in such a brash fashion. An obvious moment of nervousness found its mark on both sides of the desk. Momentarily, she was at a loss for words. Glancing down at the fliers in her hand gave her the initiative to begin the scripted conversation, some of which Sue Ellen gave her and some she improvised on her own.

"I need, or I should say, the residents at Whispering Pines need your help with something. I'm sure you're aware McClain's has closed its doors for good. Most of the men who worked there are my friends and members of our community. They'll find jobs in Atlanta, but for right now, they're a little short of cash and Christmas is bearing down on them like a mother grizzly protecting her cubs."

Mr. Morgan, shifting his weight in his oversized leather chair, covered his mouth to stifle a yawn, real or pretended.

"We've decided to have a tour of homes at Whispering Pines," Eula continued, "much like the tour of homes the town has each year. It would solve the immediate financial crisis, and might just give the trailer park residents and the folks who live in town a chance to meet and, who knows, find out they might have a few things in common."

"And just how do I fit into this picture?" Mr. Morgan asked.

Handing him a stack of fliers, she said, "You can make it happen!"

"There's no way in hell I'm going to pass out these fliers, or put any pressure on any of my friends or customers to visit your trailer park let alone pay you to do it. Are you out of your mind? I don't want this bank or my good name associated with you or anyone else in that damned old trailer park."

"I figured that would be your response," Eula said as she stood, preparing to leave.

"I made a deal with your father and paid a premium to make you and your kind go away. You got your hooks into my son and I paid dear to get him out of what would have been the biggest mistake he would ever make in his entire life. I have no obligation to do anything for you, or your tenants, this Christmas, or any Christmas, for that matter. I'll not tarnish my good name messing around with your kind."

Leaning over, Eula put both hands on his desk.

"My father has passed away," she said softly, "and your name would look tarnished next to his, so please refrain from ever mentioning my father again. This is not about any obligations you owe me. This is about doing the right thing because you can, that's all."

Eula started for the door and Mr. Morgan stood up and said, "Here, take your fliers with you."

It had happened almost to the letter the way Sue Ellen had imagined it would. And, now, it was time to play her trump card.

Pausing and turning around to face him, she asked, "Does the name Lewis Padgett mean anything to you? We can keep this between ourselves or we can let the whole town know, or would you prefer to give the good people at Whispering Pines a little endorsement regarding the upcoming Trailer Park Tour of Homes? Your choice. If it's the latter, then be at my office, that's my office at the trailer park, at nine o'clock in the morning. And, Bank Daddy, don't be late."

She had a sudden impulse to slam the door behind her, but thought better of it. She never dreamed she would face off with the wealthiest man in town, but she could tell the Lewis Padgett name shook him to his core. He didn't follow her, which told her she'd better get home and clean up her office for their meeting. She winked at his secretary as she walked out of his office. Sue Ellen was meandering around behind the teller windows in hopes of seeing Eula come out of Morgan's office. Eula spied her first, and without looking at her, gave a very quick and simple two thumbs up. If anyone else had seen it, it would have appeared she was giving a thumbs up to no one. Sue Ellen saw it from a distance and smiled, knowing she had done well.

Going straight back to her office, she heard her phone ringing off the hook. It was Mr. Morgan.

"Where the hell did that Johnson woman get Lewis Padgett's name and what possibly could she know?"

"Well, she didn't get it from me," Sue Ellen said, crossing her fingers and smiling at the same time. "Padgett had some relatives who at one time lived in that old trailer park. Maybe she met some of them. Why? When did you see her and what did she say about Padgett?"

"It's not important. I'll take care of it. I knew it didn't come from you. You're about the only person on earth I have complete confidence and trust in. She wants a favor from me, something about helping the riffraff down at the trailer park with some kind of tour of homes. I'll check it out and let you know if I need any help with it."

"Just let me know," Sue Ellen told him. "I'll be happy to help any way I can." Sue Ellen hung up and immediately felt bad for lying to him. She knew how much he trusted her and the same was true for her. He had kept all of his promises, made so long ago, concerning keeping their secrets from the Beamer and the world in general. And now she was the one to break the trust. Sometimes, she thought, the overarching good of the whole requires sacrifice. She would have liked to have told him that Eula had a name and nothing else. But she knew that wouldn't fly. In essence, she had not broken her word given so long ago. The name by itself had no meaning or connection to anything.

❧❧❧❧❧❧

When Eula got back to the trailer park, two cedar trees were by the office, and she saw LJ bringing the decorations from the shop building. Most of the residents must have been watching for her return. They started coming out of their homes and making their way toward the office. Eula was proud of them and decided to give them an update. Bubba had arrived and was standing near the back of the crowd gathered by the deck.

"Listen up," Eula told everyone and smiled. "In the morning, at nine o'clock sharp, Mr. William Morgan, Sr. will drive into the trailer park and stop at my office. He has graciously offered his help with getting the word out and in convincing the townspeople and his friends to come out to our tour of homes."

To Eula, it sounded like everyone took a deep breath at one time and exhaled in unison.

She continued, "His help will make this a huge success. He already has a stack of fliers and will make sure they get distributed in town. Here, LJ, give everyone a copy of the flier." The residents were spellbound at the thought of Morgan coming to the trailer park, but Eula could tell the troops were rallied and willing to make the Christmas Tour at Whispering Pines a success.

"One more thing and I'll let you go. Mama used to say, 'always be yourself and never forget your raising'. You're great people and this will be a wonderful opportunity to showcase not just a few of our homes and the trailer park, but also to show everyone how our Mamas raised us. Any questions?"

"I got one," LJ said, smiling. "How in the heck did you pull this off?"

"We probably don't want to know," Bubba said. The entire group broke into laughter.

"You probably don't," Eula replied and laughed with everyone else. "I can tell you're all standing here rearing to go, and you can't go for rearing. Get out of here and get to work. Mr. Morgan will be here first thing in the morning, and I want this place looking good."

They scattered quickly and seemed energized and ready to make things happen. Bubba was the only one who didn't leave.

"You must have burned a pretty big trump card," he said with a somber tone in his voice. "I won't let you down. I have my doubts about this, but I have faith in you. What about the Beast? Think those *hootie tooties* would like to take her for a spin?"

The Beast was a monster pickup truck some of the residents had built from scratch. They entered it in contests, climbing over cars, and also entered it in mud-bogging events. You had to use a ladder just to get inside the thing.

"That's a great idea," Eula said. "That's exactly what I'm talking about. Can you imagine how excited some of those guys from town would be to ride in or to drive the Beast? They see y'all driving it and wonder why. But what if they could drive it? Wow! What a touch that would add to the tour."

Eula started to go inside her office. She turned and said, "Hey, Bubba, you got a minute? Come inside and let's have a beer. We need to talk."

Her tone was a little disconcerting. It sounded motherly, and sad, both at the same time. Bubba went in and had a seat across from her at her desk. She returned from her fridge and handed him a beer. Pulling the tab, she took a long draw from the can, and then sat down hard. Bubba was almost hesitant to pull the tab on his beer. This sounded serious and he had flashbacks of being in the principal's office.

"Do you mind me calling you Tom?" she asked.

"Not at all. No one ever calls me Tom anymore. I'm just Bubba to everyone."

"Exactly," Eula agreed, "but for this conversation, I need you to be Tom, not Bubba, okay?"

"Okay," he said.

"I'm smart, Tom, but so are you. In high school we hung out with our kind, or at least what we perceived was our kind. For most of us, kind was defined by money, cars and homes. We knew who we were and, more importantly, we knew who they were. But, Tom, we were so wrong."

She paused, as if collecting her thoughts. Bubba finally pulled the tab on his beer.

"We were the ones who built the fences separating us, not them. We like to remember our experiences as being extras on a movie set, with the others the stars. That wasn't the case. They're not the *hootie tooties,* as you jokingly call them. While some may have used money and possessions to make them feel superior, the vast majority of folks who have money are great people and will befriend anyone who is open to their friendship."

"Where is this going?" Bubba asked, "and what does it have to do with now? That was a long time ago, or at least it seems like it was."

"I have a secret to share with you, Tom. My William is like that."

"Your William, as in the William who's the father of your son?"

"Here's the secret I'm going to trust you with. Only one other person knows about it, and if his father found out, William would have hell to pay. Okay?"

"Okay," Tom said. "You're one of my dearest friends. You know anything you want me to keep to myself is safe."

"I see William every week. He loved me in high school and still does. The feelings are mutual. He hasn't married and you know I haven't married or dated anyone. Luke knows him as Henry and doesn't know William is his father. He pays Luke's tuition and lives in the Atlanta area. I have a house there as well. That's where I go every weekend. We do things as a family, even though we aren't legally married. Mr. Morgan is a hard man and there's a lot to the story I can't tell you. I have fixed it legally so if something should happen to me, then William will have custody and paperwork proving Luke is his son. The headmaster at Luke's school also knows William has legal rights to pick Luke up at school or to authorize medical treatment should the need arise. We've covered all the bases, except marriage. We're working on that one."

"Wow," was all Bubba could muster.

"I need to ask you a favor. I need you to be Bubba to your friends, and especially Bubba to our visitors who'll be coming to tour our homes. But, for just a little while, I need you to be Tom for me. Do you understand what I'm asking and why?"

"You know I do. It's a whole lot easier to be Bubba than to be Tom. But for you, Tom will leave your office, but Bubba will go to work. And thanks for telling me about William. I really did like the guy. It's a great love story, but a sad story as well. Bubba would cry, but Tom won't let him."

Eula laughed a hearty laugh, finished her beer, crushed the can, and shot a two pointer in her waste basket across the room.

"William's a lucky man," Tom said as Bubba left the office.

He knew what she needed him to do. Not to be Bubba or Tom, but a little of each. Assembling his friends, he gave them a speech of his own, declaring the utmost confidence in Eula's idea. After delegating jobs to each one, he began laying out a course for the Beast. The wives of the selected tour homes were busy cleaning and decorating. There was a hum of activity in the trailer park he had never witnessed before. Little Jimmy was singing Christmas carols as he strung the garland on the split rail fence.

That night, Eula had a hard time going to sleep. Just like Bubba, she hid behind a tough, I don't give a damn exterior. But, inside, in the recesses of her soul, she was caring and vulnerable. Why else would she wait, pray and hope one day William would find the courage to stand up to his father? She could probably marry any number of available men in town but she only loved her William.

"Would Mr. Morgan actually show up in the morning?" she asked herself while staring at the clock next to her bed. "Listen to me," she scolded herself. "I gave Bubba all this advice on building fences between ourselves and others, and I'm the architect of a fence that should have been torn down years ago. Hypocrite," she said out loud.

⟨∞⟩⟨∞⟩⟨∞⟩

Eula got up early, dressed, and was in her office by 8:30. At 8:50 still no Morgan. She was about to second guess her privileged information when a shiny, new Cadillac Escalade pulled up in front of her office. It was Mr. Morgan in the flesh. She knew every eye in the trailer park had seen his arrival. With reluctance, which was visible on his face, he got out of the car and came up the steps to her office door.

Again, forgetting the advise she had given Bubba, and forgetting her own introspection the night before, she threw up a fence of her own and changed into a genuine *hootie tootie.*

"Have a seat," she said, pointing to an empty chair in front of her cluttered desk.

Eula spent several minutes adding up columns of meaningless figures, in an attempt to make Mr. Morgan feel as uncomfortable as possible. She knew it was wrong but enjoyed it immensely. Finally, laying the paperwork aside, she addressed him.

"Mr. Morgan, thanks for coming. With your endorsement, our tour will be very successful, and I want to tell you in advance how much we appreciate it."

"Let's just get on with your demands. Sorry about that, I mean your requests. Just tell me what I have to do to keep my world intact. I can't imagine where you get your intel, but I'm sure you'll protect your sources. So, tell me, how can I help?"

Eula was caught off guard by his statement about keeping his world intact and the remark about the intel.

"It's really pretty simple," she said. "My mother always told me to be honest and forthright in all my dealings with others, and I've found it to be good advice. While the families in the trailer park are in a Christmas pinch, if you will, they still have pride and aren't looking for charity. We don't want to take money from people who tour our homes unless we feel like we can give something back in return. We are planning to showcase twelve homes, and to have all the beer, hot dogs and burgers anyone might choose to consume. We'll have trailer park horseshoes, and anyone with a valid driver's license can have the thrill of a lifetime driving the Beast."

Mr. Morgan didn't know, or want to know, what the Beast was. He just wanted out of Eula's office and back in his.

"I will, as a special favor to you and the residents of the trailer park, encourage all the members of the country club and the Chamber of Commerce to attend this most gala event. I won't mention the reason for the tour, but only that perhaps it's time the two parts of the city came together in unity and in the spirit of the Christmas season. I'll make the fliers available at every teller window in the bank, and also in the three branch locations."

"Thank you for doing that," Eula said. "I personally want to extend an invitation to you to be our guest of honor. I think it'll show sincerity and will help to solidify two distinct segments of our community. It will also show how little where we live defines who we actually are."

"Very well," Mr. Morgan noted as he stood to leave. "I must be getting back to the bank. I look forward to coming back on the seventeenth. And I'm sure everyone attending will have some-thing to remember well past the Christmas season."

Eula wasn't sure what something to remember well past the Christmas season meant.

Driving out of the trailer park, Mr. Morgan couldn't help but reflect on the fact that Eula was well-mannered and articulate, not at all what he imagined her to be like.

Mr. Morgan, Bubba and the residents of the park didn't know she had been taking on-line courses for three years and would soon graduate with a college degree. William had insisted she take the courses and had gladly paid the tuition.

When the Caddie was out of sight, the office was swamped by curious residents, with Bubba arriving first.

Eula, who had worried herself to death wondering whether Mr. Morgan would show or not, was cool under fire.

"How did it go," Bubba asked, "is he helping or not?"

"It went fine," she said almost absentmindedly, "just like I knew it would. And, of course, he's willing to help us any way he can. He's coming as my special guest, and I may take him for a ride in the Beast."

"Who would have thought it?" was all Bubba could muster.

The residents were now both pumped and frightened. Eula had delivered the bank president to the trailer park, just like she had promised. They rolled up their sleeves and went to work harder than ever, getting the park ready for the tour of homes. People living in very expensive homes and neighborhoods were about to descend upon Whispering Pines Trailer Park for tours of their twelve best homes. While people from both sides of the track put their pants on the same way, the closets those pants hung in were light years apart on an economic scale. That was the only part the residents were concerned about—could they actually connect with each other?

By December twelfth, the trailer park had been transformed into a place of beauty. Every single aspect of the park and everyone living there was ready to entertain the people from town. Extra grills had been borrowed from friends and provisions were ready for a feast.

Bubba, with the help of some of his friends, had laid a course on the back acreage, adjacent to the park. The Beast had been gussied up and even had twelve-volt Christmas lights around the cab that twinkled when she was running. Bubba got a friend, who owned a junkyard, to bring over three old clunkers for the Beast to climb over. A mud bog to die for was on the other side of the clunkers.

Eula prayed for good weather, and her prayers were answered. It was a mild December day and only a light windbreaker was needed. Seems like even God wanted these two groups to find common ground. It was to be an all-day event, starting at 10 AM and ending with a bonfire and a marshmallow roast. Old galvanized number-two washtubs would hold the ice and the beer.

Bubba selected a number of residents, mostly forced, to lead the tours. Eula made up an outline for the tour guides, and they rehearsed it at least a hundred times. She stressed over and over for them to just be themselves, and to embrace the visitors as they would any friend or family member. Little Jimmy had to go and point out that none of his friends or family members drove fancy cars, lived in nice homes or had money. Eula told him to pretend they did.

Eula answered the phone early on the morning of the sixteenth, the day before the tour was to take place. When she heard Mr. Morgan's voice on the other end of the line, she expected to hear bad news.

"Miss Johnson, thought I'd give you a call, or maybe it could be a warning." His laughter seemed genuine enough. "Expect at least four hundred people to tour the park, maybe more." Her first thought for a reply was classic Eula, but she managed to refrain and be business-like.

"Thanks for all your help. We look forward to having them on this special occasion, and we'll do our best to entertain them and make sure they have a memorable time. Thanks for calling."

After she hung up, she couldn't decide if it was great news or terrible news. Then she had a Bubba thought. "They had probably always wondered what those trailer park people were like and were willing to pay thirty bucks to find out and sneak a peek inside their trailers."

Bubba walked in just about the time she finished her negative thoughts, picked up on her countenance and said, "Are you having a Tom moment or a Bubba moment?"

"Both," she told him and laughed. "Mr. Morgan just called and estimated approximately two hundred people would be coming our way for the tour."

Bubba about had a fit. "You gotta be kidding me," he said. "Two hundred! Wow!"

She knew better than to give him the real numbers. He might saddle up the Beast and ride away for good.

On Saturday, the seventeenth, cars started lining up early. It was evident that curiosity was a driving force, second only to Mr. Morgan burning up a lot of capital. At first, Bubba and the tour guides were a little reluctant to let their hair down and be themselves. After an hour or so, the genuine friendliness of the residents and the beautifully decorated trailer homes soon won everyone's heart. The burgers and dogs were a hit with the visitors, and the trailer park horseshoes seemed to go over better than tickets to the Masters. The guests weren't leaving fast enough, and soon the county sheriff's office had half their force out at the park trying to direct traffic.

And the Beast! What can be said about the Beast? Grown men became little boys again, and it was really Christmas in a new and different way for most of the townsfolk. The big, ugly, often misunderstood truck had a personality of her own, and soon won everyone over.

Mr. Morgan arrived as promised and stopped at Eula's office. "I don't know what's happening out here today, but those returning to town seem to have really enjoyed the tour and are excited about making so many new acquaintances."

Eula was visibly shaken by his honesty. Her eyes filled with tears. "My turn," she said. "Christmas brings out the best in all of us," she began. "I want to ask your forgiveness for harboring so much animosity toward you over the past few years. I don't know why you did what you did back then, and truth is, I might have done the same thing if I had been in your shoes. There's so much I'd like to tell you, but it's not my place. Let's you and me go meet some really nice people who, like the townsfolk, have made some great new friends today. And when the tour is over, I'm gonna take you on the ride of a lifetime. Disney has nothing on us."

After the tour, Eula and Mr. Morgan stopped by the cookshed for a Bubba Burger. They were about to go find the Beast when Eula received the shock of her life. She stood up so quickly, she startled Mr. Morgan.

"Mother," Luke called out as he came toward the cookshed. William was right behind him. Eula ran to meet her son and gave him a hug. Mr. Morgan followed her over to where they were standing. "Mother, Henry picked me up at school and said you were having a Christmas party, and we were going to surprise you and come to the party. Are you surprised?"

"You have no idea, Luke, what a happy surprise this is."

Mr. Morgan had walked up and William smiled at his dad.

"Son, I have something important to tell you, and Christmas makes it even more special," Eula said, while holding her son close to her. "Henry is not just your friend, he's your father." Putting her arm around Mr. Morgan's shoulders, she said, "And this nice man is Henry's father, and he's your grandfather."

Knowing his father was scheduled to be there, the Beamer had called Sue Ellen and told her his intentions were to pick Luke up from school and take him to meet his grandfather. He purposely didn't tell Eula to keep her from being any more stressed out than she already was. Sue Ellen said a prayer and decided to go to the Whispering Pines Tour, which was quickly turning into a family reunion.

Mr. Morgan's eyes were full of tears. He had just met his grandson for the first time, and he was a beautiful young boy, reminding him so much of William when he was that age. Looking up, he saw Sue Ellen walking toward the family gathering. The good man, hid somewhere deep inside was about to surface. Stepping over to William, he put his arm around his son's shoulders and motioned for Sue Ellen to come over to them.

"William, just as you have pretended to be young Luke's friend, Sue Ellen Thornton has been doing the same song and dance routine with you for nearly thirty years. Son, she's your birth mother. And, young Luke, she's your grandmother."

There wasn't a dry eye among them except for Luke. It was Sue Ellen's turn to make an announcement. "William, you were indeed adopted by the Morgans. However, there's one little caveat that makes the adoption so special. I am your birth mother, but Morgan blood flows through your veins. Your real father adopted you and was gracious enough to allow your birth mother to raise you. How special is that?"

"My turn," William said, putting his arm around Eula and drawing her up close to him. "Dad, may I introduce you to my soon-to-be wife?"

EPILOGUE

T hings were never the same again. City Bank & Trust now sponsors not just one, but two annual Christmas Tour of Homes. Whispering Pines Trailer Park is by far the most popular. The number of Beasts has grown considerably and many are parked by some very expensive homes. *Hootie tootie* has disappeared from the vernacular. Bubba went to technical school and now has a successful heating and air conditioning business—Tom's HVAC. Several of his friends work as technicians.

LJ and Janice manage Whispering Pines for Eula. William and Eula live in Atlanta, where William has risen to vice-president of a large pharmaceutical company. Grandpa Morgan turned over the reins of the bank to someone else. Three grandchildren keep him plenty busy. Sue Ellen passed away, taking a dark secret to her grave.

The God of the manor house is also the God of the trailer park, and all who dwell therein belong to Him.

Amen and Amen.

ABOUT THE AUTHOR

Gene Vickers lives in Young Harris, GA and claims to have only two hobbies; work and writing. He has been married to Elaine for 54 years and they have two children and seven grandchildren. *Amen and Amen*, a work of fiction, is his second published work with two more to be published in the near future; one, a book of short stories, and the other, a fictional work on John Wesley.